MAFIOSO
PART 6: Who Shot Ya?

NISA SANTIAGO

ISBN:978-1620780855

This is a work of fiction. The characters, organizations, and events portrayed in this novel are either the author's imagination or used fictitiously.

Mafioso 6: Who Shot Ya? Copyright © 2020 by Melodrama Publishing. All rights reserved.

For information, address info@melodramabooks.com

ISBN: 978-1620780855
LCCN: 2020917263

First Edition: April 2022

BIGGIE SAID, "NIGGAS ARE ACTORS. THEY DESERVE OSCARS."

Chapter 1

The unknown assailant walked through the ritzy high-rise building with impunity. The polished imported marble floors led past a doorman, concierge and finally arrived at three mirrored elevators. Stepping into the lift, he scoffed when he pushed the top floor; the penthouse wasn't in his foreseeable future. The doors opened, and he stepped onto a tightly woven, plush carpet bordered with silk stitching in a Greek geometric design. *This was fucking luxury.* His keys opened a door where he didn't live—his code deactivated an alarm he shouldn't know.

Once inside, the décor gave him pause. He stood silent and just stared—no, he actually glared at the furnishings, amenities, and tchotchkes. The walls prominently displayed authentic Picasso, Basquiat, Banksy, and Warhol paintings; bookshelves had first edition rare collectibles—most notable, The Brothers Grimm fairytales, and cocktail tables held exquisite statues. The expansive foyer's overhead lighting was punctuated with a tasteful crystal chandelier. There were two woven silk couches in the living room area, positioned parallel, just like the White House. A buffet of custom Hermès pillows was strategically placed, giving the room an Architectural Digest vibe. This was the type of home you took your shoes off at the front door.

Eventually, he allowed himself to tour her whole condo, but not before removing his Glock from his shoulder holster just in case something popped off. Each space he entered competed with the room he'd just left; five-star everything was an understatement. He couldn't believe that a thuggish, gangster bitch was living this high up on the hog. Once he swept the apartment and confirmed that he was, as he had known, alone—he veered away from his agenda because the lure of her wealth was too enticing to just ignore.

On Lucky's dresser, he spotted a wad of cash. He counted just over nine thousand dollars haphazardly left in plain sight like it was lunch money. Although he wanted to take it all, he couldn't. He was a ghost and needed to be inconspicuous because he was creeping. Twenty crisp one hundred dollar bills were stuffed into his sweatpants pocket, but he couldn't stop there. Lucky's walk-in closet was opened, and it resembled an upscale boutique. She had installed three lighting levels; ambient was for the glass shelving, soft light was for her shoe collection, and daylight was for her clothing. A traditional crystal chandelier with smoke gray glass anchored the space. She had more clothes than she could wear in two lifetimes—gluttonous hoarding was this spoiled bitch's favorite pastime.

Glass display shelves held pricey $30,000 handbags—too many to count. Her clothing was color and season coordinated, most with price tags still on. Lucky's shoes and boots collection was every woman's dream, including his wife and mistress. His eyes scanned labels: Balmain, Balenciaga, Gucci, Louis Vuitton, Prada, Christian Louboutin's, Fendi, YSL, Versace, and a slew of others. There had to be over a million dollars worth of shoes and clothing there. His jaw tightened so aggressively his clenched teeth trickled blood. He opened a custom-built watch drawer and saw the obligatory staples of a drug hustling queenpin—Rolexes, Cartier, Chopard, and Bvlgari. His eyes were mesmerized by the Chopard watch with dangling pink diamonds on the dial. It had to cost at least six figures. He flipped it over, and it was engraved. It read: *To baby girl, my Luck...from me....*

Whoever had bought this gift wanted to remain a secret.

Another drawer held several sets of diamond earrings, diamond chains from dainty to gaudy, and platinum ring sets. He saw all the trappings of wealth, and then he noticed what every hood nigger or hood bitch did who thought they were clever—the hidden safe in the wall, behind a picture with a stash presumably inside. If all these items were in plain sight, his mind expanded to the possibilities of what was inside the safe.

Again, he hadn't come there for this, but it is what it is. The default plan was now to come up off this bitches wealth. He wanted it all; to clean her out because he felt she didn't deserve these things. He tried for nearly two hours—ear to steel, fingers twisting the spinning biometric lock—to open the safe, and although he knew he was almost there—he wasn't, and he couldn't risk getting caught. He knew Lucky and Bugsy were laid up in New-York Presbyterian, but there was always Meyer—the loose cannon.

Reluctantly, he had to give up on the safe and refocus. He grabbed one of the three Louis Vuitton garment bags and stuffed it with expensive outfits he knew his wife would kill for. He noticed his heart had accelerated, and he'd started to perspire. It wasn't a heavy sweat, just enough dampness around his hairline and armpits to quicken his steps. He raced into the kitchen, grabbed several trash bags, and focused on her heels. He loved a woman in stilettos, and Lucky had the sexiest array of five and six-inch pieces of art he had laid his eyes on. Lucky wore a size six shoe—his wife, a size nine, so no Red Bottoms for her. However, his mistress and Lucky were nearly identical; height, weight, shoes. He couldn't wait to see her naked with only Lucky's shoes on.

Great care was taken to not take any items in display cases because it would make the theft obvious, and he pulled a small amount of clothing from each section and a few shoeboxes from the numerous stacks. All this thievery didn't barely make a dent in Lucky's wardrobe when he stood back, even though he had a designer garment and nine full trash bags worth of merchandise. Several trips had to be made to his car, and on each visit, he told himself that he was done robbing the place; but he wasn't. Greed kept calling his name. The familiar voice was loud, succinct, and persuasive, telling him that his life needed these upgrades to feel like new money. The thirst for her shit was real; like an addict, he was addicted to Lucky's drip.

There was a pair of diamond earrings that he felt he had to have. An exquisite, 10-carat pair of platinum VVS diamonds was off-limits because he knew she'd eventually miss something so ornate. However, the temptation was more than he could resist, and the pink diamond earrings were stuffed into his $40 sweatpants pocket. His heart raced, feeling unusually giddy as he continued to rummage through Lucky's belongings. He was turned on when he stumbled upon three drawers of her lingerie— silk and lace panties, thongs, and bras. The drawers smelled of vanilla, and each item was neatly folded Marie Condo style. His masculine hands rummaged through her nipple pasties, his index finger outlined the opening of her 'eat me out' panties, and his thumb clicked on the huge vibrator that was in plain sight. Instinctually he picked up the object, which had weight and girth, and gave it a sniff to see if it had her scent—it didn't. He shut the drawer after fumbling over her rabbit toy, pussy, and nipple clamps. *So Miss Lucky was a little freak,* he thought.

The assailant circled back to Lucchese's room and briefly wondered about her fate. The streets said she was murdered over a kilo of cocaine; some said it was a botched ransom. He looked around at the custom crib set, tasteful cream, pale green, and dusty rose interior colors—and felt a fleeting moment of empathy for the kid. Fate had teased Lucchese West, dangling privilege and wealth before her; to have her born an heir to such lux and snuff her out before she could live to enjoy it was intentionally cruel.

He walked over to a baby hutch and dresser combination decorated with family photos, books, and teddy bears. Three African American dolls were strategically placed in the center—as a message, maybe? One doll's eyes were covered, the middle had her ears covered, and the last doll covered her mouth. It was clear that Lucky wanted to teach her daughter the rules of the family business early—to sum it up, don't snitch. You don't see, hear, or say shit in the drug game.

Before he left Lucchese's room, something caught his attention. At the very top of the hutch was a large mason jar. He picked it up and felt the weight in the palm of his hand. On its lid, he read: *To my big sister on her 16th birthday from your favorite and only sister, Bonnie.* The glass jar had sixteen painted messages of love and adoration for Lucky from her now-deceased sister. There was also a picture inside of Lucky with her arm around Bonnie, broad smiles, and deceivingly innocent eyes. It was clear that Bonnie had gone through a lot of thought into making this special gift for Lucky, and it was evident that this jar held sentimental value. It was a love letter to Lucky that he would use. With tremendous and unnecessary force, his arm raised, and in one swift movement, he smashed the jar on the imported marble flooring—pieces scattered like he wanted to do her sanity. He would break her just as he did this glass.

As the sun lowered in the sky, and his thieving had to end, he still wasn't done shopping. He picked up a Dyson vacuum for his mother, a Viking refrigerator filter for his mother-in-law, a new pack of double-A batteries, a box of T-bone steaks from her freezer, and several Calphalon nonstick pans. It was petty, but it was free. He took her Beats by Dre headphones, an iPad, a pair of Ray-Ban sunglasses, and wireless earbuds. He wanted her espresso coffee maker, vintage turntable set, and classic album collection, but it was too risky. He stole things that someone with their cup running over wouldn't readily miss; he was sure of that. And by the time she did look for something that wasn't there, she'd think that it's just misplaced. Her arrogance wouldn't allow her to assume someone would be bold enough to steal from her home. He wanted it all, not to leave her with a fucking morsel to nibble on.

Except for the conspicuously missing earrings, he had left Lucky's home without a trace that someone had ever entered. Moving forward, he would come and go as he pleased. Who the fuck was gonna stop him?

Angel was irate when he heard that Lucky had pulled through surgery and was in critical but stable condition in the Intensive Care Unit. The doctors had given Lucky a blood transfusion, and the little bitch was holding onto life by the slimmest of margins. Angel had sacrificed a good soldier for her execution, and he had failed the drug lord. Although he had carried out his order and will undoubtedly keep his mouth shut, he wouldn't last long in lockup. The Juarez cartel—the soldiers housed in American prisons will do the hit for their boss. Angel had given Emmanuel Vega one job, and he had failed. In his line of business, you don't get rewarded for failure. If he allowed Emmanuel to live, his subordinates would think it was okay to *try* being a sicario. Or *attempt* to move and distribute his kilos.

Angel stood over the infant's crib that all this fuss was made over. He didn't know her date of birth; it was still a mystery. Angel wanted to know her born date so he could throw her lavish parties. He wanted to know her zodiac sign to understand why she was fussy or moody. Angel wanted to know all these things because, through DNA testing, he just received the confirmation late last night she was his child. He had suspected when Layla had shown him her pictures, but now it was official, Lucchese Lily West was also a Morales—an heir to his throne.

Angel was a hardened gangster, a killer who murdered without remorse. He could tear a man or woman to shreds with a chainsaw and have lunch a few feet from the carnage, but he felt only love when he looked down at his child. He didn't understand the connection he felt toward her. Lucchese wasn't his first child. She wasn't even his first daughter. And he loved his children by his wife, Dahlia, and would readily give his life for theirs. But they felt more like Dahlia's children, her responsibility. And his job was as the protector and provider. With Lulu, he was the *nurturer*, provider, and protector—father and *mother*; she made him feel needed. And for Lucky to choose her life over Lucchese's had him baffled. This was her first child, and she had done so much to conceal her pregnancy; it was disturbing how she placed no value on Lulu's life when challenged to choose.

Angel remembered the conversation he had with his cousin. He looked at Louis and said, "Bring me back a baby's finger of Lucchese's age and complexion."

Louis looked at Angel, confused. "Jefe, where am I to get a baby's finger of the same age and complexion? That is difficult, is it not?"

Angel was adamant. He yelled, "Either you get me what I just asked for, or I will take your finger instead, cabrón!"

Angel recalled Lucky's screams as she opened the box with the severed finger, yet she wouldn't acquiesce. Lucky was a stubborn bitch, so much so that apparently, she was refusing to die until she was ready.

He exhaled, and Lulu's eyes popped open. As soon as she saw her father, her tiny mouth spread wide into a grin. She had all of her incisors, but her molars hadn't come in yet. Instantly she reached up for him, and he scooped her up into his arms. Angel showered her with kisses as he held her firmly.

"Buenos dias," he said. "Lulu say, 'buenos' for Papí." All his children were bilingual, and she would be too.

Lulu smiled and said, "Bu-no-no-no-no," and puckered her lips for a kiss. "Um-ma!" she said after their lips touched and giggled.

"Say, Papí," he encouraged again. He desperately wanted to hear his baby girl acknowledge who he was.

"Ma…ma…ma…ma…," she babbled.

"No, mama!" he corrected. "Mama is locá. Say, Papí."

Lucchese just nodded and smiled, making her father work for his title.

Angel traveled through the large mansion carrying his now spoiled child, heading toward the kitchen so he could fix her breakfast. He had nannies and servants but rarely used them for her. They were for his other children, and his wife was the overseer.

Lucchese was placed in a highchair, and Angel quickly warmed up organic apples and oats. As it cooled down, he opened a kitchen drawer and pulled out one of the fifteen burner and satellite phones. Angel sat in front of his daughter and said, "Open," and she did. Lucchese opened her small mouth wide for the spoonful of warm cereal and nodded her delight.

"Good, sí?" Angel asked as she devoured her morning meal. Simultaneously he reached Louis on speed dial. He instructed, "We end this with the Wests while two are down, and their parents are out of the country. Hire no less than a thousand soldiers from Juarez, Sinaloa, and Tijuana. Speak with Félix. He runs a militia group out of Mexico City. Those men are always looking for work. I want every stash, trap, and warehouse obliterated. Bring me back their heroin, cocá, and cash."

Louis asked, "And what about the young Wests? Do you want me to send men to the hospital and finish what we started?"

Angel thought for a second and then replied, "For now, they live. I will allow them life as beggars to know how it feels to be poor as we were, Louis. Remember when we had no shoes on our feet and ate only rice and beans for nourishment?"

"But that was so long ago, Angel. We were just kids."

"And I can still recall the hunger pains. Imagine how devastating it will be to fall from grace as an adult."

It wasn't Louis's job to imagine, hope, long for the past, or make decisions. His only job was to keep his boss alive and follow orders. He said, "As you wish," and hung up.

Dahlia came into the kitchen in her silk robe and heeled

slippers. She looked like one of the exotic beauties from a 1960s film: Sophia Loren or Rita Moreno. He knew his wife was only up this early to fuck with him. Lucchese had been in his custody for weeks, and he hadn't given a definitive answer to why she was there or to whom she belonged. Haphazardly, Angel had said that the infant was the catalyst that had launched his current war but refused to go into more detail.

Dahlia had a sickening feeling in her stomach but didn't want to believe her lying eyes. She stared at the baby her husband had been doting upon and refused to see his eyes, nose, and mouth. She said, "We have staff to handle her feeding."

"I know what we have because I pay them," he said and continued spoon-feeding Lulu.

"Then why don't you let them feed her pendejo! Who is this baby? Why is she in our home! Is she the heir to a Queen?"— Dahlia twirled her hands above her head, signifying royalty. "Because you're treating her like Mexican monarchy!"

"Stop it, Dahlia."

"Is she the child of an enemy?" She walked aggressively toward her husband. "Then kill her already and be done with this!"

Angel stood up and grabbed Dahlia's forearm, "She won't ever be touched, do you hear me? Ever!"

His wife yanked her arm from his grasp, her eyes storms of rage. She called, "Rosalina, fix me a large breakfast and bring it to my room. This kitchen needs to be exterminated before I'll ever eat in here again!"

Their chef, Rosalina, came rushing into the kitchen, adjusting her apron. "Yes, Mrs. Morales. Right away."

Angel didn't acknowledge her departure, and Lucchese was unfazed by Dahlia's outburst. The two were in their own world.

Rewind: Week one after Scott and Layla's acquittals

15

∞

The horizontal pull-up bar was mounted on the bathroom's doorway of the shabby, two-bedroom home he was squatting in. The veins bulged in his neck, his triceps and biceps flexed as he rapidly pulled his body weight up and down. Naked, beads of sweat traveled down his dark chocolate-colored skin, his perspiration a reminder he was putting in work. His firm physique was sculpted through battle wounds and muscles. He was turning his body into a weapon—solid and impenetrable, it would never fail him again. This morning, rage would allow him to surpass his average one hundred reps as he stared at the newspaper clipping he had taped to a wall of Scott and Layla's acquittal. The couple had beat the gospel of the streets, which said that in the game, you either ended up dead or in jail. Scott and Layla weren't either.

The Delaware house was foreclosed on by the bank and had been vacant for months. Whistler had found the property after he willingly signed himself out of the Witness Protection Program. Leading to the trial, Whistler was treated like a star athlete; LeBron James or Steph Curry—all his needs were met. The Bureau kept him in five-star hotels with around-the-clock agents to protect their indispensable witness. The government picked up the check for all his amenities. He dined on seafood and steak dinners, housekeeping kept his room immaculate, and the FBI had sworn an oath they would take a bullet for him.

The V.I.P. treatment was halted the second the defendants were found not guilty. Agents Randall and Devonsky stormed into his hotel room with scowls on their faces. Whistler was in the middle of eating an early dinner, a medium-rare steak—knife, and fork held firmly in his hands. He was seated at the round table in his suite. The white linen tablecloth was crisp, napkin placed eloquently on his lap. Although it was late afternoon, Whistler was still in his expensive silk pajamas, finding no reason to get dressed each day.

"Get up! Get dressed!" Agent Devonsky ordered. His face was beet red, his palpable anger directed at his witness. "Now!"

Whistler was startled and confused. He was still recuperating from his gunshot wounds; his coordination wasn't sharp, his mind had dulled like an overused knife.

"Can I finish my meal first?" He thought this was a practical question until Agent Devonsky barreled across the room, yanked him by his collar, and tossed him like a ragdoll. Whistler stumbled before falling on all fours. He was humiliated. His pride—what was left of it had dwindled, dissipating like sand through an hourglass. *Who was he?* He wanted to know because, at this very moment, he despised who he had become. Wasn't he Whistler Hussain—a muthafuckin' killer!

However, on that day, he wasn't murdering anyone. Reluctantly, he got dressed and was driven from Manhattan, New York, to Wilmington, Delaware, with Agent Randall at the wheel of the Lincoln Town car, and Agent Devonsky sat shotgun. The two-hour drive was ridden in silence as each man was encapsulated in his own thoughts. Whistler was confused when Randall made a right turn into a mobile trailer park. His eye quickly darted around, landing on each light blue mobile home with wooden steps and unkempt lots. The trailer Agent Randall parked in front of was sandwiched between a mobile home with an above-ground kids pool, dirty water, a rubber duck, and another house with an immovable vehicle on the lawn littered with a motor and a transmission. This was a nightmare for Whistler, who had become accustomed to luxury and opulence, whose hands had touched hundreds of millions, who had distributed tons of kilos and heroin. This couldn't be his last station in life.

Both agents got out, and doors slammed before Whistler moved to follow. The ground was a mixture of gravel, mud from recent rain, patches of grass, and overgrown weeds. He walked into the single wide, one bedroom, one bathroom trailer, thin prefabricated walls, linoleum floors, and thrift store furnishing. Dingy wallpaper from the early nineties was stained with memories from the other unfortunate souls that had occupied the space. A full kitchen with a white refrigerator made a loud sound—a buzz and hum that would fuck with anyone's sanity. The manufactured white cabinets had grease stains on the upper doors, and the ceramic kitchen sink had rust stains, albeit from the leaking faucet.

Whistler felt claustrophobic as he was led throughout his new residence with its low ceiling and compact square footage. He saw secondhand furniture, lace dollies, and religious artifacts everywhere he laid his eye. White Jesus hung over the sofa, and a cross was placed over his bedframe. The stale, funky air combined too many things to sort through. He was livid.

Back in the cramped living room, kitchen area, Agent Randall finally spoke. He exhaled dismissively and said, "You get a nine hundred dollar stipend per month that you'll need to budget for food, clothing, and utilities. Whatever's left, you can do whatever you want with it. This home is paid for, so you will live rent-free. All compliments of the taxpaying citizens of the United States of America!"

His tone was snarky and condescending, and it didn't go over Whistler's head. Randall continued with, "There's a working vehicle parked in the back for you. Any repairs are on you, and I can promise it will need repairs. You need extra money—don't call us! You're free to get a job for extra income, but you'll have to run it by us first, and we'll have to approve. If you get arrested for any reason, you're out of WitSec. You hang around anyone with a criminal record, and we find out—you're done! You go back to your old neighborhood, and we'll drop you like a bad habit."

Agent Randall tossed an envelope on the table with the keys to the vehicle, mobile trailer, new identity, and paperwork needed to start over. "You're officially Donald Williams. Have a miserable fucking life."

Chapter 2

The ocean was gentle. The sunset looked like orange paint on a blue canvas. The whispering wind was calm, and the horizon was a beautiful thing to see from a 100-foot luxury yacht. Deep royal blue waves moved toward the idling ship that sat fifty miles from the Australian coastline. It was a vast ocean for miles around, and Layla and Scott had a panoramic view of God's creation. Layla sunbathed in her two-piece bikini on the ship's deck, and Scott smoked his cigar and stared at the sea, almost in a meditative state. They were having the time of their lives until they got that fateful information. Mason called and told them about Avery's strange murder weeks ago. His body had been found in the hospital stairwell, strangled, and discarded like trash. There were no suspects—no one was apprehended. Scott and Layla believed the Juarez cartel killed Avery. Scott and Layla had set the events in motion, and sadly, Avery was one casualty. They assumed that Angel sent his henchmen to the hospital to finish what he'd started—to make sure that Bugsy, Lucky, and Meyer were dead, and they figured that Avery somehow had gotten in the way.

And then Meyer called his mother with week-old news.

"Bugsy and Lucky got hit...shit looking critical. We at NewYork-Presbyterian Hospital. I'ma need you and Pops to come home," he screamed frantically into the phone.

Layla had to cover her mouth to prevent herself from laughing out loud. In a saddened tone, she asked, "How critical?"

"Life support critical!" Meyer yelled. "Your kids might not make it through the night. Y'all need to get here asap."

Meyer explained Lulu's kidnapping and severed finger, the

bizarre murder of Avery by an unknown assailant, and the war with Angel Morales while his mother listened intently.

"We're coming, son!" Layla assured him. "Your father will get us on the first thing smokin'. Tell Lucky and Bugsy to hold on...."

Layla took a sip from her pricey champagne, Dom Perignon Rosé, $850 a bottle, and basked under the lowering sun reliving the conversation. The desperation in Meyer's voice was so pathetic. She hated to put her favorite child through so much agony, but one had to charge it to the game.

"Come, my love...come join me, enjoy the day," she said to Scott. "I know you, and you're strategizing when you should be relaxing."

Scott turned and stared at her. Layla was untroubled by the recent events. But Scott couldn't stop thinking about things going on in the states.

"It's been seventy-two hours since we heard from Mason," he said.

"I'm sure he's fine, most likely workin' on getting a beat on those sicarios. That's hard work lookin' for Mexicans in Mexico."

"He's our eyes and ears over there, Layla. We need to know everything that's going on," Scott said. "He usually calls every day. Where the fuck he at? Some shit has gone down. I can feel it!"

"You can't worry yourself, Scott. He will call, but relax and keep me company in the meantime. Come over here and enjoy your wife."

Scott took a strong puff from his cigar and exhaled the smoke. What his wife didn't know was that he also had Mason looking for Maxine. Her body never washed ashore or turned up in any hospital or morgue in the tristate area. Scott couldn't burden Layla with his suspicions that Maxine was still alive; he felt confident in his decision to allow her to believe otherwise. But for Scott, his anecdote was *never trust, always verify.* That's how he stayed alive.

Maxine had proved to be a cunning adversary. She had not only managed to outsmart him, his wife, and his son—which was a feat not to be overlooked, but so far, she was undefeated in the ring with heavyweights; pound for pound, she kept taking those hits, and presumably, she was still standing. No one had ever done to them what Maxine did, not even the feds. And although, at a time or two, he felt love for her, he couldn't await the day he could erase her from her remaining timeline.

Scott's eyes swept over the calm waters and then back to Layla as she removed her bikini top. Her large, tan areolas and erect nipples glistened in the remaining sun. She grabbed more suntanning oil and massaged the thin liquid into her supple skin, circular motions meant to entice her husband.

"Come here and chill wit' me," she said. "Or come fuck me, baby. Let's not allow this yacht to go to waste."

Before anything sexual could get started, the satellite phone rang. Layla answered it and was surprised to hear his voice on the other end of the phone.

"Meyer…," she called out in disbelief, wondering how he got that number.

His voice boomed, "Where the fuck y'all at? Y'all been playin' games for weeks. Why ain't y'all here?"

"Calm down," she scolded in a motherly tone she had perfected throughout the years. "We had some issues…our passports were stolen from our beach rental, and we've been waiting on the United States Embassy to send out our replacements!"

Scott raised his eyebrow at how quickly his wife thought under pressure. He stood, walked over to her, and gave her a dap mid-conversation.

Meyer's voice lowered a few octaves. "My bad…but Ma, like I told you weeks ago, we at war. Bugsy and Lucky ain't pulling through. It's not a matter of if; it's when they're gonna take their last breath, and I don't wanna go through the burial processes alone. I need you…I need y'all."

This information had piqued Layla's interest. She needed clarification. She placed Meyer on speakerphone. "Meyer, your father's listening. Explain what's going on with your siblings."

"Like I said, they're almost gone. Lucky's lost too much blood, and Bugsy's bullet in his face has traveled to his brain."

Scott spoke, "Meyer, what can we do?"

Meyer cleared his throat to distract himself from lashing out. He couldn't wait until he lured them back on American soil. He simply said, "Y'all can come home."

"Your mother just explained our dilemma, and until the U.S. Embassy sorts this out, we're still on vacation. You and your siblings are grown now, and I'm sure whatever is happening, the three of y'all can handle it."

Meyer exhaled. What part of dying did they not get? "Bugsy and Lucky can't handle shit!"

This phone call was what Scott needed to liven up his mood. To hear Meyer in a panicky plea amused him. Scott kept fucking with his son.

"You have my blood in you, Meyer. And you were always a mentally and physically strong individual. I'm sure whatever shit you're going through, you can come out of it on top. You were raised to know how to handle your own. You're a West, so don't you fuckin' forget that."

Meyer wasn't here for it. He didn't need a speech. What he wanted was revenge. He became irked because he wasn't making a breakthrough.

"We're at war with the Juarez cartel. Do y'all care? It's getting ugly over here. I can't handle all this shit on my own."

"Put more shooters on your payroll until we get there," Layla spoke up. "Let us make some calls and see what we can do about travel arrangements."

"Yeah, you do that!"

She hung up and said to Scott, "He knows."

"How the fuck that lil' nigga piece this shit together?" Scott wondered out loud. "We executed every hit flawlessly."

Layla snorted. "Apparently not."

"It had to be Bugsy, then."

"It doesn't matter how Meyer knows just that he does. And I bet that hotheaded muthafucka murdered Avery," Layla deduced.

Scott's head nodded his agreement.

With Mason giving them updates about their children, they knew what Meyer was telling them about Bugsy, and Lucky taking a turn for the worse was a lie. They both were stable and talking. So if their children wanted them to desperately return to New York, it wasn't for help. Somehow, they had connected their involvement in the murders.

Scott paced around the stern of the yacht. He was brooding again. Scott said, "How the fuck he get this number?" The question was rhetorical because Layla didn't know. "Check out the brains on that muthafucka."

Layla shrugged. She was living her best life in the land Down Under and would not let her children rain on her parade.

"Who the fuck cares? Really, Scott. Lucky and Bugsy are half dead, Meyer is stuck babysitting, Angel will continue his warpath, and Dillinger, Maxine, and Lucchese are all dead. I say we got a lot to celebrate. You're looking at this all wrong. The glass is half full—" Layla stood and refilled their glasses with the expensive bubbly— "And we control the flow."

"So you don't want to go back and finish what we started? Half dead ain't dead. Bugsy and Lucky are still adversaries, possibly plotting as we speak. Every day they pull air is an insult to our legacy. That lil' nigga Bugsy really tried to overthrow the King of New York." The mere thought of the past two years had left a bad taste in Scott's mouth. "We can do our own dirty work."

Layla was about to go off on the same tangent as her husband about Lucky, but then she looked around at the opulent yacht, the vast sea, and the champagne and caviar and thought differently. "Scott, you know that real gangstas take a tactical pause to win in a war. We use this time wisely and make sure that when we come back, we're a quiet storm."

Her husband nodded. "Meyer wants to bait us back into an ambush. That hotheaded muthafucka think he could outsmart us!"

"That lil' nigga did learn from the best." Layla smiled that her son would have the balls to go against them without Bugsy and Lucky.

Scott knew that true leaders never led their team into an ambush. He would use this time to reassess his movements. One philosophy he would call upon was Sun Tzu, who said, *"The general who wins the battle makes many calculations before the battle is fought. The general who loses makes but few."*

Scott West wasn't about to lose shit.

Félix, the head of a militia group in Mexico City, traveled Northeast in the Chihuahuan Desert in Mexico with a fleet of Hummers heading toward the Texas border. His militia group was hired to ambush two tractor-trailers carrying ninety tons of cocaine before crossing into the United States. His men were heavily armed, skilled, and deadly. As the Hummers cut through the dry landscape, dust clouds kicked up and shrouded the drivers' visibility, who used brake lights as their guide on the unpaved, rocky roads.

Félix had gotten the call from Louis, the cousin of Angel, who's the head of the Juarez cartel. Their targets were in America, and the organization was his former clients. The young Wests' empire would be on the receiving end of the wrath this sicario used to inflicting. However, by some unexplained leniency act, their instructions were to leave the children—Bugsy, Meyer, and Lucky, alive.

"Dígame, Louis, what is this? Sanction us to handle the children, and the parents too!" Félix spat a chunk of phlegm out his passenger's window, disgusted at his orders. "En este negocio nadie escapa a la muerte!" Félix told Louis that no one escapes death in this business.

"No! They are not to be touched by anyone, or you will personally suffer the consequences puta! You don't tell Angel Morales how to run Juarez!"

Félix hated loose ends. He didn't understand mercy—the concept didn't resonate with his uncomplicated way of life. Mexican born and raised, as was Angel Morales, the code was to destroy your enemy. It was total annihilation in war, so he understood little of what the head of Juarez was trying to carry out. But this mission involved bloodshed. The assignment was to infiltrate the United States of America, kill everyone working for any faction of the West organization, and leave without a trace.

He needed to call in reinforcements, his sicario brothers, for a job this big, as monumental as the Juarez cartel had asked. Félix pulled out his satellite phone, and his first call was to Arturo, "We need to meet."

Chapter 3

"They know," Meyer said after ending his call with their parents.

"Are you sure?" Bugsy asked. His deep voice was now more resonant and raspier. The bullet had shattered his jawbone and came out of his cheek. He now had a permanent dimple, and his mouth pulled to the right where the projectile had entered. He and Meyer were no longer identical twins. His lowcut Caesar had now grown out into a low curly afro. His soft coils and curls looked similar to his sister's, but the hairstyle didn't emasculate him. His beard and mustache had connected, and even though he was more than a nickel away from turning thirty, a patch of gray hair had sprouted near his left temple.

Mentally Bugsy was fucked up, but revenge had a way of keeping a half-dead man alive. "How could they know something's up? They wouldn't know that you heard Avery's conversation."

"There was something in Ma's voice when I told her that you and Lucky took a turn for the worse. I know she didn't believe me," Meyer explained. "I swear, Bee, if they come back…when they come back on everything I love, Pops can't live. I'ma blow a cannon size hole in his head." Meyer simulated holding an automatic rifle and pulling the trigger.

"That ain't your place," Bugsy explained. "This is on me, don't take that away. I buried my son. My little man is gone, Meyer. I need to avenge his death. Scott and Layla played me like a muthafuckin' fool. I got innocent blood on my hands that I can't wash off. That shit haunts me."

"Innocent? Ain't nobody innocent in this game, Bee."

Bugsy's head shook slowly like it was a hundred-pound weight. He couldn't shake off what he had done. "I broke my own code: no women, no kids—"

"Wait. You stressin' over that lady and her son that me and Avery kidnapped from Florida?"

"They said they ain't have shit to do with Dillinger's murder, they all had sworn this wasn't cartel sanctioned, but I didn't believe it. I looked that lady in her eyes and put a bullet in her head." Bugsy choked up but held back his tears. "Who am I, Meyer? I killed a kid the same age as Gotti!"

"That blood's on Scott's hands, not yours!" Meyer was amped, ready to go on a tyrannical emotional rollercoaster, when six federal agents came bursting into the room in blue flight jackets, flashing gold badges with guns drawn. Startled, Meyer said, "What the fuck!"

Bugsy jumped too. The overly dramatic ambush was unnecessary and off-putting. Meyer and Bugsy saw the recognizable faces of Agent Randall and Agent Devonsky. Meyer said, "These niggas again...."

"Meyer, glad you're here, buddy," Devonsky snickered. "This pertains to you too."

"Fuck y'all want?!" Meyer asked as he glared defiantly into each agent's eyes, demanding an explanation.

Agent Randall tossed a set of papers which landed on Bugsy's lap. He said, "We just came from Judge Kavanaugh's office. He signed off on a Temporary Restraining Order and Assets Freeze of West Enterprises, West International, The West Children's Foundation, and West Kovnavian Real Estate. In short, you have no legal liquidity."

Meyer was about to detonate, but Bugsy gave him a look that halted his tantrum. Coolly, Bugsy asked, "On what grounds?"

"You're a drug dealer."

Bugsy smirked, "Prove it."

"What do you think we've done here? We proved to our good friend Judge Kavanaugh that the seed money from all your legal business ventures is derived from drug money. In my book, that means you're fucked."

"This is weak," Bugsy continued and tossed the paperwork back at the agent. "My lawyer will eat this."

Randall's face was beet red, angered at how well Bugsy was handling that the government had just frozen nearly two hundred million of his funds.

"You better watch it, punk!" Randall yelled. "I could arrest you for assault!"

"Do you, playah!"

"Bugsy West, you're under arrest for possession of an illegal firearm and will be arraigned from your hospital bed on Thursday. You have the right to remain silent, motherfucker!" Randall began as he roughly grabbed Bugsy's left arm and handcuffed it to the bed.

"Y'all muthafuckas can't do this!" Meyer yelled, incensed. "He ain't have no gun!"

"Get him out of here!" Agent Randall ordered. One of his men roughly yoked up Meyer, his strong forearm wrapped aggressively around Meyer's neck in an illegal chokehold, and he pulled. "Resist arrest! I fucking dare you motherfucker!" the agent shouted when he sensed hostility in Meyer's body language. Meyer placed his hands up in a nonconfrontational surrender as he was pulled from the room. Agent Randall continued to belittle Bugsy. "Whatever you say can and will be used against you in the court of law. As I've read them, do you understand your rights, you narcotic pushing parasite?"

Bugsy's face was stone. Agent Randall sat at the foot of his bed and wanted to taunt Scott and Layla's firstborn son. "We got the ballistics report back, and guess whose fingerprints are all over a beautiful chrome .45?"

Bugsy didn't mumble a fucking word. His eyes glared at all the men in his room, gloating. The mention of the gun put him in a sour mood as visions of Alicia came flooding back. Agent Randall continued in a mocking tone. "Yours! Oh, how I wish you were a real man who knew how to protect his woman—"

Bugsy's mouth pulled to his right side, and he squeezed out, "Fuck you!"

Randall continued, "If you were…a real man…then, you would have got out to make the baby exchange, and you'd be dead." Randall clapped his hands together. "Welp, so much for wishful thinking."

And then Agent Devonsky chimed in. "You know my wish?" He didn't wait for an answer before continuing, "I wish this piece of shit was quicker with his trigger finger because if he were, we'd be arresting him for murder and not possession. But we've heard that Meyer is the twin with the big balls."

Bugsy wanted to get up from his hospital bed and put his paws on them. But he calmed down, knowing they were intentionally trying to incite a reaction. A gun charge was lightweight in his line of work and would also be his first offense. Plus, he was confident he would beat the case, but he would handle it if he blew trial. He said, "If y'all are done, then get the fuck outta my room."

"Aren't you gonna ask why the feds would arrest you on a gun charge? Why not let NYPD handle it? Aren't you remotely curious?" Agent Randall was tickled at his own pettiness. "Let me answer that for you since you asked. We've taken over this gun charge because once we get you, we're never letting you go. Once behind bars, Bugsy West, I promise you that you won't ever experience freedom again. So tell your homies, tell your less than smart sister and your thug brother that they're next!"

Nearly one thousand elite soldiers set out enroute for America.

The heavily armed individuals—all ranking from militia and cartel members to sicarios and federalés. Carloads drove out of Chihuahua across the Mexican border into El Paso, Texas; Sonora, Mexico, into Arizona, or Tijuana, Mexico, into San Diego, California—all heading Northeast. They entered the United States by different means: illegally smuggled past the borders, driving legally through checkpoints, or direct flights into New York. Lucky would never understand that giving birth to Lucchese had set in motion what's known as The Butterfly Effect. The unsanctioned birth of Lucchese Lily West was destined to bring forth death and destruction.

Meyer took a moment to compose himself after being tossed out of his brother's room. He wanted to curse them out, swing wildly, and act ignorant. But Meyer knew he'd ultimately end up in a jail cell. He looked around and felt only anger and disgust. A familiar stale smell lingered in the air mixed with disinfectants, an odor that kept triggering bad memories of when he was laid up. That hospital had become a hub of grief for his family.

Meyer pushed the door of his sister's private room, and she was awake. The television was on, and the volume was low. Lucky looked forlorn and sullen, in deep thought, her mind miles away. She had been leaving threatening voice messages to Angel about Lulu's severed finger until he eventually disconnected that burner.

Lucky eyes turned toward Meyer and slowly back toward the television. She didn't acknowledge him as a visitor.

"What's up?" he asked and took a seat in the unoccupied chair. Meyer still had a scowl on his face, but Lucky gave no fucks. She ignored him, and Meyer said, "How you holding up?"

"How do you think?" she snapped. "I had a blade shoved in my gut repeatedly, and with a hospital full of people, no one fuckin' helped! They all wanted that piece of shit to murder me! Those bitches at the nurses' station just stood there eye and ear hustling!" Meyer didn't feel that happened, but he allowed her to vent. She continued, "I got nearly one hundred stitches all over my stomach!" Lucky sucked her teeth. "No more bikinis for me! I'm twenty-two years old, and I got more scars than Scarface!"

Lucky was having a pity party, and everyone was invited. Meyer had walked in with an attitude and quickly adjusted it. It wouldn't help either of their situations if they both were angry. He said, "I was talking about Lulu. How are you holding up, not knowing if she's dead or alive? When did the feds say the DNA test results on the finger will come back?"

Lucky was incensed. "Are you kidding me?" she asked. "You coming in here laying what happened to my daughter at my feet when it's because of you and Bugsy that Angel went so hard! Bugsy got my daughter possibly killed because his son was murdered! And then we find out that Angel didn't even have Dillinger killed. Scott and Layla did!"

Meyer looked deeply into his sister's eyes, seeing her pain. She was young and had been through a lot. He couldn't imagine how it felt to be in her shoes and knew that judging her now would be fruitless. Everyone processes trauma and grief differently, so he couldn't understand how she was feeling inside about her daughter. Meyer kept his voice low and soothing. "Nothing I say can bring her back, but I'm going to keep this promise to you, and that's I'ma murder Angel Morales for what he did to Lulu. And I'ma murder Scott and Layla for what they did to all of us."

Lucky was tired of promises. "What do you want, Meyer? Why are you in here?" He was about to tell her what had happened to Bugsy and how the feds had frozen their assets when she said, "In fact, don't come back until Angel's dead. By your hands or someone else's! I'm serious. Get the fuck out!"

Meyer didn't object. He simply stood up, looked down at his old skool Pumas', tossed his hoodie on his head, and bounced.

Scott woke from an exhausting night of lovemaking and was starving. Layla was passed out, sleeping on her stomach with a black mask covering her eyes, blocking the light. She was lightly snoring and looked peaceful. Scott stood up, yawned, and stretched out his tight muscles. He wandered through the narrow hallway of the yacht, down a flight of steps, and into the kitchen butt-ass naked. His massive penis swung between his legs, hanging low, freely flowing from obstruction.

Scott walked into the kitchen, and seated at the table was their hired chef, Jillian. She was one of many staff members on the luxury cruiser. Jillian was born in Austria and had moved to Australia thirty years ago. She was in her late fifties and still had a voracious sexual appetite. She looked at her employer's sexy, toned body and quickly got moist. She was an older, conservative woman, but she wasn't dead. His naked physique had her flustered; she wanted to sit on his dick and dig her fingernails in his chest as she twirled her hips. Her eyes lingered on his manscaped man-bush, trimmed low, outlining his deep V.

"Good morning," Scott casually said as he made himself a Bloody Mary. He had a hangover, and this drink was always his cure.

Jillian was blushing as she stared at his round, firm ass, and muscular thighs. She perspired and fanned away her lust. Finally, she said, "Good afternoon,…um, Mr. West…are you and your wife hungry?"

"I am," he replied as he poured the Vodka into his tomato juice. "I'm starving, but my wife is still asleep."

"What would you like for lunch?" Jillian said to update him on the late hour.

"Nothing. I'm in the mood for breakfast," said Scott. He took a large gulp of his drink and continued, "An egg white omelet with ham, spinach, peppers, and cheddar cheese. And crispy bacon and a couple homemade biscuits."

She nodded. "Right away, sir. And will you want this in your room?" Jillian asked, hoping that he would shower and put some clothes on.

Scott shook his head. "I'll take it out on the deck."

Scott walked toward the stern and was surprised to see another yacht parked about three hundred yards from theirs. He heard voices and focused his attention on the movement. He could see two figures on the ship's deck: laughing and enjoying themselves. This piqued his interest. Scott grabbed the binoculars so he could spy on his neighbors. Up close, he saw a beautiful woman in a skimpy bikini. She looked in her late twenties, early thirties. Her suntanned complexion glistened under the afternoon sun, and her curves had his dick standing at attention.

"And who are you…," said Scott as he admired the pretty young thang. Next, he focused on the male. Scott could admit that the male was handsome, tall, and physically fit. He looked Scott's age, mid-forties, and had a swagger that Scott recognized as a man with means. Scott arrogantly assumed that they were the only Black people doing it real big in Australia other than Oprah. He looked at the Black male with his Barbie and wondered if he were a professional athlete. If so, Scott couldn't place him.

Scott didn't realize how long he had been staring, but he looked long enough to see the female strip naked and jump into the vast mosaic of sea colors. The male immediately followed her. They frolicked around like a couple on their honeymoon. *Who the fuck were they?* He wanted to know.

Smack! Layla slapped her husband's firm ass, startling him. "What you looking at?"

Scott passed Layla the binoculars. When her eyes adjusted, she saw a beautiful, naked woman climbing out of the water dripping wet. Her short hair slicked off her face, around her ears, and the male stayed in the ocean doing laps.

"Who the fuck are they?" Layla growled, already feeling a

way about her husband watching this naked woman.

Scott shrugged. "I don't know, but you wanna go over there to find out?"

Layla rolled her eyes and replied, "Fuck 'em!"

The sun smacked Meyer when he walked out of the hospital into the brisk air. His Ray-Bans' were put on, and he made his way toward the garage for his SUV. He could feel he was being watched, followed. Meyer pulled out his cellphone and put it near his face as he walked like he was making a call and went to CAMERA on his iPhone. He could clearly see the agent trailing behind him. Meyer kept walking around the corner, past the garage, and stopped in The Brooklyn Bistro restaurant to figure out what he would do next.

He was seated and quickly ordered. There wasn't any way Meyer was getting into his Escalade. He had two 9mms under his passenger's seat, and he wasn't about to catch a gun charge. The feds were coming after them because their parents were abroad, had gotten acquitted, and because of the melee they'd caused on the Upper Westside. Meyer knew he couldn't carry a weapon on his persons, which made him very afraid.

He called Fitzgerald. "Listen, they arrested Bugsy on a gun charge."

"Who's they?"

"The feds! Those same fucks from Scott and Layla's case."

"Okay, what do you want me to do?" Fitzgerald only wanted to talk about money.

"I want you to get this bullshit thrown out," he hollered. "Bugsy ain't doing no jail time."

Fitzgerald was always amused that criminals loved doing the crime, but they thought doing jail time was optional. He said, "I'm going to need a retainer."

"Done. How much?"

"One million."

"For a fuckin' gun? You done bumped ya head!"

"For a federal gun charge, Meyer. That's my retainer for anything federal. It's the same for all my clients. Speak with your mother for verification."

Fitzgerald knew that the family was estranged, the brains of the organization was Bugsy, and he was compromised. Dealing with the young Wests, he would do things differently. There would be no strong-arming going down, no return of monies, no feeling vulnerable. After reading online that attorney Arthur Meade had committed suicide, he hired a security team. Ex-law enforcement guarded him daily because he refused to eat a bullet and have people think it was of his own volition. He knew Arthur was murdered, a fate that would not become his.

"A'ight, but we got another problem. Them pigs froze our legal accounts sayin' some judge signed off on this bullshit! I'ma need you to handle that too."

"That won't be a problem. I'll look into it." Meyer now had his full attention. He had been eyeing a Bugatti and would factor the cost into the bill. "But double the case, double the cost."

"Damn, Fitz. You's a greedy muthafucka!"

"It's not personal. This is business, Meyer. You know that."

Meyer understood. "Well, you gonna have to take cash."

"Cash works."

"A'ight. I'll bring it to your office Wednesday morning. Bugsy gets arraigned Thursday."

Meyer ended the call.

As he waited for his food, Meyer called Lollipop. He hadn't seen her in a minute since Lucky called him to say that Bugsy was shot. He went to voicemail.

"Yo, I been leavin' messages and textin', and you ain't hit a nigga back. Don't make me come through and act a fool. Call your dude. One."

Chapter 4

The cartel soldiers and militia group took just over a week to travel from their Mexican locations to New York City. They stayed in low-rent motels, slept at highway rest stops, and took naps in their vehicles on side roads—all converging in the Empire State for one goal, to end the reign of the young West siblings with specific orders from Angel Morales. Their mission was called: *Día De Muertos.* Translated into English, it meant *day of the dead.*

Félix had handpicked them all, and the soldiers were ready. These henchmen had survived pipe bombs, turf and drug wars, and police raids. Most had been shot, had fingers removed, were tortured, or stabbed as cartels waged war against each other. Félix looked into the faces of the meanest vatos Mexico had chewed up and spit out. Angry goons who were marginalized all their lives by the stereotypical depiction of Mexicans—they only cleaned toilets, jumped the border to use up all America's resources, and were responsible for the worlds' drug pandemic. This prejudiced rhetoric placed boulder-sized chips on their shoulders, and this trip would allow them to kill American citizens who had disrespected one of their own. Someone they all held in the highest regard, the head of the Juarez cartel. These men would kill your grandma over a poppy seed, dismember your child after snorting a line of cocaine, fuck your wife with a Corona bottle if *el jefe* told them to do so. This was the drug game; violent, gritty, merciless.

Félix lectured the soldiers, all Mexican born and bred for this life. By the age of five, generally, you worked on cannabis or poppy plantations—mostly in Sinaloa, Durango, or Chihuahua in the Golden Triangle region of the mountains. If you weren't helping to produce heroin or marijuana, you were assigned to a lab that made meth by the ton or evading detection along one of the many flourishing smuggling routes. By ten, if you were resourceful, you'd earn a job couriering kilos through the jungles dodging bandits, the Mexican military, federalés, border patrol, and vice police that weren't on the cartels' payroll.

Less than a decade ago, Colombia, Bolivia, and Peru combined manufactured approximately 95% of the world's cocaine. Mexican cartels, once merely couriers for the Colombians, had evolved. And through the ingenuity and ambition of Angel Morales and the Juarez cartel at the helm of this tectonic shift, Juarez was now producing their own cocaine supply. These same boys, now men, worked in the newly minted cocaine fields pulling unprocessed cocá leaves to be manufactured and cultivated into 100% pure cocaine by Mexican drug gangs. Mexico now had it all—the product, the vast distribution routes into the United States via its lengthy border, and the clientele. Mexican organized crime had dominance over the South American criminal organizations and cartels.

"Every puta dies tonight," Félix said to nearly six hundred men who had made their way across the country for war. Almost half didn't make it to the meeting spot, detained by border patrol, murdered by bandits, or flagged by customs. But those who did were more than capable of completing the assignment. The henchmen were gathered in a large catholic church, hosted by Monsignor Francisco González Valez, who held allegiance to Angel. Félix pointed to Arturo, Raffa, and then Pedro. "My men will separate everyone into factions and assign a location. Our orders are to kill the mayates, take the cocá, heroin, dinero, and report back to Juarez."

"Este maldito bastardo!" Dahlia cursed and seethed, calling her husband a fuckin' bastard. "He thinks he can just treat me like this. *No soy su puta!*"

Dahlia was livid. She was so angry at her husband she couldn't reason. Her sister Marbella stood in the kitchen with her, wanting Dahlia to calm down. But Dahlia was fed up; she wanted to kill Angel. How dare he bring that half Negro child into their home and treat her like she was his own? Where was the mother? But the question she really wanted to be answered was, *who* was the father?

Dahlia and Angel had two boys and a girl together, ages five, six, and nine—three children who needed their father's attention.

"I'll kill him!" she cursed in Spanish.

"Dahlia, lower your voice," said Marbella, looking around cautiously.

"Don't tell me how to behave in my home! I'm tired of seeing that little bitch everywhere with him!"

"She's just a baby!"

"She's an enemy," Dahlia shouted.

It sickened Dahlia to her core to see Angel treat Lulu so lovingly. Always picking her up, carrying her in his arms, and parading her through the house for everyone to see. If there was a meeting with his men, Lucchese was right there. Breakfast, lunch, and dinner—Angel handled it. If her nanny tried to take her away from Angel, Lulu would whine until Angel would say, "Leave her…leave her with me," his grin stretched a mile wide. Angel loved the attention, but he also understood that his wife was furious and didn't want to upset her. However, today Dahlia was pushing his limits, overstepping his boundaries. She was never shy about making her feelings known—today, she was in rare form.

"She shouldn't be here!" Dahlia hollered. "I hate her! She's not one of us!"

Hate Lulu? It was her right to, but to harm the infant; Dahlia knew not to act out on those feelings. Instead, she attacked the kitchen. Dahlia smashed expensive china and crystal glasses, tossed a few costly serving platters across the room, and felt no relief. Jealousy was whirling around inside her, and she didn't like that emotion. It made her feel helpless and needy like she was the mistress and not the wife. As if she had encroached on another woman's situation, another woman's life. Each time she'd ask her husband who Lucchese was and why she was there, he'd never give her a straight answer. She now felt the truth would be more tolerable than his repeated lies.

Marbella simply stood there and watched it all unfold—like a deranged mental patient, Dahlia's lunacy was almost unstoppable. She knew once her sister became angry and felt disrespected, her temper took over, and there wasn't any reasoning with her.

Angel heard the commotion and walked into the kitchen, carrying Lulu in his arms, like always. His eyes didn't even acknowledge the fury or emotional outcry Dahlia had displayed. He glanced her way and continued walking past her toward the pool area while flanked by two of his men.

Dahlia paused her tantrum and now felt humiliated on top of all the uncomfortable feelings she had to process. The Latin blood in her body was boiling to an epic level of hysteria. She was about to implode. Angel's audacity to ignore her in front of Marbella, his henchmen, had her feeling disrespected on so many levels.

Dahlia grabbed a plate to break over Angel's head as Angel exited the kitchen. But Marbella stepped in front of her sister to prevent her from doing something stupid. Marbella knew how dangerous and evil Angel could be. He was unpredictable, and although Dahlia was his wife, there was no telling if pushed too far what he would do.

Trying to fight past Marbella, Dahlia screamed, "Move! Move! Let me at him! That fucking bastard!"

Tears were now streaming down her face, and Marbella

wanted her to pull it together. She also guessed that the baby girl belonged to Angel, and she didn't think it was that big of a deal. Men had children out of wedlock all the time, and there wasn't a mother around, so why couldn't Dahlia just let it play out. She asked, "Until he tells you otherwise, why you can't just accept what he has told you?"

Dahlia waved her hand dismissively. "Get out of my face, Marbella. You're not married, and you can't have children!"

Hurt by that remark, Marbella slowly nodded as Dahlia pushed past her.

∞

Under the cloak of darkness, something unprecedented would occur on a night no different from any other. Something so heinous, so inhumane, the carnage would go down in history as another terrorist attack on American soil. An army of Mexican killers, all wearing masks made famous in the Scream movies, swarmed the locations of every stash, trap, and warehouse owned and operated by Bugsy, Meyer, and Lucky Luciana West. The takedown was reminiscent of a raid in Afghanistan or Qatar, where insurgents infiltrated local villages. From the air, if using night vision, it looked like fire ants colonizing their nests.

The hired goons were out just as quickly as they went in, stealthily, brazen, and deadly. When the smoke cleared, no one was left alive, all kilos of cocaine and heroin were confiscated, and millions in drug profits had been usurped.

Angel Morales had masterminded the takedown of the century.

∞

NY 1 news is how Meyer got the life-altering information about yesterday's attack. News reporters from each borough gave detailed accounts of the unspeakable acts committed to the victims gunned down. White coroner vans were at each location as dozens of body bags were wheeled out. NYPD detectives, sergeants, captains, and lieutenants were all present, disbelief written on everyone's faces.

Video footage from the high-tech surveillance equipment that Bugsy had installed at each location was being rolled. Each journalist narrated their version of the gruesome events to the public. Although several boroughs and different clips were shown, they all had one thing in common—all the assailants wore what Meyer knew was the *Muerte* mask, also worn in the Scream movies.

At precisely midnight, the masked killers crept up on unsuspecting gunmen with high-powered assault weapons and unleashed war. The assassins swarmed each warehouse like a bee colony—fast and deadly and moved succinctly in paramilitary form. It was something out of a movie.

Meyer watched in complete and utter bewilderment that such a feat could have simultaneously been pulled off. This had to be a muthafuckin' nightmare, a dream that he'd wake up from. His eyes were wide as the cameraman panned the recognizable places of real estate; yellow crime scene tape as familiar to him as his own hands outlined the boundaries that had been crossed. Last night he went to bed a multi-millionaire. This morning he woke up broke. Years of hard work, sacrifices, and strategizing were wiped out in synchronized raids orchestrated by the Juarez cartel. It was all too unbelievable. Every person that worked for them was murdered. Authorities only found dead bodies at each location—no drugs or money was recovered. Frantically, Meyer got on his cellphone and went down his contact list to no avail. No one answered. What the fuck would he do now? He was supposed to put together the million-dollar retainers for Fitzgerald to represent them and Bugsy against those pigs!

Meyer paced around his apartment angrily, not knowing how to move forward. It was too early to be using his brain this hard. He wanted to get in his truck and drive to each location and perhaps see if something or someone was overlooked, had survived the attack, maybe give himself a lifeline.

He called Fitzgerald and tried to stall for time. "Yo, listen. I'm tied up…but um…handle my brother's case, and I'll meet you at your office on Friday wit' that paper we discussed."

Fitz was expecting this call, but the conversation wasn't what he thought it would be. Fitz, too, had seen the footage as he drank his morning espresso and figured it had something to do with his drug-dealing clients. He assumed that Meyer would call with news that one or hopefully more of their soldiers had gotten arrested and needed counsel. Depending on how many were detained, his office had enough attorneys to represent the organization. Now it seemed as if young Meyer was trying to skip out on a bill. There wasn't any way Fitzgerald would go on the record as Bugsy's attorney without his retainer. Sometimes judges got funky and forced large firms, such as his, to represent destitute clients *pro bono*—words that tasted like shit in his mouth.

"No can do, buddy. No retainer and I don't leave my office. For you, Bugsy, or anyone else."

Meyer hollered, "All the fuckin' money we done paid ya ass!"

"First things first, don't raise your voice to me. I'm not one of your homies, motherfucker!" Fitzgerald had found his balls after Layla had chopped them off. He continued, "And last, I was paid for services rendered…focus on the word *rendered*. Your family doesn't have any credit with my office. This is exactly what I warned your bullheaded mother would happen."

"Yo, when I see you—"

Fitzgerald ended the call.

Meyer roared, "I know that cracker ain't just hang up on me!"

Chapter 5

For three days, Scott, who had now gotten his wife involved, sat on the stern of his rented yacht, and spied on the mysterious couple. As each day passed, the Wests' vacation had seemingly halted as they had vicariously infringed on the stranger's lives. Scott and Layla now had all their meals perched on the deck because voyeurism was time-consuming. Last night, several speed boats came out, and they saw numerous people, all dressed in expensive outfits, climb onto the luxury cruiser. Laughter and loud voices could be heard as it carried across the vast ocean, and a hired DJ blared old school and R&B music. Frankie Beverly's unmistakable sultry voice and iconic Black cookout song, *Before I let go,* took Scott back to his youth.

You know I thank God sun rises and shines on youuu…you know there's nothin', nothin', nothin' I would not do…whoa, nooo…

Through the binoculars—that he and Layla now fought over, Scott could see the male surrounded by a gaggle of people doing the electric slide. Everyone was smiling up in his face, but the man seemed unaffected by the events around him. He sat sipping on cognac, his jaw clenched, his eyes alert as he saw his surroundings. There was an intensity to him that Scott could identify with. The male's movements were limited and unanimated. He behaved as Scott behaved around excited guests, underwhelmed. Scott and Layla watched the action as they ate $800 an ounce caviar and drank champagne until they fell asleep on their lounge chairs.

The burnt couple was awoken by the UV rays of the morning sun toasting their bare skin. With no sunscreen on their golden and dark brown skin were shades of hot pink and deep red.

"Fuck!" Scott screamed, looking down at his legs and forearms. "This shit fuckin' hurts!"

Layla, who had turned over onto her stomach during the night, was scorched down her back to her butt cheeks. She hollered in excruciating pain.

This was the price of stalking.

"You okay?" Scott asked as they slowly stood up.

"Hell muthafuckin' no!" she exclaimed. "I'm anything but okay."

The two begrudgingly walked like mummies—arms and legs spread apart through the ship and made their way to their room. Together, they got into the shower to cool off. The heat from the burns seemed trapped and compartmentalized, so as the warm water met their skin, it felt like being baked in an oven. Scott gritted his teeth to absorb his pain while Layla cursed a lot.

"I thought sunburn was only for white people," Layla remarked as they climbed out and opted to air dry. Neither wanted a towel to irritate or come into contact with their sensitive skin. "Since when did Black people get sunburned?"

Scott grabbed the sunblock and helped his wife by gently rubbing the lotion on her back, buttocks, and thighs before they switched positions. Oiled down, Layla dressed in a loose-fitting maxi dress, and Scott grabbed a T-shirt, Bermuda shorts, and Louis Vuitton boat shoes.

"I think we should stay off the deck for a few days until the sun sets," he said. "This shit feels almost as bad as a gunshot."

Before Layla could respond, they both heard voices. Scott paused, ready to react, when he heard laughter. And then the ship's butler came to their room. He tapped lightly on the door.

"Mr. and Mrs. West, your guests have arrived."

Scott smirked. "We'll be right out."

"Who the fuck they let on our ship?" Layla wanted to know. "You think it's Meyer?"

Scott shrugged and walked to their bed, where he kept his Glock under his pillow. The chrome handle was seemingly attached to his hand like Thor's hammer. He tucked his weapon into his waist before heading out. The two made their way down the long corridor, through a few rooms and several double doors before arriving in the living room area. A one thousand square foot duplex with large windows with perfect ocean views. Wide, deep velvet couches with silk throw pillows, a crystal chandelier, and large flat-screen television. Standing in the room were strangers—two people who hadn't been formally introduced.

Scott eyed the male. At least 6'2, he was tall with dark chocolate skin, a muscular frame, a mustache, and a beard. Scott peeped his Breitling sports watch, six figures, tasteful. He was wearing Louis Vuitton boat shoes, long, casual shorts, and a fitted Tee. His muscles could distract any woman. And then Scott's eyes darted toward the eye candy. She was a tall drink of water to Scott to be so petite. She had on a pair of stilettos, which was hardly appropriate for their situation, and was just 5'4. Her hair was naturally blonde, short, and shiny; the boy haircut contrasted her feminine facial features and enhanced her beauty and sex appeal. She had on diamond studs—at least 5-carats and a massive diamond wedding ring and band. Up close, the woman didn't look a day older than her late twenties, and she was drop-dead gorgeous with a tight, killer body. She looked like Charlize Theron on the set of a J'adore Dior commercial with her smoldering eyes, thin nose, high cheekbones, and pouty lips.

Although Scott and Layla had been spying on this couple for days, they both resented the intrusion. They were hungry, sunburned, and irritable.

Layla set the tone when she sucked her teeth, eyeing the female up and down. Scott's face was stone when he asked, "What the fuck y'all doin' here on my muthafuckin' ship uninvited."

The male coolly spoke up. "I'm not one to wait for invitations, so we decided to come through to introduce ourselves since we're the only ones out here, but I see you don't like to mix it up."

Scott was trying to figure out where his accent and verbiage were from. "Not with niggas I don't know!" Scott said and walked closer to the equally looming figure. "Now, what the fuck y'all doin' here? Don't make me ask again!"

The man shrugged. "My name's Understanding and this is my wife, Jacqueline. We meant no disrespect. We're having a kickback this evening and wanted to extend an invitation, and we wanted to come through and apologize for last night. The party went on later than we had expected. But we can see no apology was necessary—"

"It wasn't," Scott snapped, curtailing the explanation. "And I'm a grown man. I don't address men with nicknames. What's your government?"

Understanding nodded. "Let's try this again. I'm Uriel St. James, Understanding was given to me by my mom, and it stuck." He held out his hand for a handshake, and Scott left his hand dangling.

Jacqueline said in a lowered tone, purposely loud enough for them to hear. "I thought they'd be on our level…I guess we were both mistaken."

Her husband nodded as he placed that same hand protectively on the small of his wife's back to usher her out of the yacht rented by hoodlums. Jacqueline's voice was posh, uppity, and sophisticated as it cut through the tense air in the lofty room. She spoke as if her surname was legendary—Kennedy, Dupont, Rockefeller. Not liking that comment, Layla spoke up before they could exit, beating Scott to the punch.

"Listen, please excuse my husband's rude behavior. We've had quite the morning and would like to invite you two to stay for lunch." She was using her corporate voice, and Scott followed.

"Yes, please, join us. We've had a long night, and since you're neighbors, we don't want to get off on the wrong foot. Please…" Scott asked. "Stay."

Understanding and Jacqueline looked at each other quizzically. The transformation of Scott and Layla was astounding. "That's alright," Understanding replied. "As I said, we were only here to apologize for last night and extend an invitation. Again, we're sorry for the intrusion."

The elite couple left, and now Scott and Layla felt fucked up.

"You heard that bitch!" Layla growled. "We're not on their level? I should have bashed her fuckin' face in."

"I overreacted. I shouldn't have gone so hard without finding who they are and what they're about."

"That shit ain't your fault. They just came in and bum rushed our personal living space. We don't know them from Adam."

∞

Whistler shadowboxed around his bedroom in complete darkness with only a pair of boxers on. His fists cut through the air with power and precision as he bobbed and weaved throughout the residence. He ducked as he anticipated a sharp left by his opponent and then levied a succession of upper and lower body shots meant to annihilate his nemesis. He was in rare form, his footwork quick, his technique flawless. He was Apollo Creed in his prime, the nigga that would tower over Scott West as he crumbled at his feet. Whistler wanted a rematch, and no doubt, the odds were in his favor. The element of surprise was always an advantage.

Although he had tapped into the city's electrical line and illegally hooked up the home, he preferred the dark. Moving around in complete darkness had sharpened his senses; his anticipation was heightened, and he needed all the advantages with one eye.

Whistler dropped down and did pushups. He fisted the splintered wood flooring, his knuckles scraping against the hardwood as he pushed his bodyweight up and down. He'd then clap and land on a flat hand to transition back to his knuckles. The pain was almost unbearable early on, but soon, he trained his mind to overcome that and not succumb. No pain, no glory.

The bullet hole that had taken his eye had healed too. He'd done some research and found eye drops that were a mixture of zinc and vitamin E. Also, he stopped covering his eye, allowed it to breathe as it healed on its own. At first, it was a hideous sight, and he had to charge it to the game. But now, he felt it gave him character. People would cross over to the other side when he walked down the street. No one gave him eye contact—they pretended he wasn't there; he was a ghost. They feared him, and the corner hustlers, triggermen, and goons gave the elusive stranger respect they didn't know he deserved for the work he had put into the game. It was long ago, but Whistler had locked down Delaware and helped take it from Deuce and DMC under Scott's direction.

Whistler reread books he had when he was just a lil' nigga getting in the drug game during the day. Classics on strategy, battles, and war. He went over all his pitfalls, situations where he had lost control, was arrogant, ignorant, and ultimately walked into a trap. The art of seduction was a muthafucka, and he wouldn't allow them young thangs to impede his judgment again. Women were a non-factor.

He changed his diet too. Whistler now fasted and cleansed his body of red meat. Throughout the day, he drank only water, ate vegetables, and steamed chicken or fish. He stopped eating artificial sugar, trans and saturated fats, processed foods and felt a clarity he hadn't ever felt. For income, he had become adept at breaking and entering too. Whistler stole what he needed when he needed from unprotected homeowners. The house was targeted if there wasn't an alarm system or surveillance cameras. Breaking and entering had also garnered him an arsenal of weapons.

Whistler wanted a second shot at the title. To be the King of New York, he had to kill the king.

$$\infty$$

He knew the order she had given him, but their current situation had superseded the childish wishes of his sister. The door to her hospital room was pushed open aggressively, and Meyer walked in, his steps heavy. It was jean and hoodie weather for him, but he could feel the heat coming.

"Yo, when they discharging you?" he asked, getting straight to the point.

Lucky rolled her eyes. "Why?"

Meyer pulled the chair as close as possible to Lucky's bed. He got on his knees and looked underneath for anything out of place.

"What are you doing, crazy?" she asked. Meyer ignored her and continued to search the room. Lucky grabbed her remote and pushed. Her electrical hospital bed moved forward so she could sit up. Instantly she knew what her brother was doing, and it meant something had gone down. She said, "We're good. You know I sleep light. I would have heard them come in to plant any bugs."

"They could have while you were taken for tests," he said and then unplugged both the room's telephone and the television. Finally, satisfied there weren't any listening devices, Meyer said, "Shit fucked up, and I'ma need you to hold ya head. I don't want to hear no fuckin' drama, emotional outbursts, or slick-ass remarks. I'ma need your input so we can come to some resolutions."

Her eyes widened. "You're scaring me…what's happened?"

"Angel hit everything we had overnight. That shits all over

the news. All our peoples are dead, all our product stolen, all our fuckin' bread gone. We're broke, Lucky," he explained. "And by the way, those FBI pigs from Ma and Pops case locked Bugsy up on a gun charge and froze all our assets."

Lucky closed her eyes. She was tired of being tired. It was all too much. And what did broke mean? She took a deep breath and counted to ten to prevent herself from crying. Slowly her eyes opened, and she asked, "Are you sure about the money?"

"They didn't leave us wit' a fuckin' crumb."

"Damn, Meyer…what are we gonna do?"

Meyer scratched his head. He wished he could go downstairs and politick with Bugsy. "Please say you still have some of Layla's money stashed somewhere."

Lucky's head shook rapidly. "That shit been gone," she explained. "Angel's men had gotten what I took from Layla and what Bugsy had taken from Scott right after y'all went to war with him over Dillinger. But…."

Her voice trailed off as she wrestled with whether she should mention her side hustle and stash.

Meyer's eyebrow raised. "But what?"

"Don't hate..."

"Just spit it out."

"I branched out from wholesale distribution to retail for rainy days like these. I've been hustling without you and Bugsy, and I have a fleet of block huggers moving my product, selling crack from the Bronx to Brooklyn. Yusef and Opie were running my crew before they were murdered." Lucky thought it appropriate to pause for a moment of silence to at least pretend she was affected, saddened by their demise. And she continued, "I couldn't make any pickups because I'm in here, but I have a couple million out on the streets. I'll give you my cellphone, names, and locales, and you can go and collect my money."

"Goddamn, I'm shocked, shorty!" Meyer felt a surge of

energy course through his veins. "You just saved us! You muthafuckin' saved the day Lucky…shiit, I was ready to do this the ski mask way to get my brother's bail."

"That's what I do," she boasted. "But, seriously, we gotta be frugal with this money since it's our last until we get back on our feet. We'd need to flip it as soon as possible if we're to come out of this shit. Two million ain't shit with all our expenses, so once you collect, make sure you call your connect in the Helguero cartel and re-up."

"You think that's wise with the feds on our backs? They goin' hard right now."

"What other choice do we have with our bank accounts frozen? The maintenance and mortgage payments on all our condominiums, property taxes, cars, and property insurances, and what about our real estate holdings? How would we maintain all this on a measly two mill? We'll be broke within four months. We gotta flip it. You just gotta be careful. Give me a few days, and I'm going to sign myself out of here so I can help you. I just need to wait until my next set of tests come back."

Meyer thought over everything she had said. "We won't even have that. If we do one thing, we need to give Fitz a million on retainer to rep Bugsy. Once he's out, we can focus on the frozen assets."

"A million dollarssss!" Lucky did the Soulja Boy scream. "For a fuckin' gun? Who he think he's talking to? That's a ten-thousand-dollar case!"

"I said the same thing, but he's convinced that it will be more than that, and he doesn't take less than six zeros on a fed case."

"Until it's more than that, then drop his ass ten stacks!" Lucky was ready to discharge herself now. Her brother was going to need her help.

Meyer got amped. "That cracker was getting all cocky too."

"Well, when you drop him the ten bands, you need to send him a strong message. Remind him who the fuck we are!"

Meyer nodded. "A'ight. I gotchu. Let me go and handle these pickups." He tossed Lucky his cellphone, took hers, and said, "I'll holler at you when I'm done."

Scott and Layla became obsessed. Still dealing with their burns, they donned large hats to block the Sun and sat on the deck wrapped up in long-sleeved T-shirts and long pants while watching the movements of the competing yacht. Scott had ordered a second pair of binoculars for his wife to be delivered, and the two continued bonding on their vacation, doing nothing more than eye hustling.

They watched as men in expensive speedboats and suits came and went at all times of the day and night. Some looked like businessmen, some looked like the underworld.

"What's this nigga into?" Scott wanted to know, now kicking himself for his rude behavior. Scott didn't dick ride, but this man was holding it down in the Australian ocean like a local street in Brooklyn.

Layla, too, was curious.

Chapter 6

Meyer didn't get far as he headed North, driving to the Bronx's first location before the blue, red, and white lights began to flash. He was pulled over and harassed for allegedly speeding. Yanked out of his driver's seat on the shoulder of a busy highway, he was illegally stopped and frisked. Although he didn't have a gun on his person, it didn't stop the uniformed police officer from slapping handcuffs on him and tossing him into the back of the police cruiser.

Meyer bit his tongue damn near off to keep from lashing out. The last thing he needed was to spend the next twenty-four hours in lockup for bullshit. He realized this would be his new normal. Getting followed, stopped, and frisked. The harassment would be limitless.

It didn't bother him when the two police officers illegally searched his vehicle for a weapon, drug paraphernalia, or drugs. When he left his apartment this morning, he thought five moves ahead. After the fed followed him out of the hospital, he realized how close he had come to catching a gun charge; against his survival instincts, he left his burners at home. It was risky and less than smart to be in his line of work and not always have at least one gun on you; Meyer sometimes carried three—depending on the circumstance. Now he felt naked and vulnerable, but what choices did he have?

The door was opened, his handcuffs were removed, and the insults came next. "You lucky today, motherfucker!" the police officer yelled. "But we'll get you! You're going down!"

Meyer gritted his teeth and didn't remark. The cop tossed

his license at him, and it fell on the pavement, dangerously close to the ongoing traffic. They chuckled and then hopped in their cruiser and peeled out, leaving the disgruntled Meyer on the side of a busy intersection.

Meyer took numerous turns and detours to ensure that he was no longer followed by pigs: state or federal, it didn't matter. Finally, he arrived at the first location in the Bronx. He parked behind several cars and could see two hoodlums not too far from the corner store. One was sitting on top of a green commercial trash bin drinking quarter water, and the other was posted up against the graffiti-laden brick tenement building. If he were a guessing man, he figured these two dumb fucks couldn't be more evident that they were selling hand to hand and that they worked for his sister. But he needed to be sure. He pulled out Lucky's cellphone and dialed. Meyer watched as the young goon sitting atop the trash dug into his jeans and pulled out his cell. Within a few seconds, Meyer went to voicemail. The young goon turned and spoke to his partner. Heated, Meyer called back. The block hugger repeated the action, and this time he jumped down from the trash and peered up and down the block. He then got animated. His hand gestures were aggressive as he simulated an automatic weapon and mowed people down.

Meyer could hear the bass in the young man's voice from his position halfway up the block. He was talking tough—murder was in everybody's future if they fucked with him. Meyer's Timbs hit the pavement, and he proceeded toward the knucklehead who went by the street name, Gonzo.

"Yo, bruh," Meyer said, interrupting the goon midsentence. "You gonna do what to who?"

Gonzo spun around and met the menacing eyes of Meyer West—the nigga he just said he would murder should Lucky send anyone to collect her bread.

"What?" he aggressively asked as he sized up the stranger.

Gonzo placed his hand close to his waist where his 9mm was resting and his man, Triz, inched closer to back him up if something jumped off. He continued, "Who the fuck is you?"

"I'm the nigga that's comin' to collect my sister's muthafuckin' bread!" Meyer's eyes were deep holes of darkness chipping away at the hardened exterior of the young thug. Still, Gonzo would not come up off that amount of money without exchanging bullets. He owed Lucky two hundred thousand, and when he had heard that Yusef and Opie were murdered and then the attempted murder of their boss, Lucky, it felt like Satan had answered his prayers. Good things did happen to bad people if you only believed.

"I don't owe nobody shit!" he spat, "Now get the fuck up outta here. You're scaring off my customers!"

"Or what!" Meyer said aggressively and took a few steps forward, so he and Gonzo were staring eye to eye. Meyer knew the block huggers were armed and dangerous, but he refused to back down. Had he been carrying, he would have squeezed off a few shots and bodied the disrespectful, young punk.

"Yo, who, dude?" the sidekick said, wanting to get in on the action. Gonzo ignored his partner, not wanting to hand his glory over. This was his moment, and he tried to seize it. He lifted his shirt to flaunt the burner he had tucked in his waistband. He and Meyer both still aggressively eyeing one another.

"Don't pull that shit out if you ain't gonna use it!" Meyer challenged the local thug, "Do it muthafucka!"

Just then, they heard, "Meyer!"

Bak! Bak! Bak! Bak! Bak!

Meyer spun around and saw what appeared to be Unlucky Larry squeezing off shots in his direction. Gonzo and Triz pulled out their burners and let off return fire before fleeing in separate directions. Meyer ran to his SUV, and Larry followed. They jumped in, and Meyer slowly peeled out, not wanting to attract any attention to his vehicle now that Larry was in it with a smoking pistol. When they got far enough away, Meyer asked, "You can't aim nigga! You ain't hit near one!"

"You welcome muthafucka!" Larry returned.

Meyer thought for a second and said, "Yo, good lookin' out. What the fuck was you doin' there?"

"I was passing through on my way to this shorty's crib when I saw you. I pulled over so we could kick it. I haven't seen you in a minute, and then I peeped that some shit was goin' down."

"My nigga!" Meyer said and gave Larry a right-hand dap while simultaneously steering his vehicle with his left.

"I wasn't gonna intervene 'cuz I know you get busy but, um, why you ain't handle them fools? You ain't got your Ninas on you?"

Meyer shrugged. He felt naked without his guns and didn't want an armed dude—cool or not, to know he wasn't carrying his heat. He said, "What you been up to?"

"I been doin' me." Larry exhaled. "You know shit rough out here. I heard what's been going on wit' ya family. How you holding up?"

"Shit crazy," he admitted. "The feds banged Bugsy on a gun. They actin' real aggressive right now."

"Where he at?"

"He's still in the hospital. He gets arraigned soon, and if he doesn't make bail, then they gonna remand him to MCC."

Larry smirked. "Why wouldn't he make bail?"

Meyer's voice deepened. "He's gonna make bail. I was just saying if…you know how petty those peoples are." He had said too much and didn't want to give any more details.

Larry thought quickly and said, "If you need to hold a lil' sumthin,' you know I got you."

"We good."

"A'ight, cuz you know you can always come to me if you need anything. We peoples."

Meyer smirked. This dirty, bum ass nigga made it seem like

he needed a handout. Meyer gave him the side-eye at the traffic light and noticed that Unlucky Larry had made a come up. His left wrist had a platinum, iced out Rolex, and he wore a diamond pinky ring. Meyer could see Balenciaga sneakers, which made him want to see more. Meyer's head swiveled, and he saw layers of platinum and diamond chains draped around his neck. A pink diamond Jesus piece looked at least six figures. Larry had nickel-sized diamonds in his ears that would work best on a female. Meyer, for once, was at a loss for words.

Meyer needed to drop this nigga off so he could get his mind right. He was just in a gun battle, and he didn't have a gun. Lucky workers thought they could say no backsies like kids and keep what belonged to them. And out of the blue, a low-level nigga seemed on the come-up while Meyer and his siblings were on the fast track in the opposite direction.

Meyer asked, "You still fuck wit' Bridget? You want me to drop you to her crib?"

"That dirty bitch," he exclaimed. "Nah, you should see this new chick. She a dime piece."

"Word?" Meyer replied, uninterested. He had shit to do and wanted Larry out of his truck. He asked again. "Where you want me to drop you off?"

"Nah. Let's catch up; go grab something to eat. What you into? You still fuckin' wit' the cartel?"

An uncomfortable silence lingered in the air and fell between the men, making the two feet gap in the car feel magnified. Meyer came to an aggressive stop at the corner of 158th street and said, "Yo, I got shit to do. You gonna have to make your way to your peoples on your own."

"You a'ight?" Larry asked, stalling.

"Yo! Get the fuck out!"

"Then take me back to my whip, man, damn."

"Nah, fam, I can't do that."

Larry reached for his iPhone. "Fuck!" he exclaimed. "I

dropped my cell at the shootout!"

"It ain't like its evidence," Meyer said and then added, "You ain't body shit!"

Larry shrugged, "You seemed stressed, so I'ma disregard the disrespect. You know we're like fam…I was just lookin' out…remember that."

Meyer smirked and decided that Larry wasn't worth a rebuttal. As soon as his door closed, he peeled out.

Meyer would get the same reaction from everyone that owed Lucky money, and without a burner, he couldn't strongarm these dudes. By the time he pulled in front of his high-rise, he was exhausted and mentally fucked up. He took a couple steps out of his vehicle before he was shoved and tossed on the hood of his car, and frisked.

"What the fuck!" Meyer yelled as the cop forcefully kicked his legs apart while slamming him on the hood of his car. "Y'all keep violating my rights, and my lawyer gonna have all y'all badges!"

After they confirmed that he had no weapon, he was free to go. One said, "Hey, Meyer. How long you think you gonna last on these streets if you can't carry a gun? With your temper…" the detective whistled, "I say one week. Two tops!"

Rewind: Week one after the Amber Alert

∞

The DEA had set up a task force called Operation: MAFIOSO. The brutal and blood-spattered war between the cartel and the West empire had created negative attention on the city. Charles Mercury, the Special Agent in charge of the Drug Enforcement Administration's New York Division, the largest DEA Division in the United States, wanted all those responsible for bifurcating his city to be captured and prosecuted. Special Agent Mercury was livid at how the FBI had handled the Wests' prosecution and was eager to hand down life sentences.

After the drug war deaths on the city street of a registered nurse, Alicia Fletcher, and the kidnapping and presumed murder of an infant; along with the brazen attempted murder at a public hospital, word had come down from the top they wanted the West family stopped, dismantled, and brought to justice. No expenses would be spared. Agents would work around the clock to secure indictments. It was embarrassing for the city, for the nation, to have such savagery and buffoonery play out like a Hollywood film. The Westside of Manhattan had turned into a Martin Scorsese movie where criminals had free reign to terrorize New York.

The mayor made a public announcement about his war on crime. He had the police commissioner and the district attorney right by his side as he spoke to the public. He stood in front of crowds and cameras steadfast—decisive about bringing justice to the animals out there.

The mayor also acknowledged the underworld, speaking to the people and the media. He said, *"Federal agents apprehended one member of the Juarez cartel, Emmanuel Vega. He's being held without bail for a brazen attempted murder. This city, the people of New York, we are not afraid of the narcos, and we will fight to rid and prosecute every member of the Juarez cartel starting today. So, I'm sending out a message that you will pay significantly if you come to my city…to our city to try and destroy it with crime, drugs, guns, and violence. We will find you. You will be captured and tried, and we will imprison you for the rest of your natural life."*

There was anger in his tone. Yes, the FBI had arrested a cartel member, but unfortunately, he wasn't cooperating with the agents. But the feds bumbling their investigation didn't discourage the DEA task force; it made them hungry to dismantle the two powerful organizations.

The DEA had implemented Operation: MAFIOSO and their focus was on the West family, who some considered a bunch of street thugs rather than an elite criminal organization. The DEA had set up base in a warehouse in Williamsburg, Brooklyn. It would become the hub for their operation. There were over a dozen agents assigned. They were good agents, hard-working men, and women that wanted to see justice happen. They wanted to become like the men who brought down Pablo Escobar, John Gotti, Lorenzo "Fat Cat" Nichols, Bumpy Johnson, Nicky Barnes, and others. They all dreamt of book deals; mics thrust in their faces as cameras rolled. The agents wanted movie deals with A-list celebrities depicting their image, like Denzel or Russell in American Gangster. Documentaries and docu-series were in their futures, and multi-million-dollar deals were on everyone's mind. Why else do it if not for a big payday?

Two men, agents Tannery, and Brown, were in charge. They were both white males in their early forties. Tannery had fifteen years with the DEA, was an average male with a thin hairline and a protruding belly. He was proficient at his job—always focused on capturing the bad guys. But his effective work came at a high cost. He was going through a contentious divorce, and there were three children in the mix. His wife hated him. He had continuously put his job before home, steadily trying to climb the ladder to the top. He'd drown his issues in a bottle of whiskey almost daily, but Tannery was one of the best to ever do the job despite his problems.

His partner, Agent Brown, was equally ambitious. He was a charismatic man with a head full of thick, black hair. He was always in the gym, working out, keeping his fat to muscle ratio low. He was single, but some might consider him a womanizer, as he had affairs with many of his female subordinates. Many ladies on the job and outside of work wanted to lock him down, but Agent Brown was a male lion that couldn't be contained inside the cage called marriage.

Both men stood in front of two large bulletin boards smattered with pictures of the West family and the Juarez cartel.

The first board had the patriarch and matriarch, AKA Scott, and Layla. Under Scott and Layla's pictures were Bugsy, Meyer, and Lucky. To the left of Scott were his henchmen, the ones that the government knew about. Mason's mugshot was an 8x10 blown up glossy, and Avery had a giant red X crossed over his face. And under Mason and Avery were Kane and Zaire. Below Bugsy's picture was the deceased Chopper with a massive red X crossed over it, his son Dillinger was a red X, and Maxine with a large red question mark. Meyer's picture was on top of Luna's, and Luna, too, had a red X crossed over his face. And finally, there was Lucky. Her picture was flanked by Yusef and Opie—both with red exes over their faces. And under Lucky's picture was her daughter, Lucchese, presumed dead with a red question mark.

The second board was pictures of the Juarez cartel, and Angel's picture was pinned at the very top. His pyramid had his cousin, Louis, his half-brother, Alejandro, with a red X over his face, and numerous associates and underlings. Angel was the main target, and he was isolated inside a giant bubble of extreme wealth, loyal men, expert lawyers, and power. It would take skill, ingenuity, determination, and technology to build a case against Angel and his cartel, and Tannery and Brown knew they were both the right men for the job. Though they had vital information on both organizations, they were still in the dark. They knew that both criminal organizations used to do business with each other; now, they were at war. They didn't know why Lucchese Lily West had been kidnapped and presumed dead or who was the baby's father. They were still trying to attain information on that. With their massive operation, they had nothing really. But it wouldn't stay that way for too long. Tannery would push the boundaries of "legal" to get what he wanted.

The briefing on the organizations went on for nearly two hours. Tannery wouldn't waste his budget on round-the-clock surveillance of the West family—because surveillance wouldn't be enough. To take them down completely, they would need undercover agents to infiltrate the criminal organization, and it wouldn't be easy.

Going after the Juarez cartel was ambitious. The DEA partnered with the Mexican federalés, and most agents were on the cartel's payroll. Tannery and Brown had to build their case in New York and get Angel on American soil to make the arrest—a feat that would be difficult.

Tannery and Brown invited two DEA agents in when everyone cleared the room. It was a private meeting, and Tannery and Brown were ordered to keep the undercover operatives' involvement a secret to the task force. Their government names were classified by the director, even above the pay grades of Tannery and Brown. The two undercover men had directly or indirectly taken down many cartels and drug empires, too many to count. They were masterful at how they blended into the underworld. Their covers gave them license to murder, distribute narcotics, demean women, terrorize men—take what their badges stood for and ignore.

Pablo and Diablo walked into the lofty room with a self-righteousness that irked Agent Tannery. Their smug faces told Tannery he needed them, and he didn't like that. Pablo was a forty-three-year-old Colombian-American male with salt and pepper hair. He was of average height and suited up sharply. His expensive tailored suits were compliments of American tax dollars, as were all the other benefits that came with looking the part of a narco. Pablo only drove fast cars, drank the finest wines, and ate delicacies that most would find offensive. Pablo looked, talked, and smelled like the real thing. He'd been undercover for so long as a cartel member he even picked up a manageable drug habit. Pablo would dabble now and again in a line of the purest grade-A cocaine to keep him alert and on his toes.

Also, there was Diablo. He was Colombian-American but often mistaken for Guatemalan or Mexican because of his height and darker skin tone. He was thirty-eight years old, with weathered, naturally tanned skin. He was an outdoorsman and loved working with his hands. Whether that meant dismembering a body or building a shed, he was down for muthafuckin' whatever. Diablo didn't use sunscreen or take pride in his appearance as his partner did. For his cover, he dressed in a cowboy hat, his jet-black hair slicked back into a ponytail, worn cowboy boots, and denim jeans. His thick, unruly mustache caught everyone's attention, a signature he refused to shave off.

Pablo and Diablo supposedly had Texas and the Midwest locked down with pure cocaine and heroin. Their new cover would be that they were cousins who'd branched off from the Los Pepes cartel and were steadily building a name for themselves. They were expected to infiltrate the West criminal organization and bring down every member via snitches, wiretaps, surveillance, and direct sales. The DEA deduced that the young West faction was in the market for a new connect due to their war with Juarez. All that was needed was the proper introduction to one sibling where someone could vouch for the two undercover agents. And Tannery knew the right man to go to, to make that meeting happen.

Chapter 7

Meyer went into his condominium, and the first thing he did was bag up all his weaponry and take it to the outside dumpster but not before removing all his fingerprints. It was only a matter of time before the feds got a warrant to search his shit. He knew that's why they had local cops trying to catch him slipping—it was because no judge had signed off on a warrant for his residence. They didn't have probable cause, and he would not give it to them.

Meyer kicked off his Timbs and made himself a tall glass of Lean, and ordered Chinese food. As soon as he powered up Lucky's cellphone, it rang.

"Yo."

"Where's Lucky!"

"Who the fuck is this?"

"Oh…Meyer? Is that you?" Her voice was curt, angered, and she didn't wait for confirmation. "This is Glenda, Reggie's mother. I've been callin' Bugsy and Lucky! Why haven't they called me back?"

"Shit crazy," he explained. "You do know they both got hit."

"I didn't call to discuss some other woman's kids," she screamed. "The streets said Bugsy and Lucky are still alive, so again, why ain't nobody called my Black ass back!"

"Well, ain't nobody ducking you." Meyer placed a Jolly Rancher candy into his mouth and took a large gulp of his Lean. His mind was drifting back to his brother, his bread, and his enemies. "Look, what the fuck you want?" He was blunt.

"My son was murdered at your spot, and I wanna know who's payin' for his funeral?!"

"Glenda, you know better than to be talkin' reckless over the phone!"

Glenda became belligerent. "Ain't nobody talkin' reckless, nigga. We starvin' over here and wit' Reggie gone the rent money is now gone too! And Keisha has his two sons, and she needs shit...milk, pampers, light, and gas money. All I'm askin' is what are you gonna do about this? We need to eat one way or another...so you better think long and hard 'bout ya next move."

"Yo, Glenda, chill wit' ya threats bitch!"

Meyer hung up before he said something he'd regret. But as soon as he ended that call, it rang again.

"Glenda, when I see ya old ass—"

The gruff voice didn't hesitate to go in. "Meyer dis Rakim! I know Lucky and Bugsy are down for a minute, but my moms over here buggin' the fuck out about what happened to my brother, Slim!"

"And?"

Rakim didn't expect that cavalier response. He remembered who he was talking to and lowered the bass in his voice because he was showing off in front of his girl and his moms. Rakim said, "And we ain't heard from you."

"You hearin' from me now, my condolences."

"True...true...," Rakim was stalling for time. His eyes peered into that of his mother's as she was expecting him to negotiate a six-figure payday for his dead brother's life. His mother's emotions were raw, but money could always dull the pain. "So, um, we wanted to know if you comin' through to pay respect at his funeral and also so we could politick about a few things?"

"Nah, I ain't comin' through cuz ain't shit to talk about."

"Oh, right...right. You holdin' down Lucky and Bugsy right now. My bad, I know you tied up."

"Bruh, that ain't what I said," Meyer corrected. "And why you hittin' my sister's jack anyway? You thought you was gonna extort Lucky, nigga?"

"It ain't even like that we tried to holla at Bugsy, first. We know y'all always take care of y'all peoples when a soldier falls. We ain't lookin' for a handout, but shit kinda fucked up over here. My moms didn't want y'all to forget about us."

Meyer's long pause was intentional, which gave Rakim hope. As he took several sips of his Lean, Meyer felt the codeine kick in; his body relaxed. Finally, he replied—"Tell ya moms that she's gonna have to charge it to the game"—and hung up.

Within seconds, the burner phones he had in his kitchen drawer began buzzing. Meyer pushed himself off of his sofa and retrieved his burners. Each phone had hundreds of text messages and hundreds of missed calls from angry mothers, brothers, sisters, and baby mamas, all wanting the same thing, money. Everyone thought they were due death benefits, like the dead worked for a tech corporation instead of a drug organization. The Wests had enormous expenses—business expenses, lawyer, bail, housing, transportation, insurance—a host of bills to pay. Meyer took the time to remove all his sim cards and Lucky's. He placed them into his garbage disposal, which chewed them up. He needed peace and quiet.

Meyer tried to relax, but the run-in with Larry kept fucking with him, and he couldn't understand why. There was something about the exchange that felt inauthentic. Maybe it was Larry's new money; a come up always had niggas actin' brand new. Frustrated, he tried to sleep. He tossed and turned for hours before he got up just after one in the morning. Dressed in all black, he crept out of his building, down the service elevator, and out the side entrance. He had shit to do. Meyer walked a few blocks, hopped on the subway, and rode a couple of stations. And then, he exited and took a taxi uptown before getting out on 3rd avenue in the Bronx and taking another taxi a short ride to his destination. All this cloak and dagger shit was because Meyer had murder on his mind, and he wasn't about to get caught. The four-inch pocketknife would have to do.

Under cover of night, he saw Gonzo still chilling on top of the garbage bin. Earlier, Meyer had peeped their operation. The fiend would pay Gonzo, and then Triz would serve them in the alley just in case the undercovers were watching. At this time of night, the fiends were out in droves. Meyer grabbed one with a pep in his step, making his way to cop, and gave him fifty dollars to lure Triz into the alley. The fiend was glad to oblige.

The crackhead gave Gonzo the money, and off Triz and the fiend went for the drugs. Gonzo began counting a wad of bills. His fingers and mouth were moving so fast it was like he was a human money counting machine. Meyer came up to Gonzo with his hoodie on low, digging deep into his jeans as if he was looking for his bread.

"Yo, hurry up. I ain't got all day," Gonzo said.

When Meyer lifted his head, Gonzo's eyes grew wide. Before he could reach for his pistol, Meyer shoved the four-inch blade into his jugular, hitting his carotid artery and twisted. Meyer yanked the knife out, and blood squirted like water gushing from a fire hydrant. The young thug couldn't believe he was dying. Clutching his neck, he stumbled forward and then fell against the bricked wall. He took a few steps hugging the wall for support before his legs went limp. The young goon was fighting to stay alive. One leg buckled, and then the second. On his knees, he was wiggling and jiggling, trying to stand back up, but Meyer knew he was gone.

Meyer reached in his waist and pulled out that same gun he was threatened with several hours earlier and then dug deep for the paper. He made his way toward the alley, and the crackhead was stuffing his drugs in his pocket. When he saw Meyer, he scurried away. He was a dope fiend, but he wasn't dumb. Triz was posted against the wall, his left leg bent for support. He gave the next fiend a head nod, which meant he was ready to service his next customer.

Meyer walked up with his head low and placed the barrel of Gonzo's .357 to his head, *Bak!,* and dropped shorty where he stood. His head jerked back before he fell.

Meyer exited from the back of the alley with Gonzo's smoking gun tucked in his waist. He wiped it down several blocks over, removed his prints, and tossed it in a nearby trashcan. Down in the subway, Meyer went into one of the disgusting restrooms and washed his hands, removing blood and gunpowder. He took off his hoodie, turned it inside out, tucked it under his arm, and made his way home. As soon as he entered his apartment, he stripped naked and placed everything in a plastic bag. It was just after six in the morning. He retook the service elevator, but this time to the basement where the furnace was. The door was locked, but that didn't stop him from getting in. Meyer broke the lock and stood in front of the fire until every article of his clothing had incinerated.

Meyer counted the proceeds from his recent jux in his apartment and totaled three thousand dollars. About one percent of what their bitch asses owed his sister. He then grabbed his Louis Vuitton knapsack and tossed all his jewelry inside. Three watches, several chains, rings, and earrings. Next, he opened his messy kitchen drawer and searched for Bugsy and Lucky's spare keys. By eight that morning, Meyer had every piece of jewelry he and his siblings owned and had also disposed of their weapons. Next, he headed to the Diamond District. Meyer had just a little over eight-hundred thousand dollars by ten in the morning. Before returning home for some much-needed sleep, his last stop was to Fitzgerald Spencer. Meyer separated ten stacks from his money, wrapped a tight rubber band around the crisp hundred-dollar bills, and stuffed the cash into his jeans pocket. The law office was less than a ten-minute drive.

Meyer tossed the knapsack over his shoulders and headed south toward the outdoor parking lot. Once inside his SUV, he called Fitzgerald. "Yo, I'm on my way." Meyer's voice was hoarse from a long night of murder and mayhem. He had been up for 24 hours, and he could feel his body breaking down.

Meyer could hear the delight in Fitz's voice, thinking he was about to receive a large retainer for little work. He couldn't wait to get there and smack the shit out of Fitz. The Michelin tires rolled out of the lot, and Meyer made a quick right and then proceeded straight on 5th avenue. Less than a minute from *Spencer, Donnelly, & Bridges*, the familiar scene took place. Meyer quickly redialed Fitz.

"Five-oh just pulled me over!" he screamed frantically into the phone.

"What's happening?" Fitz asked, unable to glean the magnitude of the situation.

"I said the cops just pulled me over! I'm on 5th and 41st. I'ma need you to come here now!"

"Do you have a weapon?"

"Nah, but I got cash, and I don't trust these crackers! Get here now!"

The days that Fitzgerald Spencer went above and beyond for anyone with the West surname were long over when Layla smashed him upside his head with her pistol and treated him like her bitch. There wasn't any way he would take the three-block stroll for Meyer. If Meyer didn't make it out of the traffic stop with his millions today, then he would need to go to one of his drug dens—where dealers hold their blood money and grab a couple million for him. And if the young thug didn't realize it, he, too, was a cracker. Tired of being interrupted, he called his secretary and told her to hold his calls.

From the back of the cop car, Meyer watched as one officer

opened his knapsack and saw the money after they had dug in his jeans and had taken the ten thousand. Now he waited in angst to know how this would play out.

The two officers got back in the squad car. Meyer expected name-calling, threats, and to be locked up. Instead, the officer in the driver's seat said, "Mr. West, you know it's illegal to carry sums over ten thousand dollars unless you can show where the money came from. Do you have a bank statement or teller receipt for this?"

"Nah, I just sold some jewelry at the Diamond District and was going to the bank to make the deposit. We can go there now, and y'all can speak to them. The jewelry was bought on credit cards throughout the years from business accounts. My jeweler will vouch for me."

"Uh, huh. So how much is here?" The officer continued, treating him respectfully.

"It's eight hundred and thirteen thousand, sir."

"You sure? Because we don't have time to sit here and count all of this, but we can if you want us to."

"That's the correct amount. And that includes the money you took from my pocket," Meyer added.

The second officer was scribbling feverishly on a large stack of papers. The car fell silent for a while. Eventually, both cops got out of the police cruiser and left his knapsack in the front seat. The passenger's door was opened, and the cuffs were removed. Before Meyer could start beefing, the second cop handed him three pieces of paper. He scanned over it and quickly saw they were confiscating his money.

"You'll need to show proof of where you received this considerable sum of money, son, and come down to the precinct where it will be vouchered. I'd hire an attorney to help with this matter if I were you. You don't want to be charged with tax evasion. Good citizens always lose against the IRS."

Meyer didn't like how nice they were now treating him. That

'son' was over the top.

Meyer finally arrived at Fitzgerald's office so he could give him the paperwork and he could work on getting his money back and preparing for Bugsy's arraignment tomorrow, but he was told he had left for the day. Meyer was so irritated and bothered that he wanted to go all Hulk on them and just smash shit. He gritted his teeth, left the paperwork with his legal secretary, and bounced.

As soon as Meyer left his office, Julia, Fitz's secretary, walked in and handed him the paperwork.

"What's this?" he asked.

"Meyer West just left these papers for you. He said that local cops confiscated his money, and he wants you to make some calls to get it back. He also said he expects you to be there to represent his brother at his arraignment." Julia pursed her lips tightly together to show her annoyance at all his demands. "He wasn't happy that you weren't here."

Fitz leaned back in his expensive, tufted leather chair and said, "He'll learn the hard way that money, not man, can dictate what I will and won't do…fuck him."

Fitzgerald was talking tough in front of Julia. She had no idea that Meyer's mother had reduced him into a whiny man-child last year. Julia walked seductively toward her boss with her brunette hair, pulled tightly into a bun, form-fitting pencil skirt, and a crisp white shirt. Her red lipstick was from Kim Kardashian's new cosmetic line, and although she didn't need to wear body contouring under her clothes, she had on a pair of nude Skims. Her five-inch black Christian Louboutin's was a staple in the office. All the women wore Red Bottoms and expensive purses. Each day she walked out of her small, New York apartment, she wondered if today would be the day she would meet her millionaire.

Julia was on trend with everything from wellness practices: yoga, meditation, organic vegan diet. She volunteered and did charity work and rubbed elbows with New York's most elite. Her twenty-ninth birthday was steadily approaching, and she vowed to be married before thirty. Her issue was that everyone was doing the same thing, so how would she stand out? She sighed and handed Fitzgerald the paperwork, and sashayed out his door.

Fitzgerald quickly scanned the three pages and immediately noticed what the dimwitted Meyer did not. The papers omitted the two most important things to locate his confiscated funds. The precinct where the money would allegedly be held, and the name and badge numbers of the officers that had taken it. The paperwork was useless. These cops had scored the biggest payday they'd ever receive working for the NYPD. And it didn't go over his head that the amount on record was far less than the millions he'd expected to receive. Did Meyer think he could negotiate Fitz's fee?

Fitz got on the intercom and called Julia. He said, "I want you to come back and get this paperwork and send Meyer West by messenger three bills outlining my fees for representation. Please note a one-million-dollar retainer for Bugsy West, a one-million-dollar retainer for the frozen assets, and a quarter of a million dollars for his case about his money."

"Yes, sir. Right away, Mr. Spencer."

Fitzgerald was ready to fuck Meyer over. Reparations for his mother's vile and abhorrent behavior.

Bugsy pled not guilty to the charges against him with a court-appointed attorney, and his cash bond was set at $500,000 at the arraignment. The moment his doctors cleared him, he'd be shipped off to MCC if bail wasn't met. The United States judge appeared via Skype, and his lawyer, DeSean Johnson, stood by and didn't object to anything United States Attorney Gloria Scheindlin had to say. Bugsy would have fended better had he represented himself. Still shackled with the handcuff and uniformed officers guarding his door, Bugsy felt like a caged animal.

He wondered where was Fitzgerald Spencer but more important, where was Meyer? He couldn't allow negative thoughts to infiltrate his mind, but he had a bad feeling. Now that he was arraigned, he was allowed visits up to one hour per day. Hopefully, Meyer will come soon and fill in the gaps.

Chapter 8

Meyer pushed open the hospital door to his brother's room. It was early in the morning, and Bugsy was still asleep. The medication flowing through his veins had him groggier than he liked to be. Meyer listened to the machines' familiar beeps tracking his brother's vitals and wondered when he or one of his siblings would flatline. It was always a thought hovering in the deep recesses of one's mind that you didn't discuss. Speaking of your death was like an omen. Once you put it into the universe, it was just a matter of time before the universe came to collect. So you tried to bury it, sweep it under the rug, and hoped you didn't trip over it, and you'd live a long, prosperous, fulfilling life.

Meyer tapped Bugsy's leg after sweeping the room for bugs and sat down. His brother's eyes lazily opened, and then he smiled. Bugsy hadn't seen Meyer in days.

His low registered voice pierced through the hospital sounds and connected with Meyer.

"I saw the news footage," Bugsy acknowledged. "Angel?"

"He's too powerful," Meyer admitted. "I didn't think shit like this could be done, Bee. Not to us…we were born into this life. We all came out of Layla's womb fuckin' hustlin'. How the fuck we let that spick crush our whole organization in one night!"

"How bad?"

"Everything!" Meyer was sitting close to his brother's bed, speaking in an angry whisper. His eyes and facial expressions manifested what his voice could not. "They took everything and murdered everyone. Please say you got something stashed away to put us back on our feet, or else we're broke, bruh."

Bugsy could see that Meyer slowly realized the magnitude of his words. Broke was so foreign, so far removed from their lives, it was the first time he'd used it in a sentence to describe his family.

Meyer continued, "Why you think I ain't have Fitz repping you at your arraignment? You know I wouldn't leave you—"

"No need to explain," Bugsy cut his brother off. "That thought never crossed my mind. But to answer your question, I took that bread I had at Scott's crib when it all went down with Maxine. I moved it to the warehouse in New Rochelle because Pops didn't know about that location, and Juarez got at it."

Meyer was broken up inside, and he couldn't understand how his brother remained levelheaded. Meyer wanted to get a reaction so he didn't feel like an emotional bitch. "We don't have a muthafuckin' dime."

"Chill, Meyer. Rundown everything that's happened since we last kicked it. Together we gonna figure a way out of this shit. Scott always said it ain't over until he says it is. We gotta feel the same way."

Meyer explained the authorities' constant harassment, Fitzgerald Spencer's insane retainers, selling their jewelry, the confiscated money, Lucky's side hustle, and the after-midnight murders.

"So they trying to jam you up on a gun charge too," Bugsy agreed. "You can't let that happen, Meyer. Lucky won't last long out here with you and me doing time."

"You ain't doin' no muthafuckin' time for no gun! On my life, I'ma get you bailed out and get Fitz to rep you. If I gotta shove a broom up his ass like a fuckin' puppet, I will."

Bugsy's head slowly shook. "Don't worry about me. I can do a bid for a gun—"

"You ain't, though!" Meyer was adamant. He would not see his brother locked in a cage. "These crackers ain't playin' fair, Bee. I swear on everything I love, I'm ready to go on a murder spree.

Kill those fuckin' pigs…those agents…by the time they assign new ones, we'll have our organization back on our feet and put our murder game down again and again until they learn to stop fuckin' wit' us!"

"You not thinking clearly, Meyer. That's what we not gonna do. Right now, we're cash poor, we don't have any liquid, but we have assets to liquidate. Whatever Lucky had out on the streets, consider it a loss and move on. Let it go…fuck those corner boys. It's not worth twenty-five to life. We're Wests, and we don't do retail…we're wholesale, and we'll get back on our feet."

Meyer wasn't as confident as his brother sounded. He needed convincing. "How?"

"We own properties with equity in them that we can use as collateral. Times like these are why it was important to wash our drug money and invest it in assets. I'll tell you which commercial properties to put on the market to sell and which ones to get a line of credit against from the banks. And our condos are residential, in our names, not under a company, so you can apply for a HELOC on each one. It'll take at least a month before any loans are approved, so I'm going to need you to be patient."

"I can't do all this financial shit, Bugsy. That's not me. That's not what I do. All our bills are due soon…I need to get you up outta here so you can deal with all this shit. I gotta get you bailed out. I'm ready to take it to the streets, the ski mask way!"

"Look, they can't transfer me until my doctors clear me. I'm still fucked up, and I will stall my recovery for a few weeks. That should buy you enough time to get at least one loan to use for my bail. And as I said, if I'm remanded, I'll handle it but what I can't handle is if anything were to happen to you. Meyer, promise me…we've already lost too many, too soon. I can't lose my right rib too. We started out in the womb together, came into this world together—listen to your older brother for once. I got this."

Meyer gave Bugsy dap and promised to do things his way. "A'ight, what else?"

"We gonna need enough money to lay low for a while until all this shit blows over. The Picassos, Basquiats, Monets, Van Goghs should be auctioned off with Sotheby's or Christie's. I have the contact information of the curators for both. They'll need to authenticate—"

"Don't put that on me, bruh. You tryin' to teach a Pitbull to curtsy."

Bugsy nodded his agreement. "Okay, so I'll handle our assets when I make bail. I want you to take our vehicles to Gino. He'll get us the best prices and should have a quick turnaround. Take Maxine's Bentley, her white BMW, my Bentley, and my Escalade. Leave my Range for now because I'll need to get around when I'm out. Keep one of your vehicles and leave Lucky's G-wagon. Those cars alone should be more than enough."

Scott woke up to find that the neighboring yacht was gone. The days of spying ended abruptly. He would no longer get to see the sexy Jacqueline emerge naked from the ocean. Her slim waist and perky breasts were always a nice treat. He shrugged off his disappointment. Maybe now he and Layla could get back to enjoying their own vacation.

He woke up his wife. "They're gone," he said.

Layla was less affected. "Good fuckin' riddance."

Scott nodded. "What we gonna do today?"

Layla shrugged. They'd been out at sea for nearly a month. It was only so often you could go snorkeling, sunbathing, and get drunk before it became stale. The isolation was welcomed at first, but now they needed some action. They realized that they would have already returned to shore had the other yacht not arrived. Byron Bay had excitement, a mixed crowd, and adult interaction. "Let's go back. I'm fuckin' bored."

Scott agreed.

As the ship set sail, Scott received a call from a blocked number. He answered immediately.

"Holá, Scott."

"Javier…good to hear from you, brother. What's up? How's business?"

"Glad you asked because, yes, this is a business call."

"It always is," Scott acknowledged. "Talk to me."

"The Garcia cartel will need you to come to Mexico right away for a meeting. You have two days to settle your situation in Australia and get here, my friend. A car will be waiting."

Scott smirked, and Layla noticed her husband's expression. It halted all her movements, and she sat down.

"Why would I want to do that when I'm on vacation. I don't have plans to leave until my villa's lease expires in four months."

"It's only money, is it not? You have plenty, and this is not a courtesy. It's a request."

Scott's jaw tightened. "Javier, let's get one thing clear. I don't work for you; I work *with* you, so you can't muthafuckin' order me to do shit. Now I like the business arrangement we've had for decades, and you've always had my loyalty, but my Black ass will get on a flight if or when I choose. Now, what's this about?"

"I don't like your tone."

"Get to the point, Javier. My patience has limits."

"So if you will not meet face to face like a businessman, then we will have our meeting now. I will place you on speaker, all notable members of my cartel are here with me, but before we proceed, I will need your word that this is respected as a formal meeting and all meetings are private."

That meant that Layla or anyone else couldn't listen in on the call or be privy to what occurred during the meeting.

"You have my word. Give me a moment." Scott got up from the bedroom, leaving his wife behind, and walked through the corridors, down two flights of steps to the ship's den. He walked in and closed the door for complete privacy.

"Let's talk," he finally said.

Now on speakerphone, Javier's voice echoed. "The first matter is that we've been hearing that your first-in-command, Mason, has been inquiring about the four sicarios who abducted you and your wife."

"So?"

"You want them dead, do you not?"

"This doesn't concern you, Javier. This is West organization's business, and we're handling it."

"Those men are now under the protection of the Garcia cartel, and they will not be touched."

Scott gritted his teeth and fisted his left hand so tightly his nails dug into his palm. Scott's nose flared, but he remained levelheaded. Revenge could take decades if you're passionate enough. Like a leaky faucet, if you stay the course, there will be a breakthrough. He would tell Mason to fall back for now and would keep tabs on his enemies, and whether it was five, fifteen, or twenty-five years from now, they all would be handled. Scott didn't question Javier's decision to back the sicarios. Instead, he agreed. "If they're under your protection, then my beef with them is paused."

"Glad to hear, my friend. As you've said, I've always had your loyalty."

"You have."

"Now to our last matter. You know that my nephew, Hector, a civilian, was murdered, sí?"

"Yeah, and I gave you my condolences. What's that got to do with me?"

"Well, it has come to my attention that he died by your daughter Lucky's hand."

Scott shrugged. It was news to him, and he didn't know why she would cross that line, but he gave no fucks either way. "I already told you where I stand on the issue of my kids, but um, again, I'm sorry for your loss. You still seem broken up about it."

"I am Scott. It was a great tragedy for mí familia; my wife cries every day."

"We all take losses in this game. As you know, I lost three children who also were civilians."

"Yes…yes…but let's stay focused on Hector," Javier rudely stated. "Angel Morales was also involved in Hector's murder, and he's made amends by giving us his brother, Alejandro. A life for a life is Mexican cartel law. We've adopted the ways of our ancestors, and our heritage is preserved through strict enforcement passed down for generations."

Now it made sense as to why Lucky murdered Hector. Angel was involved. Scott thought he had taught his children to be wiser, but apparently, they were susceptible to subterfuge.

"I understand."

"Good, so it's agreed," a voice said.

"Who's speaking?" Scott asked.

"This is Gustave."

"Gustave, what's agreed?"

"Well, the Garcia cartel has discussed this disrespect, and we've all agreed that you care nothing for your remaining children. We've heard the stories from Angel about infighting, murder plots, your son's betrayal with your woman, your daughter's betrayal against her mother."

"Again, my business."

"Correct. But since you've already given us our understanding that should we kill one of your children, none of their lives have meaning."

"Get to the muthafuckin' point!" Scott's voice bellowed. His face had distorted into an unrecognizable expression pattern, his rage palpable, inching toward imploding.

Javier spoke. "It is clear, is it not? The life we will need from you is your wife's. Layla's life for my nephew's."

Scott bellowed, "Javier, I'm warning you! Don't go there!"

"You are in no position to make threats, Scott. You cannot

win in a war against us, and to prove that you are a dear friend to me, my brother, I will give you a choice. You can kill Layla however you want, quick and painless—a bullet to the head while she's asleep. You can also hand her over to us and allow us to dispose of her. Remember that you can always get another wife. However, my wife cannot get her nephew back. So, let's not make things tense. Sí? You have one week to complete your assignment and prove we still have your loyalty. Don't let me down."

Scott said, "My great-great-grandfather was born on American soil a slave, Abraham Winslow. He was emancipated in 1865; he was three years old. My father instilled his grandfather's wisdom into me until he passed on. A man is a man of his own decisions, and if not, then that man is really enslaved. A man understands his friends' and enemies' thoughts, motivations, and brain intellect. He decides whom to trust, to kill, whom to befriend. If his actions are dictated, then the man doesn't have free will. My family's surname was Winslow, a British name given to us by their slave master. My grandfather changed our surname to West. West symbolizes my ancestors' journey from our native land as the ships sailed them to two hundred years of servitude. The name West broke the chains; my family was no longer in bondage. My full name is Scott Abraham West, and I'm nobody's muthafuckin' slave. Come for my wife, and I'll kill you!"

Scott's threat against the head of the Garcia cartel boomed throughout the vast meeting room in Tijuana, Mexico. Javier Garcia was anything but shocked at Scott's defiance, but he did feel disrespected in front of his men. Scott was always a hardheaded negro. "I understand," Javier replied. "In my country, we have a saying, 'the devil walks among us seeking someone to devour.' Scott, my friend, I am that devil. It would be wise to fear me."

"The devil is feared because he can't be killed, not because he's the devil. You bleed just like me!"

Scott heard movement, chairs being moved around, and

shuffling of unrecognizable sounds. And then Javier politely asked, "Do you know what *más vale mala suerte y buena muerte que buena suerte y mala muerte* translates to in your language?"

"You know I don't."

"It's a Mexican proverb. It means bad luck, and a good death is better than good luck and a bad death. Your wife had the unfortunate bad luck to be the mother of Lucky, who murdered my nephew, so we were going to give her a good death." Javier paused to puff on his Cuban cigar and then continued with, "Enjoy today, my friend. You may even enjoy tomorrow…who knows…but death is sure to catch up to you. That's why it gives us a head start!"

Scott disconnected the call and turned around to see Layla. She had been standing there only for a few moments. She thought she couldn't love her husband more, but her heart had expanded beyond measure.

"You heard?" Scott asked.

Layla nodded. "What the fuck did I do to get on his hit list?"

"It wasn't you; it was Lucky. Apparently, she murdered his nephew."

"Of course that bitch did!" Layla growled. "This should be on her!"

"It doesn't matter. It's on us now whether we like it or not."

"What are we gonna do?"

"Not get killed," Scott said, knowing that the Garcia cartel had an army.

"Whatever we do, we do it together. We live together; we die together," Layla said.

Scott found levity in the grim matter. "We bad boys for life, huh?"

Layla smirked. "I'ma bad *bitch*…why do I have to keep reminding folks."

Scott walked over to his wife, wrapped his arms around her, and grabbed two handfuls of her juicy ass. He softly kissed her lips and said, "I told you, it's over when I say it is. I can only die once, and it will be on my terms."

"So, Scott West...is our vacation over?"

"Absolutely not," he replied. "We stay on our timeline. We're paid up for the next four months, and that's what it is. Murder is a patient man's game. We stay here and enjoy ourselves, and it will give me time to strategize."

"You think he'll send someone here?"

"Is it possible?" Scott said. "Yes. But it's unlikely. You have nothing to worry about except these muthafuckin' bugs and crocodiles."

Chapter 9

The nurses' station that sat approximately thirty feet outside Lucky's hospital room was always abuzz with gossip about the young queenpin who had survived a cartel hit. All the RNs and LPNs felt that the West family should just rent permanent residences at NewYork-Presbyterian Hospital as it seemed they were always there.

"She's a mean, spoiled little bitch," RN White made known. "Each time I go in to take her pulse, I dig my nails extra hard in her wrist just to cause her evil ass more pain."

LPN Baker snorted and then whispered to her peers, "God, please forgive me, but before I bring her any meal, I spit in it. A huge chunk of my phlegm is mixed into her applesauce, mashed potatoes, or gravy…I know it ain't right, but I do it."

Most nurses chuckled, but some didn't find it amusing. A few nurses at the station felt that Nurse Baker had gone too far with her disgusting antics, which was ultimately a criminal assault, but they remained mute. It wasn't their fight. Besides, they were outnumbered because most of their colleagues agreed with the egregious behavior.

"Girl, you don't have to ask for forgiveness. I promise you that God understands. All the murders her family probably committed…." Nurse White's voice trailed off.

Whatever was said at the nurses' station never left that area. Any hostility, curt remarks, or vile behavior was put on pause. Nurses White and Baker's allegations were false against the drug heir to the throne. In fact, when the doctors and nurses entered Lucky's room, there was a lot of ass-kissing going on. They all feared the family named after real-life legendary mobsters who had beaten federal charges and allegedly had ties to the Mexican cartel.

The chitchat was halted when someone rudely demanded, "Tell me what room Lucky West is in!"

The nurses all looked the ghetto girl up and down, and her eyes dared someone—anyone, to say something slick. She looked like she got out of bed just to fistfight, and no one wanted to give her an excuse to act ignorant.

Nurse Baker smiled and replied, "It's the first door on your right."

They all watched as the hood chick went marching into the room, and all guessed she was some sort of drug mule.

Rewind: The Brooklyn Bridge

∞

Maxine had washed ashore on Brooklyn's side of the bridge, barely breathing. It felt like her windpipe had been restricted as shallow bursts of air struggled to escape. She turned over on her stomach and regurgitated gulps of contaminated bacteria-laden water. Maxine's whole body felt like she had fallen several stories and crashed landed on an indomitable surface—which is precisely what had happened. She rolled over again and looked up. Her body was tucked discreetly under the bridge, hidden from her enemies and law enforcement alike. She heard the helicopters and police sirens and willed her body to move. She could not. Her whole body felt mangled not only from the beating she had taken from Bugsy but from the fall. A throbbing pain pierced her lower back—solid blows, like a fist to flesh, hammered on her spine. An indescribable sensation that made her wish she were dead.

"Fuck," she cursed out and then winced from the sting she felt from the large gash she had inside her mouth. Maxine didn't know if she would make it out of this one. She knew she had a broken foot, unable to move her toes. The discomfort was beyond any pain she had felt before. Maxine laid there for what seemed like an eternity, going in and out of consciousness. She dreamt of her parents, her first love, Scott, and looking forward to her law school graduation. Maxine knew this wasn't real, that she was in a state of oblivion. Her spirit willed her to wake up and snap back to reality, but she was too weak. Eventually, the coast guard's loud siren and sight blinding scope light pulled her eyes back open.

Maxine had been in a state of delirium, but somehow she mustered up the strength to use her arms as legs and drag herself across the grassy knoll until she had put a considerable distance between the crime scene. Evidently, her looming murder was the motivating factor. Maxine wanted to live if only to seek revenge for her son because clearly, this was all God's plan. No one had to affirm that a miracle had taken place—that every bone in her body was supposed to break on impact, including her neck. Maxine should be dead, but she wasn't. She had an angel on her shoulder. Maybe more than one who was rooting for her to once and for all beat the Wests.

The night Bugsy almost beat her to death, the night she jumped off a bridge, the night her son was murdered, the first night she spent in prison were all forged together to make her almost inhuman. She felt only hate. If she bled, she would bleed revenge. Had she sneezed, she would spew venom. If she cried, she would shed tears of acrimony. Her life choices had done a number on Maxine, and she was too mentally fucked up to return back to normal. She was a ticking timebomb, biding her time for the precise moment to detonate.

Lucky gagged when a woman pushed open her hospital door. Her presence was an unwelcome, unwanted surprise.

She got straight to the point. "Who the fuck are you?"

"Well, damn," Markeeta said. "Good mornin' to you too,

cousin."

Lucky sat straight up in her bed without help. She was growing stronger by the day. Finally, she recognized the face. "Seriously, why the fuck are you here?"

Markeeta smirked. She didn't understand why she was spoken to so aggressively. Quickly, Markeeta rushed toward Lucky and embraced her in a bear hug. "I came to see a friend of mine who just had her first child when I heard these nurses talkin' about y'all and what happened and knew I had to come through and see what's what. You got beef, then we got beef. You family...we blood. I will whip a bitches ass for family."

Lucky was flabbergasted by this huge display of emotional shenanigans. Her gut told her this wasn't random, but Lucky played along.

"I'm good," Lucky said. "Thanks for having my back, though."

Markeeta removed her baseball cap, placed her handbag over the chair's arm, and got comfortable. She sat on the edge of the hospital's bed. Her thin, limp ponytail was lifeless, but her eyes had a peculiar gleam like the cat that ate the canary. Markeeta said, "No doubt, you know how we do."

"How've you been? How's your family?"

"We good. I have a son now...he's big as shit."

Lucky pretended to care. "Tell him I said hello."

Markeeta nodded. "Any news on Lulu? What's going on wit' that?"

The familiarity in her voice, the comfortability in Markeeta's actions stirred up emotions in Lucky. Markeeta didn't know Lucchese, hadn't ever met her child, and had only been around Lucky a handful of times over a decade ago. They were cousins, yes—but they weren't friends.

Lucky said, "I don't want to talk about my daughter."

"But do you at least know why she was kidnapped? Streets talkin' crazy about you owing money to the mob."

"The mob?" Lucky snorted. "Niggas need to keep my name out their mouths."

"Exactly."

Lucky continued yapping. "And how's it now mob-related when feds locked up a cartel member?"

Markeeta shrugged. "This shit's crazy…what her father say?"

Lucky's eyebrow raised, a barely noticeable act from the side of her low eye. However slight the movement, Markeeta recognized it. She pushed some more. "I mean, that nigga must be goin' ham right now."

Again, Lucky didn't like how Markeeta was acting like they were besties when the last time she saw this bitch Lucky was seven.

Lucky barked, "What part of *'I don't want to talk about my daughter'* was hard to comprehend?"

"I hear that," she replied and changed the subject. "When you get outta here? You want me to pick you up?"

"I can manage. I'd be a fool to sit here and wait for you to come from Brooklyn."

"Brooklyn?" she said with disgust, as if the borough was somewhat beneath her. "I live in Harlem now. I'm at Regency Heights."

Lucky's eyes widened with a surprising curiosity. She knew that historic building in Harlem and wondered how her cousin afforded it. Lucky looked at her nails—polish was chipped, peeling. Her footwear was basic, no jewels, no staples of wealth. She pushed, "I know that building. What scam you got going on?"

"Scam?" Markeeta looked offended. "I work for Verizon now."

"Verizon," Lucky repeated, now wondering how she could be of use. "Nice. Are you customer service? If I gave you a telephone number, could you bring up the address?"

"Nah, that ain't me. I'm a tech. The peoples you see outside climbin' polls n' shit to connect the wires."

Lucky quickly lost interest but couldn't help but say what was on her mind. "Isn't that above your educational jacket? You got a hookup, didn't you?"

Lucky was far from a fool. She knew that job took electrical knowledge, fiber optic skills, experience in telecommunications, and education—high school, associate, and/or bachelor's degree. Lucky's gut said Markeeta didn't have any of that, but she wasn't about to hate on her hustle.

"Gurl, I turned my life around. I'm chilling, makin' well over six figures, and my nigga hits me off."

"That's cute."

Markeeta snorted to stifle her rebuttal to the 'cute' remark.

Lucky didn't ask for the family reunion and was ready for it to end. But she appreciated seeing a face that wasn't one of her brothers. Lucky realized that she didn't have any female friends.

With a forced smile, Lucky replied, "I'm happy for you—" she paused and then said, "Now, what were those bitches sayin' about us?"

The two shared a lengthy conversation about the nurse's station, Lucky explained how she was almost murdered, and they laughed about family drama.

"You remember when Grandma beat the shit outta Aunt Betty at the cookout?" Markeeta asked, feeling nostalgic.

Lucky was laughing so hard now, reliving the spectacle. "She put those paws on her like an Old G. Grandma wasn't no joke. Where you think Scott got his anger issues from?"

Markeeta nodded. "Damn, I miss those days when we all hung around each other, back when our family was close."

Lucky shrugged. They were never close. Scott and Markeeta's mother, Diane, were siblings, and without explanation, he forbid his children to be around her. However, when Scott and Layla would drop Lucky and her brothers off at their grandmother's house, Diane and her kids would always show up. This happened one time too many before Scott cut them off from the whole family—his mother included.

"People grow up, grow apart, and move on. It's a normal part of life."

"Yeah, but our generation can change shit. You and me can bring the family back together."

"That ain't happening," Lucky said, not caring that they were estranged. "Look, I appreciate the visit, but our family reunion ends today. Scott doesn't fuck with Diane. Therefore, I don't fuck with you. The catch-up was cute. I ain't sayin' you gotta go home, but you gotta get the fuck up outta here."

Lucky's smile had dissipated right before Markeeta's eyes. Lucky was always a moody, two-faced bitch and could vacillate between hot and cold like no one else. Markeeta grabbed the cheap flip phone lying on the small table and called herself without permission. "I'll call you, Lucky. I miss you. You can choose your friends, but not your family, and I'm always gonna go hard for us."

Lucky's face was stone. She didn't mumble a fuckin' word. She wondered how many times she'd have to say get the fuck out before Markeeta would listen.

"A'ight, I'm out. Give my family my love," she finally said and leaned in again. This time she snapped a quick picture of them together and shoved her iPhone into her pocket. Without looking back, she left.

Lucky thought about the odd exchange. Why was Markeeta really there?

Markeeta wasn't gone for long when Meyer came through. Lucky didn't even want to ask because his face said it was more sad news. Lucky said, "What's happened now?"

"Shit fucked up."

"A fucking understatement," she replied, knowing what he was about to say would leave her in a foul mood. "Our cash flow is down to a trickle, so as far as I'm concerned, it can't get worse unless Bugsy's dead…he ain't dead, is he?"

"Nah, he cool. Chill wit' your bad omens."

"My bad omens? Nigga, what is you talkin' about!" she screamed. Meyer had a way of getting under his sister's skin in a nanosecond. Lucky was having a bad morning and was about to tell him about Markeeta's visit when his news took precedence.

Meyer exhaled. "Those lil' niggas turned out to be a problem," he began. "They ain't comin' up off your bread."

Lucky gritted her teeth and then looked at her door to ensure no one was coming through. "Make them come up off of it."

Meyer understood. "I put Gonzo and Triz down, but Bugsy and I kicked it, and I can't go after these corner boys because those peoples are on me hard. I had to empty out all our cribs—.45s, nines, threes, assaults, everything poppin'."

Lucky was livid. "Ain't nobody on you!" she challenged. "You're paranoid, Meyer. They don't want us. They want our parents. I got two million on the streets that we need to get back on our feet. I'm not living my life as some bum bitch."

"It is what it is," he calmly retorted. "You want your bread. Go get it."

"Maybe, I will."

"Do you," Meyer said and shrugged. "And you had seven large lying around. I took half for pocket change."

"You mean nine large," Lucky corrected. "I had nine grand, and you left me wit' a measly $3500. Just say that."

"Look, I count quicker and more accurately than a money machine. I know what was there, so let's not debate this petty shit. We got—"

"Forget it," Lucky said dismissively. She knew she had $9000 and wouldn't be convinced otherwise.

"But I ain't finished. I had to sell all our jewelry to bail out our brother, and then I got jacked by the same peoples you claim ain't on me."

Calmly she asked, "When you say *our* jewelry, please

explain."

"Ya shit, too, Lucky. Those diamond and platinum chains, your earrings, tennis bracelets—all your shit is gone."

"My watches?"

"Gone bitch!" Meyer snapped.

Lucky leaped from her hospital bed, and when her bare feet hit the cold, tiled flooring, she cringed. She didn't know how many germs were now touching her skin, but she was too incensed to care. In her room, she let out a long-overdue scream. Lucky hollered at the top of her voice until half of the hospital staff came bolting through the door, including the local feds one floor below, after the nurses' station notified them.

Meyer looked at the crowd and said, "Pardon me…excuse me…pardon me..." as he left. His sister was a drama queen, and today he wasn't here for it.

Layla watched Scott from the sand. She watched him paddle energetically on the surfboard and travel farther into the ocean to catch a wave. She couldn't believe that he was actually going to surf. They'd been off the yacht for a month; he'd been learning the sport, and he seemed to catch on quickly. Layla couldn't help but smile, watching her husband paddle to catch a wave with a crew of white boys. In their late teens or early twenties, they all were young, and there was Scott, the elder of the group, ready to keep up with his peers. Scott sat on his midnight black and yellow surfboard, waiting in the sea for the giant wave to come.

With her eyes on her husband, Layla stood out. She had become a pearl on the sand. Dressed in a skimpy two-piece bikini, showing her curves and ample breasts, the Australian men couldn't keep their eyes off the exotic-looking beauty. They wanted to taste her chocolate cake until they got to the cream in the middle. Some smiled, flirting with their eyes, and some boldly asked the married woman if they could buy her a drink or dinner.

Layla was flattered by the fuss and enamored by their accents, but she was sitting pretty on that beach looking for Thor. However, any one of the Hemsworth brothers would do.

Layla observed Scott and the others prepare to ride the approaching wave from the white sands. They paddled rapidly toward the beach, ready to poise themselves on the surfboard and put on a show. Behind them was the ocean wave quickly forming. They chased it. Now it was chasing them. And it happened, after a month of practicing, Scott was ready to take that ocean wave head-on, and he did—man against the ocean. He rode that wave, almost like a bird gliding on the wind with its wings spread. Scott felt nature's energy in the tide, and he cut through the water and glided almost effortlessly. He was shocked by the realization he had actually caught a wave, and it felt thrillingly surreal. And then, just like that, he wiped out. The ocean swallowed him up quickly as he plunged into the azure-colored sea.

Layla quickly stood up, her eyes scanning the area he went under, hoping he would resurface soon. Her breath hitched as her husband was taking too long to crest his head through the water. Scott was a good swimmer, but the Australian undercurrent was strong, and he had to fight his way back to the top. Scott's head came crashing through to the surface, and he inhaled and exhaled air as he fought his way back. Scott soon paddled to the beach with his surfboard attached to an ankle rope. He surfaced from the sea, dripping wet, carrying his board in his arm, almost looking like a professional surfer. Layla exhaled and smiled his way.

"You did great," she called out.

Scott felt invigorated. His endorphins were surging through his body, and he felt like he was intoxicated. That mellow high where you just wanted to chill. "That was almost better than sex." He leaned in and gave his wife a quick kiss on her lips.

"Nothing can ever be better than me," she countered.

He chuckled. "I need to go to the house. I need a drink and

to change out of this wetsuit."

"Hurry back," she said.

When Layla didn't offer to walk with him, his eyes lingered on her for a moment. He then glanced at certain men on the beach, captivated by his wife. He said, "Don't make me act ignorant out here."

"Please act ignorant in our bedroom tonight," she said wickedly.

Scott didn't reply, pivoted, and marched toward the house in the near distance.

He stepped onto the deck and slid the glass door back. Inside, he propped the surfboard against the wall and walked to the kitchen. Instantly, Scott was attacked. A baseball bat connected to his lower back, sending lightning bolts of pain throughout his body. The harsh blow made him fall to his hands and knees. He looked up, glaring at a familiar attacker, Arturo. Arturo and Raffa scowled down at him. They spoke Spanish, and then they continued to beat him severely. As each weapon met his flesh, Scott found himself losing consciousness. When his eyes eventually closed and Scott blacked out, the sicarios finally stopped swinging. Their orders were to torture and then kill Layla first, make him watch, and then kill Scott next. So Scott was left alive, savagely beaten, and he knew who'd sent them—Javier Garcia.

Chapter 10

Maxine woke up to a gag-inducing funk that nearly stopped her breath. Her nostrils inhaled an odor of feces, urine, dead vermin, rodents, and moldy food. Maxine's eyes snapped open only to be met by filthy, sweaty socks less than an inch from her face. She bolted straight up, her back erect, her eyes wide, round, shrouded in fear. *Where was she?* Maxine realized that she was unmistakably inside a shelter made of large cardboard boxes held together with duct tape, and someone was sleeping next to her. She didn't know how long she'd been there or gotten there. Maxine was lying inside a soiled sleeping bag, tattered and discolored with dirt and stains, placed on top of an air mattress. The frigid air was so brisk, the makeshift house shook like clothes on an outdoor clothesline—she thought the house would be lifted away and taken to Oz.

Maxine didn't know who the stranger was sleeping next to her and couldn't see a face. The person had several layers of jackets, and two wool hats pulled so low that Maxine couldn't even see skin. She spoke, "Excuse me." Maxine could see her breath as her body trembled uncontrollably. "Hey!"

Wearily, the body moved, begrudgingly on its back to face the guest. The hats were pulled up, and Maxine saw the squinting eyes of a woman. She was light-brown, with ashy skin and dry, cracked lips. Her eyes were sunken in and punctuated with dark circles and crow's feet. Her nose was broad, and her face was gaunt, but her eyes lit up despite her circumstance when she smiled.

"She lives," the woman said. "It was touch and go for a while, but I knew you were a fighter."

"Where…am…I?" Maxine's teeth chattered now, feeling like she was seconds away from frostbite. "And who…are you?"

"I'm Wendy," the woman said. She pointed to a pile of clothing that she had gotten from the Goodwill clothing drop box bins she breaks into. "And you better layer up before you catch an ammonia."

Maxine looked down, and she still had on her jeans and sweater. "Where's…my coat?"

"I sold it."

Maxine smirked, and Wendy wasn't about to be disrespected in her own home. She said, "I repeat, I sold your coat because it was a good coat. How do you think I can afford all these amenities? You think this room is all I got?"

Maxine was too tired, too weak, and shellshocked to argue or fight. She didn't want to seem ungrateful, and right now, she needed this woman until she could figure out her next move. She began grabbing wool sweaters, sweatshirts, and then a man's ski jacket. The awful stench didn't bother her as much as the biting night air. The oversized ski jacket allowed her to layer six sweaters underneath, and soon she could feel her body temperature warming. She scoured through the items and found a pair of gloves and a hat. She rubbed her frozen ears with friction from her hands that felt like they could shatter like glass until they stopped stinging.

"Who you running from?" Wendy eventually asked. "And what's your alias?"

Maxine paused and said, "What are you talking about, alias? I ain't running from anyone!"

"That's a lie."

Maxine was trying real hard not to turn into Max. This lady was older than her, maybe by ten years, but she didn't need to be respected as her elder. "Look, if you want me to go, just fuckin' say it!"

"You can try, but I don't think you'll get far on that foot of yours."

The mention of her broken foot brought an added level of pain to her. Maxine looked down, and her boot was removed. Her foot was wrapped in thick bandages, two rulers for support, and set in a used splint.

Wendy said, "You're welcome."

"Thank you," she quickly spat out. "How did you know to do this, or how to do this?"

"I'm a nurse." Wendy smiled, and her teeth were surprisingly white.

Maxine smiled, too, beginning to relax a little. "No, really, who set my foot?"

Wendy sat up and felt around for a solar-powered lantern and turned it on. The only lighting was from the moon squeezing through the cracks until now. Maxine squinted before taking a look around. The makeshift home was bigger than she had thought. Wendy had used the boxes to build her bedroom, where she and Maxine were. They were sleeping on a blowup queen-sized mattress with many blankets and pillows. There was the lantern and two plastic bins filled with clothing. To the left was a tent that appeared to have kitchen utensils, a cooler, and a few other amenities she couldn't make out from a distance. She saw two buckets, toilet tissue, a few toiletries, Clorox bleach, and other cleaning products to the right. That tent was used as her bathroom.

As far as homelessness goes, Maxine felt it could be worse.

"What's your name?" Wendy asked.

"It's Max…well, Maxine. Call me, Maxine."

Wendy nodded. "Maxine, you're old enough to know that people usually lie to gain something or get out of something. Tell me one good reason on God's green earth that I should lie to you?"

Maxine looked down at her foot, and then her eyes went

back to Wendy.

"I know what you're thinking. You can say it. If I'm a nurse, then why am I homeless?"

Maxine nodded.

"I don't have a sob story. I worked in the Trauma Unit at Kings County Hospital, long hours, too much death. My rent and car note had me working double shifts; after work, the doctors and nursing staff would go into the city and run up large tabs trying to forget the past twelve hours. One day I just snapped. I could not get out of my bed. One day turned into months until I lost my job, apartment, friends, boyfriend—my identity. I didn't have any children, so I only had myself to look after the first night I slept on the street. I knew I had suffered a mental breakdown and being homeless actually helped me get my sanity back."

"How long have you been out here?"

She shrugged. "Not important. What's important is who are you hiding from? The police? A boyfriend? Drug dealers? I need to know what I'm up against allowing you to sleep here."

"How—"

"When I found you, I told you that I would call for help, and you begged me not to."

Maxine didn't even remember that exchange. "A boyfriend who's also a drug dealer."

"Oh, one of those." Wendy tossed her eyes in the air and then smiled. "Why is an attractive, seemingly smart, African American woman like yourself dealing with a dangerous man?"

Just thinking about Bugsy, what his family had done to her would send her to a place she didn't want to go. "It's too raw for me to talk about right now."

Wendy nodded and didn't push further. She reached under her pillow and pulled out a sandwich that she had foraged out of a dumpster and began to eat, not offering.

Maxine's stomach was rumbling. She didn't know how long she'd been without food, but she suddenly felt faint.

"Do you have any money left from the sale of my coat?" she asked.

"Why?"

"Because I would like to buy something to eat."

"Oh, you're hungry?"

"Of course, I am."

"Well, a closed mouth don't get fed. You want something, you'll need to ask for it 'cause I ain't no mind reader."

"I just did."

Wendy reached under her pillow and tossed Maxine her backup sandwich. She opened the aluminum foil and saw a half-eaten, soggy tuna sandwich and was visibly repulsed.

"I can't eat this."

"Can't or won't?"

The reply was swift, "Both."

Wendy asked, "How long are you staying with me?"

"I'm out of here tomorrow."

"Good. Because if you stayed longer, you'd realize that meals come few and far between per night, so you never pass up food. But I get it. You're a drug dealer's wife, so you're used to that five-star dining," she remarked. "Hold on, I got something for your prissy ass."

Wendy crawled into her kitchen area as you couldn't stand up in her home. She returned with a few items and gave them to her guest. Maxine looked at the Snapple Iced Tea, an unopened chicken salad from a supermarket, and a Drakes cupcake. Maxine teared up. "I couldn't...this food...you'll need it, right?"

"Don't worry about me. I'll survive. Eat your dinner and wake me in the morning before you leave. Don't go sneaking off like you stole something." She then tossed Maxine an expired prescription bottle of Vicodin for her pain. "Only take two!"

Rewind: Week two after Lucchese's Amber Alert

∞

Markeeta sat in the back pew of Brooklyn's Family Court on Jay Street, waiting for her son, Ralph, to see the judge. He had been in Crossroads, a juvenile facility, for a few weeks. Ralph had a couple fistfights with Brian, a boy in his homeroom period, and things had quickly escalated. Tired of being bullied and on the losing end of Brian's fists, Ralph brought a serrated kitchen knife to school in his knapsack and menaced his classmate.

"I should kill you!" Ralph threatened. "I'm gonna stab ya ass!"

Brian's eyes popped open in horror. Smaller in stature than the husky Ralph, he now feared for his young life. He didn't want to die. Unable to move, his legs felt like boulders anchored to the cement. Brian listened as his classmates egged Ralph on. They wanted to see death.

"Do it! Do it!" they all chanted in their young teen voices, pressuring the emotionally unstable Ralph. "Kill him!"

Sabrina, Brian's first girlfriend, went running for school security to help her boyfriend. When the guards arrived, they witnessed Ralph brandishing the weapon spewing threats. The knife was quickly confiscated, and Ralph was arrested.

With no money to hire adequate counsel, Kevin, the legal aide, only spoke gloom and doom to the young mother. "The D.A. will ask that this case be moved from family court and your son be tried as an adult."

"Yo, I know my son, and he didn't have no knife!" Markeeta hollered, unable to speak in lowered tones. "That fuckin' boy been messin' wit' him all year! Where his moms, yo…I swear. I'ma beat the shit outta her!"

Kevin exhaled. A lengthy gush of wind escaped his lungs as he expressed his annoyance. Why couldn't his parents afford to send him to more than a CUNY law school? He continued, "So, the weapon didn't look remotely familiar to you? It didn't come from your kitchen?"

"I said he ain't do shit," she roared. "That ain't his knife! You better get my son off and do your job!"

The lawyer nodded. Her continued outbursts and disrespect just guaranteed that he would throw the case. He would hand Ralph to the A.D.A. gift wrapped.

Kevin walked out of the room, and Markeeta impatiently waited for him to come back with good news. She wanted to take Ralph home today.

The door pushed open, and two men walked in. Her large lips twisted, and her downcast eyes rolled. She was lifted.

One man asked, "Are you high?"

"Excuse you?" she retorted.

"High? I smell weed."

"And?"

The man shrugged. "Not a good look. You're supposed to be here representing your son."

"Don't fuckin' talk about my child," she bellowed. "Who the fuck is you anyway!"

The second man spoke up. "We're federal agents working for the Drug Enforcement Administration. I'm Agent Tannery, and this is Agent Brown, and we're going to make you an offer you can't refuse."

"I'm listening."

"We need help with your cousin, Lucky."

Markeeta sucked her teeth, made the most grotesque sound the agents had ever heard, and said, "Fuck that bougie bitch!"

"I hear you. But we're going to need your help to do so."

Markeeta knew the assignment. The agents needed an informant. It was the new side hustle in the hood. Her sister, mother—both were snitches. Her friends and frenemies were all secretly informing the government. The federal government was the Illuminati that people kept whispering about but didn't understand. What people got wrong was that they thought *only* certain celebrities were in a secret society that guaranteed them starring movie roles and high-paying entertainment contracts. Whispers of this cult, better known as the Scientology religion, had former members who outlined the particulars and furthered the mystery. *Another* Illuminati is the government, which used its secret society to gather people willing to work as informants and get paid. Those people were rewarded with tangible objects, monies, free housing, job promotions, and many other perks if they did their job well. This Illuminati—not Scientology, run by our government, got individuals close to celebrities, the underworld, and tech giants monetizing the affiliation.

"What y'all need me to do? Record conversations, entrapment, plant evidence?"

Agent Tannery and Brown both looked at each other in disbelief. Where had she been all their lives? They thought they would have to strong-arm her, make threats, promise her a life of misery should she refuse.

Tannery nodded. "We'd need you to do all of the above."

"And what do I get?"

"What do you want?"

"Y'all here to offer to make this case go away for my son, right?"

Brown didn't like her attitude. She thought she had the upper hand. "We might get that arranged...maybe speak to a few people, but it's not up to us."

"Listen, let's not play games here. Y'all came to me, and I'ma straight shooter and not in the mood to be pullin' fuckin' teeth. Y'all need Lucky, and I'm the bitch who's gonna twist the key on her jail cell. So all that *'might'* shit, remove it from our conversation."

This is a tough broad, Tannery thought. And she must be if she would be successful.

Tannery stepped in. "Okay, fair enough. Your demands, list them."

"This case goes away today. I wanna walk outta here wit' my son. Periodt."

"Done."

"And—"

"And?" Agent Brown interrupted.

"And!" Markeeta rolled her eyes. "I want money each month put into an account for me and my son so we can do us."

Agent Brown's head shook rapidly. "That's not how we do things anymore—no paper trails. Your cooperation is off the record. Therefore we all have plausible deniability."

Markeeta asked, "Plausible what? I don't understand them big words."

"We barter through favors," Brown explained. "I have an imaginary Rolodex of affiliates that can grant me things. We're a tight-knit club, and all help each other; one big happy family."

Markeeta didn't care about the particulars. She was looking for a come-up, and it seemed like they were offering her a handout. "So if you ain't gonna hit me off each month, then I want a better job 'cause me and my child can't survive on ten dollars an hour."

"We'll find you something."

"I want NYPD. I want to *legally* own a gun and protect and serve my community. Be in charge of niggas…."

"A cop?" Tannery asked incredulously. "With your criminal record?"

"So what! I'm ready to turn my life around, and these are my *demands*." Her voice elevated when she said demands, indicative she had quickly settled into her role. Markeeta would cash in her lottery ticket, and Lucky West was the winning number.

"We're not going to sugarcoat this. There's no fucking way you're getting on the force!" Agent Brown didn't mince his words.

Markeeta's thick lips twisted, and her bloodshot eyes rolled. "Oh, well, I guess we ain't got shit more to politick about. Ralph is my son, so he can do a bid in juvie."

Agent Tannery exhaled and took a moment to weigh his options. He had the pay grade, authority, and connections to give her what she wanted. He was her fairy godfather and had the discretion to grant more than three wishes if that's what he chose to do. He said, "As stated, you're not getting NYPD, but we can find you a high-paying job."

"Then federal corrections," she negotiated without hesitation.

"Not going to happen," Tannery repeated.

"Then, no deal. I want what I want, and I'm not settling for less."

"Listen, bitch. Five minutes ago, you didn't have shit. Now you're acting like you got leverage!" Brown's voice was noticeably irritated. He spoke in a low husky voice, almost a growl. "Don't get cute because anyone could fit in your shoes. Get this through your head—we don't need you!"

"Federal corrections or kiss my Black ass!"

Tannery said, "Listen, Markeeta, be reasonable here."

Markeeta leaned backed in her seat and crossed her legs, getting comfortable. She morphed into a boss bitch at the helm of a boardroom meeting and kept negotiating. Her eyes squinted as she tried to block out the noise, pleas, and shenanigans at the front of the courtroom. Markeeta held eye contact with Tannery. He had a jowly, pudgy round face that matched his soft, mild voice. Although he was suited up, he had a bloated stomach that hung over his belt buckle, thinning hair, and pedophile eyes— leery and low that gave him a slovenly appearance.

And then she looked at Brown, the cute one with anger issues. He had thick jet black hair, a trendy haircut, a tailored suit, an expensive watch, and icy blue eyes. He had no respect for Markeeta—none whatsoever and had no reservations in telling her so.

"Check this. Ain't nobody scared of you! I can make threats too—fuck outta here wit' that. Because, um, I think Lucky would love to hear about how y'all feds recruiting muthafuckas." She threatened, "If I don't eat, nobody gettin' fed."

Brown wanted to smash her fucking face in. He was in law enforcement all his adult life, so he was used to people cowering before him, especially in the Black community. His usual verbiage was, *Shut the fuck up! Sit the fuck down! I'll blow your fuckin' head off!*

Tannery leaned in and whispered to his partner, "Let me handle this," because he knew Brown was about to blow it. Abruptly, Agent Brown stepped out into the hallway, leaving his partner to seal the deal.

Agent Tannery finally sat down next to Markeeta. He, too, crossed his legs and led with what he felt would be a deciding factor. "I can get you a position that makes approximately one hundred thousand a year. Right now, you're making what…twenty-two?"

Markeeta added up the large salary and foolishly thought she'd have a million dollars in ten years. She nodded.

"Well, I can get you corrections if that's what you truly want because I want you on my team, but the pay is significantly less," he paused, reading her body language before continuing. "It's your call, but you seem like a smart girl. Do you really wanna be locked in a tomb for one-third of your day with criminals, a bunch of disrespectful predators. If you think Brown used harsh language toward you, just remember I told you that you'll be called a lot more for saying or doing a lot less."

Markeeta liked Tannery. He was the smart one. And so far, he was respecting her and had said yes to all her demands. "What job can you get me makin' all that money without a college degree?"

"Let me worry about all the particulars. I just want you to focus on Lucky."

"And I will. That's my word."

Tannery nodded. "Anything else?"

"I want to be friends wit' Nicki Minaj. She be around peoples that y'all should want, wit' me on the inside, I can do some damage. Help y'all take them down, get your names in the press. I'm tellin' y'all, I can do more for your team than Tekashi 6ix9ine."

"You're reaching too high. Maybe Meghan…or Iggy, but on Nicki, that's an affirmative no."

"Nope! I want Nicki. And I'm askin' because I already know what y'all can do. Y'all been planting people wit' celebrities for decades, and the celebrities don't even know. DaBaby, Kodak Black, Meek, Fifty—every third celebrity has a rat in their camp. Get me, Nicki!" Her voice now exuded desperation; a whiny moan had overshadowed her tough exterior. Nicki was her idol.

Tannery wondered how she was privy to such classified information. It was true. As far back as Hoover, the federal government has been illegally tapping the phones of people of interest for decades and placing moles in the entertainment, political, and business industry. The internet, email, and smartphone technology have made illegal surveillance much more accessible. The press reported a few incidents. Most notable was the British scandal with Piers Morgan and *The News of the World*, where Rupert Murdoch's print media allegedly had a host of celebrities, politicians, and businessmen's phones hacked and then printed the damaging information to sell papers. Then Edward Snowden did an interview for CBS. He outlined how easy it was to illegally tap into and record smartphone conversations, log into a person's laptop, desktop, or phone's camera and watch your entire day unfold. Another notable scandal was the Ring video doorbell and surveillance debacle, where men with creepy voices were scaring young children who were innocently in the rooms of their residences. The feds thought that the public wasn't listening nor cared. But Markeeta was.

Tannery's office recruited individuals to get close to celebrities by tapping into the famous person's life through telephone calls, emails, even browser history. They discover their likes, dislikes, intimate thoughts, fears, political views and then fed that information to the informant. Armed with all this knowledge, this person now has the tools to infiltrate—become besties, lovers, or business partners. Then the informant is skillfully placed in the immediate proximity of said mark, and the plot unfolds. Once they're in the celebrities' inner circle, information is disseminated, traded, or sold for profit. It's big business.

"I already said no to Nicki because we need to focus on Lucky."

"Think about that no for a while because not only will I get y'all my cousin, but my friend, Shirelle, she fuckin' wit' this dude from LG projects. He's moving a lot of weight, and they live together. I be over her house all the time. I can set him up too."

"What's his name?"

"He goes by Manny Machiavelli."

Tannery grinned. Manny's name had been circulating for a while. He wasn't on the Wests' level, but his conviction would be a win for the DEA.

"I like you," said Agent Tannery. "We're going to have a long, long business arrangement."

He handed her a cellphone that the agency had supplied. It looked like an average smartphone, but in reality, it was an ultramodern listening and tracking device that cost the government merely pennies on the dollar.

"Give the number out freely; the more street thugs, the better. Every call and text is automatically saved and sent to me. In fact, this phone is a live recording device that archives any and every noise or conversation. Everything said during a call or around this device twenty-four-seven is kept, the audio is uploaded to our network for further review. And should you get into trouble—any trouble, call me. My number is programmed under Pizza Delivery, but you should memorize it for emergencies.

For their informant to work effectively, Agent Tannery called on his connections to get a Section-8 housing voucher approved for Markeeta and her son. It was for a two-bedroom luxury apartment in Harlem, the same building Shirelle and Manny paid twelve thousand per month to live in. For Tannery to keep Markeeta off his books, again, he was able to pull strings with the private developer who'd owned a portfolio of mixed-income rentals. These developers had apartment lotteries, and the City of New York gave the developers tax breaks. Markeeta wasn't entered into any pool nor had to cross her fingers or pray to God to win. She was now affiliated with people in high places—a secret society, and that, evidently, was all she needed.

It was a hike on the train from Brooklyn and an adjustment for the Brooklynite, but it was luxury. Ralph entered a new charter school founded by the Sean Combs organization with a clean slate. His mother threatened, "I'ma buss your muthafuckin' ass if you act up in there, boy!"

Chapter 11

Layla repeatedly looked back toward their beach house, but still no Scott. She knew something was wrong as an hour was steadily approaching. Layla wasn't sure if it was her children or the sudden phone call from Javier, but whatever it was, their past most likely caught up to them.

She marched away, moving toward the house. Her senses were heightened, and she sensed trouble brewing as her eyes darted in all directions. Her heart beat faster. *What if Scott's dead,* she thought? She hated to think the worse, but she had to prepare herself for everything. She cautiously approached the beach house. The benefit for her, their residence was surrounded by shrubberies that concealed particular angles of the home. And hidden in one of the nearby shrubberies were two guns in case of an emergency—and Layla felt this was just that. Being in Australia didn't mean the couple was out of harm's way. Crouched low, Layla reached into the potted plant and removed a Beretta gun. It was loaded with hollow-point tips, and it took Scott weeks to obtain these illegal firearms. She stared at the house, observed the windows, and saw no movements inside. Carefully she continued toward the location with the gun by her side. There was no one around the proximity. It was her and her worries, and it was quiet—too quiet, which made Layla even more nervous.

Slowly and carefully, she slid the glass sliding door back and stepped inside the home, with the gun clutched tightly in her grip. Layla thought she was ready for anything that came her way until Raffa came from behind and yoked her into a tight chokehold. Startled, Layla was nearly overpowered. An intense struggle ensued between Layla and the sicario. His forearm was against her throat, closing her airwave. Her neck felt like it was being crushed as Layla desperately fought being subdued. He was strong, but she was determined not to die today.

Gripped tightly, there was no way she could get a clean shot off. Layla wiggled like a fish out of water in his grasp. With the gun still in her hand, she haphazardly aimed it down toward a part of him, any part, and let off two rapid shots—*Bak! Bak!*— two bullets pierced Raffa's leg, and finally, he released his grip. Layla stumbled to the floor in pain. Arturo saw the melee and quickly steadied his gun on Layla. However, a quick-witted Scott, who had regained consciousness, used his body weight and the last of his strength to slam into Arturo, tossing him against the wall as several wild shots went off from Arturo's gun, missing his target.

While Arturo struggled with Scott, it gave Layla enough time to compose herself, and she aimed the Beretta at Arturo, who was fighting with her husband and winning. She couldn't find a clean shot until Arturo brought her man down with a right-hand punch, his fatal mistake. Scott fell beneath his feet, and it left Arturo wide open. Layla didn't hesitate. The moment he spun to attack her, she fired a hail of bullets into him, with one piercing his heart. The sicario stood stunned, his chest and abdomen full of holes, and then he dropped to his knees and collapsed on his side.

Scott looked up at his queen, and his relief was short-lived. There was still one more issue to deal with. Raffa was still alive. He'd been crippled by the two bullets in his leg with his gun far away from his reach. Now he was at Scott and Layla's mercy, but he knew there would be none.

Layla went over to him and kicked him in his side. She screamed, "Who sent you?"

He refused to answer her. He was loyal to the game until the end, and he knew the end was now. He cursed at Layla in Spanish.

"Mierda puta!"

"Fuck you, too!" she shouted. Layla put two more bullets into his head. She stood over the body, seething. Sweat slid down her cheeks, and her body was soaked in perspiration. Layla was breathing rapidly from the intense battle. She glared down at Raffa and recognized him right away. Raffa and another sicario had kidnapped and tortured her.

"These muthafuckas again!" she said.

Scott was incensed. Javier had sent sicarios halfway across the globe to kill them. Layla stood in silence with the smoking gun still in her hand. Their beautiful vacation in Australia was officially over.

"We can't stay here," said Scott. "We need to pack up and leave right away."

She agreed.

The beach was a reasonable distance away to drown out the sound of gunshots. So it was unlikely that anyone heard the ruckus that went on in their beach home, but they couldn't be too sure. Nor could they be sure that more assassins weren't coming. They were caught in a difficult situation.

"What do we do, Scott?"

"We need to get the fuck outta here but not before we clean this shit up. They find these bodies, and we're internationally known as fugitives for a double homicide."

Layla was scared. This wasn't her turf. "What if the cops are already on their way…we should just run now. Wipe everything down and just go!"

Scott looked at his wife, and he saw fear, and Layla wasn't afraid of shit. He nodded. "Look, leave this here with me," Scott began and took the Beretta out of her hand. "I want you to go back to the beach, get in the ocean, and don't come out until you're sure you've washed all the gunshot residue off. Take off your bikini and throw on a sundress. Come back at midnight to get me. Don't wait for me if I'm not outside waiting for you.

Charter a private plane and head back to the states."

Layla objected. "I'm not leaving you. We live together; we die together. I meant that shit."

"If the heat is around the corner, ain't no need for us both to get jammed up. I don't ever want to see you with anything but diamonds around these wrists."

Layla had to fight back the tears. The sincerity in her husband's voice nearly opened the floodgates. "We can either stand here wasting time or get this place cleaned up. And I mean it, Scott. I'm not muthafuckin' leaving you!"

Scott was bruised and injured, but he was well enough to help clean things up. Layla locked the doors and closed the blinds, shutting out any view of the place from outside. She and Scott wrapped the two bodies in black garbage bags and sealed them with duct tape. Clorox and several rags sopped up the blood, and with a few hours of focused and concentrated cleaning, all signs of homicide were gone. Scott and Layla removed their bloody clothes and tossed them into a trash bag. He would set everything on fire tonight. And as the day transitioned to evening and then late night, the two sat around and contemplated their next move as their clothing was set ablaze in the firepit. They would leave for the airport first thing tomorrow.

In the wee hours of the morning, the couple loaded the men's bodies into the sicarios rental trunk. Scott drove the hour's drive to a remote location while Layla drove their rental closely behind her husband. It was dark, and a few feet ahead was a steep cliff that led straight down into jagged rocks, and the ocean waves crashed against the rocky shore. Scott climbed out of the car and put the car into neutral. He opened the fuel gauge, stuffed a rag in it, and lit it on fire. With Layla's help, they pushed the car off the edge and watched it freefall toward the rocks. It exploded on impact. Their eyes lingered on the jumbling mess of twisted steel for a moment. They knew that their past would catch up to them no matter where they were.

"Let's go," Scott said.

He and Layla left the area in the second car and drove straight to the airport. They were ready to put Australia in their rearview. However, they weren't prepared to fly back to the states, so Scott said, "How about Dubai?"

"Abu Dhabi's more us."

"Then, we do both."

"Like the ballers that we are!"

"Then that's what it is."

While waiting for their flight to board, Scott felt it was time to call Javier. Three rings in, Javier answered and heard a chilling, "Two devils down, more to go!"

Bugsy was jarred awake when several agents backed up by NYPD came bursting into his hospital room. Loud voices combined with radios crackling stormed the modest square footage and filled the room. Bugsy glared at the spectacle and already knew what this was about. Even though he was handcuffed to a hospital bed, unarmed, and unable to put up any resistance due to his gunshot wounds, law enforcement couldn't resist being petty. They lived for childish antics. These theatrics belonged in a stage play, a book, a movie, not his life.

"Wake up, motherfucker!" Agent Randall said, sneering. "It's jail time."

Bugsy's mouth twisted as he said, "I'm still fucked up. I shouldn't be cleared yet for transport. Where's my doctor?"

Agent Devonsky was already removing the handcuff. He roughly yanked Bugsy's arm and yelled, "Get up! Put your hands behind your back."

Bugsy looked into everyone's eyes. Ten sets were glaring his way. The hate was palpable, heavy dark energy that could suffocate the hardest gangsta, but Bugsy wouldn't fold. He could crack, but he'd never break. He realized that his doctors had cleared him, no doubt at the federal government's persistence. There wasn't anything else he needed to say. He mustered all his strength, determined to not look weak, and stood up. Authorities had confiscated his clothing and shoes after the shooting for evidence, so with a pair of tube socks and hospital slippers, gown opened toward the back, and boxers, he was escorted out of NewYork-Presbyterian Hospital surrounded by pigs. Handcuffed, he was shoved and led to the black Crown Vic that sat outside the hospital. New Yorkers were shocked to see the half-dressed African American male being perp-walked out of the hospital. It was a warm day, and pedestrians had better shit to do than to waste their valuable time watching an arrest. Someone called out, "Sucks to be you!" And kept walking.

He watched from the back of the unmarked car as a gaggle of blue and white police vehicles and a handful of cars driven by feds followed them. The procession of cars with sirens and flashing lights was just a taste of what the agents had planned for him. Bugsy seethed but said nothing even as they continued to berate him.

"They gonna fuck you up real good when you get inside. Those MCC boys don't like men like you. Men who are used to running things."

Bugsy didn't mumble a fucking word. His silence was triggering. They wanted a reaction.

"And a pretty boy like you who has a daddy with lots of money…oh, you're marked. First, they'll fuck you. Oh, I see gang rape in your future," Randall said. "Then, they'll extort you!"

Bugsy's gaze was out the window. His mind was elsewhere. He was thinking of ways to keep his brother in check while he rode this situation out. And then there was Lucky, Angel, Juarez, and their unresolved beef with Scott and Layla. His father had a hollow point bullet with his name on it. Bugsy would shove his burner so deep into Scott's mouth he wanted to break all his muthafuckin' teeth. Have him choke on the barrel of his gun.

This kill would be up close and personal. Bugsy wanted to stare directly into Scott eye's as he pulled the trigger and watch his brains ooze out from his ears. His mother would die too; how wasn't as important. Bugsy wanted—no, he actually needed his revenge but not at Meyer and Lucky's expense.

"You must be. How do they say in da hood," Devonsky mocked the culture. "You must be shook! You haven't said a word since we took possession of your Black ass."

Randall said, "You not so tough now, are you? You back there shaking in your panties, huh? Huh, motherfucker!"

The insults were limitless. Bugsy wondered how they had passed their psychological exams if this exchange of insults had them feeling all warm and fuzzy inside.

Bugsy felt relieved when he was turned over to the federal corrections officers for processing. He was given his orange jumpsuit, tube socks, rubber slippers, and sent to holdings.

Let the muthafuckin' games begin.

∞

"Jesus…this is fuckin' beautiful…ohmygod," Layla announced, standing by the large floor-to-ceiling windows in the hotel room with a sweeping view of a picturesque Dubai. They had miles and miles of unobstructed views. Layla was in awe of the city's ultramodern architecture. Dubai seemed something out of a fairytale, like the unbelievable Emerald City in The Wiz.

The Burj Al Arab was the third-largest hotel in the world. It was on an artificial island from Jumeirah beach and was connected to the mainland by a private curing bridge. The hotel was shaped to mimic a ship's sail—a billowing sail, a nod to the nation's seafaring heritage. The hotel's interiors screamed over the top with a soaring atrium flanked by golden columns, over thirty different marble types, and vibrant colors inspired by the elements.

The suite they were in was the best that money could buy. It had two floors with a sweeping staircase and a private butler. The room entrance was bejeweled in shades of royal blue, deep red, and bright yellow with oversized sofas, gilded furniture, and a giant mirror on the ceiling over the bed.

"You see this gaudy shit," Scott asked.

"These sand negros are muthafuckin' paid!" Layla said, grinning. "Why are we just getting here?"

"Get comfortable and relax, baby; we're gonna stay here for a while," Scott advised. "I'm gonna make some calls, make moves while we're here. We're not leaving until I've closed on a deal. There's billions out this bitch," Scott said.

Layla had no problem getting comfortable in Dubai. After their violent incident in Australia, she wanted to linger in paradise for a lifetime. She was shaken up by the cartel hitmen coming after them, and she was worried about being tracked again, but after a few hours in the city, she was back to her old self and was ready to drown in the life of sheer luxury.

Immediately Scott walked into the suite's office and got on the computer to do some research. Shortly after that, he was busy on the phone, making power moves. Layla made herself at home by peeling off her clothes and taking a hot bath in the giant Jacuzzi. There was a lot to learn about Dubai, a place known for luxury shopping and lively nightlife. There was a stack of complimentary magazines, and Layla flipped through them.

In one day, Layla instantly learned that she would have to tone down her outfits and curb her tongue. Islam was the traditional religion of Dubai. Dubai attracted many outsiders—mostly tourists, and residents were seen wearing an Abaya—a long elegant cloak worn by women in the UAE. It was considered the national dress. And the clothing banned from Dubai was Daisy Duke Shorts, miniskirts, tube tops, crop tops, and mesh dresses. These garments violated their dress code and could get an individual in trouble. Men could wear shorts to their knees and T-shirts that were respectful, and for the female visitors, the tourists, it was respectful to wear skirts or shorts that came down to their knees and to have their shoulders covered.

Layla had to take it all in, their strict clothing tradition, but she welcomed their practice and didn't plan on violating any dress codes. The last thing they needed was negative attention on them.

Scott emerged from the office nearly ten hours later. He was exhausted and now jetlagged.

"You want to stay in for dinner?" Layla asked, noticing her husband was fatigued.

"Yeah, I'm beat."

Layla was too. They both needed time to rejuvenate between the long flight from Australia, the time change, and the attempted assassination.

Scott and Layla slept on and off for nearly forty hours, only ordering room service. Finally, the couple was ready to see what Dubai offered.

Layla wanted to tour the city and go shopping. She and Scott rode the elevator down to the lobby. He wore an expensive linen pants suit and Ferragamo shoes. Layla settled on a Diane Von Furstenberg maxi goddess dress and pulled her hair into a messy bun. Outside the hotel was an impressive fleet of Rolls Royce Phantoms—all white like heavenly chariots ready to fly anyone off to their destination in style. So far, the Burj Al Arab was prepared to deliver on self-indulgence for their high-profile guests. Scott handed the valet a tip of four hundred Emirati dirhams, over one hundred American dollars, to have a chauffeur bring one of the vehicles. Scott was dropping cash just as carelessly as the obligatory drug hustler. While waiting, he struck up a conversation with one doorman.

"Is there a cigar lounge around here?"

"Yes, sir. There's Above 21, which is close, not too far from the mall. And there's Vault, which is a little farther from us."

"How the fuck they get here!" Layla cursed, and Ahmed cringed. "Are they following us?"

Scott swiveled to see who his wife was referring to, and his eyes landed on Uriel and Jacqueline. He caught a glimpse only of them as they climbed into the back of one of the complimentary Phantoms. Scott instantly felt uneasy. He angered quickly but remained stoic. He asked Ahmed, "The couple that just left, do you know them?" Scott was peeling off hundreds of dirhams for the information. Ahmed nearly broke Scott's fingers, snatching the tip.

"Yes, sir. Mr. and Mrs. St. James is one of our best customers. They're here all the time."

Scott didn't like the answer. This was his first time there, and this couple was regulars? "When did they get here," he wanted to know. He knew the intel couldn't be trusted if Ahmed said dates that the St. James's were in Australia.

"They arrived two weeks ago on a Wednesday. I was here when they arrived. Mr. St. James is a big spender and big tipper. Everyone here loves them."

Scott's interest was piqued. So the couple had arrived here after they left them on the water. "What does he do?"

"Excuse me, sir?"

Scott sounded like a dick rider, but he needed to know. "Mr. St. James. What's he into?"

"I don't know, sir. He's a businessman. I think he has ties in the oil industry like most businessmen who come here. He's seen around with Basheer Bin Qassim. They are good friends. Basheer is an oil tycoon and has real estate investments."

Scott had just researched that name online and wanted to connect with him. Basheer Bin Qassim was a billionaire, and he and Uriel were friends. *Who was this nigga*? Scott wanted to know?

Layla was ear hustling while her husband did his due diligence. That couple needed to be vetted because neither Scott nor Layla believed in coincidences.

The chauffeur drove their car around and quickly hopped out and opened the back passenger's door. Scott gave Ahmed a departing handshake before peeling again. He handed the driver five hundred dirhams, and Scott and Layla climbed into the backseat of one of the Rolls Royce Phantoms. The driver was eager to take them wherever they wanted to go. Their first destination was the *Mall of the Emirates*. It wasn't too far from the hotel.

"You asked all the right questions," Layla whispered to her husband as they rode in opulence. "What were you thinking?"

"I wasn't sure. But if they got here after us, then they were either fed or sent by the cartel."

Layla shook her head. "Not cartel. They don't move like that. They would have come after us on the yacht."

"Agreed," Scott said. "So, feds?"

"Maybe? But now, after what Ahmed had to say, it seems we've followed them, and this dude is a businessman. We should get to know them. Maybe he has connections."

"Maybe..." Scott said, curtailing that subject.

Nurse Baker came gliding through Lucky's hospital room door with her shrill voice and beady rat eyes. She was carrying the patient's lunch tray. Sliced turkey, mashed potatoes with gravy, string beans, and a healthy glob of phlegm. It didn't matter, though. Lucky's food was delivered daily through Grubhub; the drug queen didn't eat hospital food.

Nurse Baker smiled as far as her pursed lips would allow and placed the tray on the table. As soon as she was in front of the queenpin, Lucky rolled her eyes.

"Not feeling well again today, huh? Still anti-social?"

Lucky ignored her as she did every day she came through. Nurse Baker continued in a mocking tone. "I understand why you wouldn't be in a talkative mood after what happened to your brother and all...."

Lucky sat straight up. "What did you say?"

"Oh, she speaks," she said condescendingly. "She finally graced me with the privilege of listening to her voice."

"You don't know who you fuckin' with bitch!" Lucky threatened her eyes wild with rage. "Now, what happened to my brother! Don't make me ask again."

Nurse Baker was quiet for just enough time to check her attitude. She had ventured into dangerous territory, feeling powerful, cocky, thinking there was strength in numbers—that her coworkers would have her back. The readjustment was quick. "I meant no disrespect," she said. "But your brother was remanded into custody this morning. He's gone. The FBI took him, and I thought you should know."

Lucky signed herself out of NewYork-Presbyterian Hospital, and Meyer picked her up curbside. Her curly afro had grown some, so she put it into a high ponytail and tied a silk scarf headwrap into a bun. Her baby hair was laid, zigzagging down her pretty face. Her Fendi shades covered her insecurity, and throughout all the drama, she still took time to pause and put on Violet Fury Fenty's new lip shade. She stepped out into the warm air, got into her brother's SUV, and embraced him.

Chapter 12

Inside the mall, like the hotel, everything screamed high-end and elegance. It was a multi-level shopping mall that featured over six hundred retail outlets, over one hundred restaurants, cafés, and twice as many flagship stores. The mall was a playground for Layla. She gobbled up item after item, taking in store after store. It was like Alice in Wonderland—how deep down the rabbit hole was she willing to go. Shoes, clothes, jewelry, it was some of the best.

Scott's mind remained on Uriel. He just couldn't reconcile how this African American man had superseded him in business, where he was making deals with billionaires. How did he climb the ladder? What was Scott missing? Maybe he was an early investor in a startup company or received a large inheritance. His guesses were limitless, so Scott figured the only way to know the answers would be to ask.

He pulled out his cellphone and called Mason. "Any news?" Scott asked.

"I was just about to call you. Word is Juarez hit your kids' stash and trap houses in one night. Shit made all news stations. Meyer wasn't there, but there were no survivors."

Scott was taken aback by this information. But, with Bugsy and Lucky down, it was a strategic play on Angel's behalf. "You sure it was Juarez?"

"Who else?" Mason answered Scott's question with one. "Those cartel niggas brought the '80s back to our borough. There were over two hundred workers murdered—a bloodbath. Who has that kind of manpower, shooters on payroll that they're beefin' with?"

Scott was impressed that the residuals from the plan he and Layla put forth by blaming Angel for the murder of Dillinger was still reverberating through his children's organization.

"I think this warrants a bottle of an aged Scotch to be sent to Angel as a sign of my appreciation. I didn't even have to get my hands dirty."

Mason wasn't through with his updates. "The feds froze their legal tender, and Bugsy got remanded to MCC on a weapons charge."

Scott frowned. "On a gun? That lil' nigga ain't have bail money."

"It appears that way, but that seems impossible. I checked, and his bail is only $500,000. It is a cash bond only, but still, that's chump change."

"Something ain't right," Scott worried. "You think they working with those peoples…freezing assets, locking him up to cover up that he's informing?"

"Bugsy?" Mason said. "No fuckin' way, Scott. He'd die first. You ain't ever gotta worry about Bugsy or Meyer snitching. No disrespect, but Lucky…you might have a problem."

Scott no longer wanted to pat Angel on his back. "Then those ignorant muthafuckas let Angel take all my fuckin' bread. They didn't have anything hidden away from their stash and trap houses for rainy days? I thought I taught them better."

Even though Scott was at war with his kids, he still felt a way about Angel and the feds taking their cash flow unless he had a hand in it. Somehow he thought it reflected on him, his tutelage. A part of Scott wanted to throw his hat in the ring and go after Angel. But he was already at war with one cartel. Two would-be suicide.

Mason said, "They'll figure it out."

"Fuck 'em," Scott finally replied. "But, um, listen. I need you to get our peoples to dig up any and all intel on this nigga we met out here. He's doing it real big, rubbing shoulders with billionaires. I want to know everything about this dude. Where this nigga from, where he rests his head. The broads he's fucked, all his affiliations. There's something too good to be true about this muthafucka."

"Latin dude?"

"Nah, he's Black."

Mason whistled. "Like Barack Obama Black?"

Scott chuckled. "Nah. Like Whistler Hussain, Black. Like you and me, muthafuckin' Black."

"Billionaires?"

"Exactly."

Mason affirmed. "I'm on it. What's this niggas name."

"Uriel and Jacqueline St. James. She's his wife." Scott added, "Oh, and she's white."

Mason remarked, "White? You sure he's not an athlete?"

Scott laughed and gave Mason more details while Layla finished her shopping. She wanted to buy a few dresses to pay homage to the middle eastern culture.

Leaving the mall, Layla wanted to see the world's tallest building: the *Burj Khalifa*. However, Scott was in business mode. He wanted to make money. If he, Scott West, could become a self-made billionaire, he would solidify his legacy. He joined his wife in her sightseeing expedition to keep a happy life, happy wife adage.

Lucky walked inside her apartment and smelled the familiar scents of lavender and vanilla. Warmth enveloped her as soon as she walked through the threshold. It felt great being out of the hospital, surrounded by her personal belongings in her own home. She was miserable at NewYork-Presbyterian. Even in a private room, it was difficult to sleep with conversations from the nurses' station right outside her door. She could hear the constant dinging of the elevator doors opening and closing and an occasional 'code blue' over the intercom system. The firm twin bed was uncomfortable, so getting sleep was sparse, and when she finally got to close her eyes, she was always awakened by a nurse or doctor examining her.

She inhaled. The first thing Lucky wanted to do was soak in a luxurious bath filled with bath oils, salts, and a glass of Rosé. Her eyes drank in her well-appointed apartment, and she felt grateful to have lived through this last ordeal. She knew that she didn't have nine lives, and she had now escaped death twice. Walking to her room, she had to pass by her daughter's nursery. Lucky wanted to ignore it, maybe close the door to shut off her feelings, but the emptiness pulled her inside. She stood staring at the dusty rose and yellow jumbo letters on the wall that spelled out Lucchese's name. The colossal teddy bear from F.A.O. Swartz sat in the corner wearing a tutu, and a bib tugged at her heart. All that custom furniture and bedding for an infant who was no longer there.

This is my fault, she thought. *Her death is on me.* What type of mother places herself before her child? Lucky walked to Lulu's armoire and opened a drawer. It was filled with layers of clothing—the best that money could buy. She grabbed a sweater and hugged it close, inhaling the fabric. It didn't have her daughter's scent; it was gone too. Lucky got choked up and felt tremendous guilt. It felt like a landslide as all emotions hit her at once; shame, fear, desperation, anger, pity, remorse—how could she have been so heartless? She kept trying to tell herself that her daughter's father had a responsibility to his child, which was to not murder her. This was all on Angel. And then that small voice said, *you're a mother. You carried that baby…the obligation is different.*

Lucky's tears had blinded her. She couldn't wipe them away fast enough. She would never show this amount of hurt and vulnerability in front of anyone. Her mind wouldn't stop replaying Angel's offer: *Your life for her life.* She had to admit that she was frightened beyond measure. She just couldn't do it, and most telling, she didn't *want* to do it. Lucky couldn't willingly be murdered. Not for Lulu…not for anyone, and it was something that she would have to live with until she didn't.

As she turned to leave, simultaneously, she heard and felt glass crunch under her shoe. Lucky looked down and saw the only sentimental object she owned smashed to pieces. Without any thought, she dropped down to her knees and began picking up the shards of glass, nicking her hand in the process.

Lucky left the mess and shook off her guilt trip, barreling to her kitchen to get her cell. She dialed her brother. On the second ring, she heard, "Yo, you good?"

Lucky was hysterical. She didn't realize she was this emotional until the tears flowed out again. "How the fuck you gonna break my gift that Bonnie bought me and not tell me!"

"What are you talkin' about? I ain't break shit."

"You had to! Who else? I wasn't here, and it's in pieces. It's the only thing I had left of her!" Lucky's face had transformed into that ugly cry that one releases when there are no other options except to just give in to the emotion, defeated.

Meyer listened to his sister weep and felt her pain. He knew what that mason jar gift meant to Lucky; it came with her to every apartment she owned, and had it not been broken, he had no doubt that it would have remained in the family and passed down through generations.

"Lucky, I swear on everything, I didn't even go in Lulu's room."

She wasn't listening. She needed someone to blame. "Then how did it break?! It didn't jump off the ledge, Meyer. Stop lying and just admit it!"

Before he could continue his defense, she hung up and powered down her phone.

It took a hot bath and a few glasses of champagne for Lucky to calm down. She gathered the shards of glass and placed them into another mason jar, but this time she added it to her safe. Lucky twirled the round dial on her safe and opened it as she had done on numerous occasions. She checked to see that her five million dollar emergency fund and several fake identifications were still there. She didn't know if her brothers were smart enough to plan for rainy days should you ever have to run if the heat was around the corner—but she did. And a stash wasn't a stash if you told muthafuckas about it, so Meyer wouldn't be privy to this information. Besides, he had already robbed her.

Lucky saw her jewelry drawers were opened, all her valuables gone; earrings, watches, chains just as Meyer had said, except he had left one trinket that he didn't mention. It was her Chopard watch that Whistler had given her. He had it engraved, it read: *To baby girl, my Luck...from me...*

Meyer didn't know who it was from; he knew how much it meant to her, and her brother loved her enough to not sell it. Suddenly she felt terrible for accusing him of breaking the gift she received from Bonnie. But if not him, then who?

Lucky went to one of her many hiding spots. Her guest bathroom's toilet tank held a Ziploc bag, and there was her 9mm and chrome .45—her brother was a stupid muthafucka if he thought he left her naked.

Scott thought the elusive couple had left after not seeing the St. James's for over a week. And then, one night, Scott and Layla went out for dinner at the Cavalli Club—launched in collaboration with famed designer Roberto Cavalli, one of the most expensive restaurants in Dubai. Scott and Layla exited their chauffeured Phantom, and things quickly got uncomfortable. They walked up to see a host of armed men in suits, with holstered guns, speaking into their wrist radios. Although they had a reservation, they were detained, and before they could enter, Scott and Layla were frisked and scanned for weapons.

Scott was annoyed at being frisked. He said, "There had better be a president inside this joint, a king, queen, some upper echelon peoples to lay hands on me like this." Finally, they were cleared, and their host walked them toward their table. As Scott and Layla followed, a large dinner party was seated in the center, anchoring the room. Security stood conspicuously bookending the table, protecting the encapsulated dinner party. Scott could see top tier two hundred thousand dollars a bottle wines and champagnes by the dozen and unlimited seafood and steak dinners. The men spoke boisterously while the women were silent, almost used as decoration.

Scott made eye contact with Uriel and then Jacqueline as they passed by. They looked at Scott without recognition—as if he were a stranger, and he was, somewhat. The St. James's was having dinner with all the major players, and   Understanding stood out as he engaged in light banter with billionaire Basheer Bin Qassim, laughing like friends do. And then there was Ibrahim Bijan Maktoum, who had an estimated net worth of $3.5 billion. His money came from investment companies, sports teams, and stadiums. And last, there was Hosaam Nahyan, who had an estimated net worth of $10 billion.

Scott was stunned, silent. He could have had this man's ear just last month, and he squandered that opportunity. Layla could see her husband was aggravated, and it was her job to turn things around.

"So how we gonna play this?" she asked after they were seated. "We can't go to them grinning with our tails between our legs. They won't respect that."

Scott agreed. "You do realize that if I make a business deal with any one of them, then we're out the game. Fuck the cartel and all that violence that comes with it. We'd be straight for life. Imagine it, Layla. Us, legit billionaires!"

"I can," she smiled. "Again. How we gonna play this? We need to move in the same circles."

"We will," Scott promised. "I'll find a way."

Scott and Layla ordered a feast, if only to prolong their stay inside the restaurant. Plated John Stone Côte de boeuf, Canadian lobster, seared foie gras with balsamic onion jam, sturia caviar, organic clementines, and black summer truffles were devoured. *Balthazar* of *2009 Château Margaux*, which retailed for $200,000, was ordered with a staggering upsell of a quarter of a million U.S. dollars. Scott couldn't shutter at the price tag, not if he wanted to rub shoulders with the real deal.

Scott threw his money around to the support staff at the hotel, bars, and lounges because they were the ones to quickly disseminate information. Their orders were to engage the major players, the billionaires who frequented all the hot spots in Dubai, and drop his name as someone who's a wealthy American businessman—which was true. The support staff was more than willing to play the game because Scott was the most generous person they'd come across in years. Multi-millionaires and billionaires were cheap. They rarely tipped, and when they did, it was maybe a couple dirhams. Just enough to maybe buy lunch, but not at the hotel because their lunch wasn't affordable.

It didn't take long for Scott and Layla to walk into Billionaire's Mansion Dubai, a restaurant for dinner, and were waved over to a table of businessmen. Hosaam Nahyan sat at a beautifully decorated table with Understanding, Jacqueline, and a few others Scott didn't recognize. He and Layla walked over, and Hosaam did the introductions.

"Hello, my friend," he said. "I am Hosaam Nahyan, and this is my lovely wife, Faaria. I would like you two to join us as our guests." The female smiled graciously. Hosaam continued, "We've heard many good things about you. My country loves that you are here. Your money keeps our economy healthy. Since you're over here spending so lavishly, the United States must be in a recession."

Scott forced a smile. "I'm Scott West, and this is my wife, Layla."

Understanding said, "Scott, nice to see you again. Layla," he nodded toward the couple.

Hosaam said, "Uriel, I didn't know you knew them. Why didn't you say something?"

"Nothing to say," he replied sarcastically. Understanding eyeballed Scott. Scott knew the look. His eyes were those of a man who had killed before. Scott had to swallow his rebuttal. Understanding continued, "Please, join us. Unless our invitation is too forward."

Again, another jab. This nigga was on a roll. Evidently, he was still salty about their last exchange.

"I think tonight we could manage this intrusion."

Scott called the maître d over, and two chairs and dinnerware were added to the mix. Scott and Layla quickly ordered *Balthazar* of *2009 Château Margaux* and their meals to catch up with the others. It didn't take long for the ice to be broken. Layla watched as her husband blended in with a table full of billionaires. They all spoke business, politics, oil, stocks—Scott was on his A-game. He was a born leader and wouldn't squander his chance at helping them ascend.

It always amazed Layla to see Scott work, to see him charm his way into these men's lives, mingling with the cream of the crop, not just in Dubai, but in the world was a master class. They were far away from the states—feeling like they were light years away from Brooklyn, New York. The men at this table—moguls, sheiks, princes—it was part of a world that only a few would be lucky enough to partake in. Layla said little. She was afraid that she would say the wrong thing or someone would agitate her, and her Brooklyn vernacular would come spilling out.

After dinner, Scott picked up the hefty check totaling nearly two million U.S., and not one billionaire objected. His black American Express Centurion card was swiped as the table occupants quickly made their exit but not before exchanging contact information and warm handshakes. This was how business relationships were forged, and Scott West was on the precipice of a breakthrough.

Scott and Layla were driven back to the hotel and opted to stay out front to grab a smoke. Layla lit a cigarette and took in the environment—palm trees, exotic cars parked everywhere, and a regal structure. It was a balmy and cloudless night in Dubai. Scott stood next to his wife and lit a cigar—both in deep thought.

Layla spoke first. "I know how important it is for you to have a seat at the table wit' these tycoons, but if you ever pick up the check again for these sand niggas I'ma hurt you! Next time sit your Black ass there and don't reach unless it's to pay for us! We've been in this game for too long, and we ain't ever been somebody's trick."

Scott understood his wife's perspective, but she was thinking small. He explained, "What's five, ten million on restaurant bills compared to five, ten billion in potential business deals?"

"A lot," she deduced. "Fuck outta here wit' that logic, Scott. It ain't adding up yet because right now, ain't no deals being made. It was just dinner wit' strangers."

"You wouldn't understand—"

"I do, though. And if this was you picking up the check *after* a windfall, then I would cosign, but we don't gotta impress them on that level. I get you dropping a few hundred here and there but let's put a cap on our spending because guess what? We no longer have a connect, and we still got a team of triggermen on payroll back in the states, and most importantly, we're at war and war costs. So all I'm sayin' is fall back a little. Let's see if Understanding will dig deep and observe what he's really workin' with."

Scott had to agree with his better half. Layla would always

peep what he couldn't. Just as they were about to go to their suite, Mason called.

"Yo, I finally got that intel you wanted."

"Talk to me," Scott said, all too ready for the bad news, thinking Understanding was an informant or an agent or a conman.

"Uriel St. James was born in Haiti. His mother was a maid to a wealthy couple, and his father was a tourist from the states. In his early life, he went to a private school that the wealthy couple paid for. At fifteen, he moved with his parents to Chicago and went to a private high school on scholarship. Within one month, he was arrested, but he's never done any jail time. He and three other boys got caught with a firearm in a vehicle, one man copped to it, and the other three were released. By the time he was eighteen, he had begun applying for several LLCs. Each business he opened blew up. Per year, he saw expansion."

"So, he's legit?"

"I called out to the Midwest to our contacts. Although no one has ever met him, they all knew of him, and he is a businessman, but his seed money is through distribution. This dude moves major weight, but his education allowed him to flip that into profitable businesses. Just like you, boss."

That last line fucked with Scott's ego. "Who's his supplier?"

"I heard he fucks with a new faction of the Cali cartel. Everyone who's heard of him said he's like a ghost. He's tightlipped about his distribution and won't ever talk about any illegal activities. That's how he's been able to remain above the law. Folks said he's hardly on American soil. This nigga is internationally known and keeps a tight circle, small and defined. If he didn't know you from grade school, he ain't fuckin' with you."

Scott felt like he had Understanding's ear. "Anything else?"

"Yeah. In legit funds, they said Uriel's worth a half-billion from oil deals and real estate investments and is on the trajectory to clear one billion in the next year. In illegal funds, it's rumored he's worth that already. You thinkin' about fucking with him?"

"That's the plan." Scott acknowledged. "What about his wife?"

"Oh yeah," Mason continued. "They met five years ago, and he married her after two weeks. Jacqueline is a former cheerleader who, oddly enough, went to an HBCU, pledged a sorority, and then met Uriel at a fundraiser. She subsequently dropped out of college, and her parents have disowned her. Her father is the same age as Uriel and couldn't wrap his mind around the nigga. Her father didn't care how much money he made and had an inkling that he dabbled in the underworld."

"So daddy was right," Scott said. "Good work."

"A'ight, holler if you need anything else."

Scott hung up and absorbed the information. It was fucking with him; there was a smarter criminal. Their lives had paralleled, but Understanding's timeline was far more superior than Scott's. Understanding got a formal education while Scott got schooled on the streets of New York. Both had inroads to major cartels; Scott got his distribution through a Mexican faction, while Understanding had a Colombian connect. Both men parlayed their illegal funds into legitimate businesses. Scott's companies were worth two hundred million; Uriel's nearly tripled that. And while Scott had several arrests under his belt, spent a year incarcerated and had the federal government on his ass, and also had his wife roped up in his mess, this nigga had one run-in with the law and amassed a fortune with just a mild reprimand.

Suddenly Scott felt inferior.

Chapter 13

Lucky walked into Callie's restaurant like she owned the place. The owner was an affiliate of Bugsy's, so she got V.I.P. treatment whenever she went through. A light rain had fallen, and the meteorologist had threatened a massive hailstorm before the night's end. She was bundled in a silk wraparound dress with YSL high heels—hardly what you wear with tonight's forecast. Lucky held her Hermès bag snugly clutched under her arm, her .45 waiting for someone to try her.

A man was standing at the bar, unassuming and gawking her way. Lucky saw him staring and scoffed. Her evil eyes rolled, and she shifted her weight so he was now staring at her back. Management saw her come in, and quickly she made her way over. The model slim woman with the trendy skirt and shirt approached with a welcoming smile.

"Ms. Lucky, nice to have you with us tonight." She smiled warmly. "Is anyone joining you?"

"No, just me, and I'm feeling peckish."

"Good. I'll let the chef know that you're here. Follow me."

Lucky was led past the looky-loos and was seated at one of the most prime seats in the establishment. She was given a menu and quickly ordered an Appletini, rock shrimp tempura, and a garden salad.

"You too pretty to make such faces."

Lucky stared up at the bugaboo. "You? Again?"

"Guilty," he said and gave a warm smile. "My name's Ragnar."

Lucky couldn't deny that he was cute. *Ridiculously cute.*

Ragnar had smooth reddish-brown skin, the color of southern clay dirt—rich and creamy, which glowed naturally either from lots of water or simply good genes. A smattering of freckles was on his broad nose and cheeks, accented by his thick, reddish-brown eyebrows. Ragnar was an older man, mature like Scott. An aged bottle of wine was just the way Lucky liked her men. He had unbelievably white teeth, a strong, square jawline, with full pink lips. His mustache connected to his goatee, and his low, soft hair had spinning waves. He wore a thick, dark gray sweatsuit, and she couldn't see a dick imprint—so she wasn't remotely interested. A pair of Pumas, no watch, no jewels. He wasn't her type—she liked gangstas, but she had to admit the stranger had a presence.

He sat down uninvited. Lucky snapped, "Excuse you!"

His pearly whites displayed again, and he said, "Oh, pardon me, but I can't stand up and have a conversation with you. That's rude."

"We're not conversing."

He smiled. "What we doing then?"

"Cute." She exhaled. "What do you want from me 'cause I'm not giving you my number."

Ragnar's eyebrows connected as he considered the question. His head tilted to the side, and he clasped his hands together. Lucky didn't think the question was that serious, but he seemed to put thought into his words.

"Initially, I wanted you to help me pass the evening after getting stood up. But as I sit here and stare into your pretty face, I'm glad my date isn't here."

"Date? Who ghosted you?"

"Someone I met online. We were supposed to meet for the first time, but here I am, and she's not."

Lucky laughed. "You too old to be out here swiping right."

Ragnar laughed too. "No, it's not like that. I was on a good site looking for my life partner. But I'm already over it." He stared intently at Lucky.

The waiter approached and gave Lucky her Appletini, and Ragnar ordered a Dr. Pepper in the can.

"Are you serious?" she asked.

"What?"

She shook her head. "You're sitting at my table *and* ordering shit?"

"I'm going to pay the bill."

"I can pay my own bills," she snapped.

He looked at the bougie young lady and said, "It's only a meal, not your mortgage."

She asked, "What type of name is Ragnar? I've never heard of it before."

"It's Norse from Icelandic stories. My father was into Viking and 9th century Norse literature. Growing up, my friends called me Ray, but as an adult, I prefer my government." He leaned in and gave her his undivided attention. "So, I've told you mine. Now tell me yours."

He was a nerd, one part clueless, a smidgen of self-confidence, with a smattering of dark energy. Those factors meshed together Lucky found herself drawn to. She took a sip of her drink and wondered why she was entertaining this scenario. She hesitated. Lucky wrestled with whether to be truthful or not. She felt her family was under siege like she was a fugitive, yet there wasn't a warrant for her arrest. Finally, she replied, "Lucky...my name's Lucky."

"You know I'm going to ask, so just explain."

She chuckled. "After Lucky Luciano...."

His eyebrow raised. "The gangster?"

"Is there anyone else?"

"Noted. So Gangster Lucky—"

"Just Lucky, but if you must, then 'Gangsta Lucky.'"

He laughed. "What do you like to do for fun?"

The simple question had her stumped like Fermat's Last Theorem in high school. Her brain cells fizzled. All the men she had been with never asked or never cared what she liked. It was always dinner and then dick. To think of it, her dudes never took her to the movies, parks, museums, or anywhere to enjoy herself. When she didn't answer, he said, "Are you always so serious?"

"With strangers? Yes."

The waitress brought his Dr. Pepper, and he ordered a steak and asked, "Would it be possible to have our meals come out together. I don't want this beautiful lady to eat alone."

The waitress nodded. "Of course, no problem," she said and looked at Lucky and winked, approving the cute dinner guest.

Ragnar looked around and asked, "Is it too bright in here? Take off your shades so I can see your eyes."

Lucky was tipsy off her one drink, medication remnants still in her veins. But she wasn't drunk enough to willingly take off her YSLs. Just as she was about to object, he leaned in and gently removed them for her. Lucky's hand immediately went up to shield her low eye.

"Don't, please," she begged in a lowered, insecure voice. She didn't want Ragnar to stare, to see her without her security blanket. "I had an accident…."

"You're stunning…so beautiful." He stared at the young woman, her imperfection, and said, "The next time I see you, you better not have these on indoors."

Lucky snatched her shades and quickly put them back on. He was getting too familiar too quickly. Besides, she wasn't ready to be her authentic self on his timeline. Ragnar noticed how uncomfortable she was; her body had stiffened, her lips were pursed tightly together, and her hands were now fists. He said, "You know who Aaliyah is?"

"Who doesn't? The singer, right?"

Ragnar nodded. "Early in her career, she would use her hair to cover her left eye. Eventually, either sunglasses or a long bang over her eye became her signature."

"So? What does that have to do with me?"

"Aaliyah had a lazy eye, where one eye isn't as open as the other. Not many people have symmetrical eyes, breasts, fingers, toes, et cetera. What she considered an imperfection was actually what contributed to her beauty. When you walk around with shades on, you look like every other woman walking. But, if you see your accident as an accent, a mark that accentuates what God gave you, then what sets you apart is also what makes you stand out."

They continued to converse as their meals came. Lucky found herself relaxed and comfortable with someone she didn't know from a hole in a wall. Ragnar was intelligent, college-educated, and had a sense of humor. During dinner, Lucky was used to talking about moving ki's, trap house shenanigans, and rival drug hustlers. Now she was engaged in grown-up conversation, and she liked it.

"Since we've been here, you've mentioned God a few times. Are you religious? Or spiritual as Oprah likes to say?" she asked.

"I'm both."

Lucky pushed back in her seat and stared intently at Ragnar. *Why not?* She thought. "Do you really believe a God is hovering in the sky, granting prayers like a wizard, banishing those who do evil to hell, which is ablaze in a fire?"

Ragnar got serious. "I believe there is one God that is in all things, not just the sky above who sees and knows everything."

Lucky nodded. "Do you practice what you preach?"

"I try, but I'm not perfect. I go to Saint Gabriel's Catholic Church on the Westside. You should come."

Lucky's head shook. "No, thanks," she replied dryly. "But, Catholic? I thought Black folks were Baptist or Pentecostal? Maybe, nondenominational?"

"Ah, look at you," he sang. "You know your stuff, huh? Let me find out you be singing hymns on the weekends. Rolling out of the club into the pews."

"I see you got jokes."

He sang Marvin Sapp's hit, *"Never would have made it…never could have made it without youuuu…I would have lost it all."*

"Ohmygod, you sound terrible!" Lucky was a little too enthusiastic.

"Look at you. You're a believer and didn't even know it. Calling on the lord when the mood is right."

"Okay, fair enough. But you sounded like trash."

"Thank you." Ragnar took another sip from his soda. "What do you do to make an honest dollar bill Miss Lucky?"

The calculus equations kept coming. Lucky needed to be better prepared to interact with civilians. She needed a believable cover story. There was a pregnant pause as she thought about saying she was a nurse. Maybe she'll go next level and say, lawyer. Instead of a barrister, Lucky settled upon, "Barista. I work at Starbucks."

Ragnar stared at her for a long moment. "You don't like talking about yourself, do you?"

Lucky shook her head. "Actually, I don't."

"That's different. Pretty women usually won't shut up, but you're a breath of fresh air. You're sweet and modest. It's rare, and I can dig it."

Sweet and modest? Lucky wanted to laugh out loud. Who was she on this random evening? She liked the role she was playing; it was much-needed escapism.

"And you?"

"I'm a scientist," Ragnar said, reaching into his wallet and pulling out a business card. As Lucky read his details, he pulled out two hundred dollars and dropped it on the table for the bill. "Call me Miss Lucky so we could have lunch, maybe coffee, if you'd feel more comfortable."

He nodded, stood, and exited, making Lucky yearn for more. The abruptness of his departure had her feeling weird. She couldn't understand why she wanted more of him. Lucky continued examining his navy blue linen cardstock with raised silver lettering. It read: Ragnar Benjamin, Head Researcher, J.L.R. Laboratory.

What do scientists do? She wanted to know. *And do people still carry business cards?* And finally, *why didn't he ask for her cellphone number?* These questions were fucking with her.

∞

It was late. And Scott and Layla found themselves with guests in their hotel suite. The couples weren't ready to end the night, so Scott suggested they come to their place for a nightcap, and they agreed.

Layla was trying not to rain on her husband's parade because she knew how important connecting with Understanding was to Scott. He not only wanted to do legitimate real estate and oil business, but Scott also wanted in on his Colombian connect, the Cali cartel. Because the war with the Garcia cartel had left their supply dried up, and his men back in the states needed to eat. It was only so long Scott could keep his soldiers on payroll without moving product.

But Layla didn't like them. Especially that Jacqueline bitch. She refused to be called Jackie and had this air about her that triggered every raw emotion Layla had. They went from having an occasional dinner to making dinner plans every night. That transitioned into dinner and lunch, and then they called to have breakfast too. Mason had told Scott that the St. James's was standoffish and didn't allow strangers in; then why were they so special? Layla tried to get Scott to see things her way, but he was up their asses. She'd never seen him so happy with anyone other than family. The prospect that Understanding could help Scott reach billionaire status had changed him somewhat.

Layla played the hostess. Anything to give her a few minutes away from the fake smiles and snobbish bitch. She walked to the bar and asked, "Understanding, what you drinkin'?"

"Drinking," said Jacqueline correcting her English.

Layla smirked and looked at her husband. Scott's eyes told her to chill, and she did. Understanding replied, "I'll have Scotch if you have it."

"We sure do. Is Macallan rare cask single malt good enough for you?"

He nodded. "It'll do."

"I'll have the same," Scott said.

"Jackie—"

"It's Jacqueline, sweetie."

"I'm not your muthafuckin' sweetie!" Layla snapped, ready to call her more names than Jackie. Like, cracker ho! But she counted to ten to deescalate her rage.

"Well, then you see my point," Jacqueline explained. "I won't call you, sweetie, so don't call me outside my name either. It's simple etiquette."

"She'll have a white wine spritzer," Understanding responded for his wife and squeezed her hand, hoping that the two could bond as he and Scott had.

While Layla made the drinks, her guests indulged in light conversation with Scott. They liked him, and he seemed to like them too. Layla felt like the fifth wheel and wanted to go inside her room and crash. She was beat. She walked around with a tray, handed everyone their drinks, and joined the conversation.

Somehow a conversation about who Scott and Understanding both knew in the business world turned into a discussion Jacqueline decided to hijack. "Layla," Jacqueline asked, "Where did you go to college?"

Layla smirked. "I didn't," she announced proudly.

"You never wanted to further your education?" she pushed.

"Why the fuck do you care?" Layla asked. "Seems that even if I'm uneducated, I still managed to be in the same room as diplomats and billionaires. So to me, I'm the smart one."

"Yes, that's true," Jacqueline said and took a sip from her glass before clearing her throat. "Would you agree that being in the same room isn't quite the same as having a seat at the table?"

What the fuck was going on? This bitch had Layla's head spinning.

Understanding said, "Jacqueline, don't be anal."

She grinned and said in a low purr, "Ooh, you know I like anal."

And both Scott and Layla cringed. But the torture wasn't over. Understanding replied, "Me too," and Scott and Layla were ready to end the night. This was about to go left.

Layla said, "Only lil' dick niggas like to give anally!"

Understanding let out a guilty chuckle, and Jacqueline glared.

Scott yawned, "It's getting late, right? We should turn in."

Layla watched as Understanding looked to his wife, and she spoke up. "Why don't we join you two."

Layla exploded. "Bitch is you stupid! It ain't that type of par-tah, you hear me ho? I don't know what type of kinky shit you and your husband are into, but me and mine ain't down!"

Jacqueline ignored her outburst and turned to face Scott. She said, "Well, it could be. We could switch partners for tonight if that made everyone more comfortable."

Jacqueline was giving off all types of *fuck me* vibes. Layla looked at her husband, and she saw a look only a woman could decipher. Layla's hand reached far back, and when she swung, it landed across Scott's cheek. The slap echoed throughout the quiet room. She went to slap him again, and this time Scott caught her hand, stopping the assault.

"I told you what the fuck I'd do to you if you *ever* put your dick in another bitch!"

Scott was composed. "You're embarrassing yourself, Layla. Why don't you go and sleep it off?"

"Don't fuckin' try me, Scott!"

Scott gritted his teeth. "I said, let this shit go!"

"We're just going to leave." Understanding stood up and gave Scott a firm handshake before escorting his wife out the door. When they left, Layla went into a rage.

"I don't like that bitch!" she roared. "And these little rendezvouses are over."

Scott smirked. "It ain't over until I muthafuckin' say it's over. Know your place, Layla."

Layla was incredulous. "My place," she spat. "Nigga is you stupid? You done bumped your fuckin' head, Scott. My place is by your side. You don't walk in front of me. You walk beside me, and if you don't know that by now, after all these years, all my sacrifices, then you ain't shit!"

Layla was near tears, but she refused to cry. She fought hard to hold back her emotions as she stormed into their hotel's bedroom, slamming and locking the door shut.

Scott exhaled. He took one last swig of his single malt Scotch, looked at the spare room, and knew he would need to make himself comfortable.

Chapter 14

"Can I buy you an Appletini?"

Lucky spun around to see who had violated her personal space, and it was Ragnar, the guy she'd quickly forgotten. His reddish-brown skin glowed under the restaurant's dim lighting, and his freckles danced a happy dance as his smile widened to a full grin. Lucky had quickly lost interest in him seconds after their first encounter, but he was again standing before her. Lucky's eyes drank him in; fresh haircut, fitted suit pants, and Louboutin hard bottoms. His Patek Phillipe watch was classic, tasteful, baller. Ragnar had done a one-eighty from their first encounter. He was on-trend, clean-shaven, and looked and smelled like money. He was definitely worth a second glance.

Lucky finally responded, "You can buy me dinner and a few drinks. I'd like to get fucked up."

"I can do that," he said and looked for the hostess to seat them.

Lucky's head shook. "Let's eat at the bar." She didn't want him thinking this was going somewhere, eating dinner in a cozy booth again.

Ragnar needed no time to contemplate his dinner order. He waved the bartender over.

"Let me have a Dr. Pepper in the can and an Appletini for the lovely lady—" he turned toward Lucky and asked, "What will you have for dinner?"

"I'll have the rock shrimp tempura and a garden salad."

Ragnar said, "Scratch that," and turned again toward Lucky. "You probably order that all the time, right?"

Lucky shrugged. "It's what I like."

"If I never see you again, at least I can say that I got you to try something new." Ragnar got up and ushered the bartender out of earshot of Lucky, and placed their order. He came back and said, "This should be interesting."

Lucky crinkled her nose.

He saw her face and said, "What?"

"If being extra was a person." Lucky was used to calling the shots in her business and personal life. And although she no longer had a roster of shooters to control, she certainly could still order her own food. She wasn't about to be subservient for no nigga. "I know what I like."

"Time for you to try some new things." His sleepy eyes almost lulled her into a trance, hypnotizing her to let her guard down. His lips curled slightly, amused at how everything was monumental. He assessed that she felt disrespected but couldn't glean why. "Can you just trust m—"

"I don't trust anyone," she said, curtailing his speech.

Ragnar nodded. "It's food, baby girl. Something to be savored, explored, tasted…just like a woman."

Lucky blushed. She hadn't expected that response. Ragnar was giving her grown and sexy vibes.

"Why are you here again?" she asked.

"I don't know what you mean."

"Straight up, are you stalking me? I've never seen you before and now twice. And please don't say it's a coincidence because, like God, I don't believe."

He grinned. "And I thought you were sweet and modest. You got a slight edge to you, huh?"

"Your words, not mine!"

His head nodded. "Got it. Well, if moving directly across the street last month from the best restaurant on this side of town somehow equates to stalking you—then I'm stalking a lot of people."

She felt stupid. "You live in Borough Park Towers?"

"I do."

"Expensive...um, I should have paid more attention in science class."

He looked her up and down. Lucky had on thigh-high Balenciaga boots straight off the runway. The diamond watch she had on could purchase his apartment and still have money left over. Lucky's Birkin bag and designer shades could put him in a custom Range, so she didn't need science.

"You look like you're doing well for the coffee business."

"I'm managing."

"And that watch," he whistled. "Exquisite."

"Thanks." Lucky changed the subject, "I asked before, and I'll ask again. What do you want from me?"

Ragnar cocked his head to one side, and after some serious thought, he said, "I don't know...everything...nothing. Maybe I want to make you smile, cry...feel pain...feel ecstasy." His voice was low, self-assured, with a hint of arrogance. Ragnar had leaned in, placed his hand on her upper thigh, and continued with, "But ultimately, I may want you to call out for *mercy*."

"You'll be hard-pressed waitin' on me to call out for mercy." Lucky chuckled dismissively at the thought. Was he serious? Did what he was spewing work on other women? She realized that he had no idea who she was or what she could do. Although she felt like a shell of her former self without her security blankets: money and power, she was still Lucky West—firstborn daughter of Scott and Layla West and the baby mama of Angel Morales, head of the Juarez cartel.

"You asked."

Lucky nodded. "I did."

"So, Lucky, I have to admit that I've thought about you since we were last here, and straight-up, why didn't you call me? Please tell me you lost my number so I can feel less rejected."

"I didn't lose shit," she said evasively.

"You have a man?"

"No, I don't have any attachments."

His eyes were like lie detectors searching for her truth. "Entanglements?"

Lucky inhaled and took another sip of her drink. She hadn't been with anyone since Packer died and didn't like where this conversation was heading, but Ragnar didn't seem to pick up on her discomfort. "Why would that matter to you?"

Ragnar thought about that. "Because it would explain why you didn't call."

"I didn't call because I didn't want to," Lucky said flatly. "If you were so pressed to get to know me, you should have taken my number too."

Her response said she wanted to be chased. "I was being respectful."

"But you're not, though. You keep pushing the issue until you hear what you want!" Her eyes rolled. Lucky had been through a lot, more than most. She was at war with her parents, her daughter was presumed dead, she'd just survived her attempted assassination, and this nigga wanted his ego stroked?

"Not at all," he said, defending his line of questioning. "I'm asking because I thought we had made a connection. And just for clarification, I didn't ask for your number because I didn't want to watch your sexy lips say no."

His voice was calm, his words seemed honest, and he was self-effacing. Lucky realized her outburst didn't unsettle him at all. Sometimes she could be too explosive, too emotional, or too disrespectful for no reason. She needed to chill. Lucky stared at the scientist with the smoldering sleepy eyes, freckled face, and athletic body and knew he was a catch—if you liked *good* guys, which she didn't. Lucky was into bad boys who drove expensive toys.

"May I?"

She was perplexed. "What?"

"Get your number?"

Lucky grabbed a new burner, unlocked her phone, and handed it to him. Ragnar quickly dialed himself and then saved his name in her contacts. When he handed her back her cell, he had this smug look like he had done something groundbreaking.

Lucky was on her third drink and feeling nice when the array of dishes was brought out. Thanks to the cocktails, she had loosened up and found herself forgetting about her troubles. Maybe dating a civilian could be just what she needed. Ragnar had a legit career, seemed to have the trappings of wealth, and certainly didn't seem like he was hurting for money.

The large white platters were sitting between them, and she couldn't help but giggle. There wasn't any way she was eating this slimy shit. Her eyes scanned the delicacies Scott and Layla always ordered and passed. The unmistakable aromas of foie gras, oysters, caviar, steamed octopus, roasted Peking duck, and a side of French fries were revolting. Ragnar definitely had a sense of humor.

"I got dibs on the fries," she said, smiling.

"Absolutely, but only after we tackle this right here."

"I'm not eating this." Lucky could see the steam coming off the food, how the chef had plated each dish, and couldn't believe she was about to try it after years of Layla's urging. "If I eat this, I'll turn into my mother."

"Is she as pretty as you?"

"She's dead."

"Dead?" his eyebrow raised and then relaxed. "Oh, I'm sorry."

"I'm not."

He nodded. "And your—"

"He's dead too."

"Any siblings?"

"None."

"I understand now why you're so mean...distant. You don't

have anyone to share yourself with."

"I'm not mean. I'm cautious." Lucky marveled at how he thought he knew her, could assess who she was—likes, dislikes, personality, characteristics from a few words, a couple of sentences connected by a thread of lies. If she learned anything, you genuinely don't know anyone; their proclivities, triggers, or what they're truly capable of. What they do in the dark is usually a stark contrast to what's done in the light. She thought she knew Whistler—would have placed her life on the line that he would never turn snitch, but there he was up on that stand singing like Sinatra.

"Okay, so full disclosure cautious, Lucky. I've never tasted anything here, so this is as new to me as it is to you. I want to experience this with you. So," Ragnar stared into her eyes. "Lucky are you down to have this mouth orgasm with me…I know we just met."

This guy was a freak. Everything circled back to sex, and after three drinks, he was starting to look like a snack. It had been too long since she felt the pressure of a thick dick opening up her cave. *But he's so corny*, she thought. He couldn't possibly fuck—not this pretty boy.

"I'm ready," she said. They started with the oysters and squeezed fresh lemon juice and sriracha sauce on top before sliding the delicacy into their mouths—both looking in each other's eyes. The oysters slid around on their tongues, bursting with flavor before they finally swallowed. Both were pleasantly surprised at the taste.

"It's good, right?" he asked. "You like it?"

"I do!" she said enthusiastically. "I didn't know what I'd been missing all my life."

"All your life…you're all of what?" he asked. "Twenty-five?"

"Excuse you," she said, offended. "I'm twenty-two, and I don't look a day older than nineteen."

They chuckled. "You right. I was going to say nineteen but

didn't want to seem like a predator."

"You good," she admonished. "And how old are you, if you don't mind my asking?" Lucky was already loosening up another oyster, drizzling it with the condiments.

"Not at all. I'm forty-one."

Lucky nodded knowingly. With her daddy issues, he was just the right age.

They tackled the foie gras next. "Isn't this supposed to be banned in New York?"

He placed his index finger over his full lips and said, "Shhh. I don't want to turn you into a felon."

She giggled again. "I would never knowingly break the law."

"I like that."

"What? That I'm a law-abiding citizen."

"No, your laughter...well, your giggle. It's endearing. And what did I tell you?" Lucky was clueless until he reached over and removed her Chanel shades. "There...that's better. Now I can see your beautiful face."

Dinner was a pleasant surprise for Lucky, so she didn't want the night to end. And the thought of going back to her empty apartment wasn't appealing. She knew what she wanted and was ready to shoot her shot.

"Take me home," she said, her hand finding its way to his lap not too far from his manhood. Lucky sucked her bottom lip in between her teeth and then bit down as her mind went places it hadn't gone in a while.

"I'd love to see you home safely," he announced as he waved to the bartender and then motioned for the check. "Where do you live?"

Lucky felt uninhibited and alive. She wondered if what they said about oysters being an aphrodisiac was true because her deep cave was throbbing. She wanted to be held, kissed, licked, and caressed with deep, penetrating strokes. Bluntly, she said, "Take me to your home so I can show you a few things, old man." Ragnar grinned and then snorted. Lucky's eyebrow raised. She was intrigued. "Or you can show me a few…?"

"Maybe another time," he said. "You're not ready yet…or ever, who knows? You come home with me, then you'd have to be ready to surrender."

Lucky frowned. He was a weird one. Who turned down no strings attached sex? Once again, she was over the choir boy.

"Your loss." Lucky stood up, grabbed her handbag, and walked assertively toward the front door. Ragnar pulled out his wallet, dropped thirteen crisp hundred dollar bills on the bar, and ran after her.

"Don't be mad," he said when he finally caught up to her. "Let me drive you home so I can explain."

"Mad?" she snorted. "I'm drunk."

"More of a reason to allow me to drive you home."

Her eyes rolled. "I can walk…I'm only a few blocks over."

"Then let me walk you."

"Dude…chill. The moment is gone. Just let it go." Lucky took a few steps ahead and then spun around and said, "And thanks for dinner." As she backpedaled, she couldn't help but still want him. Lucky turned her back on Ragnar and decided to leave well enough alone.

He called after her. "You're welcome, Miss Lucky…anytime." When she didn't respond, he said, "Pick up when I call."

Without turning around, she tossed her middle finger in the air.

He called out. "Soon Gangsta Lucky…I promise I'm worth the wait!"

That last line made her laugh out loud. Who was this clown nigga?

Rewind: Week three after Lucchese's Amber Alert

FBI agents Randall and Devonsky put in exhaustive hours to pursue Scott and Layla West, who fled the country. It bugged Agent Devonsky these two murderers and drug traffickers were enjoying the southern hemisphere on vacation while they were up to their eyeballs in the carnage. The bureau was giving them one last bite at the apple to prosecute the couple, or they'd be demoted to desk duty and shipped to shithole territories like Fargo, North Dakota, or Laramie, Wyoming.

The pair had sat through numerous meetings with top federal officials, and FBI behavioral analysts to form a strategy on how best to move forward and ensnare the Wests in a trap. The room was filled with a gaggle of middle-aged white males, and then there was Franklin Garrett, an African American man, and Kimberly Cooper, an African American woman. Franklin and Kimberly wanted to use this meeting wisely, hoping their input could impress their superiors.

An idea was tossed around to use one of the oldest tricks in the book; trojan-horse deception, commonly known in street terms as a snitch.

Agent Randall spoke up. "No, that won't work. They'd see an informant coming from a mile away."

"I agree," Agent Devonsky concurred. "But what else can we do? We haven't been able to get them on wiretaps, through surveillance, or gotten anyone remotely close to this family to flip except Whistler Hussain. And we all know how that turned out."

There was a pregnant pause in the room as everyone weighed their options.

Agent Randall continued, "Look, what do we have here? Who are these people?"

Jacob Fuhrer was one of the top analysts in the room. He finally spoke, "They've been in drug distribution all their adult lives, and Scott has transitioned into a businessman. He's arrogant, a megalomaniac, and an alpha male. Let's use this to our advantage."

"How so?" Agent Devonsky asked.

"Well, he and his wife have insulated themselves from everyone; their children, soldiers, and connect, Javier Garcia. So we infiltrate the impenetrable fortress he's placed around him and his wife with competition."

"Competition? Like a drug dealer?" Kimberly called out.

Jacob shook his head. "Like a businessman who hides his drug distribution just as Scott West."

"Not to sound dense, but how does that get us closer to a conviction?" said Agent Devonsky.

"His ego will want to get to know him, see what he's about, and the more our businessman pulls away, the more Scott should pursue. And then we'll allow Scott to 'find out'"—he did air quotes and then continued, "that our guy is shady. That our guy is pushing major weight, and at this point, Scott should want to do business, grandstand on the male, and display braggadocious behavior."

The room got it.

Franklin asked, "So this businessman, a Latino? Hispanic?"

"No. I think an African American male would provoke Scott. He'll compete with this man and not even know he's in a competition," Jacob deduced.

"And what will Layla be doing while all this is going on? She'll need to be distracted, or she might see something that her husband won't if she's far removed from the situation," Agent Randall asked.

Kimberly answered with her two cents. "Let's not make it one individual but two…a couple, and both should be attractive. When Layla and Scott were separated, she had many lovers. Maybe, the male could do some flirting to keep her engaged. And, if no one objects, I could be the undercover female agent."

"That won't be enough. I've studied Layla's profile, and she's a vicious woman. She shot Whistler at point-blank range. Not many women could stomach what she did, not to mention our informants said she committed a murder with her bare hands and allowed her best friend to take the weight. She is cold and calculated, so the person we plant as the wife needs to give Layla a run for her money. Have her and Scott so confused that they won't see the double-cross coming." Franklin sat forward in his seat. His smooth voice had captured the room's attention. "And no disrespect, Kimberly. But you're not that attractive."

All males turned toward the subject. They examined her without tact; squinty eyes and pursed lips scanned the average-looking woman with the above-average intelligence. Kimberly could feel the judgment as heads slowly nodded in agreement with Franklin's assessment of her. Kimberly's round face was flushed. Her hazelnut coffee-colored complexion deepened a shade. She was embarrassed and humiliated, but she wouldn't act indignant. Nor would she just take the insult.

"Franklin, your opinion of Black women isn't without bias, correct? I don't think you've ever found an African American woman attractive. And just so there's no ambiguity, your opinion of me holds no weight, and I should hope my colleagues aren't persuaded by your narrow views. I've been studying the files on each member of the West family, and I know that I could do my job effectively and help lead us to an arrest and a conviction. Please, Agent Randall, just give me a chance."

Franklin cleared his throat and decided not to rebuttal her quip about his romantic tastes. It was no secret that he was married to a white woman; Martha was his high school sweetheart. Nor did he make apologies about being attracted to Caucasian women. He couldn't help who he loved. Franklin spoke, "I think we should take a different approach with Layla West because she's just as sharp and cunning as Scott. We'll need her off her A-game, have her insecure and emotional. And I know just the agent to have Layla distracted—Agent Gwyneth Sullivan. She's beautiful, intelligent, and quick-witted. I can guarantee that her blonde hair and blue eyes will have Mrs. West seeing red."

The office didn't know that Franklin was having an affair with Gwyneth, and if he could help her climb the ladder, he would.

"You can't be serious!" Kimberly blurted out. She knew she had to bottle up her rage and swallow it, or she'd be labeled an angry Black woman. Her words needed to be succinct yet persuasive. She dialed it back a bit and spoke to Jacob, looking only at him. "There's this myth that African American women feel inferior toward Caucasian women, especially those with blonde hair and blue eyes. And as a Black woman, I'm here to affirm that that's not remotely true. And Franklin is helping to perpetuate this fallacy by suggesting that Agent Gwyneth Sullivan could do a better job than I could in the field. The skin color won't matter to Layla; she's territorial over her husband and will react the same way to a woman—*any* woman. Let's not make this about race. I'm sitting in this room—not Gwyneth, and I'm highly qualified."

"I think that Franklin has a point," Jacob said, supporting his male colleague's position. "An interracial couple could be just the ruse that we need. We use agents, deep cover field agents who're trained to extract the indictable information, and should Scott or Layla smell a rat, they're also trained to protect themselves. And I concur. Gwyneth Sullivan is gorgeous. She's a real looker." There was a pervy undertone to his voice when he mentioned Gwyneth.

Franklin knew the men in the room would all see Gwyneth as he did. He took it a step further. "I'd like to throw my name in the hat as the male agent. I think Gwyneth and I would work great together."

Kimberly seethed. "Of course you two would."

The room watched amusingly as the token Blacks both jockeyed for positions in this career-making case.

Agent Randall now had to step in. It wasn't lost on him that

Franklin was too eager to pair up with Gwyneth. Married or not, Franklin was a heterosexual man, and Randall would not send Gwyneth on an all-expense-paid work assignment in Australia with a Black man—not a straight one. Randall had been trying to bed Gwyneth for nearly a year, and she'd always turned him down because Randall was her boss. No, the agent he had in mind was a gay Black male agent who tried to hide his sexual orientation. He said, "That's a generous offer, Franklin. But we need you here. We'll send Agent Laurence Warren from Chicago. He's experienced, tall and handsome, and can pull off the callousness needed to be a believable dealer."

"I think Laurence is perfect. He's handsome and tall, as you said, but you left out that he's masculine!" Kimberly added inference on masculine because that was the one thing Franklin wasn't, and nobody in the room could debate otherwise. Franklin was effeminate, soft-spoken, and an ass kisser.

They kept talking as they drank lukewarm coffee. All the men with their suit jackets off, ties loosened, and sleeves on their crisp white shirts rolled up thought they had everything figured out.

"So, we're settled then." Jacob pushed back from his chair, which was indicative that the meeting was over. His input was greatly appreciated by Randall and Devonsky.

Everyone filed out of the room, but Franklin lingered behind to accost Kimberly. Her remark about his masculinity had struck a nerve, and he felt her input had cost him a chance to work with Gwyneth abroad without the prying eyes of his wife.

"Don't fuck with me," he said in an aggressive whisper.

"Excuse me," Kimberly spun around. "What did you say to me?"

"I said, are you flirting with me?"

Kimberly stared into his wild, crazed eyes. He was inches away from her face—so close it felt like an assault. She realized he wanted her to *fear* him.

"I know exactly who you are, Franklin. You may have everyone fooled, but not me!"

Chapter 15

After spending an hour there, Meyer came out of the boxing gym, letting off some steam. He had on ball shorts, a white T, and a pair of Uptowns. Sweat trickled down his face, which he wiped away with the front of his shirt. His back and armpits were soaked with perspiration, and his breathing finally slowed to an average pace. Meyer lit up a Newport and took long drags of the carcinogen. His thoughts were on his family's finances, his brother's incarceration, his war with the Juarez cartel, and his parents' unmitigated violence against their children. The only thing that could save them was a new connect so they could have cash flow. With money came power. Meyer could put shooters on payroll, bail Bugsy out, and keep their investment properties.

Meyer started to feel insecure. He felt naked without his jewels gleaming—his chains, Rolexes, and diamond rings were a part of the fabric of who he was, his image. And not having his ninas or .45s left him vulnerable. He had a lot of enemies, and this felt like suicide. At any moment, he could be fired upon by Angel's men or anyone affiliated with his parents. Meyer felt like he had acted irrationally by dumping his guns. The street rule was that you'd rather be tried by twelve than carried by six.

The bass from the speakers pulled Meyer's eyes down the street. He saw the McLaren crawling up the block before it slid into an open park right in front of him. The pearl white exterior and the custom white leather interior with black stitching was beautiful. The windows were slightly tinted, just enough to keep the UV rays out from the sun. Meyer saw the back of a female facing the driver. When she stepped out, he had to do a doubletake. She had a waist that few women got from genetics. It was through surgery or a waist trainer, but she was looking right, whatever it was. Her ass was phat, thighs were thick, and she had two bee stings up top. When she turned around, Meyer's bubble was burst. She had those wide eyebrows tattooed on, fake eyelashes too dark and thick, and she needed to tone down the glossy shine on her full lips. Meyer was into a more natural woman. He didn't need all that ass if it was fake, huge breasts if they were filled with silicone, or hair if you had to buy it.

Meyer flicked his cigarette and was about to bounce when he focused on the driver. Who was dude, and why didn't he know him or know of him? And then he recognized Larry was behind the wheel. Unlucky Larry had glowed up. Larry's lean was different; his body language ran on pure ego and arrogance.

Meyer made his way to the vehicle, and as he approached, Larry reached for his burner as if he didn't recognize him. Meyer's hands went up in surrender.

"Yo, money, it's me, bruh." Meyer was now standing at the passenger's door.

Larry feigned bewilderment. He gave a quizzical look before his face softened and showed recognition.

"Yo, Meyer," he finally said. "Bruh, I was about to let that thang go. I didn't know who was walkin' up on me." Larry pointed toward the gun in his waist.

Meyer whistled at the car. "This you?"

"Yeah, just a little sumthin'…tryin' to keep up wit' you," he said with false modesty. "Get in for a minute so we can politick."

Meyer climbed in, and his eyes scanned the car's interior. The dashboard looked like a spaceship. He wondered why he didn't buy one when he had it. He could have bought ten of these in one day if he wanted to.

"Yo, what's up wit' you?" Larry wanted to know.

"Whatchu mean?"

"You lookin' a little different lately," he began. "Where ya,

159

jewels? You good?"

"Nigga why is you on my dick?" Meyer barked.

"Come on now," he said, rubbing his chin, flossing his diamonds on his wrist. "Do I look like I need to be on any niggas dick? I heard some things, streets saying y'all ain't takin' care of ya fallen soldiers fam."

"So!"

"So again, you good? As I said before, you like family. I've been doing my thang lately, so if you need to hold sumthin'—"

"Hold somethin'?" Meyer gritted his teeth to stop himself from smashing Larry's teeth out. If he had his burner, he would have robbed him. Shoved a .45 in his gut and told him to run his shit.

"No disrespect, Meyer. It's all love, my nigga."

"Yo, how you went from a nigga wit' nothing but lint in ya pockets to all this drip?"

Larry grinned. "I'm hustlin' nigga. What you think? My parents finally gave me my trust fund money." Larry laughed at his own sarcasm. Meanwhile, Meyer's face was stone.

"You ain't hustlin' for me, so who's ya crew?" Meyer sized up the bling, and this wasn't corner boy dough. This was wholesale profits. "Who's ya connect?"

"It ain't Juarez…fuck those Mexicans."

"That wasn't my question!"

"You heard of Los Pepes?"

"Colombians?"

Larry nodded and remained silent. He was making Meyer pull the information out of him.

"You fuckin' wit' Los Pepes? That's your connect?"

Larry shrugged; his face was smug. He was leaning so far back in his seat; it was almost a bed.

"How long?" Meyer asked.

Larry blew out air. "For a minute now."

If Larry could move weight with his limited street

knowledge, Meyer could only imagine how quickly he could get back on his feet with his infrastructure. They needed a new connect, and he needed his brother home.

"I wanna meet them…make the connection."

"Los Pepes?"

"Yeah, nigga."

"Nah, we boys, but that's my connect. You know how the game goes. If you wanna buy weight, then you gotta go through me. My numbers are low—"

Meyer bashed Larry in his mouth, knocked out one of his front teeth, and simultaneously grabbed his burner from his waist and pointed it toward his head. Larry spit out his tooth and held his mouth, which was leaking blood.

"Yo, what is you, doin'?" he asked. "You buggin' right now!"

"Shut the fuck up nigga!" Meyer barked. "And run ya shit!"

Larry's eyes were wild. This wasn't supposed to be happening. "Chill, Meyer."

The barrel of the gun went upside Larry's head. "Tell me to chill again, nigga, and see if I don't push ya fuckin' wig back."

Larry nodded his understanding.

"I don't got all day."

Larry stalled. When Meyer nudged him with the barrel, he realized his former boss was serious.

Larry removed layers of chains, unclasped his watch, and slid off his rings. He'd never felt so emasculated in his life. Meyer ran down his demands as he put a chain around his neck. "Now, what ya gonna do is make the introduction to Los Pepes."

The Rolex went on Meyer's wrist. "And you better vouch for me nigga because I want a low number." Meyer inched the pinky ring on his trigger hand. "And if you ever don't respect me like the boss nigga I am, I will lullaby you nigga. You hear that? Ya momma won't be able to recognize you—closed casket nigga!"

The last two expensive chains went around his neck.

Calmly, Meyer exited the vehicle, tucked the .45 in his waist, and slammed the passengers' door so hard, the window nearly shattered.

∞

Scott and Layla saw Uriel and Jacqueline being chauffeured away in the backseat of the luxury Bentley. They didn't know the couple U-turned and headed right back to the hotel once Scott and Layla left.

Two field agents were tailing the couple on their lavish shopping spree while agents Laurence Warren and Gwyneth Sullivan, aka Uriel "Understanding" and Jacqueline St. James, entered their hotel room. The FBI agents stealthily went through their luggage and planted bugs and video surveillance equipment. It was an executive decision by their director to not plant the bugs until after the couple arrived, just in case the couple had the room swept. Now, after they'd been in Dubai a couple of weeks, the agents were confident that Scott and Layla had let their guard down and got back into vacation mode.

The ornate, gaudy, gilded furniture inside the hotel suite made hiding video surveillance cameras much easier. And they hid plenty, even in places that clearly violated their privacy rights, like the bedroom and bathroom. The couple's intimate moments would be captured, reviewed by many, and illegally analyzed.

The feds were going hard. They had fucked up by only planting bugs at the couples' beach villa. The Australian rental was modern and had no pictures, vases, or tchotchkes to sufficiently hide tiny cameras. So when they listened to the bugs and heard an argument, several scuffles, and gunshots, they knew they had missed capturing a double murder. Listening to the tapes, Layla was once again the ringleader; she wielded the gun that took the life of two men with Mexican accents. No names were spoken by the couple, and little was discussed.

Luminol would outline the bloody carnage, but unfortunately, no bodies were recovered, no missing persons reports to move forward on arrests.

∞

DEA agents Tannery and Brown went to one of the many warehouses with several desk agents. The warehouses were filled with confiscated furniture from white-collar crime criminals, drug lords and donated by companies for tax write-offs. They needed to furnish Markeeta's apartment with some decent pieces; otherwise, Lucky wouldn't believe that Markeeta could afford the building.

Two women, Karen, and Christin, had pads of paperwork. They would need to add each item number and bring it back to the agency for the vouchers, careful to add the furniture under another case per Tannery's instruction.

"I like this set for the main bedroom," Karen said, and Tannery agreed. The king-size bed had a beige linen fabric, tufted headboard with antique bronze nail heads that outlined the hexagon structure. The nightstands and tall dresser were mirrored. It was an expensive set.

"She doesn't need all of that," Brown griped. "All this opulence. She's not married to a brain surgeon."

"No, but she's supposed to be dealing with a hustler. They buy things like this to show their wealth."

Brown was the only one taking this process personally. The building had imported marble tile in the lobby, laundry service, dog walking service, a rental car agency, concierge, gym, indoor pool, and underground parking. Her two-bedroom apartment that the taxpayers were paying for was ten times better than where he lived. He would die for the silk couches, high-quality linens, and crystal chandeliers. The apartments came with a gourmet kitchen and had Sub-Zero appliances. Would Markeeta even have a clue how to maintain such expensive luxuries?

Christin picked out the drapes, area rugs and found towels monogrammed with Markeeta's initials, MW. The women had a fantastic time shopping for the day, even if it weren't for them. All the men heard were oohs and ahhs throughout the shopping excursion. With shopping concluded, agents Tannery and Brown went back to the office to tie up loose ends while the rest of the staff went home.

Chapter 16

Lucky walked into Ragnar's apartment and felt the whole seduction thing going on. Sweet and savory smells floated throughout, and with the dim lights, she had no idea it would be that kind of partay because he seemed stingy with his dick. Always acting like a virgin on Prom night.

A 90s R&B playlist was on low, and Lucky listened to songs recorded before she was born. Ragnar had on an apron and handed Lucky a glass of Jesus juice—a full glass.

I guess I'm getting fucked tonight, after all, Lucky thought.

"Sit down, relax. I'll be in there in a moment," Ragnar said. "I hope you like steak. That's about all I can cook."

"Steak is fine."

Lucky walked farther into his apartment and sat down on his leather couch. Her eyes scanned the furniture, the room, and everything looked new, pristine, preserved. Lucky called out, "Give me a tour of your home. It's nice in here."

He called back. "Go ahead…walk around. I don't have anything to hide, baby girl."

"Well, since you insist," she mumbled.

Lucky walked through the one-bedroom apartment and examined the contents from top to bottom. She opened his closet and stared at his dark-colored suits hung four inches apart. His hard-bottom work shoes were color-coordinated, as were his shirts and ties. Yet, there wasn't much of anything. That meant little, but it also meant everything. Lucky ran her finger along his dresser, and a light film of dust picked up. She had to admit that if her senses weren't heightened, these were things she could have easily overlooked. Lucky made her way to his linen closet, and it was sparse. He had just enough towels, washcloths, and blankets for 72 hours before he'd have to do laundry. Was he a minimalist or just a busy man who needed a woman's touch? The quintessential bachelor? When she walked back into the living room, Ragnar had set the table. He'd prepared medium-rare steaks, asparagus, and baby carrots. It wasn't Lucky's favorite meal, she was more of a soul food and seafood type of woman, but she would eat.

"Who's singing?" she asked.

"You serious?"

"I asked, didn't I?"

"Oh, I forgot. You're just a baby."

"That sounds a bit pervy, especially since you're trying to get me drunk, and I know you wanna fuck tonight." Lucky smirked. "And moving forward, don't call me baby-girl either. An ol' beat of mine used to call me that."

Lucky saw a darkness in his eyes that was easy to read. He didn't like being spoken to the way she talked to him. She waited for the witty rebuttal, but none came. Finally, he forced a smile and said, "Aren't you presumptuous. But to answer your question, it's a group called Silk. They had another hit but didn't really make it. In the 90s, there were so many great groups that they faded. But this song, *Lose Control*, it's deep."

Lucky listened, "*Last night, we had an argument; you told me you loved me. All the things I said I never meant…nah, baaaaby.*"

She said, "Alright, that's a bop. I like it."

The harmony was the best she had ever heard in her generation. "That's talent," she agreed. "If those voices can't earn seven zeros…there's always hustling."

Ragnar snorted. "Said the dead man."

"You think all roads of a hustler lead to the grave?"

"Or jail, right? Isn't that the mantra of the streets?"

"I don't know anything about that life. I'm a church girl,"

she teased.

Ragnar seemed pleased with her response. "With a foul mouth." He stuffed a mouthful of medium-rare steak into his mouth and then continued, "You should come to a service with me."

"You got jokes," she concluded.

"You mean to tell me that your grandma never kept a Bible in the house, never dragged you to church?"

Lucky exhaled. "You're starting to sound like a religious zealot, a fuckin' nut." Lucky got up and grabbed her Chanel bag that held her .45 and placed it on the back of her chair just in case. Ragnar noticed the movement and asked, "What's in the bagggg," he hollered. "What's in the bag?"

He was a fool, but he could make her laugh.

"Where do I know that line from?"

"Brad Pitt's movie, Seven. His wife's head is in the box."

"Oh, yeah. That was a good movie." Lucky finished her Merlot and wanted something more potent. "You wanna watch Netflix and chill?"

"I don't have Netflix. I just moved in, remember."

"Forget it," she said dryly. She was flirting, and it went over the old man's head. Who didn't know what Netflix and chill meant? "You got any weed?"

"I don't, but I can try to find some or buy some for you if it helps you relax and be a little nicer to me."

Ragnar was kissing her ass, and she liked it. She said, "Nah, that's okay. You'll probably get jacked."

"Good point." Ragnar's voice deepened as he opened up the conversation for more dialogue. He continued, "So you drink, smoke weed, don't trust anyone, are an orphan, living in an expensive condominium, and work as a barista. Is that about right?"

"Okay, so three questions. Ask me three questions you want to know, and then cut this shit out."

He nodded. "How old were you when your parents died?"

"My father died when I was nineteen, my mother, I was twenty."

Ragnar's face showed deep concern, but he didn't expound. Next, he asked, "How can you afford your expensive lifestyle working as a barista?"

"My father left me an inheritance," she replied. "This is your last question, so you better make it good."

Ragnar mulled over her answers. Lucky could see his mind racing as his eyes darted quickly like he was calculating equations. Finally, he said, "I'll save my last question for another time. You want more to drink?"

Lucky did. Ragnar cleared the dinner dishes and returned with another glass of wine for her and cognac for himself. He wasn't smiling, nor was his body language readable. There was a hint of something sinister lurking behind his eyes, dark and cold. There was a tectonic shift. The warm, gentle, clownish persona had unraveled as a gloomier side of Ragnar had appeared. He had gone from a summer breeze to a winter storm in a matter of moments. His mood was transformative, eerie, blunt like a solid fist to her gut; she felt numb. The comfortability was fleeting for Lucky as she watched Ragnar seemingly revel in the awkward silence.

She wondered whether the liquor had altered his vibe. She said, "I thought you didn't drink."

Ragnar stared at his guest. His eyes slowly rose from the bottom of her feet until he landed on her curly mane of hair. Finally, he said, "Why would you think that?"

"Because you always order a soda."

"I don't drink when I'm working."

"You mean you don't drink on *work* nights, correct?"

"Isn't that what I said?"

Lucky didn't answer; she just stared. The temperature of the room had shifted from seduction to a snooze fest. Lucky was ready to go until Ragnar asked, "Do you find sexual pleasure in pain, Lucky."

She shrugged. "It depends…"

"On the level of pain?" he probed.

"Where's this going?" She wanted to know.

"I want you."

"Then let's fuck."

"Not like that…I want you. All of you…but my way."

Lucky stood up. "Again, let's fuck, or I'm out," she said, almost exasperated with his mood swings.

Ragnar said, "I don't fuck."

"Well, we won't be making love."

"I have sexual experiences, and I want to experience you without inhibitions, which might be a challenge because you said you don't trust."

"I don't."

"How about you don't trust me with anything except your body. You seem like a tough woman, are you?" he challenged.

"More than most."

"Show me. Take off your shirt," Ragnar ordered and then demanded, "Just your shirt."

Lucky stood and pulled her shirt over her head. The silk blouse fell at her feet. She was wearing a Savage Fenty lace bra, the new collection to go with her new breasts that had gone up two sizes since having Lucchese. Her once firm size A cups had blossomed into C cups that hung lower than she had liked without bra support.

"Good girl," he said. "Now take off your jeans, but this time do it slowly, more seductively…make me wait for it."

Lucky stepped out of her Louboutin heels one by one, her bare feet resting on his plush carpet. She undid the top button on her jeans and slowly slid down the zipper until her matching lace panties were revealed. Lucky used her thumbs and twirled her hips to guide her jeans past her thighs. She inched her jeans off and stood before him in her bra and panties—the most vulnerable she had ever felt with her newly minted scars across her flat stomach. A few tan stretchmarks outlined her navel, just enough evidence of the daughter she no longer had. Lucky conspicuously placed her arms in front of her to hide her imperfections. Ragnar noticed at once.

He stood up and walked toward her and pulled Lucky's chin up so she could see his eyes, how much he wanted her.

"Don't," he said. "You have nothing to be ashamed of. Every line on this sexy body, any shadow, every scar is perfect to me. You're a real woman."

Lucky bit her lip in anticipatory pleasure as Ragnar walked behind her. She could feel his breath on her neck. Hovering over her by at least ten inches, he unclasped her bra. The heavyweight of her breasts dangled freely. He grabbed both straps with steady hands and slid them down her arms, his hands brushing against her skin. Ragnar leaned down and planted wet kisses from the nape of her neck up to her ears as she murmured her pleasure.

"Shhh," he breathed. "Not yet."

Lucky nodded, realizing that he wanted to take things slower than her usual lovers.

"Don't move," he said, still giving orders as he took her bra and tied her hands behind her back. Lucky wondered, if only momentarily had she walked into a trap, but the sensuality of the situation was too tantalizing to object. Ragnar walked back around to face her. His eyes were hungry for the young woman nearly half his age. He bent down on his knees and was at eye level with her sweet box. He could see her stomach muscles contracting. She wanted him.

Her panties were next to be removed, sidled down her toned thighs until she stood before him naked.

He stood up.

"Open your legs…wider…wider…stop." Ragnar never lost eye contact with Lucky as he placed two fingers into his mouth and then inserted them into her deep cave. "You're already wet," he breathed.

Ragnar twirled his fingers opening her up while massaging her clitoris with his thumb. The sensation was hypnotic, and she wanted more.

"Fuck me," she murmured, almost begging it had been so long for her. Ragnar scooped Lucky up. Her petite body felt practically weightless in Ragnar's arms, and he carried her into his room. She was placed face down on his plush king-size bed, hands still clasped behind her back. Her head was facing away from him, toward the windows, the light from the moon illuminating the large room.

The sting across her ass was jarring, unexpected, and painful. Lucky tried to wiggle free and shouted, "Are you crazy, muthafucka!"

"Relax," he urged. "Act like a woman and learn some things...I can teach you if you let me."

Lucky was furious. She wanted this corny nigga dead! But *and* however, she was still horny, and so far, he had her aroused. What could he teach her that Whistler didn't? She decided to see this through.

"Untie my hands first," she said warily, giving into his challenge.

Ragnar removed her lace bra from her wrists and removed all his clothing. Lucky was unimpressed with his manhood; he was average length and girth and suddenly understood why he had to go above and beyond in the bedroom. Ragnar reached into the nightstand and pulled out two things—a condom and a bottle of body oil. He placed Lucky back on her stomach and straddled her; his dick dangled near the opening of her vagina.

Ragnar poured the oil on the small of her back and took his strong hands to kneed the liquid into her supple skin. He massaged from her neck, tracing the curve of her back until focusing on her tight, round ass. Ragnar palmed large handfuls of her buttocks, opening, and closing her cheeks while blowing softly into her cave. Lucky's whole body was stimulated, and he hadn't even entered her yet.

She felt the sting again as he smacked her across her behind; her ass cheeks wiggled. Lucky stifled her response as she clasped the sheets to dull her pain.

He leaned forward, down by Lucky's ear, and whispered, "You better not scream...you hear me. Don't make a fucking sound unless I tell you to. Understand?"

"Yes," she breathed, and he smacked her again harder. The feeling was intense and sweet at the same time. The agonizing pain swam through her body, awakening something carnal she hadn't ever experienced.

"I said, don't speak!"

Lucky quickly nodded. Her body felt flushed, raw, alive. Right now, at this moment, she was ready to submit.

Ragnar spanked Lucky until her ass was the same hue as his reddish-brown skin. His tone was authoritative when he said, "Get on all fours, doggy-style,"—and she did. Ragnar rolled the condom back and positioned his dick near her throbbing pussy. Lucky was wet, juicy wet, dripping wet, and ready to be explored.

Ragnar grabbed Lucky's hips and slid into her with ease. He quickly grabbed her lace bra, expertly, wrapped it around her neck, and pulled it while slamming into her again and again and again. Lucky felt her breath becoming shallow as Ragnar controlled her airwave, tightening and then relaxing his grip. He was mercilessly exploring her cave, hitting all her sensitive buttons.

Lucky wanted to scream, moan, or call out for Jesus as her body responded accordingly. Waves of pleasure enveloped her body, and the intensity was magnified by suppressing her verbiage.

Her pussy muscles contracted around his penis as she pushed back against his pelvis. Lucky was peaking, her body responding in ways she hadn't felt before. Ragnar smacked her ass one last time before she shuttered and orgasmed—a sweet release of satisfaction nearly wiped Lucky out. She collapsed face down, eyes closed, trying to regain a steady air stream. Lucky was panting, in a delirious state of euphoria.

"Turn over, face me."

She couldn't. Lucky was spent. What more did he want?

"Don't make me ask again," his voice stern, throaty, sultry. "I want more, Lucky…much more from you."

Warily, Lucky flipped over onto her back and stared up at him.

"Open your legs," he breathed. "You can't sleep until you come in my mouth."

There wasn't any way she thought she could have another orgasm. Her pussy was sore, her clitoris swollen, her body content.

Ragnar buried his head into Lucky's neatly waxed pussy, biting licks around her vulva as she squirmed underneath him. Her swollen clit was almost too sensitive to be touched, and Ragnar was sucking and nibbling on her ecstasy button with a hunger only she could satiate. There was decadence between her thighs, and he wanted to conquer it, selfishly take it all for himself. From tonight forward, Lucky would be no one else's.

Astonishingly, she came again. Lucky couldn't move, and within seconds she was asleep.

Inside the McLaren, Larry was nervous. He had tried to stall Meyer as he waited for the federal cavalry to come and rescue him. He thought they would drag Meyer out of his vehicle and manhandle the parasite at any moment. But minutes later, the gun was still pointed to his forehead. When Meyer nudged him with the barrel, he realized his former boss was serious, no agents were coming, and his life meant nothing to the government.

He yelled into the wired car at the video footage he knew was rolling, "Y'all ain't shit! Y'all just gonna let that nigga do me like that? I'm a valuable asset! Y'all let that shit happen again, and I walk! Y'all here me? I fuckin' walk! He should be locked the fuck up for how I was just handled!"

In an unidentified van parked two blocks up sat DEA agents Tannery, Brown, Pablo, and Diablo. All men were laughing so hard at the live footage and audio it was hard to hear Larry's threats.

"I like this kid, Meyer," said Diablo.

"And he's fast too," said Agent Brown. "You saw when he snatched his firearm!"

More laughter.

"I think he knocked out his tooth," Pablo commented.

"No…you think so?"

More laughter.

"About last night," Ragnar said as he walked into his room with a cup of coffee. He was fully dressed as he sat on his bed, startling the sleeping beauty. Lucky pulled her eyes awake and desperately reached for the hot liquid. She was parched, her ass was sore, and her neck was bruised. "Did I hurt you?"

Lucky only remembered being pleasured with the level of hedonism that went on last night. There was a pleasurable pain, but she would do it again—in fact, she couldn't wait to fuck him again.

She said, "It was cool. I liked it."

"Good, now get dressed. I leave for work in five minutes."

"I can't be out of here in five minutes, Ragnar. Just leave me here, and I'll lock up."

He smiled. "That's not going to happen."

"I hope you know that you can trust me. I'm not gonna steal shit."

Again, that smile. "No can do, Miss Luciana. I thought you took trust off the table. Now, come on…get up, get dressed. I can't be late."

Lucky didn't like the single standard, but she curbed her witty remark. He was right. She wouldn't trust him to stay in her apartment alone. She exhaled and said, "How did you know it's Luciana?"

"What?"

"You said, 'Luciana,' not Luciano. My name's Lucky Luciana. How did you know that?"

"It's called a guess," he sharply replied.

His response was a little too sarcastic this early morning for her tastes, but Lucky didn't want to be that girl who took things too personally. She explained, "Yeah, well, my parents were going to—"

"Another story for another time." Ragnar's patience was now paper-thin as he glanced down at his watch.

She placed the coffee down and quickly dressed.

Before she left, he said, "Just note, you ever walk back through my front door again, and I own you for life, baby."

Lucky smirked. She had no idea what that meant. "Okay, crazy."

"Brat!"

"Scientist!"

Chapter 17

Lucky walked into Markeeta's plush apartment and had to admit that she was stunned. The well-appointed, two-bedroom was no less than impressive. Lucky's eyes scanned her surroundings and saw a tufted silk sofa, matching wingback chairs, a Persian rug, a glass coffee table, and a traditional chandelier. The open concept showcased a gourmet kitchen with Sub-Zero Wolf appliances and Corian countertops.

Markeeta saw the look of pure shock and bewilderment on her cousin's face and felt a surge of good energy.

"Lemme give you a tour of my shit," she said, her gloating tone cutting through the moment's silence like a sledgehammer. Her voice was a constant irritant to Lucky, but it was something she would have to deal with.

Markeeta led the way into the primary bedroom that displayed the furniture the two female agents had picked out. The headboard to the custom king-size bed was a statement piece. It stood eight feet high and was tufted in beige linen fabric for $800 per yard. The room was reminiscent of old Hollywood glamour with silk, throw pillows, fur area rug, silk settee, and balloon drapes.

Lucky's mouth was gaped open, so it was crucial to say something. "This is cute," she squeezed out.

"Hmph…cute?" Markeeta snorted and rolled her eyes. "Come on," she now demanded as she led the way to her son's room. Markeeta opened the door, and Ralph was sitting on his bed with his dirty sneakers, watching YouTube on his phone, eating a Hot Pocket. He had two bags of chips to his right, a package of Oreo cookies, and a cold glass of chocolate milk sitting on his nightstand without a coaster. She waited for Markeeta to correct his behavior, but Markeeta said nothing. Lucky wondered how they kept the furniture and apartment so pristine, remembering her family's hygiene habits. It wasn't any of her business, but it was just a microscopic detail you placed on the back burner until it produced something or dissolved into nothing.

"This is your cousin, Lucky," Markeeta said. Ralph just shrugged his response. Finally, he spoke. "You never cook! What we havin' for dinner?"

Markeeta exploded as abruptly and deadly as a time bomb. "Muthafucka, I ain't cooking, damn! All you wanna do is fuckin' eat, yo. Ya fat ass! Lookin' just like ya father…order some Chinese food later after our company leaves!"

Ralph just nodded, seemingly unaffected by the outburst. However, Lucky was taken aback. That elevated level of explosive rage was normal for Markeeta, Lucky too, but for Lucky, never around kids.

Ralph was a husky teenager bordering on fat, and if Lucky was honest, he wasn't a cute kid either. His hair was unruly, and his hairline could use a shape up. His thick, chapped lips couldn't hide the brown and yellow stains on his teeth that looked like he drank several cups of black coffee a day. And to compound his dental issues, his mouth was overcrowded with buck front and crooked teeth. It was a shame, really, that he looked so neglected. Lucky deduced Ralph was a pitiful sight, but he wasn't a lost cause. You couldn't just say to your child, go brush your teeth. As a parent, you had to make sure they had good hygiene habits. If Ralph were under Scott and Layla's tutelage, his ashy skin would be moisturized, his teeth cleaned and straightened with braces, and his clothes would fit. It looked like he had grown out of his shirt a couple years ago, squeezing his chunky chest for mercy. Ralph seemed like a kid with little adult supervision in her short observation. He was raising himself while his young mother ran the streets.

Everything Ralph said and did irritated his mother, his mere presence was a constant reminder of her regrets and failures. She regretted giving birth at thirteen, being a single mom, and she, too, regretted he wasn't a cute kid. His face was his father's face—the face of the man that had taken her virginity at twelve, impregnated her, and then told their peers in the housing project that Markeeta was a slut, and the baby wasn't his. The moment she gave birth to Ralph, Markeeta knew it was a mistake. She thought a baby would keep her man, but it only managed to sever the nonexistent bond they never had.

By the time Markeeta was fifteen, her son had taken the brunt of her discontent. If he cried or whined too much, he was beaten. When he could go to school and didn't excel, he was beaten and verbally abused. If he lost a fight in school, he was beaten again, and then Markeeta would seek out the mother of the child who had whooped her son and beat the shit out of her. You see, the only person that could abuse Ralph was Markeeta. She felt she had earned that right after spending nineteen hours in labor before his large head came bursting through her vagina.

Markeeta led her cousin back into the living room and asked, "You drinkin'?"

"What you got?"

"Henny and coke."

Lucky frowned. "Nothing else?"

"I said what I said." Markeeta's voice was sharp and laced with resentment. Lucky wondered where the anger had stemmed from.

"I'm not really here for the Henny. You don't got anything else up in here…in your palatial estate?" Lucky's voice dripped with sarcasm, amused at her cousin's discomfort.

"I said I got Hennessy and coke," she repeated and glared at her overreaching nemesis. Lucky glared back—the tension had escalated; they were like bookends with nothing but hatred between them. And then Markeeta remembered she had a part to play and smiled warmly. "You want me to run out and get you sumthin' else?"

Lucky thought about the question trying to connect the randomness of her cousin's hospitality and also the timing of Markeeta's reintroduction into her life. Usually, Lucky would have drunk the Henny, but since Markeeta was kissing her ass, she said, "Yeah, could you go out and get us a bottle of Macallan 25? I know since you love cognac that you must drink that too."

Markeeta wasn't familiar with the brand but would rather die than admit it. Nor could she believe that this privileged bitch wanted her to leave her home and go fetch this liquor. But Markeeta knew that Lucky's mere presence with her was a win for the feds. She would get her fucked up and see if she would divulge any information that would ultimately help put her family behind bars.

"Macallan is my drink, yo," she lied. "Anything else while I'm out?"

"Bring us back some Chinese food," Lucky ordered. "Make sure you bring enough to feed your son. He seems hungry, and there's no home-cooked meal prepared."

Markeeta glared, flaring her nostrils, and clenching her teeth at the disrespectful comment. "Of course, I'm gonna feed my child."

Lucky nodded. "I know you know this, but I don't eat corner store Chinese food. Please bring back either Nobu, Mr. Chow, or Philippe Chow." Lucky watched as Markeeta's chest began to heave up and down. She was muthafuckin' livid. Lucky continued, "And I know you don't eat that roach-laden cat, not pork meat Chinese food either. I know we're on the same level."

Markeeta nodded, did this thing where she smacked her tongue against the roof of her mouth, making an awful suction noise. "Yup…I don't. Anything else?"

"Nah, I'm good. Hurry back so we can catch up."

∞

Bugsy had been medically cleared from the 9-South wing and was transferred to Gen-Pop a couple weeks ago. He rubbed shoulders with inmates in this unit, from traffickers to murderers, but mostly kept to himself. Bugsy's arrival was the new headline, gossip that spread faster than an oxygenized fire—the backdraft that explosive. The consensus was that the feds always get their man one way or another.

Everyone wanted to befriend the heir to the West throne. However, Bugsy was unsociable. It was who he was—a boss. And boss niggas didn't cozy up to new niggas, especially not ones who had something to gain from his affiliation. When he walked into the gym, TV room, or the kitchen, a cold chill followed, mostly oozing off the scowl on his recently marred face, the railroading from the federal government, and the loss of a child.

Bugsy was unapproachable, inmates knew he was untouchable, and COs treated him respectable. He didn't need a corrections officers badge to be in charge; his résumé would do.

There was one inmate that Bugsy found himself catching eye contact with. The man, too, was a loner and spent most of his time in the law library. Occasionally he would be seen counseling men on their cases, reading Clancy novels, or watching the news in one of the TV rooms. He was a tall, slender, white male with carefully tapered dark hair, slightly graying at his temples. Gold-rimmed glasses sat on his broad nose, his thin lips shut tight, eyes wide, alert with anticipation. Although he was in prison garb, he looked displaced, like a poodle amongst Pitbull's. The man knew anything could jump off at any time, and even if he couldn't do much to defend himself, he at least wanted to be aware his death was coming.

As Bugsy stared, he felt a presence approaching him from

behind but refused to flinch. Soon the figure was standing shoulder to shoulder with him staring at the same man as he was.

"That's Kenneth Collins," a voice said. Bugsy cut his eyes sideways and saw a CO was speaking. "I'm Corrections Officer Mahan."

Bugsy gave a barely visible nod.

CO Mahan continued, "He's a former federal prosecutor. He's in here for some serious shit. Word is he's on the shortlist, so if I were you, I wouldn't fuck with him. He's a real piece of shit and most likely informing."

Bugsy inhaled his frustration. Standing next to this pig was triggering; however, he didn't react. Bugsy continued to ignore the CO, and then he heard, "I knew your father when he was in here, and I looked out—" Mahan nudged Bugsy and tried to discretely place a cellphone in his hand. "I'll look out for you too."

Bugsy's eyes bore holes into Mahan's before he finally spoke. "I'm not my father," and walked away.

Markeeta slammed the door on her brand new Jeep Cherokee that the DEA had supplied her with. Just a few weeks old, it still had that new car smell that she liked. She looked at the leather interior, piping stitching, navigation system, and wood grain and felt like that bitch. You couldn't tell Markeeta that she wasn't pushing a Bentley or some other six-figure exotic whip. She wasn't about to put her vehicle in drive without calling her handler, Agent Tannery.

Tannery picked up. "Gino's Pizza Delivery."

She barked, "I'ma beat the shit outta that bitch!"

Agent Tannery was no longer shocked or unnerved at Markeeta's disposition or outbursts. Calmly, he asked, "Who? Lucky?"

"Yeah! That bitch got me runnin' fuckin' errands for her bony ass like I'm some fuckin' bird bitch! I'm a West too! She ain't no better than me."

Tannery wanted to sift through the facts first. "She's with you now?"

"She's up in my crib."

He smiled. Markeeta was moving swiftly and without provocation. Tannery was working late on this very case against the West organization he was trying to build. He sat back in his chair, placed his feet on his mahogany desk, and relaxed. "Tell me, what's going on?"

In a rushed voice laced with no less hate than her gruff voice could muster, she ran down the wordplay exchange that had just taken place a few moments earlier. Markeeta felt slighted and was furious at her cousin's elitist attitude. Agent Tannery listened intently at the petty diatribe of events through Markeeta's lens, and when she paused for air, he said, "This is what you're going to do...."

His voice was self-assured, confident, and warm-toned. Markeeta instantly calmed down. "Go and get the Macallan and Mr. Chow's Chinese food. I'll call ahead and place the orders for you and text you the addresses for pick up—"

Markeeta interrupted. "For free, right? I don't gotta pay shit?"

"That's correct. It's on us."

"And what about the weed? She wants that too." Markeeta didn't admit that she wanted the Kush.

Tannery thought about that request. "Do you have someone you can get the marijuana from?"

Markeeta considered how she would answer, not knowing if Agent Tannery would want her to snitch on her weed supplier. She said, "I do, but I don't wanna jam shorty up. He good people and only sells recreational weed. He ain't big-time at all."

"You don't have to worry about him. I only go after people that will land my name in the papers, so get the marijuana too, and I'll make sure to reimburse you for the expense."

Agent Tannery felt like Santa Claus to Markeeta, and it wasn't even Christmas. He continued, "See if you could get her to talk about the unsolved murder of Avery Jackson at New-York Presbyterian around the same time Lucky and Bugsy were admitted. Avery had allegedly switched sides from Scott to Bugsy and was killed under mysterious circumstances."

"But how do I do that? I didn't know, dude? Wouldn't it look suspicious if I bring up his name?"

Tannery thought Markeeta was a savvier snitch than this. He didn't realize he'd have to do this much hand-holding. "Don't be assertive when you're fishing for information. Lead the horse to the water and then allow it to drink in its own time. You understand?"

She did.

"A'ight, cool." Markeeta wanted to stay on this winning team and knew she had to start producing. "What else? Just give me everything you need outta this bitch now, and I'll work it in my own way."

Tannery didn't need to understand why Markeeta hated her family this much and wanted to play such an intricate part in seeing them incarcerated. But he did understand the psyche of these situations and what it took for loyal walls to collapse, and it's as simple as you're either a snitch or you're not. Self-preservation. People with the propensity to inform on others always have some grand, logical excuse for why they started talking. The most common defense is the Sammy Gravano's reason. This is where the person is played the tape, usually by law enforcement of a friend, foe, or family member speaking distastefully about them. Hearing the disparaging remarks about themselves, a preemptive strike is teed up, and they snitch in a retaliatory revenge move.

Another common reason is just good old-fashioned jealousy. A jealous person would rather see someone dead or in jail than for their nemesis to keep living their life to the fullest. Jealous informants' information is unreliable because they will do or say anything to get their arch enemy locked up. Sometimes the news is embellished—at best, a straight-up lie—at worst. Nevertheless, if it can be used to secure a conviction, it is.

And the last reason is to barter. Informants will easily exchange someone's livable years behind bars if it makes the snitches' life that much better. It's like an auction; what can the snitch get if their information leads to the person getting locked up? This is Markeeta's motivation. Hired at their dream job— done! A home with no payment—muthafuckin' done, done!

The world also gave birth to those who, under *any* circumstance, would never inform on others no matter how hard they're pressured or how much there's to gain. That same person—male or female, could have been in Gravano's shoes, listening to Gotti throw him under a bus, and wouldn't have opened his fucking mouth to mumble a word. That person won't trade in their moral code for the monetary perks the federal government could shower upon them. That population was thin, rarer than type AB negative blood. It's easier to find Muslims who eat pork than find someone who won't bend for the government, but they do exist. However, Markeeta West wasn't one of them.

Tannery broke down Markeeta's agenda. "Let's see if you could get her to open up to you, to trust you. We've analyzed your cousin, and she doesn't have any female friends or a woman in her life after she planned a coup against her mother and her mother's organization. She doesn't know it, but she needs estrogen in her life. And that's you."

Markeeta was taking mental notes and appreciated the guidance. Speaking with Agent Tannery, she felt important, respected, and seen. He continued, "You're rough around the edges, Markeeta, so you have to keep shooting from the hip, or Lucky will pick up on your acquiescence. Whatever energy she's on, make sure to match that same energy."

"So why am I gettin' this bitch dinner and drinks?"

Tannery exhaled, "Why do you think?"

"Because that's what she's used to and also cause if she's fucked up, she won't see the double-cross comin'."

"That's my girl," he said, and she could tell he was smiling through the phone. Markeeta had pleased him and didn't realize how good that would feel to her.

"What else?"

"For tonight, let's not overwhelm you or her. Focus on Avery, get her talking, make sure you take a photo with her for our records, and last, tonight would be a good night to introduce her to the Instagram page."

"Oh, y'all set that up already?"

"We did." Agent Tannery was just about to hang up when he finished with an afterthought. "Oh, and Markeeta. Should Lucky go after your parenting skills again, go after hers. Not many people knew she had a child, and those who did say the nannies were raising Lucchese, and no one knew who the father was. Our guess is she doesn't either. And let's not forget her child was kidnapped, tortured, and is presumed dead, and she's worried about Chinese food and cognac? It practically writes itself, right? Like I said, keep her same energy."

Tannery continued to fill his informant in on the complicated drama surrounding Lucchese's birth, the unknown father of Lucky's child, how Lucky managed to have her child in the middle of a shootout, and, as witnesses reported, never left the safety of her vehicle to save Lulu.

Markeeta was hyped to get the dirt on her cousin and hung up, thinking, *I wish this bitch would try and come for me again!*

Chapter 18

A room full of FBI field agents sat in a luxury Dubai suite, furnished with high-tech surveillance equipment, watching Scott and Layla have angry sex. It was half-past three in the morning, and Scott had just come in from having drinks with the St. James's. The live footage showed Scott opening the bedroom door to a visibly angry Layla. The agents could almost feel her wrath through the computer monitor. Layla wore a blood-red negligee, robe, and scowl etched on her pretty face. She sat catacorner on the edge of the bed, a Newport pinched between her fingers, eyes dark like night devoid of the moon and stars.

Scott glanced at his wife dismissively and began loosening his tie. He was beat and mistakenly assumed that Layla would be asleep. She placed the Newport to her tightly pursed lips and deeply pulled—the cancer stick sparked and lit up in an orangey hue before she exhaled clouds of smoke into the tense atmosphere. Layla's manicured nails stomped out her cigarette in the ashtray before she finally spoke.

"Where were you?"

Scott slid his suit jacket off and tossed it on the arm of the chair. "Why are you still up?"

"Where were you nigga?" Layla asked again. Her voice was choppy; high and low tones spewed out—a mixture of rage and hysteria. "I done told your ass that I don't want you spending so much time wit' your new homies! I don't fuckin' like them!"

Scott removed his tailored slacks, unclasped his cufflinks, and took off his shirt before his icy words ripped into her. "Fuck you think you talking too? I'm not one of our kids, bitch! You fuck up my business deal, and I'ma fuck you up!"

Truth be told, Scott was also tired of the St. James's. He didn't feel he was gaining any traction but was too stubborn to admit that. Layla was right. He was spending far too much time and too much money for no results. Their mere presence had put a strain on his marriage, and Dubai no longer felt like a vacation.

Had Scott not been fatigued, he would have known to not turn his back on his wife after disrespecting her. The unmistakable force from the barrel of a Glock smashed into Scott's skull. The pressure thrust him forward two steps before he spun around, wrapped his masculine hand around Layla's throat, and squeezed. He could feel the muscles in her neck moving as her head twitched. She was gasping for air—however, Layla had the wherewithal to point the Glock to his temple.

Both fiercely stared into each other's eyes, exchanging powerful looks before Scott knocked the gun from his wife's grip. With great force, he slammed her back up against a wall; her sharp nails dug into his skin, drawing blood. Layla could barely breathe, but Scott refused to acquiesce. He wanted her to fully submit to his authority, act like a lady, cower at his strength, and when she wouldn't, he was turned on.

Scott could have squeezed the life out of her or snapped her neck for pointing a pistol at him. Instead, he released her. Layla sucked in air, quickly filling her lungs before Scott aggressively parted her lips with his. His long tongue explored her mouth until she bit down on his lip just hard enough for a reaction.

"Fuck, Layla!" Scott yelled angrily and was assaulted again when Layla's backhand flew across his jaw. In a reactionary movement, Scott slapped her back. Layla swung wildly, beating on her husband's back and chest before he grabbed a handful of her hair and yanked her head back. Scott's strong fingers gripped her long locks while his free hand held her chin so she couldn't wiggle free. Forcefully, he kissed her again, this time more passionately. Layla finally responded accordingly. Scott pulled away and shredded her negligee off her body, ripping the expensive silk to pieces; she was naked underneath. Her full breasts hung low but still had definition; her large tan areolas and nickel-size nipples perked up. She wanted to be manhandled, and Scott would not disappoint.

Gwyneth watched as Scott stepped out of his boxers, his porno-size penis was fully engorged, and it was an unbelievable sight. She'd fucked many men, preferably Black men were always on her menu but had yet to be blessed to sit on a dick this big. At that moment, she understood why Layla was so possessive of her husband. Scott, completely naked, had a body that looked like a sculpture—chiseled, muscular, perfection.

Layla resisted as Scott pushed her up against the wall again, her palms flat, legs apart like she was under arrest. Scott sucked on her neck as his strong fingers kneaded her breasts, flickering her nipples.

"Is this what you want!" Scott's manhood opened her up as he vigorously entered her sweet cave. Layla was dripping wet, her pussy stretching wider with each thrust. Scott's penis was hitting all her sensitive buttons as he circled his hips, slamming into her again and again with an unbridled force, sensational waves cascading throughout her body. Scott pulled out of her and then pushed into her again, causing Layla to cry out.

"Oh, shit, Scott…" she breathed.

Scott groaned loudly, his voice hoarse —"Fuck me back!"— thrusting so deep, so wildly, that Layla was overcome with mind-blowing pleasure spiraling through her body, swirling around her belly, moving toward an anticipatory orgasm.

Layla lifted her left leg, and Scott's arm gave her the balance she needed. She contracted her pussy muscles, gripping his dick and then releasing her Kegel muscle the way she knew he liked it.

"Oh, shit…" Scott moaned. "Do that shit, ma," he encouraged.

Layla was throwing her ass back into Scott's pelvis as he

controlled her wide hips, her whole bottom wiggling with each thrust, each stroke more potent than its predecessor. Scott had that grade-A dick and knew how to use it.

Deep waves of pleasure were brewing; Layla purred, "I'm about to come!"

With that, Scott unexpectantly pulled out of his wife, curtailing her epic explosion. In pure anger, Layla spun around and slapped Scott across his face again before she was lifted up in a bear hug and tossed on the king-size bed. Layla tried to crawl away, but Scott grabbed her ankles and pulled her back toward him. He flipped her over, with her face-up upon her back, he positioned himself between her shapely thighs. Angry, lustful eyes glared at each other, and Layla slapped her husband again, each sting more provocative than the last.

Scott absorbed the blow and grabbed both her wrists, pinning them on the bed, wrestling to enter her again. His mushroom tip struggled to penetrate, as Layla wanted to make him work for her sweet nectar this go around. Scott sunk lower, deeper, completely into his woman and began a slow grind that drove her crazy. Her thighs curved around his backside as Layla dug her fingernails into Scott's muscular, masculine ass.

Scott's head was buried in his wife's neck, inhaling her scent—Chanel No. 5, his favorite perfume, classic and seductive. His voice was low, gritty, controlling. "You not gonna fuck up my deal—you hear me!" His strokes hit her walls, punctuating his point.

"Fuck you…nigga," Layla whispered almost inaudibly. "And fuck…me, shit..."

Scott's hands dug into Layla's mane and twisted. He fisted her hair and gripped tight, increasing his rhythm; strong, vigorous, hardy, unrelenting strokes drove her crazy. Scott wasn't playing fair. He demanded, "Tell me you're gonna behave."

Scott kept bringing Layla to the brink of an orgasm, a tidal wave of feelings before cascading to a low tide, riding her almost into submission.

Layla wasn't about to surrender; she wasn't that bitch. She switched positions and climbed on top. Leaning over, she sucked on Scott's bottom lip, her long, tousled locks falling into his face, brushing against his cheeks. Layla's hand wrapped around her husband's girth and guided him into her.

The agents watched Layla skillfully ride her husband from the suite several floors below. The way she popped her hips had every man in the room wanting to show this clip to their significant others as a tutorial. Gwyneth, too, wanted pointers. If she wanted to keep a Black man in her bed, she had to keep up with what Black women were doing in and out of the bedroom.

By the time Scott and Layla finished their lovemaking session, everyone in the room needed a cigarette.

"I need to go slap my woman around and call her a couple bitches to see if it turns out like that just did," one agent said. "Goddamn, that was hot."

Another agent chimed in, "I see a cold shower in my future."

"Do married people still fuck like that?" another agent wanted to know.

Gwyneth, not a fan of Layla, had other issues. "If we don't get them on conspiracy, that bitch is going down for that gun she managed to obtain in this Allah-loving continent. How did we miss that?"

Gwyneth's comments fell flat. No one in that room was working on a gun case; Scott and Layla West could do no less than life.

Larry looked past Tannery and Brown and fixed his eyes on the two strangers standing behind him. Larry knew they were bad news from their demeanor, nothing to play with. Both undercover agents stood firm, with a glare aimed at him—no emotion poured from them since the meeting started.

"This is Pablo and Diablo, the two men you will connect Bugsy and Meyer with," Tannery said. "Make it happen."

Larry nodded. "I will, but um, y'all know Bugsy is jammed up, right?"

Tannery smirked. "What do you mean 'jammed up'?"

"Your peoples got 'im. He's in MCC on a gun charge."

"Motherfucker!" Tannery yelled. "My peoples don't *got* him! If we knew that Bugsy was incarcerated, would we ask you to make the introduction?"

Larry shrugged. How was he to know what was going on if they didn't?

Brown asked, "How long have you known about this information? You holding out on us?"

Larry didn't like all the finger-pointing. "Why should I drop dime on something I thought y'all already knew! He's in the feds. Aren't you a fed?"

Tannery gritted his teeth. "How long have you known is the question?!"

"Meyer told me about his brother when I rode wit' him uptown—"

"Something you weren't supposed to do!" Brown reminded the dim-witted flunky. "You were supposed to get him into your vehicle, so we could video your exchange. We would have heard this information weeks ago had you listened to us!"

Pablo chimed in. The premium line of cocaine he had snorted before the meeting had his patience waning. He wanted some action, and this little punk was withholding pertinent information. Pablo's cold dead eyes, expensive tailored suit, and Colombian accent startled Larry when he spoke. Larry could hustle a hundred years without being fully convinced this man was an agent. His narco authenticity was unmatched; how could you learn and not live this? In a measured, surly voice, Pablo asked, "You were debriefed after your encounter with Meyer, were you not?"

"Look, man. I said what I said, and I don't answer to you. You ain't my handler! I ain't gonna be havin' all y'all muthafuckas tellin—"

The slap was firm, dizzying Unlucky, and now toothless Larry.

"Owwwww!" he hollered, looking to Agents Tannery and Brown for an intervention.

"Listen to my question, sí." Pablo nodded and repeated, "You were debriefed after your encounter with Meyer?"

Larry reluctantly replied, "Yeah." Pablo thought; his lips were poked out, rubbing his bruised cheek like a little bitch.

"And you didn't think to mention to my colleagues that Bugsy West was apprehended? Meanwhile, Diablo and I have been preparing for weeks for an introduction to Bugsy that *only* you knew wouldn't be taking place. Tell me why I shouldn't break this chair over your fucking head, maybe bury your pitiful body alive?"

"Because you 'posed to be the good guy!" Larry deduced.

"Good guy?" Pablo chuckled. "You crazy."

"Okay, I gotchu," Larry said. "I don't wanna make excuses, but bullets were flyin' 'n shit. I dropped the cell Tannery had given me that would have also recorded the conversation...right, Tannery? I told y'all I had dropped the phone. It wasn't my fault."

Diablo spoke, "This is who we're relying on? Chivato has no balls...I can't have my life in his hands. He's stupid."

Larry blew out air, which was the most he could do under these circumstances. He felt emasculated, belittled, and now he felt regret for whatever part he was about to play in taking down another Black man for these unethical muthafuckas. But he was handcuffed, without many options, he reasoned.

Brown sarcastically asked, "Anything else you think we already know?"

"As a matter of fact, there is. The shootout y'all put me in the middle of—"

"The one where Meyer didn't kill anyone? Of course, we know," said Brown.

"Yeah, so that's the thing. It's not like Meyer to not handle his business. The man I know would have bodied those block huggers wit' the quickness."

"And?" Tannery said.

"So, I'm thinkin' he wasn't strapped."

"Again, and!" Tannery was losing his patience. "So the thug left home without his illegal weapon. It happens."

Larry shook his head. "Not with Meyer. I think something's up, that's all."

"Okay, we'll look into it," Brown said. "Now, back to business."

Pablo and Diablo started to school Larry on their cover story about Los Pepes. They described their fake operation to Larry in full detail, and if Larry didn't know any better, he would've sworn the two men were the real thing—cartel men that were deadly, dangerous, and making tons of money in drug trafficking. Their clothing, accents, steely gaze was all official. Larry knew this would work. All he had to do was remember everything the two undercover agents told him to sell the story to Meyer.

"You have three weeks to make the introduction happen," Tannery told him.

Three weeks? Larry knew that it would be a short three weeks.

It didn't take long for news to circulate that the man who had tried to murder the only living daughter of Scott West was housed in the same unit as her brother, Bugsy. Emmanuel Vega sat at the rectangular-shaped table during chow with his amigos surrounding him. Hispanics in orange jumpsuits, canvas footwear, and sleeved tattoos shot menacing looks toward the kingpin as they whispered threats in Spanish to Vega, vowing retribution.

Bugsy, too, was encapsulated by several henchmen, those who would die for the mere affiliation with him. These men also had résumés stretched as long as I-95, punctuated with murder, RICO, kidnapping, and torture. Bugsy and Vega's eyes spoke from across the room, promising a bloody demise. It was cliché—kingpin versus cartel, Black versus Hispanic, mono y mono. Who would win?

Vega had no idea that his days were numbered and that Bugsy's incarceration was actually his saving grace. Juarez could not allow a rival inmate to live; the decision to now assassinate Bugsy was only business. Angel would give him redemption as long as he murdered Bugsy, and this time Emmanuel would make sure his target would fall by his hand.

Bugsy left chow and made his way, alone, to the library. It was either a sign of strength or stupidity—the conclusion was relative. Bugsy perused the shelves and grabbed *The Autobiography of Malcolm X*. He was only a few pages in when Kenneth Collins approached.

"Bugsy West?"

"Yeah." He looked up. "How do you know me?"

Kenneth shrugged and sat down, uninvited. "I know everyone I tried to prosecute."

Bugsy smirked.

"Oh, come on. Don't look so surprised. Feds got me too."

"Who's they?"

"My former colleagues. The feds." Kenneth exhaled in a defeated yet pugilistic way. As if he had a few more rounds in him. "I heard they got you on a gun charge, and its absurdity is actually a smart play."

"It is what it is," Bugsy replied. "Tell me about my failed prosecution."

"We roped you in when you were a mere eighteen…tried relentlessly to build a case against you, your siblings, and your parents. Nothing ever stuck."

Bugsy snorted. "We don't leave any witnesses."

"Witnesses, no. Your father taught you well. Informants…that's a whole other beast and just like the forefathers that came before you, will be your downfall."

Bugsy's interest was piqued, but he remained cool. "Is that so?"

"You tell me? If history has shown us anything, it's that it repeats. There is no 99.6% conviction rate without the rat. You can't build a drug empire alone, and an empire can't rise without those willing to help it fall."

Bugsy absorbed his nuggets of wisdom, allowing Kenneth to do most of the talking.

"Why'd they turn on you?"

"We had a good racket going. We took our power and monetized it. Our federal badges and connections allowed us to rob dealers like yourself before we had them sentenced to life. We made deals with defense attorneys to railroad their clients while charging them exorbitant fees where we'd get a cut. The defense attorney would run up the bill with bogus man-hours. We'd schedule fake motions before the court that the defendant was told they didn't have to attend," he laughed. "We'd enter the residences of kingpins and stole whatever we wanted, they'd never miss anything, and we knew that because we had their homes and phones bugged. You wouldn't believe—actually, you would. We'd walk into a home, and there'd be stacks of cash sitting on tables, jewelry, watches, you name it—we'd take it. And suppose they did realize that something was missing, which was rare. In that case, they'd blame their housekeeper, gardener, babysitter, family member…so many migrant workers were accused of theft and ultimately maned or murdered because of us."

Bugsy couldn't glean whether he saw pride, amusement, or both in his eyes. "Y'all was making a killing, huh?"

"Ab-so-fucking-lutely," he admonished. "And we weren't

just robbing drug dealers."

Kenneth adjusted his gold-rimmed glasses on his nose and leaned in. Bugsy could smell the lingering odor of coffee on his tart breath, so he tilted his head sideways to cut the stench. Kenneth continued, "We had many lanes of income coming in…there was this rapper…don't ask his name because I can't remember, but the incident made the papers. He'd received a watch from some super-producer worth half a million dollars. We went in, switched the watch with what we thought was an identical fake. Rapper goes to get the watch appraised, and it's a certified fugazi."

"I heard about that," said Bugsy.

Kenneth chuckled. "Yeah, we got away with a lot."

"So, how did you end up in here?" Bugsy wanted to know.

"You have to ask?" Kenneth replied. "Greed. I got greedy and decided to cut my compadres out of my deals. I wanted it all, so I took it. And my ill-gotten gains didn't sit well with my coworkers. They set a trap, and I walked right into it."

"If you have all this information against your colleagues, why tell me? Why not tell your lawyer and have them as cellmates and not witnesses scheduled to testify against you?"

"I think we're more alike than you think."

Bugsy nodded. "You're not a snitch."

"And therein lies my downfall."

Bugsy sat back and knew that this was a pivotal moment. He was schooled about the game by his father, a Brooklyn-born hustler. On the flip side, he was getting the game from a criminal with a badge. Class was in session, and he would attend every day to save his family, even if that meant he wouldn't be able to save himself.

Chapter 19

Lucky was soaking in a warm bubble bath, reliving the sex session she had just had with Ragnar. She had been spending her nights in his bed, and each morning at first light, she would be ushered out so that he could get to his day job.

A legit working man, she thought. Lucky found herself intrigued with his routine, that nine to five monotony employees loathed had her wishing she could shadow him for a day. Ragnar would tell her about office antics, meetings, and, most interestingly—his research. He was intelligent, different, funny, sarcastic, friendly, mean, freaky, but above all, he was a distraction. This thing they had—that couldn't be quantified with labels was good for her. Was she a jump-off, side-piece, his bae, or boo, his woman, or baby-girl? What was Lucky to him? She didn't know. And what she couldn't understand was why he wouldn't accept her invitation to come to her home. She didn't mind her morning walk of shame out of his residence, but it would be nice if he showed an interest in seeing how she lived.

When Lucky's toes began to prune, she knew it was time to get out of the tub and get dressed. But not before sending Ragnar a naughty emoji text: *an eggplant, handclap, and the smiling face with the tongue out.* She hoped the old man understood that this was how her generation held conversations. In any event, she had company coming in less than an hour. Markeeta invited herself over, and Lucky wondered why she had said yes. *I know why,* she thought. *I want her to see that we glow differently. I own, while she rents. I write checks while she receives them. I'm Lucky West, and she's Markeeta Winslow.*

Lucky was about to break out into a sweat looking in her closet for a Prada one-piece jumper she owned. She knew where it should be and was mystified why it wasn't. It wasn't the first garment or item she couldn't find lately. Things were missing that she couldn't explain. Lucky was about to call Meyer and accuse him but realized how ridiculous that would sound. Accusing Meyer of boosting her clothes was some crackhead '89 shit. Strange things were unfolding, and she couldn't put her finger on why. Like when she came in the other day, Lucky would have bet her life that she'd left all lights off. When she walked in, her apartment was lit up like Christmas lights, and the television in her room was on. Odd?

Markeeta came with a broad smile and a tight hug. The fact that Lucky was affiliating with the enemy—blood or not was less than smart. Which was the sole reason Lucky had yet to mention her chitchats with Markeeta to her brothers.

Markeeta said the expected oohs and ahhs while walking through Lucky's lux condo. And truth be told, she was impressed. Markeeta wasn't acting as her mouth gaped open at such opulence. Lucky popped open a thousand-dollar bottle of champagne, rolled up premium Kush, and steamed a bucket full of seafood. The two tore open king crab legs boiled in beer and Old Bay seasoning and dipped large chunks in melted butter. The corn on the cobb and red baby potatoes were devoured as Markeeta kept cracking jokes keeping her cousin highly entertained.

"Yo, you check out that Instagram page I told you about?"

Lucky's head shook. "I told you I don't do social media...I ain't got shit to sell."

Markeeta snorted and said, "Except them ki's," and laughed.

Lucky didn't find anything to laugh at. "I don't sell drugs," she aggressively replied and then relaxed somewhat. "I smoke 'em." Lucky held up her blunt, and they both giggled.

Markeeta's fingers began moving quickly before she walked

over and gave Lucky her phone. "So you don't know about this? None of ya peoples hit you up?"

Lucky read the handle: *hoodfellas_waybackindaday*. She saw pictures of hustlers from the early '80s up to date post after post. Legendary gangstas posed in mink jackets, thick rope chains to mink coats, and platinum Jesus pieces. Most were dead, some were incarcerated, only a few had survived their era. And then she saw Scott. Her father looked younger than she was now. It looked like he was in a nightclub holding a Magnum bottle of Moët, surrounded by his crew. Scott was crouched low, mid-center, with a scowl on his face. Lucky recognized Whistler, Mason, and Avery but not anyone else.

Lucky kept scrolling. There was a picture of Scott with his arm draped around Layla's neck. Her parents looked so young, so in love. Scott had on an Adidas tracksuit and matching sneakers. His hands had several chunky gold and diamond rings and a phat gold chain. Layla had her hair in a mushroom-style, a side part, silk blouse, tight jeans, and bamboo earrings. They were posted against a Benz that Lucky was sure her father owned. Next, Lucky stopped at a picture of her father and Maxine, a white BMW with a bow was on display, and the two looked just as in love as Scott did in the picture with Layla. Maxine's hair was cornrowed in Cleopatra braids, her baby hairs snaked down each side of her face. Her dark chocolate skin glowed against the red Fila sweatsuit she wore. Maxine had hoop earrings, a nugget watch, and a wrist full of gold bangles. Scott wore a matching Fila suit, Rolex, and his neck was draped in several rope chains.

Why was this online, Lucky wondered? She kept scrolling until the nineties reached the twenty-first century. And there were her brothers, all iced-out in various photographs, in numerous cars, and with different women. These were personal pictures, not meant for the public's consumption, but they were. Finally, her face began showing up. There she was—long hair, short hair, unmarred-faced, scarface, childless, post-baby—this Instagram handle had documented it all.

"You read what they sayin'?"

"What?" Lucky whispered, somewhat taken aback.

"The captions, each picture has one. They sayin' Uncle Scott and Auntie are snitchin'."

"You can't be serious," Lucky replied while still scrolling. She quickly landed on the picture that ran in the newspapers of Scott and Layla's acquittals. The person behind the page had captioned the post: NOBODY LASTS DECADES IN THE DRUG GAME UNLESS SNITCHIN'!

Lucky read comment after comment, the harshest words, the harshest critics. Everyone spoke like they knew her parents, knew that they were cooperating with the feds. People were using this forum under fake accounts to spill what they felt was all the tea. Any tidbit of information, dirt, hearsay was posted as the gospel. Those quiet hating hoped that the feds were also privy to this page and their information could lead to an arrest.

Thinking quickly, Lucky unlocked her phone and tossed it to Markeeta. "Make me an account, a fake one, of course, and make it so I can see this shit."

Markeeta nodded and went to work while Lucky continued reading one horrible lie after another.

"I guess you don't know what the streets are sayin' about some dude named Avery. You know him?"

Lucky didn't confirm nor deny. She responded with, "What's being said?"

"They sayin' you was fuckin' him, and Uncle Scott found out and had him murdered at the hospital."

"What!" Lucky bellowed. "I ain't ever fuck Avery. That's on my child. Where are they getting all this bullshit?"

Markeeta wanted to crack the fuck up at Lucky's outburst, but she couldn't. Tannery had concocted this story because it was alleged that Scott West and Whistler Hussain's acrimony stemmed from Whistler fucking his boss's underage daughter.

Markeeta's head swung left to right quickly as if she empathized. "This the first you hearin' this?"

"I *never* heard no shit like that!" Lucky was amped. "Make it make sense!"

"But you was there, right? How you ain't hear nothin'?" Markeeta pressed on. "Who would want to kill dude...you think it had to do with Lulu?"

"Lucchese...you never met her to call her by her nickname."

Markeeta sarcastically replied, "I can't even pronounce that shit, so I'll just say your daughter."

"Works for me," Lucky said sarcastically.

"So if the streets got it wrong and Avery wasn't killed over you or your daughter, why is he dead?"

Lucky paused momentarily. She was fucked up, but she wasn't dumb. "You act like I was at the murder scene."

"Nah, I know you ain't kill 'im."

"You know a lot then. More than most...."

Markeeta realized that she may have overplayed her hand, underestimating Lucky's tolerance to alcohol, and weed and overestimating her hugs and company. It was time to fall back.

"Here," she said and handed Lucky back her phone. "Your password is your daughter's nickname, which you can change. Your handle is *disney_princess1998*, and *hoodfellas_waybackindaday* isn't private, so you're following him. You will see each post."

"Thank you," Lucky said, and not much more for the next hour. Lucky answered Markeeta with one-word responses before she got the hint and decided to leave. As soon as the front door slammed, Lucky was back on Instagram. She was going to figure out what the fuck was going on one way or another.

Agent Brown sat behind a Dell computer with Bose headphones on as Larry dialed Meyer from the bureau's cellphone. The recorded call was automatically stored in a cloud owned and operated by the DEA and protected by a firewall system that Russia and China thus far found to be unhackable. Agent Tannery was also at the warehouse, both men becoming impatient with the pace of the operation. They had Pablo and Diablo at the ready, but they weren't being used so far. Their skills as undercover operatives were sitting dormant because Meyer wasn't behaving as they assumed he would. He was a drug distributor who wasn't making any effort to distribute drugs.

They figured that after the assault and robbery of Larry, Meyer would press him for the Los Pepes connect, especially after the urgency that Meyer displayed. They allowed a week to pass, but that call never came. The DEA wanted Meyer to chase Larry, so they used a few of their confidential informants to spread the word that Larry had blown up with his new connect. Men and women in Meyer's circle began namedropping in hopes to pique his interest again. They allowed another week to pass and, again, silence from the young West. The agents were perplexed. After Larry gave them the intel about Bugsy's incarceration and Meyer being weaponless, Tannery dug around a little and found out that the FBI had been busy. So he contacted NYPD and told them to fall back on harassing Meyer and was also trying to get the judge to allow Bugsy to be released on his own recognizance. These conflicts arose because the DEA didn't inform the FBI that they, too, were investigating the Wests.

The streets said that the Juarez cartel had not only murdered Lucchese, shot Bugsy, and stabbed Lucky, but they were behind the most recent stash and trap house robberies owned and operated by the young Wests. So if they no longer had a cocaine supplier, what the fuck was Meyer waiting on?

"Make the call," Tannery instructed. He sat catercorner on the desk, his right leg planted firmly on the ground, his left leg dangling as he faced Larry.

Larry was their yes nigga. Whatever they asked, the nigga had to say yes. He had done a one-eighty since they had first approached him after illegally detaining him for the fake traffic violation. Larry now wanted to please them. He was all in. Larry was going above the call of duty to help them secure an arrest. He was mixing it up with every street thug, fucking all the get-money chicks, and the West crew was brought up during each interaction. *What's up with them? When was the last time Meyer came through? Y'all heard from Bugsy? What's up with Lucky?* Any and everything was relevant.

The agents also noticed his new enthusiasm. They figured it had to do with Meyer leaving him toothless, but it didn't. Larry had gotten addicted to the infamy and notoriety they had given him. He was now the man—toothless or not. Bitches wanted to fuck him, and niggas were all riding his dick now. Larry didn't want it to end. Tannery had gotten him more jewels, and if he got robbed again, more would follow. They kept stacks of money in his pockets—he had to look the part. He was now popping bottles at the club, making it rain in the strip clubs, and they had added a black Range to his repertoire. Unlucky Larry was the muthafuckin' man, the biggest dope distributor on the east coast, and he didn't have to move weight. It was all an illusion.

Larry was planning to stay connected for life. He had an extensive list of niggas he was ready to help them take down after they got Meyer. Hustlers from all parts of New York. Dealers he once envied and wanted to be as his sneakers leaned, and his stomach growled. Niggas who shitted on him and never helped him come up in the game. It was time for payback.

Larry made the call. "Yo, what's up, playah?" he asked when Meyer answered.

"What up, nigga?" Meyer casually asked.

"Those peoples I told you about…I can make that happen," Larry spoke in code because Meyer would know he was being set up if he didn't.

There was a pregnant pause, and then, "Word. You did that,

huh?"

"No doubt," Larry continued. "So Friday. You good wit' that?"

"Friday?" Meyer seemed distracted, almost uninterested. "Let me holla at you in a few."

"These ain't the type of peoples you keep waiting. They said Friday."

"Nigga I said what I said."

Agent Tannery twirled his index finger in circles, which meant he wanted Larry to keep Meyer talking to seal the deal.

"A'ight, but remember you came to me, nigga. Don't start beefin' if I can't get another meeting for you."

Meyer didn't address that last warning. He simply said, "I'm out," and hung up.

"Goddamn it!" Tannery yelled. "What's wrong with this kid? Why is he stalling?"

Brown said, "You think he made him?"

Larry spoke up with the quickness. There wasn't any way he was getting benched. "That nigga ain't made shit…but something is goin' on wit' him. Y'all need to do what y'all do and figure it out so I can do my job. I can't effectively work without all the puzzle pieces." Larry got cocky with it. "I'm out here wit' my life on the line while y'all sitting behind closed doors and shit…I'm serving up Meyer West, muthafuckin' Meyer on a silver platter, so I'ma need more intel on this nigga, and that's y'all jobs."

Tannery and Brown were incredulous.

"It's easy to win when you cheat, Larry. We cheat! We made you, and just like that," Tannery snapped his fingers, "We can break you! So don't get cute. You wouldn't even have Meyer's ear on this level if it weren't for us, so you better fucking check that ego of yours before I check it."

Larry relaxed. "Well, I'm gonna need more ice."

"Ice? What the fuck is that?"

"Jewelry."

"We already gave you more, and now you want more?" It was all too gaudy for Brown to understand. What was it about Black folks and their flashiness? The name Rolex was an instant trigger for him. If he saw that watch on one of them—them being Blacks, he lost it.

"It's a matter of believability. Top niggas in the game don't have one watch. They have at least two—multiple pieces of shine. I can't keep comin' round wit' that same drip. I'm thinkin' an Audamar watch will grab Meyer's attention, and he'll realize that I'm makin' money hand over fist. He'll want the introduction."

Tannery asked, "So you think a new watch will be needed to move this shit along?"

Larry nodded. "That and then some."

After their volatile yet steamy lovemaking, Layla still felt isolated in Dubai. Scott felt that her actions—constantly arguing with Jacqueline could cost him the foundation he was building with Uriel and was livid when Layla said she gave no fucks. Scott wasn't spending any time with her, leaving early in the morning, and returning long after she had gone to bed for the night. Scott didn't include her in the outings, business meetings, or dinners. This behavior went on for weeks, but Layla refused to show weakness. What hurt her the most was when she would go into restaurants and see Scott seated at a table with Jacqueline and the Billionaire Boys Club, and her husband wouldn't acknowledge her presence. Scott was a shady bastard when he wanted to be. Layla would order lavish meals and smile politely to the wait staff, but she was wrecked inside. Again, Scott had tossed her aside and allowed a female to come between them.

With no one to turn to, Layla called her favorite child.

"Fuck...you...want?" Meyer rudely choked out, no longer feeling he had to respect the woman who gave birth to him. Not when she played a part in murdering his nephew and clearly wasn't on her way to the states to help facilitate her murder.

"Watch your mouth, boy! I'm still your mother!" she snapped.

"Nah…," Meyer said slowly and didn't finish his sentence.

Layla immediately sensed something. "Are you high?"

Meyer nodded as if she could see his response. He was alone inside his apartment, lights out, television on mute, drinking Lean. Meyer had a stressful day, and he had wanted to fuck his stress away, but Lollipop was still ignoring his calls.

"Meyer," Layla repeated. "Are you high!"

"I'm smokin', so don't blow—" he took an unusually long pause and then continued, "my high…wit' your shit."

Layla figured he was smoking some potent Kush and wished she had some. "Your father and I are having issues again," she began, not caring her son didn't care. Layla just needed someone to listen to her gripes and affirm what she felt wasn't paranoia. "We met this couple out here, and I can't put my finger on it, but something ain't right with them."

Meyer gave no fucks but continued to listen.

"Everywhere we go, they're there!" she lamented. "We step on the elevator, go to the pool, the mall, the front desk, and we see those muthafuckas."

Meyer didn't understand the issue, so all he could contribute to the conversation was, "And?"

"Nigga I lived in New York all my life, and I ain't ever ran into any muthafucka like this. We been in the game for a minute, we know shit ain't random and damn sure don't believe in coincidences."

Again, Meyer nodded as if his mother could see him. "What…Pops say?"

"He has a lot to say, mainly that I'm paranoid, fuckin' up his money, and most recently, miserable."

Meyer took another sip of his Lean. The thick grape-flavored liquid had him in a chill mode he couldn't get from weed.

"You…think they feds?"

"Scott had them vetted, so no, I guess."

"You guess?" Meyer repeated. "You?!"

He hadn't said much, but to Layla, her son had said everything. She now knew what she had to do, but before she hung up, something compelled her to say, "Meyer, you do know how much I love you, right?"

Meyer snorted. "Eat a dick."

"You first nigga!"

Chapter 20

His eyes had to be playing tricks on him. There wasn't any way fate could be this cruel to someone he felt was good at her core. He had unintentionally followed her life for decades because she kept making the papers. The two were in the same classes from grade to high school but didn't run in the same circles. By middle school, she was his dream girl, wifey material—the one he wanted to put a ring on. She was his prom date, study partner, and the one who made his heart skip several beats. Then high school rolled around, and the nerd with the bifocal glasses didn't interest her anymore.

With his bad-boy image, flashy cars, and gaudy jewelry, Scott West stole the love of his life and usurped his happily ever after. There wasn't any way he could compete, so he didn't. He moved on. Shocked when he read that she had been charged with murder, stunned when decades later he read about her and Scott and the FBI raid of their lavish city dwelling.

But it was her. It had to be. Even with her hair in dreds, crusty lips, ashy skin, and layers of mismatched holey clothes, she was still beautiful to him. Sitting on a cardboard box, parked outside a Chase bank on a busy side street in midtown Manhattan, the woman panhandled nickels, dimes, and dollars.

"Maxine?" Gregory asked.

She averted eye contact and ignored the male.

"Maxine Henderson?" he asked again.

Maxine said nothing, annoyed more than embarrassed that she had been identified. She was homeless, in rags, hadn't bathed in months, and had allowed her hair to dred. *What more could she have done to live in anonymity?* She thought.

"Maxine, it's me…Gregory from East New York, Brooklyn."

Maxine continued to ignore her government because she had resigned herself to being nameless, faceless, soulless. She was a woman with a mission—two, really, and that was to see Scott and Bugsy West die by her hands. And if the murder of her son wasn't enough motivation—which it was—Maxine also had two multi-million dollar insurance policies on father and son that had an expiration date. Scott and Bugsy had to die in less than ten weeks because that's when the premiums were due, hefty sums of money that she would never be able to beg the good citizens of New York for.

Maxine would often sneak off from Wendy and stalk Bugsy's and Scott's residences, but there was no movement, no sign of the woman beaters. She became antsy as the clock ticked and expanded her stalking to Lucky and Meyer. No action until finally, Meyer appeared acting weird. Maxine trailed the killer and wasn't shocked that it led to a double homicide. Meyer hopped on a train, she followed. The young West flagged down a cab; she did too with her last few dollars. And when he dumped the smoking gun in a trash bin, Maxine couldn't believe her luck. She retrieved the .45 relishing the irony that Meyer West had just supplied her with the weapon that would ultimately put his father and twin six feet deep.

Maxine wondered how long Gregory would stand there stuck on stupid? If being ignored wasn't a subtle enough hint, crazy always worked. Maxine's eyes met his, and she growled, "Grrr,"—and then barked—"Ruff! Ruff! Rufffff!"

Gregory's eyes popped open, wild with disbelief and pity. He backpedaled a few steps before ultimately walking briskly away.

Her day ended when Wendy came ambling up the block, pushing her shopping cart that was now filled with what people considered trash. Maxine enjoyed going back to their makeshift abode constructed of boxes, duct tape, and a discarded tent to find out what Wendy had collected. They both had a part to play in life. Wendy would go through dumpsters and trash cans while Maxine would panhandle. This union was a sisterhood Maxine didn't know she needed.

The FBI was using different tactics to cripple the Wests than the DEA. They wanted to be thorns in the children's side until they had enough evidence to build cases against the whole clan. They had no issues being petty. It gave them immense joy. Locking up Bugsy on a gun, having NYPD harass Meyer to ultimately confiscate his money, and freezing their legal cash accounts was deliberate. They figured it would all make sense in the end. And while they were in the states fucking with the kids, two of their top field agents gained traction against the parents.

Agents Randall, Devonsky, Franklin Garrett, and Kimberly Cooper were going over their case in Lower Manhattan's conference room.

"So what do we know," Randall said, starting the meeting. "We know that they're at war with Juarez. One of the underlings in the cartel on wiretap took credit for the slaughters against the West organization. The member bragged that they took at least four hundred million and drugs in the raids."

Devonsky and Garrett both nodded.

Randall continued, "That explains why Meyer was selling their jewelry and why Bugsy hasn't made bail."

"They can't be broke, right?" Franklin asked. "Don't these dealers usually have safe deposit boxes? Have we run a name check for boxes?"

Devonsky nodded. "I did run a check, and we didn't find any safe deposit boxes in their names, business names, or any of their well-known associates. Meyer has a long-time stripper in his life, but nothing came up under her name either. She has a Citibank account with a little over nine hundred dollars."

Randall continued his statement, "We've run their parents out of the country, seized their business bank accounts, and locked up the brains of the young Wests' organization. Let's also mention that Juarez sucked the life out of their empire in one night—yet, they haven't made any mistakes. I have to admit I'm impressed."

"Well, don't stay that way. We need to break them so that they're desperate. Every move they make will be out of desperation," Franklin added.

Randall asked, "What do you have in mind?"

Franklin looked at all the paperwork and pretended this idea had just come to him. Truthfully, he had been thinking about it ever since he got assigned to this case. Pursuing Lucky, their intimate relationship, and every horrible thing Franklin had planned for her was his secret to keep. He said, "Since they haven't bailed out Bugsy, let's keep it that way until we're ready for him to be released. All their liquid is gone; let's now take their assets. When Bugsy is released, we want him to walk into pure chaos. We can all agree that he's the organization's brains out of the siblings."

"Well, he ain't that smart if he allowed Angel Morales to confiscate every dime to his name and murder every soldier he had," Devonsky deduced.

"Good point, but he's smart enough. We don't want him out on the streets liquidating assets. We have to contact all the banks. I'm talking even the credit unions and flag all their real estate. No loans get approved, no refinances, no pulling out equity. Once they can't get fast money, they'll want to sell. We stay on top of that and make sure the realtors keep those properties on the market indefinitely, and without a buyer—overhead, mortgages, and taxes still due, we can foreclose on the assets that way. Box them all into a corner and allow the beasts to immerge."

"Won't their parents step in?" Kimberly asked what she felt was a relevant question. Yet all the men gave her annoyed looks.

"Bugsy impregnated his father's fiancée," Franklin said dismissively, "Let's move on."

Randall and Devonsky liked that Franklin was on their team. He was thinking outside the box, and that's how you had to sometimes catch criminals. Devonsky added, "I'll contact all their credit card companies, personal and business, and have them cancel all cards. They could buy a fucking private plane with the black card!"

The boundaries of what was legal had blurred when they got a second chance to prosecute. An investigation was morphing into strong-arming, which had morphed into violating the civil rights of Americans Bugsy, Meyer, and Lucky, who were presumed innocent until proven otherwise.

Kimberly added, "Shouldn't we focus more on getting drug dealers to move drugs? Isn't that where the case begins and ends?" She didn't wait for a response. She continued with, "They've been at war with Juarez for some time, and we haven't been able to glean why? We also know they dabbled with the Kiqué Helguero cartel for distro, but Meyer hasn't reached out for any product. I think that if we keep with this petty line of harassment, although you all may find it amusing, it drags us farther and farther away from the ultimate goal. And what about their civil rights?"

"Why is she here?" Franklin boldly asked and then directly said to Kimberly. "Why are you here if you're too emotional to prosecute? I mean…was she properly vetted because she's been championing the liberties of the Wests mighty hard right now. Maybe she wants to sleep with one of the black bastards!"

"You're out of line, Garrett," she warned.

"Not even close! Unlike you, I don't want to be invited to the cookout!" he snapped. Randall and Devonsky had no idea what that statement meant, nor did Randall step in and get his team back on track. He allowed Franklin to rant. "I'm here to help my superiors make a conviction stick against the whole West organization. My only goal is to be here for Agents Randall and

Devonsky and see that all their arduous work is realized."

If *proud coon* was a person, it would begin and end with Franklin. There were nine African American male agents in that office, and Franklin wasn't counted as one. The other agents called him *Mighty Whighty* because he refused to hide that he thought he wasn't Black. He was always boasting about his *23andme* DNA test proving he had a meager percentage of the Negroid gene.

Franklin was that 'yes nigga', *king coon,* as the other African American males in the office called him behind his back. He heard the smears but didn't care. He was climbing up the ladder and liked the view from up top. On the weekends and holiday's he was invited to the homes of the upper echelon. Often he was the only Black man there. Franklin said he didn't see color, 'people are people,' he'd say. He tried to explain to anyone who gave him five minutes of their time that his white wife could easily be a Black female because he fell in love with her personality, not her race. No one listened. No one cared. It was his life, his choice, yet he had the chip on his shoulder. He was always waiting for a Black judge or Black senator to challenge him, to question his personal choice, so he studied African American history, knowing every nook and cranny to affirm his blackness when needed.

"We're both here for that same conclusion," Kimberly refuted, treading carefully. "I also have input on how to get there, but it seems that your approach is more effective."

Kimberly fell on her sword. She would lose this battle to ultimately win the war. If she got removed from this case, she wouldn't get another one of this magnitude, and if these childish antics led to a conviction, Kimberly wanted her name attached to that. So she damn near bit her tongue off after realizing her boss, Agent Randall, felt his *yes nigga* Franklin could do no wrong.

"As I was saying before being rudely interrupted. They have expensive things that they shouldn't have…items worth a lot." Franklin wasn't done blurring lines. "And we've been forgetting one thing."

"What's that?" Randall wanted to know.

Franklin asked, "Where does one go to get away from all the drama in one's life?"

Devonsky answered, "Home."

Markeeta arrived at Lucky's bearing gifts. She had a half ounce of premium Purple Haze, a bottle of Prosecco champagne, and two steaming plates of Jamaican oxtails, peas, and rice—hoping to put some meat on Lucky's bony bones.

Today, the shit had hit the fan for Markeeta's friends, Shirelle and Manny Machiavelli. The DEA had kicked open their front door a couple of hours before dawn, thanks to the information, Markeeta supplied to agents Tannery and Brown. It was far easier for Markeeta to get incriminating information against them than Lucky, and it wasn't just Shirelle running her mouth. Once the blunts were passed around, Manny couldn't shut the fuck up. He was always talking real big to impress Markeeta. Without provocation, Manny ran down murders he committed or was about to commit; who feared him, and who was stupid not to. Manny described his operation, who his supplier was, and when he let slip that Shirelle had muled for him a time or two—Shirelle put an abrupt end to their little pow wows. Not only because she was embarrassed, but Shirelle also noticed that Manny's grin was a little too wide when Markeeta came over, which was all the time. However, it was too late. Manny and Markeeta were already fucking. He'd sneak upstairs and fuck Markeeta, come back down a few hours later, and fuck Shirelle.

Markeeta was in an exceptionally good mood predicated on the fact that Agent Tannery had rewarded her for a job well done.

He'd upgraded her Cherokee to a metallic grey Range. The SUV wasn't new, but new enough. It had less than eight thousand miles on it and had been seized in a drug raid in Pittsburg. Markeeta had been doing rounds in her new whip driving through Brooklyn at all hours of the night so her friends and frenemies alike could see her come up; her son left alone, raising himself.

Markeeta grew fond of Tannery even found herself calling him for advice on situations that didn't involve DEA-related matters. Markeeta was misguided and a fool. She thought they were friends; Tannery knew she was only business. Tannery recognized her codependency toward him and understood how she could blur the lines. In her mind, he was her provider and protector. Tannery gave her more than her parents, friends, fucking, or hustling could provide. She had no idea that her apartment was wired for video and sound. Whenever he wanted—and he wanted often—Tannery would watch Markeeta in her habitat and be repulsed.

Those flat-screen Smart televisions, cable modems, laptops, desktops, chandeliers, motion sensors, appliances—all recorded her 24/7. Tannery was fully aware she was sleeping with Manny—something she did not mention. He watched her slurp up Manny's dick and swallow his seeds on many uncomfortable occasions. Markeeta would holler and moan at the top of her lungs with her son's room just ten feet from hers. She had no class and was uncouth but a great snitch. And that was the bottom line.

The girls were inside Lucky's closet while she tried on clothes for her date tonight with Ragnar. Markeeta was a nosy bitch, so Lucky told her that she was going out with Meyer and ignored her when Markeeta pressed for more info.

"This bag or this bag?" Lucky asked, holding a Fendi and a Hermès.

"Now you know nothin' compares to a fuckin' Birkin bag…you ain't even have to ask."

Lucky was standing in front of her full-length mirror. She

pulled the Fendi close to her outfit and then the Hermès. The Fendi matched. Lucky tossed the Birkin and said, "The Fendi matches this outfit…besides, I want to wear these Fendi stilettos."

Markeeta didn't believe that Lucky would go to all this trouble picking out an outfit to hang out with her brother. Unless her brother was bringing one of his friends.

"Why can't you mix the Birkin bag with the Fendi shoes?" Markeeta wanted to know.

Lucky paused momentarily and, in a rare gush of generosity, said, "You can have it if you want."

"Have what?" Markeeta quickly replied, hoping that statement meant what she thought it did.

Lucky picked up the Birkin and handed it to her. "This."

Markeeta held the ostrich, peach-colored Hermès Birkin bag and realized it was new. The price tag was $120,000.

"You'd give this to me?"

"I just did," Lucky said quickly and continued dressing.

A warm feeling enveloped Markeeta, and her heart expanded. For a moment, no matter how brief, she felt guilt for what she was doing to Lucky. She knew it wasn't for her son, not really. Nor was it because her mother spoke so distastefully about Scott throughout the years. She wondered if she was jealous of how their grandmother placed all of Scott's children on a pedestal. Maybe it was because Scott had blown up and didn't look out for her mother financially. Or was it because Lucky was the have, and she was the have-not. Markeeta couldn't definitively put her finger on it, nor did she want to. It could be a culmination of all those things or none of them. Markeeta could just be an opportunist who recognized she had to plot and scheme to get hers. But no matter how many people she fucked over, she would take her secrets of working for the DEA to the grave.

"Thanks," she replied dryly. A pang of jealousy quickly surged through her whole body that Lucky could just give away such an expensive item. Markeeta knew that she wouldn't be as altruistic if she were in Lucky's shoes.

Lucky expected a much grander response. She was about to check Markeeta's manners when one of her songs came on. It was by one of the Baby's—Lil', Da, Mo,' she wasn't sure.

I watched her twirl it slow…drop low like a thotiana…mob queen, body lean…Lucky Luciana.

Lucky sang the words to the fourth rap song her name was included in and waited patiently for Markeeta's questions to start. Lucky assumed the junior journalist would want to know how many rap songs her name was in? Did she know Baby? Was Baby Lulu's father? Something? Anything! However, no words were uttered.

Lucky knew jealousy was a muthafucka!

Layla decided to not take Scott's disrespect personally. She knew her husband loved her to his core but was acting like a fuckin' fool because he was on a paper chase. Even though Scott would never admit this, Layla also knew that the only reason he'd made it this long in the game—and vice versa—was because they were a team. Right now, her husband was in the driver's seat, and she'd be his rear and side-view mirrors. So Layla decided to behave, called Jackie…Jacqueline; said little if anything during dinners and didn't react to snide remarks.

Layla saw and made assumptions. Like she assumed Uriel liked dick up his ass; something she couldn't definitively say was true but just something she'd picked up on. Layla also believed that this globe-trotting, goddamn near billionaire drug smuggler wasn't the real deal. She couldn't verify that they were either fed or informing them, but nonetheless, it was how she felt. And she realized that telling Scott how she felt about them had gotten her nowhere. Layla wondered if she fucked Uriel would that be enough to get her husband to kill him and be done with this shit? *No,* she thought wisely. Her pussy was bomb, but it wasn't billion-dollar deal bomb.

∞

Lucky had been seeing Ragnar for some time now, she didn't want to say he was a secret, but she never mentioned him to her brothers. After a long night of what she considered good sex, she was awoken by movement early Saturday morning. Her eyes slowly pulled open, and Ragnar was moving noisily around his room, not at all mindful that she was still sleeping. Lucky stared at him for a long moment before finally asking, "Why didn't you wake me? It seems you have somewhere you need to be."

"Yeah, I was about to do just that. I need you to hurry up and get dressed so I can make my meeting."

"Hurry up?" she snapped. "If you needed me to hurry up, then you should have woken me up at a reasonable time, like when you got up!"

"Look, I'm not gonna argue with you about my schedule."

"Argue?" Lucky quipped. "I'm just assertively speaking my mind."

Naked, Lucky tossed the covers off of her lean, toned body and went to get in the shower. She took her time lathering up with the mint-scented shower gel, brushing her teeth with Tom's toothpaste, and moisturizing her skin with shea butter. Every fifteen minutes or so, she would hear a hard knock on the door by Ragnar—which she ignored. Lucky tried to understand his mood swings as she languished in the bathroom. Seemingly overnight, he had changed. Everything about who she was seemed to bug him: she spoke too loud, drank too much, dressed as he now called, *'ghetto fabulous,'* and was too hood. Lately, he made known that she wasn't good enough for him, continually criticizing everything about her.

He made quips about how for a Black female, she had no ass—yet he didn't mind smacking it. What he used to call unique—her low eye—was now a hideous sight and needed to be covered. Ragnar even suggested that during sex, she keep a shirt on to hide her unsightly stretch marks and knife wounds. He wanted her to feel uneducated, unaccomplished, unworthy, and unloved.

When Lucky finally appeared from the bathroom with a towel draped around her tiny frame, Ragnar stood at the door with a business card.

"What's this?" Lucky read the inscription of a plastic surgeon. Puzzled, she asked, "Why are you handing this to me?"

"Your eye…I noticed it when you woke up. It's lower than normal. You should go get that looked at. He's a friend…maybe a plastic surgeon can make it more symmetrical."

Immediately, Lucky felt self-conscious. Ragnar continued with, "I can't imagine how I would feel as a female being scarred for life. How did you say that happened again?"

Within a nanosecond, he had snatched all her swag. Lucky's voice was barely a whisper. "I didn't…."

Ragnar absorbed her embarrassment. It fueled him as one would a vehicle, nourishing him to go the distance. He continued with, "Oh, I think I'll ask my last question that you promised me."

"What is it?"

"I almost don't want to ask."

"Then don't!" Lucky snapped. She was still standing in her towel, her emotional pain gradually morphing into anger, sizzling below the surface. His words were like adding water to hot grease—she wanted to pop off.

Ignoring her attitude, he said, "I was at a party the other night and met a rapper named Blue Ice. He has your name in his song, so I told him I knew you, and he mentioned that when you were young, he and his friends used to fuck you in pissy staircases."

The pure rage on Lucky's face was something to savor. First, her eyes opened wide from shock as she tried to process what he'd said. And then she looked puzzled as if he couldn't possibly be talking about her. Finally, her resting bitch face settled in and got comfy. Lucky didn't say a word. She walked past Ragnar and headed to her Chanel. There she searched for her .45—only it was gone. He'd taken it last night and locked it in his hidden safe. Not because he'd predicted she'd try to kill him today. He hid her gun every night once she was asleep and would put it back before she walked out. He was a federal agent. He couldn't sleep peacefully at night with an armed thug in his bed.

She hollered, "Were you in my fuckin' bag?!"

Ragnar snorted. "I don't understand what you're asking me?"

"My fuckin' bag, bitch! My shit is missing!"

Ragnar casually looked at his watch, then exhaled. "Look, I'll disregard you calling me outside my name because I'm pressed for time. And whatever you think I stole, I'll write you a check for it. What's missing?"

Lucky glared. Her nostrils flared wide, and she'd begun to perspire. *Did she bring her gun?* She thought. *Or is it sitting on her nightstand at home?* While her mind jostled over her situation, Ragnar spoke.

"Can you hurry up?"

"You don't have to ask me twice," said Lucky as she began getting dressed, her shades immediately placed on her face.

"Apparently, I do."

"Apparently, you won't have to ask thrice." Lucky was already preparing to get Meyer to stomp Ragnar's guts out, and also, Blue Ice was a dead rap nigga.

Ragnar chuckled. "So it's over between us."

Lucky smirked. "That part!"

She quickly dressed and demanded, "I'ma need you to drop me off at the body shop on tenth."

"Why?"

"Because someone bashed out all my windows on my truck last week. I told you that!"

Lucky thought she was being driven to Mercedes when she climbed in Ragnar's SUV's passenger seat. They sat in silence as he had K-Love, a Christian radio station playing. Lucky's body was turned toward the window in a guarded, defensive manner; she had gone into protective mode and had shut down since leaving his apartment. The imaginary boundary was thick as he brooded, and she sulked. Traffic lights, bodegas, statues, and subway stations passed as Lucky felt ambivalent. She refused to capitulate to such mental manipulation, yet she felt like from the first day they were intimate, she had stepped into quicksand and was slowly losing who she was.

It wasn't the sex; Whistler was an amazing lover. It wasn't his silliness, his intellect, or his looks. The only explanation for her being in this now toxic and mentally abusive relationship was loneliness. He found her insecurities and magnified them. Ragnar gave her air, only to collapse her lungs.

The worship music was like listening to nails on a chalkboard to Lucky. She leaned in, turned down his radio, then asked, "You fuck all day out of wedlock, take a shower, and act like you've been dunked in holy water. Born again just to do it again? What religion is that?"

"You're in no position to question my piety."

"Why?" Lucky spat. "Because I smoke weed? You think you're better than me 'cause you recite some Bible verses after you fuck and get fucked up? On the weekends, you drink more than me!"

"You do a lot more than smoke marijuana."

"Like what?" she challenged. "Please, nigga, tell me what you think you know about me!"

"Don't you *ever* call me that! I don't tolerate the N-word!"

"What's your preference, huh, nigga? With your education and cheap suits, you wanna be labeled Black or African American?"

"Do I look black? Or African?" Ragnar didn't allow her to answer; his rage was palpable. "My mother is full-blooded Native American, Cherokee! And my father is German, Irish, Scottish, and Swedish. There's a tiny percentage of those black genes running through my veins. That's why I don't act like your ghetto ass!"

See, this is what happens when you fuck first, get to know a person second. Lucky wasn't down with his brand of crazy. When the car came to a rolling stop, Lucky looked up and was bewildered.

"What are we doing here?" She asked as she looked at the dreary towering building of MCC.

"I told you that I have a meeting, and you made me late," he retorted. "You're going to have to catch a taxi to your destination."

"Since when do scientists have meetings in federal jails?" Lucky challenged.

Ragnar smirked. "My meeting is in the satellite school"—he pointed past MCC and then followed up. "What do you know about Metropolitan Correctional Center?"

"Just as much as you," she said as she opened the car door. "Lose my number, bitch."

Lucky had an exhaustive morning, a challenging afternoon, and a long night. All she wanted to do was crawl into her bed and sleep peacefully. At three a.m., her alarm system blared, jolting her awake in complete darkness. Lucky scrambled to her feet, grabbing her spare 9mm from under her pillow.

Her heart hitched as she made her way through her apartment, clearing each room. No one was there, her front door was locked, no intruder had penetrated. The ringing phone was from ADT, who had gotten the alert.

"Yes, I'm fine," Lucky said. "But why does my alarm keep going off in the middle of the night, scaring the shit outta me.

This shit never happens during the day!"

"I don't know," the rep said. "But let's do a test alarm."

"We did a test alarm last night, and the night before and the night before!" Lucky snapped. "Why is this suddenly happening!"

"It could be your equipment, Miss West. I could set up an appointment to have your equipment updated."

"When?"

The agent placed Lucky on a thirty-minute hold before replying, "We could have a tech come out tomorrow, and we'd only charge for the equipment, not the service call."

"I'm not paying for shit!" Lucky screamed. Her body was still involuntarily shaking. "Not only have I been a loyal customer, but if shit is falling apart, that's not a me problem."

"Yes, of course, Miss West. We can take care of it at no charge."

Franklin watched and listened to the call in real-time as she wasn't talking to ADT. Her phone calls were routed to his network—a group of retired agents, and the agent worked for him. He was amused at Lucky's frustration. He also watched her nearly jump out of her shadow each time he set off her alarm system. Each morning Lucky would wake up exhausted from the disturbed sleep. And he also noticed that when she entered her apartment, she now checked each room to make sure no one had gained entry and triple-checked her locks. She was scared.

Franklin told her that he'd make her scream for *mercy*—he was just scratching the surface of what he was capable of.

Chapter 21

After months in Dubai, paying for million-dollar meals, Scott was on the eve of closing a deal. Uriel came to him last week and broached the subject of investing in an oil mining deal in Saudi Arabia. It was a two billion dollar deal that would net ten in thirty short months. He'd have to invest five hundred million if Scott wanted in—a sum he didn't have. Scott was on the phone day and night with Mason trying to liquidate assets, find investors to come under his umbrella, and get business loans, but the process was taking longer than the deal would wait. Uriel, noticing that Scott was having difficulty with the money, invited him to dinner.

Scott arrived alone. At this meeting, he wanted a clear mind, and his wife was a distraction. Uriel came through, suited, gold cufflinks, hard bottom shoes. Jacqueline was always at her husband's side, blonde hair slicked back with mousse, tasteful jewelry, killer body, and a mean walk.

The wait staff nearly committed a homicide, fighting to get assigned the big spender Scott West. This American was tipping damn near yearly salaries per meal. As soon as all parties were seated, drinks and meals were ordered, Uriel got down to business.

In a low voice, he began, "Issues with liquid?"

Scott nodded. "It's taking time to put that kind of paper together—"

"Time you don't have."

"I need this deal, Uriel," Scott replied, sounding unlike himself. "A few deals like this would leave my great-great-grandchildren inheritances...that generational wealth men like me don't get the opportunity to make. My great-great-grandfather Abraham set the foundation, the infrastructure, and mindset for me to want more than what my skin color dictated I deserved. I do this for him, for me, my legacy, and my successors."

In a cheery voice, Jacqueline sang, "Well, they'll be other deals, isn't that right, baby?"

Scott's jaw tightened. The snowflake, HBCU alumni, white woman marrying a Black man didn't glean a morsel of the oppression he'd just outlined. How could she? It wasn't her fight or plight. Sure, Jacqueline could sympathize, but could she empathize with how a Black person had to be four times more intelligent than their white peers to be considered just average. The struggle was real, but it was Scott's to overcome. And he planned to…he just needed time.

"He wants *this* deal, Jacqueline, and I'm going to see if I could help," Uriel said. "Scott, how much time are you talking about?"

Scott explained that he could comfortably put together two hundred and fifty million and would need to sell off some properties and get a loan for the balance.

"That could take months," Uriel concluded. "I might have to agree with my wife. This probably won't be the deal for you."

"What about your other associates," Jacqueline asked. "Couldn't Scott make the balance in a couple weeks?"

Scott watched Uriel give his wife a stern look. Then, he squeezed her hand so tightly that Scott thought her hand would break. Curious, he asked, "What other associates?"

"Nothing. Jacqueline knows better than involving strangers in certain aspects of my business. I gotta watch you around my wife, Scott. You're all she talks about lately."

Scott and Jacqueline's eyes met, and hers unequivocally said, fuck me.

"That's because he's something to talk about…."

"Well, our room is free for a few hours. As I offered before,

225

I could go and see if Layla feels about me as you do about Scott."

Scott didn't understand how all business dinners always led to swopping partners, but Layla's kitty cat wasn't up for negotiation. Scott would kill this nigga if he ever tried some freak shit with him or his. Now, if Uriel was used to whoring out his Becky wit' the good hair—more power to him, but Scott's queen was off-limits.

Scott said, "We broke bread too many times for me to be considered a stranger." He also wanted to add that he was paying for these feasts but didn't want to seem petty. He continued, "If your other associates are Cali, count me in, playah."

Uriel's face was stone. "You had me vetted?"

"You wouldn't expect less, right?"

With Scott opening the door to distribution, Uriel spoke freely about his illegal business dealings. The longer they sat at the table, the more food and drinks flowed. It didn't take long for Uriel to structure a deal. Scott would buy two tons of coke directly from Uriel's connect in the Cali cartel, flip that, and reinvest the money in the oil deal. With Scott at war with the Garcia cartel, his henchmen were in the states with no product to move, so this deal was desperately needed.

Dinner began at seven, and it was quickly approaching midnight, and the trio had no intentions of retiring back to their rooms. Even when the maître's came over to Scott with a note from Layla that read: *Bring your Black ass home,* he didn't.

The conversation between men soon dug deep into shared associates in the game. "You knew Trini from Flatbush?" Scott asked.

Uriel smirked. "Ask him how he got that buck-fifty across his face. Nigga came up short on a brick, and I opened his cranium with a Moët bottle."

Scott was too old to be asking men about their war scars, but he suspected Uriel knew that.

"He's doing life now…with, what's that niggas name," Scott

repeatedly snapped his fingers before saying, "Chauncy."

"Nah, he caught that case with Malik Brown. Them niggas doing football numbers in Ossining."

"That ain't gonna be me," Scott admonished.

"Me, either. Brothers like that had too much exposure…not learning from what the game shows us."

Scott nodded. "Malik tried it, though. I heard he had his brother, Darryl, murder Anwar Santiago, right. Anwar was a witness or something."

Uriel grinned sneakily.

"What?" Scott asked.

Uriel leaned in close, his eyes low, his voice a husky whisper. "It wasn't Darryl or that nigga, Chief. I was just a young nigga in the game, eighteen, when I took the contract. I murdered Anwar Santiago, and the feds charged and convicted his brother, Darryl."

"I think you've had enough," Jacqueline said, interrupting her husband's murder confession. She waived for the bill.

When the check arrived, it was placed in the center of the table, and no one reached. Usually, Scott would grab it, and no one objected. Tonight, as Jacqueline pulled a small mirror from her expensive purse and touched up her lipstick, Uriel looked off into space. Scott sat stone.

More uncomfortable moments would go by, yet no one reached for the check. The host came over and noticed that no credit card had been placed. He looked to Scott and then Uriel and said, "I'll give you a few more moments."

Scott nodded but still didn't reach. Scott realized that he'd need to strong-arm this nigga and said, "You got this, right?"

"What? The bill?"

Scott didn't answer his question. He stood up. "Thank you two for this lovely meal. Let's resume business tomorrow. Goodnight," and walked off.

Twelve undercover FBI agents had branched into three factions, each headed by either Randall, Devonsky, or Garrett. Four agents carrying knapsacks of essential items and vermin hidden in closed cargo boxes headed to the condominiums of Bugsy, Meyer, and Lucky West in broad daylight while the units were unoccupied. The locks were opened, and the agents gained entry with alarm codes. Franklin Garrett sat at the building's security desk in their media room and watched his men infiltrate Lucky's building. The condominiums' security was sent out on a long lunch break while the FBI handled their business. Garrett also had two field agents following Meyer and Lucky, giving them updates on their whereabouts. They had a job to do and needed to be careful.

Inside the apartment, their orders were simple. Destroy everything of value, and steal the rest. The feds didn't want the Wests to have any items they could sell for cash. They wanted to leave them penniless and destitute. And if they came upon more cash flow, the feds would take that too. The agents looked around with envious eyes, and their anger swept over them like a tidal wave. The knapsacks were opened, and numerous cans of red spray paint came out. Each man tagged every surface, wall, item of clothing, mink coats, her expensive shoe collection, the valuable paintings on the walls, the vases, chandeliers, beddings, chairs, rugs were all destroyed. They grabbed serrated knives and sliced and diced, leaving nothing salvageable. Televisions and all electronics were smashed and dosed with water. One agent opened up the refrigerator and found a dozen eggs. It wasn't a part of the original plan, but egg was difficult—if not impossible to remove. The eggs were tossed on the linen wallpaper, and you could almost instantly see the unrepairable damage.

Franklin had chosen his team wisely. They were retired agents he could trust, and among them was Eli—the best safecracker the bureau had on the east coast. Eli's orders were simple: open that motherfucking safe!

All this happened while Agent Franklin Garrett sat in the

safety of the building's security room. There wasn't any way he stepped foot in Lucky's apartment while all this went down. He wanted two words, plausible deniability.

Two final things remained. The gasoline was only to make the apartment inhabitable until it was cleared by the fire department—which they would make sure would be held up. The carpeting was soaked in the bedroom and the living and dining rooms. And finally, they opened the cargo. Inside were large, hungry sewer rats and mice. Both were needed because they reacted differently. The rats would quickly eat through all of Lucky's clothing. Rats were also stealthy. When they heard a noise, they ran away from it. However, the mice would come running toward the noise, so when Lucky came into her now vandalized apartment, she would get greeted by her new housemates.

When they were done, they left as quietly as they came. Agent Garrett erased the surveillance cameras and headed back to the office, feeling justified. Meanwhile, the same atrocities had occurred at Meyer and Bugsy's residences, with Agent Devonsky and Agent Randall overseeing those raids.

Meyer had just dropped off Lucky at her apartment and was about to head home when he pulled over to order Asian food from Philippe Chow's. He was going for takeout but had stayed.

"Fuck," Meyer said as he sat down. He had left his phone in the car and wanted to call Lollipop to see if she wanted to join him. He ordered his food and went back out to get his cell. His truck was parked a couple blocks away, and he had to admit that his first mistake was feeling safe. The gun in his back came as a complete surprise.

"Yo, what the fuck you doin'?" Meyer asked and then felt a second person behind him.

"You even attempt to move, and this nine will turn your

spine into kibbles and bits. You feel me?"

Meyer didn't recognize the voice. He sounded African American, not Black. In Meyer's book, there was a difference. The man seemed to be playin' hood, but none of that mattered because he could clearly feel the barrel pushing into his back.

"A'ight, playah. Chill," Meyer casually said as he was forced into the cut of a van and an SUV.

"Don't turn around," the same voice repeated. "And run your shit."

"*My* shit?" Meyer was stunned. He'd never been on the receiving end of a robbery. "Nah, playah, you gon' have to kill me nigga!"

The butt of the gun smashed into the back of his head, and Meyer spun around. He saw two African American men, wool ski masks covering their brown skin, their eyes wide and fearful. Meyer hit the brolic one with a two-piece—an uppercut to his chin and a solid fist to his gut. Meyer pivoted and smashed the second assailant with a hard right. His arm extended and snapped back quickly. Meyer was moving fast with two and three-piece combinations, ducking and weaving like a professional pugilist.

Soon the gunmen began fighting back. They jumped Meyer and landed numerous blows before Meyer reached. His left hand fingered the handle of Larry's .45, and with muscle memory, he pulled the trigger and fired.

Bak! Bak! Bak!

Meyer heard, "He's got a gunnn!"—as the goons took flight. Meyer gave chase, on their heels, firing.

Bak! Bak! Bak! Bak!—he emptied the clip and hadn't hit near one. Out of ammunition, Meyer tucked his pistol and halted his sprint. He knew the henchmen were armed, and they knew he was out of bullets. Both men circled back and quickly caught up to Meyer, who expected to be murdered. Meyer was quickly taken down as he was jumped and partially dazed from the pistol-whipping he received. On the ground, he was robbed of all of

Larry's jewelry.

Meyer sat on the side of the curb with his throbbing head in his hand, leaking blood.

When he got into his vehicle, Meyer saw he had missed several calls from Lucky. Just seeing fifteen missed calls had him even more aggravated. He thought about ignoring her when he began reading her text.

He called. "Who vandalized ya shit?"

Lucky was hollering and wailing so loud that he had to remove the phone from his pounding head, place her on speaker, and lower the sound. He was already heading toward her and allowed her to keep crying until she got it together. Finally, she said, "It was Angel. It had to be him. Everything is destroyed, Meyer. Everything," she sobbed.

"It can't be that bad."

"It is," she wailed. "Animal control and the fire department are on their way because that rat-faced Angel infested my place with rats."

"Rats," he repeated. "You can't be serious."

"Just get here!"

Whistler finally got movement on a member of the West clan. It wasn't who he wanted, or was it? He'd watched Meyer drop off his sister, and shortly after that, all hell broke loose. When NYPD, NYFD, and a couple wildlife vans lit up the scene, he knew it was for Lucky West; melodrama always followed this family.

His eyes darted quickly, trying to ascertain what the fuck was going on. Patiently he waited for the coroner's van to arrive because this had to be a hit, but none came, nor did an ambulance.

Whistler tried getting answers from the building's concierge, and neighbors, but no one would respond once they took a look at his grotesque face. Uppity bitches and elite men looked at him as if he were shit under their Gucci loafers.

The suspense was killing him. The commotion had heightened his animal instincts drawing him to the action. Whistler knew there was a nexus between the flashing lights and the queenpin. It was easy enough for him to slide into an open NYFD truck and suit up. He walked out dressed head to toe in the heavy uniform and made his way up to the drama without any obstruction. Within minutes he was one of many standing, huddled around a hysterical Lucky West, and she was none the wiser that Whistler Hussain, a man she once loved, a man she once fucked, a man she tried to murder, a man that had her on his hit list was inches away.

Whistler walked around and didn't fully understand what he was seeing. He didn't know what this was, but he knew what it wasn't. This wasn't a failed hit, nor a home invasion gone wrong. He couldn't figure out what was the fuckin' purpose? Who does this petty shit? And being the street nigga that he was, instantly knew: feds.

Killers kill, robbers rob. Ain't no goons successfully getting inside the secure building of someone they know is moving tons of ki's a month to wreck shit. Niggas in the game are starving, always looking for a come-up. Whistler also knew that agents Randall and Devonsky were shady as fuck. They purposely dropped him in Wilmington, Delaware, a stone's throw from New York, where he had just testified against one of the most powerful couples in the drug game. But more importantly, where he went to war with Deuce and his crew.

They assumed Whistler wouldn't last six months, but he did. He would breathe just long enough to get retribution and then some.

∞

Scott didn't go directly back to his suite after leaving the St. James's. He ended up at a cigar bar until the sun came up. And when he did enter his suite, he sat in the living room thinking. He'd been up for 24 hours and had come to a definitive decision. Scott called Mason and put him on a new assignment.

At eight o'clock, he awoke Layla.

"Get dressed. We're leaving."

"Abu Dhabi?"

"Nah…the states. We got unfinished business to take care of."

Layla didn't ask any questions as she showered and dressed. There wasn't any idle chitchat as the concierge and butlers packed up their rooms. She didn't comment on her husband's brooding manner. All that mattered was that they get the fuck out of Dubai.

As they strolled through the hotel's massive lobby, a small commotion broke out. Scott and Layla watched as support staff began running toward the elevators, and the sound of first responders could be heard in the distance. Scott gave no fucks, but Layla asked a looky-loo.

"What's going on?"

A wealthy woman replied, "They think it's a suicide or overdose…something dreadfully awful." The woman's eyes scanned the chaos. "Just dreadfully awful!"

Scott chartered a private plane for their long trip home. Layla sat in her plush chair and reclined as a half dozen Louis Vuitton and Gucci suitcases were loaded into the lower cargo deck. Scott had hired armed security to escort them to the airport hanger and sweep the plane for listening devices. She knew her husband well and felt that as soon as he was ready to open up, he'd disclose what was important enough to cut their vacation short—not that she was complaining.

A smooth takeoff and a three-finger glass of cognac later, Scott said, "I don't trust 'em."

"Who?" Layla replied fucking with him. She knew damn well

who he was referring to. Shit, she'd been hollering she didn't trust them for weeks.

"The St. James's," he replied. "We had a meeting last night that I thought went well—"

"A meet that I wasn't invited to!" Layla scowled and rolled her eyes to show her discontent. She said, "Go on."

"Uriel offered me a chance to go in on a ten billion dollar oil deal."

Oh, shit. Layla thought perhaps she'd fucked up but didn't mumble a word. She watched as Scott took a sip of his expensive drink before continuing.

"I'd need to put up five hundred million, and I couldn't get my hands on that much liquidity, so Uriel offered his connect in the Cali cartel so that I could do a side deal."

"And?" Layla feigned ignorance. "Isn't that what you wanted since day one…the Cali connect and to join the Billionaire Boys Club?"

Scott nodded. "As we kicked it, we began chopping it up again about niggas we both knew in the game, and I realized that anyone that could vouch for him, that had actually laid eyes on the nigga was dead."

This is what got Scott to run them out of Dubai on the first thing smoking like they stole something? Layla was utterly confused.

"So?"

Scott blew out air which annoyed Layla—just a lil' something because he was taking too long to get to the point.

"So as the night went on, I mentioned the highly publicized murder of Anwar Santiago."

"Scott, that murder reverberated through every hood from Crown Heights to Compton—that nigga was a legend."

"What did you hear?"

Layla sat forward. "I heard that the feds had flipped Anwar, and he was scheduled to testify against Malik Brown and that

Malik's brother, Darryl, murdered Anwar before he could get on the stand against Malik."

Scott nodded. "What else did you hear?"

"Only that Darryl swore his ass was innocent, and someone else did the hit. And none of that mattered because Darryl got life without parole."

"And who was that someone else the streets said actually murdered Anwar for Malik?"

"Chief from Brownsville, one of Malik's enforcers."

"And Chief and Darryl are both what?"

"Dead," Layla said. "Scott, don't get me wrong. I didn't like them from jump. The whole situation felt too contrived. However, you disrespected me for that Jackie bitch, ignored me when I said I didn't trust them, and continued to drop millions kissing their asses, and this is what got you to see the light? Uriel taking credit for a murder that happened…what… twenty-five years ago?"

"It was thirty-one years."

"Scott, you were just as young as me when all this happened. You can't say it was or wasn't Darryl, Chief, or Uriel who pulled the trigger."

"I can because it was me."

This was news to Layla. She thought she knew all her husband's secrets but apparently not.

"You did the hit for Malik?"

Scott's head shook. "Nah, it was on the humble. I was a lil' nigga trying to come up. I saw a man with flashy jewels and swollen pockets, shoved my .45 in his gut, and told him to run his shit."

"And that was Anwar Santiago?"

"It was," Scott affirmed. "He must have sensed that I was young—I was only fourteen—and tried to test me. Before I knew it, I'd squeezed back the hammer and emptied the clip. His body drank in all seven shots before I took flight. I had no idea who I'd murdered until the streets spoke. He was my first body."

"And no one else knew this…you told no one…not even that Maxine bitch?"

"I didn't mumble a fuckin' word until now. I wouldn't have lasted long if I bragged that I murdered Anwar; a dusty young nigga like me would have taken a dirt nap within the first 48."

Layla knew that was a fact. Even at that early age, her husband wasn't anybody's fool. Scott knew the game and had played it well. Scott continued, "The first case I caught was three years later—"

"The case your sister testified against you, right?"

Scott nodded. "So you see why Uriel would have felt comfortable taking credit for this murder because I wasn't on paper yet. If he's a fed, they don't got me getting in the game until three years after Anwar's demise."

"You think they fed?"

"Absolutely."

"Good! Because I do too! So now what?"

"Fuck 'em," Scott rebuked. "They ain't got shit, wiretap or otherwise. All they got is me discussing a potential deal wit' Cali."

"What about Byron Bay?"

"What about it?" Scott said coolly. "They don't got shit unless we talk…if they had a morsel of evidence on the murdered sicarios Agent Randall and that Devonsky dick would have met us in Dubai when we landed."

"Not to sound like a stupid bitch, but if the feds are on us, why are we heading back to the states."

"They're on us but don't got shit *on* us, and I wanna keep it that way. And to make sure niggas ain't flipping, we need to go back and make our presence felt and make amends wit' our kids. Our first stop is bailing Bugsy out of jail. Once the feds get notified we've left, they'll know Uriel and Jacqueline's covers are blown, they'll pivot."

Chapter 22

Bugsy had been in lock-up long enough, translation—Emmanuel Vega had to die. He now had a feel for who he could trust, and it wasn't Kenneth Collins, the inmates, or most of the guards. After a failed attempt on Bugsy's life in the shower and casualties on both sides—Blacks against Latinos was just warming up.

Kenneth Collins tried to hand Bugsy a filed-down toothbrush for protection; Bugsy refused. CO Mahan came to him with an icepick—Bugsy wouldn't touch it. Someone was in his ear daily about murdering Vega, and Bugsy kept the same spiel.

"I ain't murder a man in my life, and I won't start today. I'm innocent…wrongfully incarcerated."

When the alarm was sounded throughout the jail at a little past four in the morning, and the inmates had to remain in lockdown for most of the day, everyone assumed that either Bugsy West or Emmanuel Vega was dead. And they were right.

Vega's body was found hanging from a utility pole behind the food pantry in the kitchen. His death was ruled a suicide; Bugsy West's hands were clean.

For days everyone was stunned. Suicide? Never. How could Bugsy have pulled it off? Did the kingpin pay a Judas inside the Juarez cartel to kill their amigo? Did Angel Morales order the hit? Who was close enough to Vega to execute his murder?

Meyer arrived at an unbelievable scene. Two fire trucks, several blue and whites, and a wildlife van were still parked out front. He also saw that the building tenants were being evacuated. Police were regulating the location and weren't allowing anyone in.

Meyer said, "It's my apartment that's been vandalized. I live in suite P3951."

The doorman knew he didn't live there, but he was family, so he nodded, and Meyer was allowed through. He could smell gasoline when he stepped off the elevator. When he opened the door to Lucky's apartment, his jaw dropped. Wildlife had collected over two dozen sewer rats in wired cages through humane means. The mice weren't so lucky. There were too many, so traps were laid with bait, and already several were sliced in half. The firemen cut up the gasoline-soaked carpeting and bagged the pieces for trash removal. Meyer's eyes swept through his sister's place, and he was stunned silent. Red graffiti was scribbled over every surface, every wall, every painting.

Meyer went looking for Lucky and found her inside her bedroom. She was standing in front of a pile of clothing, crying hysterically. Everything was ruined. When she saw her brother, she ran and embraced him.

"I can't take much more," she admitted. "It's too much." For the first time in a long time, Lucky wanted her parents. They would fix this. They would help make this right.

"And they stole my Chopard watch!" she wailed some more.

"This right here is from the mind of a madman," Meyer deduced. "Angel is on some other shit."

"You think that's foul? Someone left a huge pile of shit in my toilet!" Lucky explained. "Shit! Who does that except a barbarian?!"

"Don't worry 'bout this," Meyer began. "I'ma—"

Lucky pulled away. "I don't want to hear it anymore! I already told you how I feel about the matter; only bring up his name when it's in the past tense!"

"Ms. West," a voice called from the living room. Lucky and Meyer walked out to see two uniformed police officers, the building's security team, and Bradley, the head of the building's Board of Directors.

"What happened to your head?" one officer asked Meyer, which he ignored.

"How could this happen!" Lucky yelled, barreling toward the head of security. "All the money I pay to live here! I could have been killed!"

"We don't know, Ms. West. We're checking the surveillance videos now."

"Somebody gonna have to pay for all this shit," Meyer threatened.

"Her homeowner's insurance," Bradley replied curtly, distancing the building from liability.

Lucky bolted from the living room with Meyer right on her heels as if she had been struck by lightning. She ran into her closet, ripped the ruined Monet off the wall, and carefully twisted the dial on her safe. And to her horror, it had been emptied.

"This can't be happening!" she wailed, her voice a loud screech that alerted authorities who came charging in. "Somebody's gonna fuckin' die!"

Meyer was concerned. "What the fuck they took?"

"My fuckin' five million dollars, that's what!"

"Your what?" Meyer repeated.

Lucky couldn't concern herself with the optics right now, she was robbed without a gun, and someone needed to pay.

The police chief stared into the empty safe and said, "Am I to understand you had five million dollars in that safe of yours?"

"I just said I did!" she hollered. "Y'all better do your fuckin' job and find out how someone could get in here undetected and do all this to me."

"Lower your voice," Captain Rourke said. He was fully aware of who Lucky West was and all the allegations of drug distribution. He'd already placed a call to the FBI and expected them to show up soon to take over this investigation. This had to be drug-related. "We'll need you to come down to the station and make a police report to list all stolen items."

"I'm listing them now!" Lucky continued to holler. "Take notes!" As she and Captain Rourke bickered, Meyer coolly interrupted.

"Pardon me, sir. But I need to speak with my sister for a moment. I'll give her back once I'm done."

Captain Rourke was already done. He and his men were all scratching their heads at this mind fuck of a crime scene. When he called the feds, he was put in touch with Special Agent Randall, who unequivocally told Rourke to instruct his men to sit on their hands, which meant don't lift a finger trying to solve this. Basically, no dusting for prints, no interviewing tenants, no bagging trace evidence.

They left the siblings alone and continued to stand around, biding their time to close this case.

Meyer said, "You had five milli and didn't bail Bugsy out?"

"Please, Meyer. Like you don't have an emergency fund should things go south. You know the game just as well as me."

"The fact that you would even question if I had money and didn't bail him out shows who you really are!" Meyer's hand wrapped tightly around Lucky's neck, and he squeezed. He moved so close to her face that spit felt like a weapon as it slapped her when he spoke. "You's a stupid, selfish bitch. I should break you in half right now!"

"I'm the bad guy?" she retorted, defending her actions. "I didn't see you running to sell your jewelry for his bail. Jewelry, you swore you had already sold, yet weeks later you came through wit' that drip, you fuckin' hypocrite. Sell my shit but keep yours!"

"That wasn't my drip!" he explained. "I robbed dude on the humble—"

"And?" Lucky spat. "It don't matter where you got it; it looked like bail money to me."

Meyer was speechless. Lucky should have been a lawyer; she

240

sure knew how to get out of shit.

It took hours for absolutely nothing to get resolved. There wasn't any footage, no one saw shit, no one would be arrested. When Agents Randall and Devonsky showed up, the siblings knew it was time to go.

Randall and Devonsky had huge grins on their faces as they looked around at the destruction. As the siblings left, Randall lied and said, "Oh, and Lucky…your daughter's dead. Just in case you were wondering."

"Then I guess someone has a murder to solve."

Lucky had the clothes only on her back as she rode to Meyer's in silence. Neither mentioned Lulu's fate, as it was what they both expected. When they got to his front door, they both smelled gasoline. Meyer looked at his sister and then opened his door to be met with the same fate.

Just before midnight, the investigation at Meyer's building was closed. He and his sister were now exhausted as they headed over to Bugsy's apartment. They wanted to shower, eat, and sleep after these recent events. They smelled the gasoline at Bugsy's door and didn't even go in. They were mentally weary and wouldn't hold up again to hours of questions and scrutiny.

The private plane landed at Teterboro airport in New Jersey, and Scott and Layla were back on American soil. The couple was well-rested and ready to put their affairs in order. Scott could see Mason parked off in the distance, the Range idling until his boss disembarked. The dim lights were switched to full overhead lighting as the passengers' and flight attendants' eyes adjusted. The quiet of the moment was interrupted as the familiar sound of sirens blared.

Scott and Layla both peered out the window, and it looked

like a movie set. Two dozen vehicles, SUVs, town cars, and NYPD pulled up, surrounding the aircraft.

Scott gritted his teeth, rethinking his earlier comment. "Maybe we fucked up in Byron Bay after all."

"You think that's what this is about?" Layla asked, a million thoughts tumbling around in her head.

Scott shrugged. "What else?"

Soon the familiar faces of agents Randall and Devonsky led the team. Flight jackets and gold badges bum rushed the jet, and Scott and Layla were promptly detained.

"Scott and Layla West, you both are under arrest for the murders of federal agents Laurence Warren and Gwyneth Sullivan—"

"Who?" Scott interrupted his Miranda Rights speech.

He was ignored.

"You have the right to remain silent…."

The Soho hotel would be their sanctuary. They rolled up to the front desk receptionist and asked to book two suites.

"Your card has declined, sir. Do you want me to rerun it?"

Meyer smirked. "Declined?"

"Yes, sir. Do you want me to rerun it, or do you have another card?"

"Run it again," Meyer demanded, and she did.

The receptionist gave a sympathetic look and asked what he wanted her to do? Meyer reached into his wallet and pulled out his American Express Centurion Card. He smacked the card down. "This doesn't have a limit."

Lucky and Meyer ran through each card, and all were declined. Embarrassed, they had to leave the hotel and get inside his SUV. "Something ain't right," Meyer said. "This shit ain't a coincidence."

Lucky lit up a Newport and inhaled deeply. Her nerves were

shot. She exhaled a couple of rings before passing the cancer stick to her brother. "How all our cards are declined. Have you been spending lately?"

"Me? Nah, no more than usual."

"Do you know if the minimums were met on the cards?"

"We could call, but I'm sure they were," Meyer said. "And that Discover card was clean. I never used it, so how the fuck did it decline?"

"Well, then it's the feds. From sending Bugsy to MCC, harassing you, and now all of this. We're fucked, Meyer."

"Nah, not yet. We'll figure something out." Meyer pulled out his phone and said to his sister, "I'ma call Lollipop and see if we could crash there for a few."

Both siblings sat in Meyer's SUV, hoping for a return call from Lollipop, but none came.

Meyer and Lucky fell asleep on a random block in the back seat of his car. They woke up a few hours later with stiff necks and tart breath. The air inside the vehicle was strangling them. The sun was high in the sky, and the city streets were busy. Meyer had forty dollars in his pocket, while Lucky was broke.

Meyer looked at his gas tank, and he was nearing empty. They needed to stretch their legs, so they walked to a local café and got breakfast sandwiches and coffee.

Lucky asked, "What are we gonna do?"

Meyer exhaled. His younger sister was looking to him for guidance, and he had none. Meyer didn't know where to begin to fix this shit. It was like the feds had pulled a thread on a garment, and their lives were unraveling at record speed. When Meyer didn't answer, Lucky did for him.

"You think we should go see Bugsy?"

He nodded his head in agreement.

New York law says a person can be legally detained for 24 hours before being arraigned or released. Agent Randall didn't take the couple to the Federal Building because he knew that's precisely where Scott's high-priced legal team would look for them. Instead, he had them held in the Midtown Precinct South so he could thoroughly, without interruption, look for evidence against them.

Scott and Layla were fingerprinted, photographed, and placed in separate cells. No one—not the local PD or the feds questioned the couple, Randall's orders. He knew it would be fruitless. Both would lawyer up, demand a phone call, and make threats about impending lawsuits for harassment.

Seventeen hours in, and they still had nothing. A gaggle of agents poured over every bit of surveillance footage they had and couldn't place Scott nor Layla anywhere close to the agents' room. The videos had Scott leaving dinner and exiting the property, and next, he showed up on video at a cigar bar until ultimately returning to his room.

They also had a video of Layla inside her suite all night, constantly calling the restaurant wanting her husband to come home. She was angered, but she was always angry. Nothing seemed out of the ordinary.

Randall was stunned but more so confused. No less than ten agents with a combined two hundred years of knowledge had formulated this takedown. Yet, a street thug with limited education had managed to murder two of their best field agents seemingly without a morsel of trace evidence? Who was this guy? And the fact they thought that they finally had Scott, had walked him into a shady deal that would take away his freedom for no less than life—only to have that implode was sobering.

Agent Warren, aka Understanding aka Uriel St. James, got Scott to want to do business with a new connect—the Cali cartel. They figured within six months, Scott and Layla would go down, once and for good.

Laurence and Gwyneth's bodies were flown back to the

states, and one of the top coroners on the east coast did autopsies and said it appeared they had been poisoned. It would take time for the toxicology reports to come back, but he was almost certain.

Poisoned? The bureau wondered how that could have happened. They weren't some crackerjack organization. The chefs were all vetted, and most of the wait staff assigned to Laurence and Gwyneth were agents. Reviewing the tapes, they saw that Scott drank the same champagne as Laurence and Gwyneth, so how did he pull this off?

If they didn't find something soon, they'd have to kick them loose.

Kimberly was at her desk reading over police reports from the horrors that had taken place at Meyer and Lucky West's condominiums. When she was brought in on the investigation, she thought it wise to reach out to the Captain of each precinct near all sibling's residences and gave strict orders that they contact her for any reason—no matter how insignificant.

As she read through the reports, she knew her department was responsible; more specifically, her team. This foolishness was exactly what Franklin had hinted at in the meeting. And the fact that she was left out of this execution didn't sit well with her. They viewed her as an outsider. Of course, she would have objected to these tactics. It was illegal and not what she had learned in the academy. She was better than this; she thought her superiors, Agent Randall and Devonsky, were better than this.

Her mouth hung open as she read about the destruction of priceless paintings, the infestations, and most jarring the theft of five million dollars. What was more disturbing were the pictures. The police reports couldn't do justice to the photographs taken.

Kimberly's mouth shut when Franklin approached her desk. His appearance had recently done a one-eighty since taking this case. He wore tailored suits, Red Bottom Shoes, and an exquisite pair of pink diamond earrings in his newly pierced ears. Kimberly had seen pictures of Scott and Bugsy West, and Franklin was jockeying to be a contender in their world.

He said, "Agent Randall asked me to come and speak with you."

"Why doesn't he speak with me himself?"

"Because he asked me," he snapped. "And he's busy investigating the murders of Warren and Sullivan."

Kimberly was in utter shock. She repeated, "Murders?"

"That's what I said." Franklin leaned against her desk and folded his arms. He was thinking, *I knew the danger...I should have never blocked Kimberly from the assignment. It should have been her instead of Gwyn.* While she was thinking, *Laurence was a good man...it should have been Franklin in his place.*

"When did this happen? Why didn't anyone tell me?"

"I'm telling you now."

"Don't be glib, Franklin. I'm a part of this team and should be in on all aspects of the investigation."

"Oh, and about that. You're actually not on the team, effective immediately."

Kimberly didn't know why she was shocked, but she was. The backbiting, glass ceiling, and discrimination ran rampant in all fields. Hers was no different. The look of pure disbelief on her face tickled Franklin. He knew he had just fucked up her world and took considerable pride in doing so. She wanted to return the favor.

"That decision wouldn't have anything to do with this, would it?" She said, tossing a stack of photos his way. He didn't have to examine the pictures because he was there—up close and personal—to take everything Lucky had. He told Lucky that he would make her scream out for *mercy,* and she laughed in his face.

He said, "Two words. Plausible deniability."

"You think this is a joke," Kimberly snapped, irked at his arrogance. "These are crimes, Franklin. And I have enough evidence to report—"

"Go ahead and see how far you get." He stared directly into her eyes so there would be no ambiguity. "I told you once…don't fuck with me. You can't imagine what I'm capable of."

Kimberly was unrattled. She knew what she could do with her Glock and refused to be intimidated by this misogynist.

"How do you casually threaten me, do this to that young woman, and report to church each week?"

"I'm an enigma."

"You're a hypocrite."

Franklin chuckled. "We all have our own contradictions."

"Have you ever seen the movie, Malice?" she asked.

Franklin didn't know where this was going, but he'd bite. "The God complex, right? With sexy Nicole Kidman and Alec Baldwin?"

She nodded. "Good movie. But there was one scene, in particular, that was why I got into law enforcement. It's the scene where they both realize that they'd fucked up. And Alec's character says he got a letter from her husband. Nicole said, *'What did he say?'* And Alec corrected her and said, *'He didn't say…it was a letter; he wrote!'*"

Franklin shrugged. "What am I missing?"

"Alec was a surgeon who thought he was better than Nicole because of her background. Her mother was an alcoholic, absent father, Nicole was a hustler. Alec spoke down to her every chance he got. But at the end of the day, she didn't rise to his level; he sank to hers. He was just as much a criminal—medical degree and all; the only thing is that at least Nicole had an excuse. I got into law enforcement not for the corner boys but for the white supremacist who wears a badge, corrupt politicians, and Ponzi scheme billionaires. Those who think they can commit crimes with impunity because they're educated, in law enforcement, or are wealthy."

"Get to the point."

"Here it is," she replied coolly. "I grew up in a household that said, *What did he say?* And I have great disdain for the; *He didn't say...it was a letter; he wrote* criminals. At the end of that movie, Alec goes down. And so shall you."

Chapter 23

The shit had hit the fan. And Meyer and Lucky were feeling boxed in, more caged than if they were incarcerated alongside their brother. The siblings sat at a visiting table, waiting for Bugsy to come through. The visiting room was crowded. Inmates in orange jumpsuits all conversed with loved ones. Bugsy came walking out, his head held high as he searched for his family. When his eyes landed on Meyer and Lucky, he smiled.

Bugsy looked good. His hairline had been touched up, his sides faded, and his mustache and beard were tapered. He was looking grown man sexy, rugged, with a swag he had earned. Meyer stood and gave his brother dap, and then Lucky stood up, and they had a warm embrace. Her soft lips kissed him on his cheek. Immediately he noticed something wasn't right. Bugsy sat down and folded his hands in front of him. His siblings looked a little worn, and Meyer was injured.

"How you holdin' up?" Meyer asked.

"I'm good," Bugsy answered. "I told y'all not to worry about me. I got this."

Meyer nodded.

"So what's up…how are things out there. You two keeping your hands clean?" Bugsy looked at his brother's bruised face. "I see you still not controlling your temper."

Lucky couldn't hold her emotions any longer. Plump tears slid down her cheeks, which startled Bugsy. He reached across the table and grabbed her hands into his firm grip.

"You won't believe what's happened," she began. Lucky explained the vandalism, rats, gasoline, declined credit cards, and how both their apartments were hit. It was all very traumatizing. She expected her brother to be equally angry, shocked, appalled, but Bugsy was different.

Calmly he said, "Let's assume they hit my apartment too."

Meyer asked, "Who, though? Cartel? Feds? Ma and Pops?"

"Feds." Bugsy's answer was definitive. "This the type of petty shit they'd do. They're jealous, frustrated...they're trying to keep us distracted while they build a case. Incidents like this are meant to force our hands, get careless, reckless. Don't give them what they want."

"Why you lookin' at me!" Meyer wanted to know.

"Because I know my twin. What's on your mind. Talk to me."

Meyer lowered his voice. "We need money, Bee. We need to make your bail. You need to be out here helping us handle all this shit."

"When I go back to court, the judge should lower my bail, maybe cut it down in half, make it more reasonable."

Meyer smirked. "That ain't gonna happen. You just said that the feds are behind all this. They ain't lowering shit. You know how this goes...they got the judge in their pockets. They ain't playing fair so fuck 'em."

Bugsy nodded.

Meyer continued, "Listen, there's this new connect from Los Pepes—"

Lucky wiped her face and asked, "Colombians?"

Meyer nodded. "If the introduction is made, then I'll ask for a few bricks on consignment. I know that's asking for a handout, but we don't got no seed money. I flip that shit and get us back on our feet. I tried contacting our Kiqué Helguero connect, but all lines of communication were shut down."

"Who's making the intro?"

"Larry."

Bugsy's jaw tightened. There wasn't any way that Unlucky

Larry could be affiliated with that caliber of cartel. It was a setup. But Bugsy knew his brother. He couldn't order him to stand down. Meyer would feel marginalized and would do the opposite. He had to make Meyer feel as though it was his choice.

"Larry's doing big things, huh?"

"Dude riding 'round with that drip, pushing a McLaren, he's got some paper."

Only fools in the drug game would push a McLaren. And although that's precisely what Larry was, it just didn't feel authentic. The car was showy, gaudy, and not something men bought to cruise the city streets of New York. The Hamptons, Los Angeles, Miami—but not Manhattan and certainly not Harlem. Bugsy looked at Lucky. "You heard the streets whispering about his come up?"

Her head shook. "This is news to me. Shit, I'm shocked."

"What about you, Meyer. Any affiliates' been noting his rise *before* I got knocked?"

"Why you askin' that?" Meyer's eyes looked wild. "You think he's a snitch?"

Bugsy asked, "What do you think?"

Meyer's judgment was biased. The realization they were broke and now destitute had him wanting to take his chances. He needed to get back on his feet, and Los Pepes was a good look. They needed a team, new soldiers, a first and second in command to keep the crew in line. But Larry blowing up seemingly overnight didn't sit well with him either, yet niggas did it all the time. They do the right home invasion, commit a profitable jux, pull off a few smash and grabs, and you got a baller.

Meyer finally responded. "It could go either way…Larry better hope it doesn't go left."

"You think I should ask around in here, see what they know about his rise to the top."

"A'ight, do that. I'ma keep that nigga on the backburner, keep stalling." Meyer liked how Bugsy asked for his permission and guidance.

Lucky asked, "What have you discussed with him so far, Meyer. Think. Did you tell him anything that could be used against you? Or us? Did he have you talking about murders?"

"Nah, nothing. Truthfully, I pushed for the Los Pepes intro...had to knock the nigga's fronts out to get him to agree to set up a meet."

"Damn, Meyer," Lucky said. "You always use your hands as full sentences."

This news made Bugsy relax a little. But he still knew it was better to *never* trust and *always* verify in his line of work.

Meyer spoke again. "One thing ain't sitting too well wit' me, though. When I smashed that nigga in his face, I took his burner. And when niggas ran up on me yesterday telling me to run my shit. I pull out and just start bussing!"—Meyer simulated firing a weapon with his left hand, and then said, "Ain't hit near one."

Bugsy said, "And you don't miss."

"Exactly," Meyer affirmed. "It's like I was shooting wit' blanks."

Lucky's nose crinkled. "You sure?"

"Nah," Meyer admitted. "Not really...."

Bugsy pushed for more information. "What's up with Gino?"

Meyer gritted his teeth. He had dropped off the cars weeks ago, but they still remained on the lot unsold. "He said he ain't gettin' no movement. Niggas are broke, or they want to lease cars now."

Bugsy couldn't believe that not one car had sold, especially now that it was spring. Niggas were ready to floss. "Call him and tell him to lower the prices." That was their only choice. With the condos vandalized and their art and antiques destroyed, they needed a Hail Mary. He still had more direction to give his siblings. "I will need either one of you to go to the office and get the insurance information."

Lucky said, "I'll do it." She needed money, and whatever she could do to expedite the process, she would.

"Good. Download a claims form for each and mail it to me. I'll fill them out and mail them back to the office for you to send off. You'll need pictures of the damage and the police and fire department reports. Lucky, this is tedious but needed. Can you handle it?"

She understood. Lucky was far from a dummy. She said, "I don't need to mail you the paperwork to fill out. I can get the claims started."

Both Bugsy and Meyer were impressed.

Bugsy said, "That's good because, for a moment, I thought I had to mansplain the process." He joked.

Lucky continued, "I want to handle getting a couple of properties sold and the HELOC loans. Meyer told me that you would handle that when you came home. I'm sorry big bro, but I can't wait. I need money now."

Bugsy agreed.

"So while you're doin' all that, what I'm supposed to do?"

Bugsy and Lucky said simultaneously, "Stay out of trouble!"

They all laughed, and then Bugsy said, "Shit went down in here last week that concerns you, Lucky."

Her eyes widened. "What?"

"Emmanuel Vega was murdered, feds calling it a suicide."

Meyer asked, "That's your handiwork?"

"It was supposed to be but wasn't. Shit strange," Bugsy admitted. "I was days away from executing the hit, and the nigga is found dangling from a bedsheet? It don't add up. I've gone over this a million times. No one had a reason for wanting him dead but me. Juarez wouldn't kill him before he got at me, which rules them out. And the feds wouldn't murder him until they got the conviction against him. So who then?"

Meyer and Lucky shrugged. If Bugsy couldn't figure it out, they wouldn't be able to.

"Speaking of strange, our cousin Markeeta came to see me in the hospital. She was all bragging about her new job and new money and how she's moved into Regency Heights."

"Markeeta?" Meyer repeated.

Bugsy's nostrils flared wide as he gritted his teeth. "What'd she want?"

"Information on Avery's murder. And much more."

"Avery?" Meyer whispered. "Why?"

"She's a snitch," Lucky surmised. It wasn't until the words fell from her mouth that she believed them. "She's definitely working wit' the feds."

"You can't be serious talkin' that dumb shit," Meyer said. "She can't be a West and have snitch in her blood."

Bugsy was quiet and then said, "Why not? We can't ever trust anyone at our level because people have agendas. You gotta believe she's no different."

"So what she came through. We all grown now. She probably just wanna see her family," Meyer added. "That don't mean she's an informant."

"She is, though," Lucky affirmed.

"Then why you fucking wit' her?" Meyer snapped.

"To keep our enemies close. Scott taught us that."

"But you're not Scott."

"Neither are you, bitch!" Lucky retorted to Meyer.

"This is dangerous. You could slip up, give her something to use against us," Bugsy deduced.

"I'll give her something to keep them engaged, just enough to keep her on their payroll."

"Wait, what?" *This was insane,* Meyer thought.

Bugsy answered for her. "The devil you know can be handled. They'll be a pattern. Look out for it. She'll use that y'all are family as a weapon and will know things she shouldn't know because they'll have briefed her."

"I wasn't planning on doing too much talking, Bugsy."

"You'll have to, or they'll suspect that you know and send someone we won't see coming, and that person can jam us up. Scott always said that a lie will show you the truth."

"I never understood what that meant," Meyer said honestly.

"It means you say a lie, and the person that brings you the truth is the enemy or working *with* the enemy," Lucky explained. "Let *that* sink in."

Meyer thought. "That shit is genius. Scott is muthafuckin' brilliant!"

Bugsy chuckled. Reminiscing about his father didn't hurt as much as he thought. He explained, "I think he got that from The Godfather. Vito tells his son Michael that whoever comes to him about the Luca Barzini meeting guaranteeing his safety is the traitor. It's the same concept."

"Scott always schooled us to never trust anyone who shows up from your past when you're in this life. It ain't random it's orchestrated."

Lucky also told them about the Instagram handle, and that information made Bugsy lose his calm exterior.

"I'ma kill that bitch when I get out," he threatened. "Feds puttin' our lives on blast, using a snitch to call our parents snitches! The wrong person sees that shit, and all our lives are in danger…niggas start thinking we hot they'll want to lullaby any one of us."

"We all need to stay on point. If feds sent Markeeta after me, they're digging in the crates. Don't be surprised if muthafuckas start coming out of the woodworks talking 'bout remember me. Your third-grade teacher, a fourth cousin twice removed, even the cute chick wit' the phat ass, Meyer…they all will want to be attached to this case."

"What case?"

Lucky rolled her eyes. Sometimes Meyer could be dense. "The case they're trying to build, dumb ass!"

∞

A dream team of highly paid lawyers entered the Midtown Precinct South, and within seconds you could hear a pin drop. All movement halted as cops—of all ranks—gawked at the spectacle. The attorneys came nine deep; tailored suits, satchels, and smug looks. These ivy leaguers had no time to waste and would not be disrespected. Their mere presence demanded their asses be kissed, and their clients were released. Not now—but *right now*, as we say in the hood.

Christopher Azul and Liam Gavalas were both high-profile celebrity lawyers known for getting their clients acquitted for anything from child molestation to murder—they were that good. Gavalas had taken the red-eye flight straight from Los Angeles to represent Scott and Layla and wanted to spend as little time in this filthy precinct and loud city as needed.

Gavalas spoke, his voice dripping with a mixture of white privilege and generational wealth. His ancestry could be traced back to the eighth century, and you couldn't find a peasant if you tried. He said, "Our clients, Scott and Layla West, are they being charged?"

The Lieutenant fumbled a couple papers, stalling, waiting for Agents Randall and Devonsky to come out and handle this situation. Lieutenant Mielle said, "Let me check with the desk clerk to see if they're—"

"They are. And if the Wests are not being charged, we demand they be released immediately!"

Azul added, "If our clients have been assaulted; if God forbid they tell me that their handcuffs were too tight—expect a lawsuit to be filed in the multimillion-dollar range."

Mielle walked off only to find Randall and Devonsky huddled behind a door, listening. This was their case, yet Mielle's ass had been handed to him.

Randall saw the accusatory look in the Lieutenant's eyes.

"Cut them loose," he simply said. "We got nothing."

$$\infty$$

Meyer and Lucky exited the federal jail to fresh air and sunshine, contrasting the dire situation before them. They had no money, no clothing, and nowhere to live. Once inside Meyer's truck, they sat idle without speaking because the same thought was on both their minds. They had nowhere to go, and his gas was dwindling. Being broke was complicated. You had to think of things that nonbroken niggas didn't ponder, like where would your next meal come from? How would rent get paid? Lights? Water? Heat? Lucky thought about calling Ragnar and asking for a handout, but when the idea popped into her head, she forced it out.

Lucky broke the silence. "Call Gino again."

Gino Salvatoré owned and operated the luxury car dealership they bought all their vehicles from. He was mob affiliated and had amassed a fortune through his underworld connections. You could walk into his office with three-four hundred thousand in cash, and he would make the transaction look legit. He was masterful with numbers, sharp, and the ladies loved him. He had dark, olive skin and jet black hair he wore slicked back. His thick Italian accent gave him an authenticity that garnered instant trust from criminals.

Meyer smirked. "I ain't gonna keep beggin' that nigga to sell our shit. Once he makes a sell, he'll call."

"What's his number?"

"Why!"

"Because I would like to wash my ass, pop tags off a few garments, and swallow more than my spit. Why is everything an argument wit' you? You love conflict!"

Begrudgingly, Meyer unlocked and handed her his cellphone. Lucky dialed and heard, "Hey, Meyer. How are things?"

"Gino, this is Lucky."

"Oh, the sexy West. Why don't you ever come up here and see your Uncle Gino?"

Gino was the sexy one. Lucky had wanted to fuck him for years, but he was stingy with his dick. He would never flirt, but she knew that was because he wanted no problems with Scott. She grinned. "I'm well, thank you."

"Good…good to hear. So, I guess I owe the pleasure of this call to these vehicles?"

"Yes, that's correct."

"Oh, why do you torture me so," he continued laying it down thick which was new behavior. "You could have lied to an old man and said you missed me."

"I do miss you," she said in a seductive, flirty tone. Meyer gave her the side-eye and saw this goofy look on his sister's face. He didn't like it. He snatched the phone.

"Gino, what up, this Meyer. Any movement?"

Gino's voice adjusted, and his bass returned. "Not yet, Meyer. I have my best salesmen on them. There's interest but no sales. We might have to come down on the numbers by ten percent."

"Do it then."

"Done."

"And Gino. Don't ever let me catch you trying to fuck my sister again wit' ya old ass. You wouldn't try that shit if Scott were around. Don't disrespect her now, or you're dead!"

Meyer ended the call.

Lucky had her lips poked out. She rolled her eyes. "That was dumb! Didn't you ever hear you catch more bees with honey?"

Meyer wasn't trying to hear philosophies right now. "So, what's up? What's next? Where we going?"

Lucky was astonished that her brother was looking to her to problem solve. But she was up for the challenge. These were her problems too. And then she remembered that she owned a residential building; she was bringing it back from dilapidation, but it was more than nothing. The other alternatives were their warehouses or the offices where mass murders were just committed, and there were no showers, kitchens, or living amenities. She said, "I own an apartment building that we can crash at for now…at least until we get our money from Gino or the banks."

Again, Meyer realized how they had underestimated his little sister. There wasn't even a need for him to ask questions or scream on her for keeping secrets.

"Head to the FDR drive and get off on 125th."

Meyer peeled out.

Chapter 24

Lucky knew they would need things before she took him to the apartment building and didn't have the money to legally obtain them. She emptied the contents of her oversized Chanel bag and said, "Come on."

Meyer asked no questions. He followed his sister into a large Walgreens. He watched as she stuffed male and female deodorant, toothbrushes, toothpaste, mouthwash, body wash, facial wash, nail polish and remover, and other female necessities. Meyer couldn't front, he was a little leery watching her shoplift at first, but this was survival of the fittest. Soon, he was browsing the aisles, looking for the hygiene products he needed. He grabbed shaving cream, an expensive razor, tube socks, cheap boxers, and lotion. Lucky saw him coming toward her with his hands full. She glanced around quickly and then opened her bag, and he stuffed the contents inside. Instantly she spotted the boxers and whispered, "Where did you get these?"

Meyer nodded toward the back, and they walked to an area with a selection of inexpensive clothing. She saw leggings, 3-pack panties, socks for girls aged 12-14, white T-shirts, and sports bras. Lucky could have kissed her brother. All these items were priced at $9.99 or less, but it felt like Saks 5th Avenue right now. Lucky loaded up on the essentials and stuffed them in her purse like they were supposed to be free. When the Chanel couldn't hold much more, her brother said, "Lucky, chill. I think we done here."

Meyer's eyes scanned the room, and he made eye contact with a worker. She called out, "Do you need help?"

Meyer couldn't front; he was scared. He had no idea what he

would do if she walked toward them.

Lucky said, "No, we don't!" Her snappy response stopped the clerk in her tracks, and she pivoted away from what she assumed was a couple. Meyer looked up and saw the cameras.

"Yo, you peeped the cameras?"

"Don't look up, Meyer. You gonna get us busted!"

"Us?" Meyer smirked. "I ain't steal shit."

Lucky stopped in her tracks. Her teeth gritted, she squeezed out, "I will take your shit out of my bag and make more room for me. Good luck with two-day-old drawers!"

He chuckled. "Nah, I'm just fuckin' wit' you. I'd body niggas if they laid hands on you. We good, let's bounce."

Lucky and Meyer casually walked toward the front door, passed the alarm box and security guard, and rang. The sound was constant and loud. Lucky paused, trying to decide what to do, and Meyer was ready to react. Lucky said, "You want to check my bag?"

He looked at the two individuals and made a judgment call. "Nah, y'all good. This been going off all day."

Lucky nodded and smiled, and they continued to her brother's SUV. Inside, they both breathed a sigh of relief.

"I was shook," Meyer admitted. "You did that before?"

Lucky shrugged. "Of course. All the white girls in my private school used to shoplift for fun. I'd hang out with them and steal petty shit; candy bars, soda, chips. They were always on some rebellious agenda against their parents." She talked to her brother but looked through her Chanel to see what rang. And there it was, Meyer's razor.

"You didn't see this big ass alarm sticker before you stuffed it in my bag! You were supposed to peel it off. How could you not know that?" Lucky was livid.

"Yo, I ain't no booster!"

"Booster?" She sucked her teeth. He had a lot to learn. "Booster's don't steal ten-dollar leggings. What we're doing is

261

shoplifting. There's a difference."

Meyer didn't care nor needed clarification. "You ready to head in?"

"Not to an empty refrigerator. We have to get food before I faint."

Meyer agreed. He was starving and was more than ready to shower and eat and then get some real sleep. Lucky emptied her bag's contents into the back seat while Meyer drove into a Stop & Shop parking lot. There they loaded up on bacon, steaks, rice, seasoning, lobster tails, shrimp, scallops, crab legs, and when her bag was packed, Lucky stole three reusable bags and loaded them up with cereal, milk, juice, cooking grease—in total, they stole more than two hundred dollars in groceries. Lucky rolled the shopping cart out the door with her brother, as her protector, on her heels.

Meyer could no longer deny it. He was getting an adrenaline rush from the petty theft he'd help perpetrate.

Angel waded in the water in the pool while pulling Lulu around on a large float. His two sons and daughter had joined them, playing with Lucchese, splashing around, and having a fun time. They, too, had fallen in love with the baby. But when Dahlia appeared from the mansion and furiously fixed her eyes on her children, they nervously swam away from the float. They knew that Dahlia hated Lulu, and she ordered her children to stay away from the baby. Angel looked at his disgruntled wife and said, "Dahlia, they're just having fun. Please, this is unlike you to behave like an infant. Who is the child, huh? You or Lucchese?"

"I don't want them having anything to do with that baby!" she yelled. "She doesn't belong here!"

"I'm tired of hearing the same thing every day," he said dismissively. "Go inside and have a cocktail or take a few of your pills. You need to take a time out, or I'll give you one!" Angel's patience was dissolving right before everyone's eyes. He was trying to remain calm on the strength of his children, but his mercy had limits.

"I know who she is, Angel, and if I tell the cartel, they will kill her!" she threatened. "You know the rules, pendejo! If I tell Juarez, maybe they'll kill you too! She needs to go, or one day you'll find that lil' puta drowned floating at the top of this pool!"

Angel went from unruffled to unmitigated anger in an instant. His face transitioned into a dark mask of fury, and Dahlia knew she'd crossed that line. Angel didn't reply right away to her threat. He coolly pulled his child into his arm and walked through the waist-level salt-watered pool. Angel climbed out, water rolling down his tanned legs. His bare feet tracked puddles on his imported marble floor into his home.

Dahlia tried to stand her ground, but she knew when Angel became this quiet after a threat, all hell was about to break loose. Marbella stood in the background, shocked by her sister's idiocies. Marbella always knew that her sister's temper could get Dahlia killed. Now with her there, Marbella wondered if her life was also in danger.

Knowing she fucked up, Dahlia turned and hurried back into the house, running in the opposite direction from Angel.

"Angel, I know she didn't mean it. My sister's just upset, but she would never do anything to harm you or Lulu," Marbella said, running behind him. "She would never tell the cartel!"

"She's gone too far!" Angel exclaimed.

Calmly, Angel took Lucchese to her room, where she had an ensuite bathroom with Marbella trailing behind. She watched as he bathed the baby, put on her PJs, and placed her down for a mid-afternoon nap. He stood over Lulu until her eyes got heavy and slowly closed.

Heatedly, he walked toward the mansion's east wing, where the main bedroom was.

Marbella said, "Angel, please…don't—"

Angel spun around and forcefully grabbed Marbella around her throat, his strong fingers gripping her slim neck as he slammed her against a wall. The back of her head connected with a loud thump. "Cállate!" he screamed, and she obeyed.

Dahlia was already in the bedroom where she had closed, locked, and barricaded the door.

Angel heatedly banged.

"Open the fuckin' door!" he ordered. But Dahlia refused. Her defiance of a direct order had only infuriated the drug lord beyond reason. He called his men to help him break the door down as he berated and threatened his wife. Several men ran up the staircase in military boots with their weapons holstered. It sounded like a small army had invaded their residence.

Angel nodded toward one bodyguard who swiftly shouldered the door several times.

"Go away!" she screamed. "Don't come in here, or I'll kill you!" Dahlia shouted, giving them a warning.

Her threat was ignored. The soldier continued to shoulder the door until it finally flew open, and the army was about to charge inside the room. The rapid gunfire put all their male testosterone and bullying to a muthafuckin' end.

Bak! Bak! Bak! Bak! Bak! Bak!

The first goon dropped face down and dove for cover while everyone else scattered like roaches when the lights came on. Dahlia turned their home into a battleground with her children standing at the top of the steps seeing the dysfunction. It was reckless and less than smart, but Dahlia felt like being wrong and strong today.

"You stupid bitch!" Angel screamed. "I'm going to fuckin' kill you!"

"Not if you die first, cabrón!" she hollered back.

"Papí, no!" his oldest son cried out, tears streaming down his cheeks. Angel paused to look at his three children, who were all hysterical. Angel was torn. He was crouched low by the doorway, gritting his teeth—his wife had gone too far. But Dahlia was a tough bitch; she'd been around the cartel all her life and learned that only the strong survive. She went 1980s "Gloria" on them, believing that Angel was coming to kill her. But he wasn't. Now, he was so furious that he'd considered it.

Dahlia squeezed the trigger until the gun emptied of ammunition—*click-click-click-click*. The familiar sound pushed everyone into action. His men immediately charged into the room and detained his wife. There was nothing Dahlia could do now but wait for it. She'd fucked up. She scowled at Angel, refusing to beg for mercy. Defenseless, she was hit by a swift and brutal right-hand punch that made her stumble and then fall. He crouched over her with his fist clenched tightly, and he continued to savagely beat her, nearly breaking her face apart. When he finally stopped, his knuckles were swollen, and Dahlia still had some fire burning inside.

"You're not a man…," she whispered. "You're a little cockroach!"

Marbella could only watch in horror as Angel went ape shit crazy on her sister. His rain of punches blackened her eyes, nearly broke her nose, and slightly disfigured her beautiful features with bloody bumps and bruises. She was barely conscious when he finally stopped beating her. She couldn't move. She couldn't pick herself up.

He looked at his men and said, "I want this bitch taken to Chihuahua. Dahlia, you hear that; you're banished back to your birthplace alone because my children stay with me. You're banned from this family until you learn how to behave!"

Louis asked, "What about her?" He was talking about Marbella. Angel thought for a second and then said, "She stays."

"We're here," she said. "Pull over."

Meyer looked at the six-story tenement building in

Soundview in the Bronx and knew this was a dangerous neighborhood. Newly gentrified, it would take time to snuff out the weeds. However, the buildings' exterior looked like a rose surrounded by concrete; it stood out.

Lucky climbed out of Meyer's Escalade on 172nd Street and grabbed bags. He followed, tucking Larry's gun in his waistband. They strolled toward the building as Meyer's head swiveled, observing his surroundings. So far, he was proud of his little sister for accomplishing so much on her own.

"Yo, how much you paid for this?" he wanted to know.

"Three hundred thousand at a city auction."

The building was all brick, which she had pressured washed and restored to its original vibrant color. She also added a new roof and HVAC system, and new ductwork. She added new, energy-efficient windows and a large black awning with beige trim. The plumbing and electrical wiring had been completed in each apartment, and new light fixtures were installed in the now brightly lit hallways.

"Get the fuck outta here." He was incredulous. "For all this? How many apartments?"

"Sixteen." Lucky walked up the front steps and used her key to unlock the newly installed glass security doors. No longer would the hallways be littered with vagrants, hood niggas, stickup kids, or other ingrates. There was an intercom system, so the tenants could buzz in their guests and a camera system. Lucky wanted her tenants to feel safe, and she wanted her property to be guarded and surveilled by her or someone on her team.

They walked into the vast lobby, and Meyer saw an area for mail on the left. The new mailboxes were Post Office style, medium size, with tables so tenants could place their bags while collecting their packages. The flooring was hand-scraped hardwood, six inches wide, with a custom mural made from marble tile with the monogram, *Château Lucchese*, in script letters. The apartment doors were solid wood with wrought iron over the peephole. There were benches in the lobby, two faux fireplaces with custom, reclaimed wood mantels, crystal chandeliers on each floor, and recess lighting. An elevator was to the right, and the building also had an open staircase that led to all six floors. He felt like he was standing in a Parisian building. It had a French country feel—warm and cozy. Maybe homelessness wasn't so bad if they had this to fall back on.

"Which crib is mine?" he wanted to know. Meyer was ready to get his fuck on, maybe call up Lollipop and see if she wanted to come through. He needed to release his aggravation, and a good nut would do that for the gangsta.

"Slow your roll, playah." Lucky knew her brother well. "We're not done shopping—"

"You mean stealing."

"Tomato, tomahto," she said and stuck her tongue out at him. "We're going to need something to sleep on."

"You crazy!" he exclaimed. "How we gonna steal beds, Lucky? They can't fit in your pocketbook!"

Lucky walked toward the elevator and pressed the button. "Relax, Meyer. We can get blow-up mattresses from any of these local stores. Walmart, Target, somewhere like that."

Lollipop was looking better and better for the kingpin. Lucky explained the inevitable as they rode the elevator to the sixth floor.

"Only two apartments have functioning bathrooms, and that's the trap house and the apartment next door. When Angel tried to have me assassinated, the renovation had to pause. My contractor had to move on to the next job, and now I don't have the money to get things complete."

"Yeah, but that won't last long. Whatever I can do, I want to see you get this place up and running. Like I said, I'm proud of you. And with New York rent at its lowest, you will stand to make at a minimum—" Meyer did the math in his head and then replied, "Nearly fifty thousand a month in passive income."

Lucky nodded as the elevator doors opened. "The trap house won't be fit for us to sleep in, so we'll sleep in apartment 6B." Lucky had a heavy chain with several keys on it. She opened the door, and instantly they smelled something rotten. Lucky was about to walk toward the odor when her brother pushed her behind him and pulled out his burner. He crept farther in, not knowing if a body was inside or not. They snaked through the apartment to the kitchen and saw a fold-up table and a few fold-up chairs. Old, molded food was everywhere. It looked like savages had lived there. Chicken wings were on the floor, wonton soup had dried out and molded, dozens of soda and beer cans were strewn about the apartment, soy sauce and duck sauce used packages were tossed everywhere. Blunts smoked down to the quick, and cigarettes smoked down to the filter were stockpiled on brown paper bags. Used condoms were on the tabletop, floor, and dropped wherever they'd fucked.

Roaches scattered as they stared in disbelief. Neither of them had ever seen a cockroach in a place where they would sleep. Lucky's skin crawled.

"Those nasty muthafuckas," she murmured, astounded at a person's hygiene habits. Lucky ran to open a window to let the funk out.

"Who was in here?"

Lucky was livid. The only two fools with the keys were Yusef and Opie. She replied, "Two dead niggas so I don't have anyone to be mad at but myself for trusting them to act like humans."

Meyer still needed to make sure that no one was hiding out. They continued to travel from room to room and stumbled upon the source of the odor. Apparently, even after Lucky had told Opie not to, he took in the neighborhood stray cat. And with he and Yusef murdered, no one had been in that apartment in several weeks. Dead next to the cat's rotting corpse was a mouse, and with the heat, the feline's insides had liquified and soaked into the hardwood flooring. Maggots were everywhere, and the pungent smell had attracted many insects, from German roaches to water bugs to mice. She would need to get the building exterminated. This made Lucky's stomach convulse. Just as she was about to run into the bathroom to regurgitate, a mouse ran over her foot. She screamed and hopped back like she had been struck by lightning. Lucky couldn't stop her tears from falling. Why would they do her like this?

"Goddamn," Meyer yelled out at the scene. Until he saw all this, he was hungry. He looked around the apartment at his sister's vision and was still impressed. She had hardwood flooring, quality amenities, spacious bedrooms, and a well-appointed kitchen. "Only jealous niggas treat nice shit like trash. I'm glad those niggas are gone, Lucky, because eventually, you would have had to watch your back."

Lucky used the back of her hand to wipe away her tears, but her hand became like a windshield wiper. It kept going back and forth because she couldn't stop crying.

"This is only material shit, Lucky. You better than that. Don't let them steal your joy. Let me walk you next door and see what's what. I'll look for some cleaning products and get all this shit cleaned up. Just chill. You've done enough."

Lucky nodded, and they walked next door. It was somewhat better, but trash from food containers and roaches scattered when they turned the light on. Cocaine remnants and paraphernalia were everywhere because this was a trap house. The upside is that the refrigerator had cases of beer, soda, and bottles of Snapple raspberry tea. A few rolled blunts were on a table and some cash. Meyer quickly scooped up the bread and counted. Someone had left $500 on the table, and that seemingly innocuous gift had placed a smile on both their faces.

"A couple ki's would have been better, but some cash is good too," she joked.

"That would mean Santa Claus existed, and Ma and Pops told us from day one that he didn't." Meyer stuffed the money in his pocket. "Take a bath and relax. I'll go and get what we need."

"You sure we shouldn't just get out of here? Go to a nice hotel for a night? Order room service and sleep in luxury until noon?" Lucky was serious. She was already over this lower-class living.

Meyer got serious too. As the older brother, he felt like he had to step up and give direction and sometimes tell the hard truth. "Sis, we fucked up right now. Last night, we slept in my truck and had to scrape together pennies to eat. Bugsy's in jail and can't make bail. We're at war wit' a cartel *and* our parents, so we can't afford luxury. We gotta eat. You don't understand how I'll never forget that you put a roof over our heads. You were thinkin' about your future when a nigga like me was living for today."

Lucky handed him the keys. "Okay, and I'll start dinner."

"Lock up," he ordered as he left.

Meyer was gone longer than Lucky had wanted, but when he came back, he had gotten everything to bide them over. He had filled up his gas tank to get them around, and although he wanted to get his whip washed, it wasn't necessary. Meyer went to Target and got the blow-up beds, sheets, towels, wash rags, slippers, cleaning products, cleaning gloves, mouse traps, roach baits, and roach bombs. He also did more food shopping.

When he got back, his sister had bathed, dressed in a pair of leggings and a stolen T-shirt, and had cooked a feast; lobster, shrimps, crab legs, yellow rice, and corn on the cob. Meyer smelled the Slap Ya Momma Cajun seasoning from the hallway. Lucky's grin was broad when he walked in with all the bags.

"I missed you," she said, and his heart felt different. He knew Lucky loved him, but the words they usually exchanged were harsh, combative. He looked in her face, and she seemed to glow. Something changed when he walked through the door.

"Oh, yeah," he said. "What you been doin' since I've been

gone?"

She shrugged. "I cooked and then painted my nails. I don't know, but I started to worry about you. I know it's silly—"

"No doubt," he quickly replied. "Ain't shit gonna happen to your big bro. I can promise you that." Meyer didn't like to talk like that. It felt like a bad omen to him.

Lucky nodded, immediately understanding why he curbed that conversation. She helped him unpack the bags. She was glad to see he had the wherewithal to buy more groceries.

"Let's eat first, and then I'll go and clean out that apartment."

"Cool," she said. "And I'll clean up here and blow up our beds."

They ate the feast Lucky had cooked and strategized about their next moves. They discussed Bugsy, his bail, Angel, Los Pepes, and cash flow before excusing himself to do the cleaning. Meyer couldn't wait to restore his sister's apartment to its original state. While Meyer was next door, bagging up the dead cat and mouse, trashing all the molded food, he took great pride in cleaning and disinfecting all surfaces. The apartment sparkled and smelled clean when he was finished, Fabuloso lingering in the air. He left the windows open while he cleaned so air could circulate because they weren't expecting rain. Meyer laid down the mouse traps in all corners because that's how they moved—they scurried along walls and hugged the darkness. Next, he placed all the roach baits before realizing he had to close the windows to let off the roach bombs. Which he did. They could move into this apartment in eight hours because he was sure any mice would be trapped, and all insects would be dead.

Meyer walked back into the trap house, and his sister had done an equally good cleaning job. All cocaine traces, crack vials, and triple beam scales were trashed. The steel tables were shining, the food was put away, and the dishes were cleaned. That apartment, too, smelled like Fabuloso. It was a two-bedroom, and Lucky had placed a bed in each. The towels and washrags were loaded in the linen closet, and it was just a few minutes after ten o'clock. They had been through a lot in one day, but the night wasn't over.

"Yo, stay up. I'ma go hop in the shower, and when I get out, I bought some cards. Let's play Spades."

They hadn't played Spades in years. The very idea of the game brought fond memories gushing back. When they had a full house, all six siblings were alive, and they had parents who loved them, and they felt the same.

"Hurry up," she coached. "So I can whip your ass!"

Meyer quickly showered and put on a pair of boxers and a T-shirt. He got the deck of cards from his pocket, made his way into the kitchen, and made him a tall glass of Lean before his sister joined him. He poured her a three-finger glass of Henny, and they sat down.

Lucky was a beast at Spades, and her winning streaks always caused arguments throughout the household because someone would accuse her of cheating. It didn't take long for her to take four books in a row as they sipped their drinks.

"What's that you drinkin'," she casually asked.

"This," Meyer slowly said after he took another sip. He didn't look up from his hand when he replied, "It's Hennessy and Welches grape soda."

Lucky crinkled her nose. It sounded to ghetto for her tastes, but evidently, her brother liked it. She was curious. Things were different. And if there ever was a time to taste Hennessy and grape soda, it was now. "Let me taste it."

"Come on now. Play the game, so I can start winnin'. You got your own drink."

"I just want a sip."

"Go make ya own," he snapped. A full-blown argument would have ensued, but Lucky fell back. Her brother had just cleaned up cat and mouse guts for her, so if he wanted to be stingy, so be it.

"You ever miss them?"

"Who? Bonnie, Clyde, and Gotti?" he asked.

"No, well, yes. I know you miss them. We all do, but I was talking about Scott and Layla."

Meyer took a moment before he truthfully answered. "I do, but that doesn't make things right. So as far as I'm concerned, our parents died a while ago. It's just us, Lucky. Mourning over what we had wit' them won't bring back my niece and nephew."

Thinking about the children, more specifically, her child, would put her in a mood, and she was over heartache and heartbreak for the evening. She didn't say this to her brother, but she'd already come to terms that Angel had murdered his daughter when she received her finger—just as he said he would.

She continued her line of questioning. "What they did was reprehensible, but I miss Scott if I'm keeping it honest. I was always a daddy's girl, and not having him in my life leaves a large void. If he were here, things would be handled. People wouldn't be disrespecting us like this. Fitz wouldn't be trying to play us, Gino would have sold our cars, and we wouldn't be spending the night in a rental. I don't know how things got so fucked up, but it all started with Maxine. I'm glad she's dead. In fact, I wish she were never born!"

Meyer listened intently as the Lean took effect. His mind opened in ways it didn't when he was sober. He sparked one of the pre-rolled blunts and inhaled the Kush. The smoke billowed in his sister's direction as she scooped up another book. The game was 10-0. Finally, he said, "This shit was already written. Maxine would always take the fall for Layla so our mother could birth us. Our siblings, Bonnie, Clyde, and Gotti, were born only to make Maxine whole before she joined Dillinger. This entire situation was written years before any of us were born. We can press rewind a million times, and it'll still play out the same way. With Maxine doing time only to end her own life, our brothers and sister in a cold grave, and us broke, destitute, and at war."

Meyer's eyes were low, and his words were slow. He was lifted but not off Kush and Henny. Lucky knew that high, and this wasn't that. She was concerned. Something else was going on. "You okay?" she asked.

Meyer's eyes closed and slowly opened again. "What?" He had forgotten the question.

"Did you take something, Meyer?" She looked at his cup, and it was empty. "Or did you drink something?"

Meyer was nodding off in his chair. Lucky snatched his empty glass and smelled it, sniffing the sweet, artificial smell of grape. She concluded that it was Hennessy and grape soda, but why was it affecting him like this. Lucky grabbed the blunt and put it out in the ashtray. She took her fingernail and sliced open the paper to ensure the weed wasn't laced with cocaine or something more potent and lethal. But the contents were only marijuana. Lucky relaxed somewhat. Maybe her brother was tired. They had been through a lot. She got up, placed his arm around her neck, and led him into one room, where she helped him lay down on the air mattress and covered him with a sheet.

She walked into the adjoining room and collapsed faced down on her bed, and within minutes she was asleep.

Chapter 25

Lucky's sleep was interrupted by voice, text, and Instagram notifications. At 3 a.m., she finally sat up. She was sleeping on her air mattress that would deflate slowly throughout the night, so she'd awake on the hardwood floor by morning.

Groggily, she logged onto her Instagram account and had over one thousand comments. Her eyes scanned the messages, and she was perplexed. People were asking if she was doing porn now. Lucky scrolled up and saw her name tagged to a video posted on what was supposed to be her anonymous page *disney_princess1998* and *hoodfellas_waybackindaday*. When she pressed PLAY, her worst nightmare became a reality. In the most intimate of positions, she was having sex with Ragnar. The video was edited to never see his face, but hers was vivid in 4K ultra HD. You could hear her moans and groans…all the sounds one makes when having sexual relations. All their naughty moments—Ragnar repeatedly smacking her ass, entering her doggy-style, Lucky riding him making love faces, and her on her knees giving him head were all spliced together into 3 one-minute posts.

Lucky's whole body shook violently. She trembled with an uncontrollable fear that stemmed from the perverse humiliation. Exposed, she felt dirty and cheap, and no amount of showering would change that.

The owner of the Instagram handle had written her whole government to his post: Lucky Luciana West, aka *Cinder*FUCKING*rella,* is Scott West's *disney_princess1998?*

Lucky tortured herself even more, reading the hateful

comments: *What's wrong wit' her eye? If she wanted a reality show, just say that! If clout chaser was a person, smh. Sis needs some a$$ shots to kickstart her porn career! Who's still getting spanked in 2020? Somebody tell this chile she ain't Kim.*

Some people commented on Ragnar: *Notice that dude with the slim di@k ain't show his face! His weak thrust is giving me old man vibes!*

But the brunt of the criticism was all aimed at her.

Lucky had too many text messages to read. A few of her brothers' old girlfriends, including Lollipop, left texts warning her of the post. Associates that she rarely spoke to also reached out. But who was noticeably absent from the flurry of texts was Markeeta?

This was the ultimate betrayal; revenge porn. Lucky would kill him. Ragnar was a muthafuckin' dead man!

Lucky exited her room and went barging into Meyer's, who was startled awake. He reached for his burner until there was facial recognition. The panicked look in his sister's eyes had him shook. Immediately he sat up, and she collapsed by his side.

Lucky felt like she had lockjaw. Her eyes were nearly swollen shut from crying her pain out, her hurt vibrating on another wavelength. She handed Meyer her phone.

"What's up?" he wanted to know. When Lucky didn't answer, he looked down and saw her cell was cued to a video. Within seconds of hitting PLAY, he shut it off. Meyer saw that his sister's sexual tryst was uploaded to the Gram. He was sickened and embarrassed.

Meyer rubbed the cold out of his eyes and cleared his throat. "Who's this nigga, and where does he live!" He would not make promises—Lucky was clear that she no longer wanted that. His actions would speak for him.

Lucky nodded. "I'm going with you." Her voice was low, weak, broken.

∞

With Kimberly kicked off the West case, it gave her more time to investigate her colleague. She used her skills and resources to keep track of Franklin and build a case against him but only if he drew first blood. Kimberly suspected that he would go through with his ominous threat, and if that happened, she'd be ready.

What she couldn't do was report him and her superiors; she'd be seen as insubordinate, and she didn't know how far up Franklin's connections went. No one would trust her, so she had to tread lightly. Her gut told her that Franklin had a hand in stealing the five million dollars at Lucky West's apartment and so much more. Her intuition also said he was the unknown Black male in the leaked porn video she'd just watched. He was an emotional masochist. These psychological games validated him, and Kimberly wanted to bring him to an inescapable conclusion.

Special Agent Franklin Garrett had targeted the twenty-two-year-old female—the youngest of the living Wests and unleashed the ultimate mind fuck. It wasn't a reach for her to conclude that he knew better than to personally go after Bugsy or Meyer. Franklin thought that Lucky was prey.

Kimberly hated that many people believed Black women were last on the list. They were behind the white male, white female, white Hispanic men, white Hispanic women, Latin males, Latin females, Asian men, Asian women, American Indian, Native Alaskan, Pacific Islanders, dogs, cats, endangered species, Black men, and finally, Black women. Kimberly was in that last box; the least respected and most disrespected person was the Black woman in America, more likely, worldwide. And that hurt that much deeper when a Black man bought into that dogma.

It didn't take long for her to find the fuck pad Franklin had rented with federal funds under the name Ragnar Benjamin, which meant Randall and Devonsky had greenlit this operation. *Ragnar?* So his alias was a Viking warrior? If she didn't believe it before, she knew Franklin had some issues.

"So there was only one person that signed the visitor's log?" Kimberly asked John, the concierge of the building.

"That's correct," he said, looking through the journal entries. "Only one, and that was a Ms. Lucky West."

She nodded. "I'm going to need a copy of all the dates and times she signed in."

"Do you want me to forward them to Agent Randall?"

Kimberly stifled a snort and eye roll. "Considering I'm the one standing here, I want you to make copies for me! Now. I'll wait."

Before John could make the copies for the agent, Kimberly couldn't believe her eyes when a disgruntled Lucky and Meyer West stormed through the doors, trying to bypass security.

John called out, "Excuse me…sir, madam. You have to sign in." He then whispered to Agent Cooper, "That's her. Ms. Lucky West."

Kimberly knew precisely who they were. Although the surveillance pictures always had Lucky wearing sunglasses, right now, all you saw were her puffy, bloodshot eyes. It was clear she had been crying, and Kimberly knew why. The young woman was tinier than her photos depicted, almost frail-looking. You could see that the toll of recent events—the sum of nonstop trauma couldn't be hidden.

Lucky walked over to the desk to sign in while her brother remained off to the side. Meyer's nostrils flared wide, his eyes lowered to a murderous squint, and his body language said he was ready to commit a 1-8-7 on an undercover cop.

Lucky said, "I'm here to see Ragnar Benjamin."

"I'm sorry, miss, but we don't have a resident by that name."

Lucky was incredulous—"But he just moved in!"—she shouted. "Ragnar Benjamin! You allow me up to see him all the time."

John smirked. His voice was an annoying mix of

condescension and snarkiness. "As I've said, no one by that name lives here, and I've never seen you before today. Is there anything else I could help you with?"

Standing two feet away from the queenpin, Kimberly noticed Lucky reaching into her handbag, undoubtedly for a gun. Gently, she placed her hand over Lucky's, halting her movement. "He's just the messenger."

This subtle action was really an act of kindness on Agent Cooper's part because she wasn't there to arrest Lucky on a gun charge, especially not after what Franklin did to her.

Lucky stared at the woman and then down at her Glock 17 holstered under her jacket. Kimberly purposely allowed her to see her gold badge clipped to her waist. Lucky exhaled her fury and acquiesced. The Fed was correct; John wasn't the enemy.

Lucky and Meyer quickly exited the building while Agent Kimberly Cooper watched them leave.

"Bugsy West, you've made bail." CO Mahan said as he watched another West get set free without enticing or entrapping him with an illegal eavesdropping cellphone.

The average inmate would have had numerous questions, mainly who posted bail, but Bugsy gave few exchanges with the guards. He didn't have any clothing on when he was processed except his hospital gown and boxers, so he did wonder if they'd allow him to leave with his prison-issued jumper and slippers. Hoping that Meyer or Lucky would think to bring him something to wear home would be a stretch. Besides, what would they bring? He assumed his apartment was just as vandalized as theirs, and all his clothing and belongings were ruined. He also wondered how they could make his bail because the judge hadn't lowered it and assumed that his brother had taken an unnecessary risk for his freedom.

Bugsy was led to a small, dingy, private room to change. He

noticed a Saks 5th Avenue garment bag hanging from a hook, a Christian Louboutin shoebox, and a leather satchel with toiletries. Bugsy suited up nicely, put on his 18k gold cufflinks, his hard bottoms, and walked out of MCC like the boss nigga he was.

He stepped into the fresh air and saw three Cadillac SUVs parked out front with familiar and unfamiliar faces. Mason, Scott, Layla, Zaire, Kane, and a gaggle of high-priced lawyers—Gavalas and Azul at the helm.

Bugsy and Scott glared at each other. The disdain between father and son was palpable. Even with Bugsy on the receiving end of his father's good will, he was unreceptive.

Scott broke the moment. He walked toward his son and whispered, "We need to kick it. I think Meyer and Lucky are in trouble."

That statement was enough for Bugsy to put his personal feelings on pause for the moment. Scott quickly introduced his son to his legal team that would take over his gun charge before everyone got into their respective vehicles and left.

Bugsy and Mason sat facing Scott and Layla in the back of the Yukon while Kane took the wheel and Zaire sat shotgun.

Layla hadn't seen her firstborn son in nearly a year, yet no hugs and kisses were exchanged. They got straight to business.

Scott said, "I had Emmanuel Vega bumped off."

Bugsy shrugged. "I was gonna handle that."

"But you didn't," Scott shot back. "What do you know about an Instagram account airing all our dirty laundry?"

Bugsy suddenly shrank under the weight of a simple question. He felt inferior when he replied, "Not much, other than what Lucky told me. I asked around, but nobody—"

Scott nodded toward Mason and then cut his son off. "Did you see this?"

Mason pulled out his cell and passed it to Bugsy. He shut it off within seconds of watching the video, visibly disgusted. Everyone in that vehicle felt anger and shame, but no one wanted this man more dead than Scott. This parasite had violated and humiliated his baby girl, his firstborn daughter, who loved and adored him at one point. Scott felt like he had failed her, allowing his love for the game to take precedence over his love for family. Dissension is bound to seep through once there's a crack in the foundation. Scott knew this doctrine like he knew his own name, yet here they were.

Scott asked, "Who is this nigga?"

Bugsy didn't even know Lucky was seeing someone, and the excuse of being locked up wouldn't fly in this arena. When they branched off from their parents, he did so under the belief that he could walk in his Pops shoes, govern, and teach simultaneously, just as Scott did. Bugsy couldn't lose control he never had. His siblings did come to him for advice, but did they *listen* to him.

The chip on Bugsy's shoulder, the bravado he had only moments earlier, the ego that repeatedly told him that he'd taken the West Organization to where it was today had deflated. He said, "I don't know."

Layla finally spoke to her son. "Where's Meyer and Lucky living? We went by their residences and found a shit show."

Stalling, Bugsy said, "Yeah, I heard about that."

His mother went off. "Where the fuck are my kids, nigga! You sittin' behind bars getting three hots and a cot, and my fuckin' son is out there…God knows where in these streets wit' nowhere to lay his fuckin' head!"

Scott said, "Do you have a way to contact them?"

Bugsy nodded, reached for Scott's cellphone, and dialed. "Lucky, where y'all at?"

The forceful, repetitious bang wasn't something that could be ignored. It shook the house awake and yanked a highly perturbed Markeeta out of her bed. She stomped to the door, her bare feet slapping against the cool marble tiles in quick hurried steps.

Markeeta needed the sound to stop and whoever making that sound was gonna pay.

"Who the fuck is it!" she roared, her voice unmistakably agitated and hoarse.

"It's me, Lucky."

Markeeta allowed a considerable amount of time to pass as her eyes adjusted to the dim lighting, and her foggy mind cleared somewhat. She turned to see the time; it was 4:48 a.m.

Lucky spoke again, "Open up."

Markeeta looked through her peephole and saw her cousin and a male. She said, "What do you want?"

"Are you serious right now? Let me in?"

"Who's wit' you?"

Lucky faced her brother and then replied, "It's Meyer. We wanted to come through and kick it…catch up."

Markeeta knew about the porn video, but she didn't have anything to do with uploading it. As soon as she saw that pitiful display of wack sex, she called Agent Tannery, who was just as baffled as she was. He said he'd look into it, and he did. Whoever uploaded the video wasn't an amateur and had covered their tracks at being found so far. But that video was a gift and exactly what creating the handle meant. Once the handle went live, so many hustlers, wannabe gangsters, mamas, and baby mamas began sending direct messages with pictures and information hoping to be posted on the site that now had over 300,000 followers in a few short weeks. These washed-up Uncles and Aunties, still reliving their glory days, wanted Insta-Fame on Instagram. When the video came through, Tannery had his IT guy do what he does best; humiliate the West family and their affiliates.

Lucky repeated, "Markeeta open up? Why you got us out here lookin' crazy."

"You actin' real aggressive at my door, yo. Get the fuck outta here 'fore I call five-oh!"

"Bitch, why you mad? You wouldn't have none of this shit if it weren't for me! You don't think I know what time it is?"

Markeeta didn't answer. Instead, she ran past her son, screamed for him to go the fuck back to bed, and barricaded herself in her room. She called Tannery and went straight to voicemail, saying the pizza shop was closed. She whispered, "Lucky and Meyer are at my fuckin' door…they gonna kill my ass! Get here now!"

Lucky would continue to bang for an additional ten minutes while screaming obscenities through the door. She was understandably upset, but Lucky did finally leave. Markeeta was now wide awake, chain-smoking, and calling Agent Tannery in five-minute intervals.

Markeeta's last message was at 1:30 p.m. She said, "You're a fuckin' piece of shit! I should have never fucked wit' the feds. Now my ass is on the line, and you don't have my back? You wouldn't have Manny Machiavelli if it wasn't for me! Remember that bitch! I should go to TMZ and tell them all this shit, how it really goes down! Tamron Hall…Don Lemon…I be knowin' shit. Fuck wit' me if you wanna, and I'll have Justin Carter reporting for TSR Investigates on y'all crooked asses!"

Lucky had to literally drag Meyer from Markeeta's building. Meyer began forcefully kicking on the door when she refused to let them in. He had just about penetrated when neighbors began opening their doors, peeking out to see what was causing the commotion. Lucky knew a couple things were true. Calls went out to not only NYPD but also the feds.

Meyer felt like he owed his sister an apology for not trusting her instincts. He'd taken up for Markeeta, vouched that she couldn't be a snitch, yet her actions said otherwise. She was definitely working with those peoples; it seemed everyone was, including Lucky's secret beat.

Meyer fixed his sweet purple drink and went to his room to get some sleep. Lucky, however, couldn't do much of anything but cry, make threats, and cry some more. Ragnar, or whatever his real name was, his cellphone was no longer in service. Lucky needed clarity. She sparked up a blunt and sat in silence for some time. Ragnar had disappeared. All traces of him were gone. Yet, Markeeta was still a sitting duck. Were the feds hoping that Lucky and Meyer would put their murder game down, ultimately handing the feds life sentences on a silver platter? Markeeta, expendable—Ragnar not expendable. Markeeta/informant. Ragnar/fed.

But why would a fed investigating me fuck me? She wanted to know. It doesn't add up. And could compromise any case they're building. Yet she didn't have any pictures of them together; he never set foot in her home, so no fingerprints to be collected, and other than a video that could be any tiny dicked Black male—it was her word against the law.

Lucky called Markeeta's phone, knowing she wouldn't pick up. At each tone, Lucky pressed PLAY, and Tupac's angst-riddled voice spat, *"Knew he was working wit' the feds, same crime, different trials, nigga picture what he said...."*

Lucky kept calling and allowed the rap song to be the same. The message: *You're a snitch. And I know this to be true*—until Markeeta shut her phone off.

Chapter 26

Maxine and Wendy were in their cardboard box home, feasting on medium-rare steaks and potatoes that Wendy had scavenged from the dump of Amy Ruth's Steak House. The restaurant was crowded that early Saturday evening, and the busboys were trashing food soon after each dish was plated. Wendy had bagged a week's worth of dinners before others came sniffing around. Maxine said, "Hey, if I came into some money, life-changing money, would you leave New York with me?"

"How much money you talking?"

"This is hypothetical…so let's say millions."

Wendy gave Maxine the side-eye. Unbeknownst to Maxine, Wendy had already found the .45 pistol and the box of ammunition Maxine had bought. Couple that with an ex-boyfriend who was a drug dealer, and it spelled a situation she didn't want any part in.

"Look, if you scratched a lottery ticket and won millions and wanted to hook a sistah up, I'd be down to leave all this behind." Wendy outstretched her hands, outlining all she had collected while on the streets. "But I won't give up my peace of mind to look over my shoulder for the rest of my life…not for money."

"It wouldn't be like that," Maxine objected. "I'm not planning on robbing a bank."

"Then what are you planning?"

"Nothing," she lied. "I was just daydreaming out loud. Never mind, it was silly."

Maybe it was best to leave Wendy in the dark about her

upcoming murder appointment. Maxine went to Scott and Bugsy's homes for months, hoping to catch a glimpse of either one before her policies expired. She couldn't gain any traction on Bugsy, but Scott popped up, and he was a sight for sore eyes. Scott was well insulated, surrounded by goons and henchmen, but she'd find a way. Because she still had the will.

Everyone stepped out of the SUV at the address Lucky had given and stared at the Bronx tenement building. Meyer's Escalade and Lucky's G5 were parked out front. Puzzled, everyone assumed that this had to be temporary lodging given by one of Meyer's jump-offs until they were buzzed in and read *Château Lucchese*. Lucky had a lot of questions when Bugsy had called, mainly who bailed him out, but he said he'd explain once he got there.

Zaire and Kane took the stairs to ensure there weren't gunmen lying in the cut for an ambush while Mason rode up with his boss. Scott and Layla were at war with their children and hadn't unilaterally squashed their beef.

When Lucky flung open the door and saw Scott, she ran straight into his arms and cried like a baby. Scott gave his daughter a bear hug he didn't know he still had in him. Lucky was heartsick. Her remaining strength, lingering anger, and defiance had been depleted. That video, that singular disgusting move from Ragnar, had reduced her to nothing. The reduction was clear to everyone. Ragnar wanted her to suffer a living death.

Layla was unmoved by the overly dramatic lovefest between her husband and daughter. She and Bugsy moved farther into the apartment, looking for Meyer. He, too, was a pitiful sight. Meyer was nearly comatose, a gun inches away from his head. He had on cheap boxers, sleeping face down on an air mattress. Layla's heart softened instantly as she bent down and tried to wake him.

"Meyer, get up," she sternly said while nudging him awake. Repeatedly, Layla and Bugsy called out to him until the others were standing in the modest-sized room.

Lucky offered up, "He's been smoking a lot lately and drinking Henny."

Layla shot her daughter a nasty look. "This ain't from Henny and Kush." She spoke directly to her son. "Meyer, what'd you take?"

Finally, Meyer's eyes lifted. He wasn't sure if he was dreaming as he looked into the faces of Bugsy, Scott, and Layla— drifting in and out of reality. But everyone was glad he was alive.

Scott looked around at their meager surroundings and spoke, "We're getting the fuck up outta here. Y'all coming home with us."

Tannery had heard all the frantic messages from Markeeta about her cousins at her door, but most sobering, he listened to her threat. It was a threat she wasn't shy about making. She'd made that same threat from day one. Markeeta, like most, didn't understand the small word: power. She thought she did. And leverage was relative. We got away with so much because people thought we were the good guys; we're not. Brown told her that anyone could stand in her shoes. A crop of informants just waiting to be chosen was younger, smarter, and more connected than her. And her cover was blown. She was of no use if Lucky knew she was cooperating with the government.

Tannery let Markeeta sweat it out for a few days while she held up in her apartment, afraid to go outside. The calls with bravado and threats had reduced to begs and pleas, all of which tickled him.

Shortly after seven a.m., Markeeta was showered and dressed for work when her cellphone rang. It was her job. Markeeta put on her corporate voice. "Hello," she said.

"Hi, is this Markeeta?"

"Yes."

"Hi, Markeeta. This is Alexis."

She was her supervisor.

"Hey, Alexis. I'm on my way in. What's up?"

"Yeah…about that. Human Resources called and said that you falsified your bachelor's degree." Alexis's voice got stern. "Is that true?"

"Wait, what?" Markeeta said. Tannery had gotten her this job; she didn't falsify shit. There was a test she had to take that he had given her the answers to, but all that other shit she was talking about wasn't even her handiwork.

Her voice elevated as if Markeeta was hearing impaired. "Do you have a degree or not!"

"Let me make a call, and someone will call you back to straighten all this out." Markeeta's voice was a panicky plea.

"Don't bother. You're fired."

Tannery contacted Alexis and told her exactly what to say and how to say it. And then he and Brown listened in on the call. Seconds later, Tannery's phone buzzed. It was Markeeta.

She was sent to voicemail, and they listened to this, "What's going on, Tannery? It ain't that serious. You gonna take my job, yo. I thought we were cool…just call me back so we can get back on track. I got some more peoples for y'all. It ain't gotta end wit' Lucky."

Markeeta was sitting on her plush sofa, cognac in one hand, a blunt in the other when she heard a commotion going on in the hallway. She'd just gotten fired a couple of hours earlier and told her son to go back to bed. Markeeta was in a foul mood and didn't want to drive him to school.

Keys jangled, locks unlocked, and a moving crew came barging in.

"What the fuck is this?" she asked as her voice rose. "I live here!"

There were nine men in her apartment, and each glared her way. The cold, dismissive attitudes, burley workers, and aggressive stares had her stomach doing flip flops. Ralph ran out of his room and stood, stunned, next to his mother. Bubble wrap, blankets, boxes, and dollies were rolled into what Markeeta thought was her forever home.

When no one said anything, and she didn't see Tannery or Brown, Markeeta yelled, "I'm calling the cops!"

No movement was halted. Everyone just kept working, breaking down room by room.

Markeeta called nine-one-one and frantically tried to explain her situation. "I need the cops to my apartment."

"Yes, this is nine-one-one," the female repeated.

"I need help! These men just barged into my apartment and are packing up my stuff!"

"You need help with your stuff?"

"No!" Markeeta shouted. "Men are in my apartment taking my things!"

"Do you know them?"

"No! I don't. They just walked in!"

"So you don't know them?"

Markeeta blew out air. "I said I don't. I need you to send the cops!"

"For what?"

"What is you talkin' about? I need you to send the police. I'm being robbed!"

"What is your address."

"7366 Mockingbird Lane, apartment 27."

"1366—"

"Seven!"

"Seven Mockingbird Lane, ma'am?"

"No! 7! 3! 6! 6! Mockingbird Lane!"

"Hold on," the nine-one-one operator placed Markeeta on hold while weird music played. Markeeta's eyes darted forth and back as her beautiful belongings were being packed up and moved out of the apartment. At some point, she realized that she'd been on hold for twenty minutes. "Hello!" she screamed into the music and then hung up. Immediately she called back, and the seemingly same voice answered.

"Yeah, I just called. Are y'all sending the police?"

"You need the police?"

"Yeah, I just called and was placed on hold. My address is 7366 Mockingbird Lane, apartment 27."

"1366—"

Markeeta hung up, realizing she wasn't speaking to actual dispatch. She pushed past the men and ran down to the lobby. She grabbed the building's phone at the concierges' desk and tried again.

"Nine-one-one, what's the emergency?"

It was the same voice. Markeeta disconnected the call. Defeated, she went back upstairs and watched all the contents of her home walk out the door.

"I'm not leaving!" she screamed to anyone who would give her eye contact. "Y'all better tell Tannery that I'm not muthafuckin' leaving!"

It would take eight hours for the apartment to be hollowed out, and just as the last dolly rolled out, in came two NYPD officers. Markeeta heard the familiar sound of two-way radios crackling and knew it was five-oh.

"You called for police assistance?" Officer Carrol asked.

"That was hours ago."

"Did you call was my question?"

"Yeah," she said sourly.

"What's your name?"

"Markeeta West."

"Any middle initial?"

"M as in Mary."

Officer Carrol had an iPad, seemingly entering her

information. He looked up and stared at Markeeta. "Any warrants?"

"What?" she questioned. "No!"

He looked back down, let a pregnant pause go by, and said, "What's going on?"

"A group of movers entered my apartment and took all my stuff! My room, my sons' room. Everything!"

He nodded. His partner, Officer Newton, said, "You got receipts for what you said they took?"

"Receipts?" Markeeta gave a quizzical look. "No, I don't!"

"Ok, so we'll write this up, and you can come down to the precinct and get a report—"

"Write what up? You didn't investigate shit! Go down to security and get the footage of all my things that rolled out of here!"

"As I said, you can come down to the precinct in two days to get a report of this incident. But for now, you gotta vacate the premises," said Newton.

"I'm not fuckin' leaving! We live here!"

"Do you have proof?"

"Proof?"

Officer Carrol snapped, "Why do you keep repeating our questions! Proof! Proof that you've been paying rent to live in this expensive building!"

Markeeta knew what this was. It was being on the other side of the eight ball. Tannery and Brown had used her; gotten the Manny Machiavelli conviction and all the accolades that came with it. Meanwhile, she'd pissed away her friendship with Shirelle, ratted on her family, and sent Manny wit' the good dick to jail. She didn't play the game; the game played her.

"Nah, I ain't got no proof."

"Then we're here to escort you out of the building."

Markeeta and her son's clothing were bagged up in large trash bags and tossed in a corner. The officers didn't lift a finger as she dragged the bags into the elevator with looky-loos turning up their noses. The humiliation of the moment had affected Ralph, and he shrunk into his quiet place in his mind. Markeeta pulled the bags that were shredding with each step to where she knew she'd parked her Range. That, too, had been confiscated.

Markeeta had nowhere to go and no one to blame but the person in the mirror. Meanwhile, Tannery and Brown not only listened to the exchange with the officers they had sent to the apartment but stuck around to see if she'd go for the Range; she did. How fucking stupid could one person be?

Back at their parents' four-bedroom palatial condominium, Bugsy, Meyer, and Lucky took languorous showers, stretched out on two thousand thread count sheets, and dined on 5-star meals cooked by their parents' housekeeper. All had agreed to a truce as Scott took over all affairs. He hired contractors to work with his children's insurance companies while realtors searched the city for suitable properties closer to his residence. There wasn't any way Scott would allow them to move back into those apartments once they'd been compromised. Their vehicles were also retrieved off Gino's lot, and shortly after that, Gino's Benz S550 lost control, and he crashed. There were no survivors.

Scott and Layla were astounded at the shenanigans perpetrated against their children, but Lucky was most violated. The feds had stalked Meyer, railroaded Bugsy, and most egregiously wanted to gaslight his daughter. Lucky told them about the missing items, her alarm going off at random times during the night, her smashed truck windows, the broken gift from Bonnie, and her lights and electronics being placed on. She told them about going to look for Ragnar Benjamin, and the building's concierge said he'd never seen her before and that no one by that name lived there. The feds were trying to make her think she was crazy, and then, in an attempt to push her over the edge, they released the tape.

As Scott listened, he had a wild look in his eyes. Mason knew that look; it meant that Ragnar's death wouldn't be quick, there would be no mercy, and those he loved would be joining him in an unmarked grave. They just needed to find this ghost.

Once Scott involved his legal team, what was meant to harm Lucky could actually end up helping the West family. Liam Gavalas, Christopher Azul, and associates met with a sketch artist at Scott's. Lucky described her former lover down to each freckle on his face. The sketch and the sex tape would be entered into a brief. The attorneys would file a preemptive motion with the federal court and demand that this agent is identified. The motion asked that his body be examined by expert witnesses and compared to the tape once he's located. If it was good enough for Michael Jackson, it was good enough for Ragnar Benjamin, aka Agent John Doe. Gavalas would then ask that any evidence collected by this agent and his colleagues working on building a case against the West family be thrown out under *Silverthorne Lumber Co. v. United States*, fruit from a poisonous tree.

The infamous Instagram handle had been taken down, sex tape gone. But luckily, Lucky had saved a copy, and their attorneys were subpoenaing Facebook for a copy of the handle's history. Scott deduced that his legal team could get the ball rolling, but his street team would bring this shit to a full muthafuckin' stop.

Scott held a long-overdue meeting with his men, only this time his family, those remaining members, were all present, just like old times.

"My wife and I ain't been home in a minute," he began. "But I kept the cash flowing even though there wasn't any product.

That means you been on a long, paid vacation." Scott looked in the eyes of many so they could feel his words. "That shit ends today!"

He continued with, "Some of y'all niggas may have heard things about my family from third parties, chitchat from grown men that works best for teenaged girls. Let me remind y'all, if you don't hear it from me, it ain't gospel."

The room was packed. All henchmen had gathered at a restaurant owned by Mason, each goon staring at the West dynasty. Scott stood in the center, flanked by Layla and Lucky, end-capped by Bugsy and Meyer—the family represented power.

"We are now at war with two cartels, Garcia, and Juarez. I don't have to break down why or what that means, just know to watch your backs," he then chuckled, "And my Black ass."

The room laughed.

"Some of y'all may have seen or heard about a video of my daughter posted online. This nigga thinks he's an Einstein, that he's covered all his tracks. He's taken comfort in feeling like he's a ghost. I'm putting a ten million dollar bounty on his head to be brought to me alive. Whoever finds this piece of shit,"—Scott spit out a chunk of phlegm—"You won't even have to get your hands dirty."

Someone called out, "How do we find this nigga, boss?"

"If we knew that answer, why offer a bounty?" Mason spoke up and then repeatedly tapped his temple. "Think, nigga! That's what you're paid to do."

Lucky wanted to show her strength since this matter concerned her. She didn't want to look weak in a room full of men who had possibly seen her at her most vulnerable point.

"We have a sketch of what he looks like…made thousands of copies, and on the back is his alias, last known residence, places he frequented, and the make and model of his car. He's a Black male with freckles, reddish-brown skin, and fiery red hair, in his forties. Anyone fitting that description needs to be captured and brought to us. I'm the only one who can definitively identify that piece of shit," said Lucky. "Y'all found more niggas with less information for my father. Find this parasite so we can show him what no mercy feels like!"

Scott didn't expect his daughter to speak but was proud she did. He concluded the meeting, and the family remained.

"Why didn't you sic them on Markeeta!" Lucky wanted to know. Bugsy and Meyer had sat on her residence for days until they confirmed that she pulled a *gone girl*.

"I want her dead, Daddy!" Lucky pouted. "I want her fingernails pulled out, her fuckin' eyeballs removed with spoons! Ooh…I want her bones broken, crunched into tiny pieces like stepping on a bag of potato chips!"

"Damn, you want a lot," Scott said and kissed Lucky's forehead. Everyone knew better than to patronize or dismiss her trauma. "If that's what my princess wants, then that's what she'll get."

Layla had to swallow the vile taste that had crept up in her mouth. She wasn't down with Lucky reliving her teens with her husband. Scott had spoiled Lucky rotten when Lucky was a teenager, but now, she was a grown woman who had reverted back to baby talk, poking out her lips, and whining. Layla was waiting for Lucky to pull a tantrum so she could slap her back to age twenty-two.

Layla said, "Markeeta is last on our hit list, Lucky! We got two cartels on our asses, two sicarios are still breathing, and we still have to clean up this mess with that Red Guard…Ray Nard…or whatever the fuck his name is! And do I need to mention the feds and no coke?"

Lucky glared at her mother as the twins remained silent. Scott said, "I give you my word she'll be handled. They both will…it's time."

Scott felt it was time to let his children know why he didn't fuck with his family.

"We grew up next door to the Valdez family. My mother's best friend was Alana Valdez and she had a son, Julio. I was a young nigga, getting money, and my money took care of my whole household. My sister, Diane, was a loud, mean drunk. The type of person who ended the party once she came through. Her and Julio had fucked with each other on and off for years, the kind of couple that shouldn't be together, but no one else wanted them. Julio was a bum ass nigga without ambition. On the strength of Diane, I tried to put him on, gave him packages on consignment, and he'd fuck up every time. Coupled with the fact that he was a woman beater, always laying hands on my sister, I'd beat his ass more times than I can remember.

"I'd been up all night hustling, had just kicked off my sneakers, and fell out when Diane woke me up. Her face was all bloody, and she was screaming, hollering at the top of her lungs. 'Julio tried to kill me! He shot me, Scott! He shot me!' Not thinking clearly, seeing blood dripping down my sister's face, I grabbed my pistol and found him in our building's lobby. No questions asked, I pulled the trigger, and his body dropped where he stood.

"Two people other than myself had seen the shooting; Diane and Valerie. NYPD came around and did a piss poor job at trying to solve the homicide, but just in case, I had stayed at Layla's for a few weeks."

Layla said, "I told him to murder Valerie because she was a witness, but he ain't listen to me."

Scott nodded. "When I went back home, Valerie, who feared for her life, came and pledged her allegiance to me. She told me the real story: Julio and Diane argued over crack. The trio was smoking, and Diane had gotten greedy. Julio and Valerie had watched Diane bust herself upside her head and threatened that she'd come to get me to fuck Julio up if he didn't give her the last hit. He didn't."

"And Scott didn't even know Diane was a crackhead at that

time."

Again, Scott nodded. "I moved out of my moms' house that day and continued to rise in the drug game. A couple of years later, my name was ringing out, and NYPD circled back around about the murder of Julio Valdez. They straight up told me that they had a witness. Out on bail, I bodied Valerie, who had gotten her life together thinking she was the informant. Arrogantly, I thought the case would fall apart. Diane broke my heart when she took the stand and testified against me. My mother came to court not to support me but to be there for her daughter."

The kids thought they saw sadness in their father's eyes.

"Layla had just given birth to y'all twins, so I had no choice but to take the stand. I spun a yarn of wanting to be a professional ballplayer, looked into the jurors' eyes when I spoke, and outlined a life of erratic behavior from my alcoholic, crack-addicted sister. How my sister came in covered in blood, saying someone had just murdered Julio. I told how the cops never came to take my statement or question me about that night. Before this arrest, I had no priors. And this was a city where the crack era had left many victims, most victimized by crack-addicted relatives. It was a slam dunk…found not guilty within three hours of jury deliberation."

Layla jumped in, "But while deliberating, Scott had to hold me back from fuckin' that bitch up! We heard Diane in the hallway hollering about her snitch money the A.D.A. had promised her for her testimony." Layla snorted and then reenacted the scene. "Where's my check! Where's my check!"

Scott continued, "Diane got paid a measly couple hundred a day for her cooperation against me. And although my mother had taken her side, I still continued to pay for all my mother's expenses and would allow her to get to know her grandkids just as long as she promised to keep Diane away when y'all were around."

"That bitch couldn't even do that. Diane's shit didn't stink to y'all grandmother, so we finally decided to cut Scott's family off for good."

"This time, I will make the separation permanent," Scott promised.

Chapter 27

Three carloads full of goons rode around the city day and night in low-riders at all the known hot spots that Meyer, Bugsy, or Lucky frequented. AK automatics, sawed-off shotguns, and chrome ninas were ready for homicide. The click-clacking of guns could be heard cutting through the silent car interiors as the shooters checked clips, chambers, and ammunition. These were members of the slain workers who were slaughtered at the warehouses owned by the young Wests. The same family members expected large payouts, but none came.

Rakim said, "I want that nigga wit' that slick ass mouth. I'ma blow Meyer's head off!"

As the FBI fought back with their own motions to protect the identity of Franklin Garrett, Lucky couldn't have delivered more shocking news to her family. While everyone dined on champagne and lobster at dinner, she announced, "I'm pregnant. And the feds the father."

"You're muthafuckin' what?" said Scott.

"Twelve weeks pregnant, Daddy. And I'm keepin' my baby."

"You didn't want the first one," Layla spat.

"No way you're bringing a half-fed into this family!" Scott barked. "No fuckin' way. Get rid of it!"

Lucky explained, "I've thought it through, and this could be a win for us."

No one said shit, but they all were thinking it. Bugsy's dumb ass already had thought with his heart and not his head with

Maxine, and look how that ended up. Everyone just kept eating.

Lucky continued, "Let's assume the feds have an airtight case against us. We'll have a better chance arguing the fruit of the poisonous tree and getting evidence thrown out if I can prove we had a relationship, right? How better to prove that than with this baby? DNA don't lie."

"Lord, please help this dummy." Layla dropped her lobster tail and glared at her daughter. "Why do you think your father got shooters looking for this fed? You think it was just to give you your dignity back?" Layla snorted. "No, fool. What the lawyers are doing on the legal end is a longshot. If the feds have a case, a solid case, then kiss our asses goodbye and ain't no baby gonna save us! Ray Negro dies, and so does his baby!"

Scott had taken meetings with other significant players in the game. He needed a new connect, so he met with Kiqué Helguero and Caesar Mingo. These were grown men who knew the game, and all concluded that it would be unwise for Scott to cop from anyone who lives on American soil because Scott was hot. He would need another connect like the Garcia cartel, where Javier Garcia didn't live nor frequent the United States. So it was a meeting he would take when Angel Morales called.

Seven black GMC SUVs traveled down a dirt road and stopped at the neutral location chosen by both parties. It was in New Jersey, on the outskirts of Atlantic City, an isolated place near the Wharton State forest. The site was a secluded log cabin that was nestled in the boondocks. It had privacy, and each organization brought security.

Scott, Bugsy, Meyer, Layla, and Lucky arrived together heavily armed with over two dozen men—a display of strength and cohesiveness. Scott wanted his enemies to know that his family's bond was unbreakable despite their past disagreements.

Angel arrived at the exact location with Louis, his trusted first in command, around the same time, and he, too, came with an army.

Already, things started off tense between both parties. Meyer glared at Angel and his henchmen, and he felt the urge to react. Meyer wanted to blow Angel's brains out for financially crippling his business, and murdering his niece. But Scott and Bugsy had given him a warning not to go there. It sickened Meyer and Lucky to face Angel and couldn't kill him. But Scott was running the show, and he wanted everyone to be on their best behavior until he told them not to be.

Angel had reached out to the entire West family for a sit-down and gave no details surrounding the meeting. No one trusted Angel, and they were reluctant to be in the same room with him, but Angel assured them that it would be worth their time.

All parties involved walked into the cabin. The soldiers took their positions outside, vigilant of each other and any outside forces—law enforcement, rival cartel, or hired sicarios looking to collect a large payday.

The influential individuals from both organizations took a seat at the large round table, Angel, and Louis on one side and the Wests on the other.

Still, everyone inside the room was on edge. *What now?*

Angel spoke first. "So much anger and bloodshed between us when I wish it wasn't. It should have always been about business, not murder."

Scott said, "In our business, you can't have one without the other."

Angel shrugged. "We are in the same business, Scott, but not the same lane." He continued to punctuate his point. "My cartel supplies cocaína, and your children's organization distributed it. We should have always been allies, not enemies. Mexican cartels should war with other cartels; mono y mono, Pitbull against

Pitbull. Juarez against your organization, empire, conglomerate—however, you choose to define yourself is like a Pitbull against a Doberman. An opponent, sí...but no match."

Scott refused to be disrespected. "Yet the West *organization*, all five members are still standing, ten toes firmly planted on the ground. I've crossed over into your terrain throughout the years, taken out cartels on both sides of the border. I've never shied away from a battle and never will. Whoever wants war can get it."

"Relax, Scott. Tranquilo...I said Doberman, not Chihuahua," Angel laughed, amused. "No disrespect, huh? My point is that we should all live to enjoy the vast amounts of money we've made."

"How do you propose we fix this situation between our peoples," Scott said coolly.

Angel looked at Lucky. The contempt she had for him was apparent. He said about her, "You were an unfortunate mistake, and that mistake produced our child, Lucchese. I wished you never lied to me but understand why you did."

Lucky glared at him. She hated being seen as a fling, and considering he murdered their child, she felt he had no right to mention her. It took everything she had not to jump on the table and vehemently slam a knife into his neck. But she would be dead before she leaped his way.

Angel continued to speak. His words now were toward Layla. "Juarez cartel has a set of rules that has survived generations...rules that I disregarded—first, by doing business with a woman, and that was you, Layla. I used to think that women were emotional until I met you. You are just as, if not more cunning than any narcotrafficante I've dealt with...and that's a compliment. So when you came to me disclosing that Lucky had not given birth to a full-term boy, but a premature girl, as indicated by Lucky, a few things were clear. By my hands, you wanted your daughter *and* my daughter dead, but most enlightening was that you knew *all* Juarez cartels' rules."

"That's a lie!" Layla snapped and was ready to leave when Scott placed his heavy hand on hers, pausing her movement. Scott knew what they'd done; he also knew that his children did too; hearing it aloud was of no consequence. As he said earlier, business and murder always collided for him.

"Layla, please," Angel said in his calm, effeminate voice. "I'm here to put everything out in the open, sí? So we can move forward on better terms."

Begrudgingly Layla shrugged.

Bugsy frowned the hardest at Angel's statement. The mere mention of his dead son and which part each member in his family had played in Dillinger's demise could be enough to finally send him over the edge. It was a fact that his parents had Avery murder his son, but what about his sister? Bugsy couldn't keep dismissing that Lucky's insistence of sharing an apartment while simultaneously telling Angel she gave birth to a boy was a recipe for murder, was it not?

The gangsta didn't mumble a fuckin' word. He just kept listening.

"Somehow, I suspect that Layla and Scott found out that another cartel rule was that we could not have any heir to the Juarez throne that wasn't one hundred percent Mexican."

"What is the point of telling us this, Angel….let's bottom line this. Why did you call us to meet?" Scott said. "Are you trying to bring dissension between my family? Why are we here?"

"Because I have decided to step down as head of Juarez, and my cousin, Louis, will run the cartel. And in my absence, Louis wants nothing but to move forward again with business—supplier and distributor. Money over everything."

Louis was about to take over the meeting when Scott spoke up again. He was the only West in the room that had solved the riddle.

"Am I to understand that Lucchese is alive?"

"She is," Angel affirmed. "And all this bloodshed between us, over Lucchese, is fruitless and absurd because Lucky didn't want the child. I generously gave Lucky an ultimatum…her life for the life of her baby—Mexican law, and she refused the deal."

It was news to everyone at the table. The Wests had no idea Lulu was still alive nor the ultimatum Lucky was given. However, Scott and Layla were privy to that law. The Garcia cartel wanted them to experience it up close and personally, with Layla taking a bullet for the life of Hector Garcia.

"She what…?" Bugsy uttered.

Angel didn't falter, he saw their questionable stares, and he confirmed by saying, "Yes, she's still alive and has been living with me, under my protection. And to keep it that way, to keep my daughter safe, I've named Louis my successor, relinquished my power in Juarez, and will relocate us to an unknown location. You all were asked to be here to end this war for good because should any one of you…anyone!"—Angel's voice rose—"Come to harm my daughter, I will come out of retirement and unleash the fury as only a parent can when protecting their niños."

Meyer was relieved while Lucky *feigned* relief. Scott looked nonchalant, and Layla looked on the fence. But Bugsy, he was a different story. He took in everything that Angel had said, finally losing it—he leaped from his chair and charged at Lucky, his large hands pounding against her skull.

"She's a fuckin' baby!" he yelled, his left fist swelling her right eye. "She fuckin' needed you, and you didn't give a fuck about her!"—Lucky's lip split, opening wide and spewing blood. "You abandoned her, you selfish bitch! You left her to die just like my son!"—her jaw jiggled, nearly breaking under Bugsy's knuckles.

Immediately, Scott and Meyer came in between the two, and Angel simply sat there and watched the show. *Lucky needed her ass whipped and much more,* Angel thought. Bugsy continued his abrupt outburst and shouted, "I should fuckin' kill you!"

"Get him off me!" Lucky hollered. She wasn't the one to back down from a challenge or fight, nor did she see herself as the culprit. She rebuked, "You killed Dillinger, not me! You should have never fucked Maxine! Had Dillinger lived, he would have never been a West! Not after what his mother did to our family!"

Lucky had learned from the best. She was trying to refocus the anger from her deeds toward Bugsy, making all family members remember her dead brothers and sister. To her count, it was three dead children to Bugsy's one—she was winning.

The intense squabble between brother and sister wasn't orchestrated by Angel. He was really there for peace. And when their quarreling peaked at the point where guns were drawn, Angel quickly saw his meeting going left.

Bugsy angrily pulled out a shiny Walter PPK pistol and nestled the barrel firmly against Lucky's temple—his finger on the trigger, her death just a squeeze away. And once that happened, Meyer pulled out his chrome ninas and pointed his guns at Bugsy, his eyes pleading with his twin, *Bruh, please, don't make me do this shit.* With the quickness, Scott aimed his .45 at Meyer's dome. Layla was the only one who spoke as her Glock 17 touched the back of Scott's skull. She spat, "Move your fuckin' gun from my son's head, nigga!"

If you froze this frame, you would see where allegiances lay within the family. And Angel was taking notes, a master class on the West pyramid. Meyer equally loved his twin but would see Bugsy dead before allowing him to murder Lucky. And Layla would die for her husband but wouldn't hesitate to slam a bullet between his eyeballs if he harmed her favorite child. And although Scott had twin sons, it was no secret that Bugsy had his loyalty.

"Everyone, just calm the fuck down," said Scott, the diplomat. "We're all getting ahead of ourselves here. Is this how we want to end things?"

"He's right, we all need to take a deep breath and relax, or we all can die right now, and then what?" Layla agreed.

Bugsy read the room and realized that he was the only one

who felt some way about Lucky. He acquiesced, and everyone followed and lowered their guns.

"It don't matter who mothered my child, bitch. I was his father, and my little man will always be a West, and your saying otherwise won't change that." He spoke directly to his sister, disregarding that his parents had Dillinger murdered. "From today on, you're dead to me."

"Bugsy, relax," spoke Scott. "We've all made mistakes."

"My son wasn't a mistake!" Bugsy corrected.

"You think you lost something? I lost three children to the bitch you had a baby with," Layla exclaimed. "You're not the only one who took a huge loss. Now let's move on."

Bugsy felt betrayed by his whole family. He could live a hundred years and never forget that his twin pointed double barrels at his head, his sister plotted his son's demise, and his parents executed the hit. They kept telling him to move on and get over it like he'd lost money in a stock trade, totaled his new whip, or caught wifey fucking his homie. He had to bury his butchered son's body six feet in the ground.

As Bugsy continued to brood, the meeting when on. Louis took the floor briefly, and it was settled that Juarez would supply Scott with tons of kilos, and their children would operate under their parents' umbrella just like old times.

The Wests were no longer two factions.

Lucky went over every encounter, every conversation, things said and not said with Ragnar, and focused on religion. Why bring it into his cover story if it were not true? She nor her family were religious, so she figured that this man was. He added a sprinkle of the truth and mixed it in with many lies. She started with Saint Gabriel's Catholic Church, hovering outside during Sunday mass and midday confessionals, but he never showed up. Lucky knew this wouldn't be easy, so she pushed further.

On her smartphone, she pinned all Catholic churches surrounding the federal building's headquarters, and within days there he was. That red-faced, fire-crotched bitch came bebopping out like there wasn't a ten million dollar bounty on his head. She fell back and watched as he got into an SUV with dark, tinted windows.

Finding Ragnar was challenging; following him home was damn near impossible. Lucky knew she was dealing with a fed, trained by the academy to avoid such pitfalls, and, most critical—protect where they rested their heads at night. If she knew his real name, she would never find him in a Google search engine. He was protected…that Illuminati shit at play. But with patience, the sheer willpower of a strong Black woman, she broke the code and his home she indeed sat in front of.

Lucky watched his routine for days; when he got home, his wife, his son—one big happy family. She didn't see any surveillance cameras, but she knew they were there. Had to be. And, of course, there wasn't an ADT yard sign, as all his neighbors had. This home was seemingly unprotected, and only fools would pay the stupid tax.

Lucky sat a few houses down in a rental, chain-smoking. A half dozen Newport's were in the ashtray, and Solange was on repeat.

I tried to drink it away…I tried to change it with my hair…I tried to let go of my lover, thought if I were alone, then I would recover…

Lucky didn't plan to wait another day for her confrontation, nor should she. Just as she timed it, the son was dropped off by a neighbor a few minutes past four. Lazily, the thirteen-year-old walked up the driveway with his cleats in his hand. His keys jangled before he opened his front door. The gun to his head startled him, and his gaped open mouth was covered by Lucky's hand. She kicked the door closed and pushed him toward the noise. Inside a lofty kitchen sat Ragnar on a stool eating a burger, and his wife was at the stove sautéing vegetables. The look on Ragnar's face was a Kodak moment for Lucky. The muthafuckin' shock of the moment was beyond belief for him.

"Take it easy," he began. "They don't have anything to do with this."

"You piece of shit…" she spat. Lucky glared, taking it all in. And then said, "Are those my earrings!" Her pink diamonds sparkled in his ears. She looked to the wife, "And that's my muthafuckin' watch, bitch! Take it off!"

"Franklin…what's happening?" Martha asked, her voice trembling.

"Franklin?!" Lucky snorted. "Not Ragnar Benjamin, the scientist!"

Franklin was still trying to see how to gain control of the situation. It was complicated with Lucky pointing a pistol at his son's head, his own gun was locked in his gun safe per bureau rules, and he was too many feet away to bumrush her. He needed to treat this as a hostage negotiation and talk her off the ledge.

"You want the earrings, here…take them." Franklin began unscrewing the precious stones and placing them on his granite countertop. He nodded to his wife to remove her watch. Which she did.

"You hear this nigga?" Her voice dripped with disgust. "This ain't a muthafuckin' robbery! This is MY shit that you STOLE from me! You hear that, boy! Your daddy's a thief!"

She continued, "You." The gun was pointed toward Martha. "Read the inscription on the watch."

Martha didn't want to. She knew what it said and didn't want to say it aloud. When Franklin had given it to her for their anniversary, she could admit that the words didn't sound like him. But the watch was so exquisite and expensive that she decided she liked the change in him; his new wardrobe, edgier vernacular, and gaudy jewelry. The gun was transferred back to her son when Martha didn't move.

"First bullet goes in shorty's head, the next in yours, bitch!"

The warm liquid made its way through his boxers, down his leg, and puddled on the floor where Lucky and the boy stood. The teenager began to quietly cry; large round tears ran down his cheeks. He didn't know what was happening and desperately wanted his daddy to save him. Lucky understood. She was just as wounded and traumatized and had wanted her daddy to save her. Then realized this was something she had to do for *and* by herself. Her family would never understand why she needed this confrontation, why she chose to have his baby, and how she ultimately believed her son could save them all. Lucky didn't come to kill; she came to confront.

"Please," Martha begged. "Have a heart! Let my son go."

"Read, bitch."

"Do it," Franklin snapped at his wife. He knew who was calling the shots.

Martha cleared her throat. "*To baby girl, my Luck…from me….*"

"Are you, baby girl?" Lucky asked. "Because I remember when my man gave me that watch for my sixteenth birthday…said I was his luck. Me! Lucky Luciana West! Yet, Franklin stole it from me and put it on your wrist. You might be thinking that says a lot about how he felt about me—" Lucky didn't wait for anyone to respond. She continued with, "No, grandma! It says a lot about how he feels about you!"

"Knock it off," Franklin bellowed.

"Or what?!"

Lucky had complete control of the room, mainly because she had control of their son. "What's your name?" she asked the boy and lightly tapped him on his forehead so he knew whom she was speaking to.

"Junior," he quietly answered.

"Your government."

Junior didn't know what that meant, so his father answered

309

for him. Still lying, Franklin Garrett replied, "His name is Franklin Washington Jr."

"Well, Franklin Washington Jr., you'll have a little brother soon. Franklin Washington West Jr. the third." Lucky chuckled.

"That's a lie!" spat Martha.

"Is it, Franklin?" Lucky asked.

Franklin and Martha exchanged glares. He knew the condom had broken a time or two.

"Do you know how to work a cellphone, Junior?"

The kid, who had stopped crying by now, had settled into being her hostage. He nodded. "Dig in my jacket and retrieve mine." Lucky gave him her security code to unlock her phone, and he did the rest. These kids these days were Einstein's when it came to technology. Junior found the video that Lucky had described and pressed PLAY. She allowed him to watch the video as Franklin stood helpless. This was the video Franklin had put out for public consumption, the video that he gave no fucks if someone else's child found it on the world wide web. Therefore his son wouldn't be spared.

"What is that? What's he watching," Martha wanted to know.

"Your turn."

Martha slowly left the stove and ambled toward her son. Lucky didn't have to bark threats; the rules of the day were firmly in place. Martha took the phone and, without provocation, walked back to the safety of the stove.

"Don't…" Franklin said before she hit PLAY. "Martha, please, don't watch it."

She didn't say a word. Martha hit PLAY and saw every cringeworthy hip thrust, ass smack, and ecstasy face one could make. She knew that was her husband. This gun-wielding thug was his mistress, and her anniversary gift was stolen. Her man, who had sworn allegiance to her, the flag, and our nation, was fucking and robbing drug dealers.

Her tears fell quick.

"Don't cry now; you married him."

"And you fucked him," Martha shot back.

"Bitch," Lucky said, "Give my watch and earrings to your son and then back the fuck up."

Reluctantly she did as she was ordered. Junior was told to place the items in Lucky's pocket since her hands were occupied around his neck and holding her gun. Next, she asked, "Where's my fuckin' five million, Franklin!"

"What?" he feigned shock. "I don't have your money."

"You think I don't know it was you behind that break-in! You fuckin' kleptomaniac!" Lucky pointed the gun at his son's leg. "I swear I'll take a toe off this little nigga!"

And then it happened. Junior took his free hands, wrapped them around Lucky's arm that was gripped around his neck, pushed his butt back, and contracted just as he had learned in wrestling camp. Lucky flipped over his shoulder and crash-landed on the floor with a thud. Temporarily dazed, she lost control of her gun.

Franklin was on her with the quickness; hands wrapped aggressively around her throat and squeezed. He straddled her and was able to feel the pregnancy bump he couldn't see. Lucky dug her sharp nails into his skin, and tiny welts swelled up instantly on his hands. Desperately, she wiggled under his heavyweight as their eyes glared at one another. Lucky's eyes darted around the room quickly and landed once again on his. This was as intimate a moment as death could bring. Even as Franklin continued to apply pressure, a huge part of Lucky didn't think he'd actually go through with this. He couldn't murder her, right? He was a federal agent, her former lover, the father of her unborn child. They had history, albeit a brief one.

It wasn't definitive that Franklin would kill her; he was just so angered at what had gone down. But when he thought about his illegal actions, he felt like he didn't have a choice.

"Let me hear it," Franklin snickered. "Beg for *mercy*, bitch!" Lucky yelped out—"Daddy!"—But Scott couldn't save her.

Franklin's hands were so tightly wound around Lucky's neck he could see the blood vessels in her eyes burst. Red vines spread over the white landscape like an invasive weed. Lucky fought to suck air through her closing airwave as the bones in her throat were seemingly crunching in his grasp. Lucky was fading away, alone, on the kitchen floor of her former lover, with her unborn son along for the ride. Eventually, her body went slack, and she stopped fighting.

Before her light dimmed, the last thing Lucky saw was Martha removing her Chopard watch from her pocket. Seconds away from being strangled to death, one shot went off, *bak!* And slammed into her already marred eye. The bullet pierced through her pupil and traveled no farther, nestling inches away from her brain. Her last breath was shallow, filled with regret, and definitively final.

On February 8th, 2020, Lucky Luciana West and her unborn son had taken their last breaths. Just as the birth of her daughter, Lucchese Lily West had ignited a war that played out on the streets of New York—this war, predicated on the murder of Lucky, would be fought in the dark. Where real hood niggas came out to play.

COMING SOON!

Made in United States
North Haven, CT
14 March 2023

34034907R00172